THE

POPPY CHILDREN

by E. B. Sachem

STEPHEN M. CREEL, EDITOR
VA DDTC
125 LINCOLN STREET
BOSTON, MA 02111
Myrmidon Publishing Co.
Milton, Massachusetts

The characters and places in this book are fictitious. Any resemblance to persons living or dead, or to specific programs or institutions, is strictly coincidental.

To all the addicts who told me their stories, without whom this book could never have been written.

Introduction

"Anyone reading this book will become an expert in the field of drug addiction practically overnight."

This was the comment made by one of my colleagues after looking at *The Poppy Children*. In telling his story, E. B. Sachem provides the reader with an incredible number of detailed facts about drug abuse. This is the result of exhaustive gathering of material. Dr. Sachem has talked with hundreds of addicts over the past few years in the course of his working with them, both in private practice and in various clinics, and he has kept careful notes on their conversations. He also has interviewed federal and local narcotics agents, and has done considerable background research on the history of heroin addiction and drug traffic.

This dramatic, documentary novel is set in the year 1971, just as the first big epidemic of heroin addiction that peaked in 1969 was waning (at present, a second epidemic is building in this country). The characters in the story are also the most typical of the kinds of addicts that one runs into either on the street, or in various treatment programs. The author has melded together many individual stories and traits in order to present composites of these addict-types, and he brings them to life for us. Now the reader lives with real addicts, and shares their thoughts, hopes, fears, desperations, and dreams. The reader will understand them as human beings, will know their psychology, their backgrounds and home lives, and he will experience with them the tragic events that led to their being "turned on" to drugs. In addition, the author has taken pains to present another, more sordid side of the drug scene, the regrettable but all too real, criminal "hustling" that most heroin addicts have to engage in sooner or later to support their habits. Once the reader shares in these illegal exploits, whatever vestige of innocence he may have clung to will be irrevocably lost. He will be shocked, yet moved by the drug scene, and will be the wiser for it.

What is the answer? Dr. Sachem discretely leaves it up to the reader to come to his own conclusions about the problem of drug abuse. Certainly, it is now a number one problem in the nation, and a formidable challenge to our generation.

Alonzo T. Hunicutt, M.D.
Consulting Editor
May, 1975

The headlights pierced the darkness, illuminated flying snowflakes as the Mercedes swerved into the winding drive. Mr. Frank was glad to be home. He did not like to be out on a stormy night. As he opened the car door the chill air blew in, driving his wife into her fur coat.

"I don't see why we had to leave so early, Si," she complained. "It really isn't snowing that much."

He pulled on his gloves, annoyed, got out and slammed the car door. In a moment he stood on the other side, gently helping her out onto the fresh snow. "You didn't see the weather report, my dear," he argued. "This is supposed to be a bad one. I say we got home just in time. Now, I'll put away the car. Make me a hot brandy, will you?"

He backed the car up, raised the garage door automatically, thankful for such a convenience on a night like this. After pulling off his galoshes he entered the house. It was strangely silent. Even with their two sons away at college his wife usually made quite a clatter. In the kitchen he took off his coat, threw it over a chair. Still he heard nothing, wondered if she might be upstairs.

"Mandy?" he called gently. "Mandy?"

He stood in the silence for a full minute, then walked into the living room and stopped short. There his wife stood, her pale, terrified face staring at him, a knife pressed against her throat. The young man who held it barked a sharp command.

"Don't try nothin'! Now go get all your money and jewelry! Quick!"

Mr. Frank recoiled, caught himself, struggled with fear. He found himself looking at a short, excited youth trembling under a heavy coat. The face made him draw back. There was a peculiar, animal look, a snarl, the eyes dilated, glittering sharply. The knife trembled.

"C'mon! Get goin'!" the youth snapped.

"Please! Please don't hurt her!" he pleaded. He turned, hesitated in momentary confusion and stumbled upstairs to the bedroom. Reflexively he reached for the telephone but his hand froze at the thought of the knife at his wife's throat. Clearing his head, he stepped quickly to the safe, crouched and fumbled at the knob. Somehow, despite his panic, it opened. But he had not deactivated the alarm on the safe and realized that the police would be arriving within minutes. Hurriedly he scooped up as much of the contents as he could carry, an armload of bills and jewelry that trickled onto the thick carpet as he ran downstairs. His wife had not moved, her eyes closed in terror.

"Lay it on the table and get back!" ordered the youth. He pulled the woman over with him to the table and with quick, ferret-like movements, seized the valuables with a shaking, clawed fist and stuffed them into his coat. Then the youth and the rigid, frightened woman shuffled backward, stepping awkwardly, halting, then shuffling together again in a tense two-step toward the door. "You, mister!" he went on. "Lie down on your belly, arms out! No funny stuff or she gets it!"

Mr. Frank obliged cautiously, but his wife panicked, began to shriek hysterically. "You—you aren't going to hurt us are you?" she cried.

"Mandy! do as he says!"

"Oh, please! Don't hurt us!"

"Shut up!" growled the youth. "Now get down!" He pushed her and she fell to the floor, lay groaning.

"Mandy!"

"Don't move!" warned the youth. "Now you better give me plenty of time, man! I don't wanna hafta come back an' use you fer hostages, see? Don't forget, I gotta gun!"

Mr. Frank lay very still, his arms outstretched. His wife began to weep loudly and out of the corner of his eye he saw that her face was bloodied. Enraged, he wanted to jump up, find his pistol and chase the intruder. Instead he stifled the impulse, shut his eyes, began counting.

The youth leaped off the porch, sprinted across the snowy yard and down the deserted street. He had not expected to be surprised, knew that the police would arrive soon. Yanking open the door of the idling Volkswagen, he got in and drove off slowly, wheels spinning on the ice.

"Sonofabitch! Should've stolen one with snow tires!" he muttered to himself, and slithered through the barren, white streets lined with naked trees. Gradually he felt more secure, protected by the heavy sheets of wind-driven snow that orbed the street lights, like a quaint, old-fashioned Christmas scene. Yet for the last two years he had scarcely known when it was Christmas, and had no recollection of its most recent passing just two weeks before. He lived only from one day to the next.

Suddenly a police cruiser angled into view, coming the other way. Startled, he stiffened at the wheel just long enough to send the tiny car sliding sideways on the ice. Bumping against the curb, he sat, wheels spinning, the engine racing, as the cruiser loomed up and stopped beside him. Fear, if it was ever present, vanished. He boldly rolled down the window and grinned. "I got turned around!" he said. "Where's Brooklawn Avenue?"

The two patrolmen studied the bearded youth with impassive, ruddy faces, waiting and scrutinizing. The cruiser door opened a crack and the youth's stomach knotted, his fingers creeping around the handle of the gun. He kept grinning, thinking how "cops and robbers" was so often a waiting game, a game of nerves. He was cool long enough for the police radio to shatter the silence with an insistent, staccato call. One of the officers took up the mike, spoke soothingly into it. The cruiser door slammed shut. "Keep going straight, four, five blocks. . . ," came a surly voice.

The patrolman behind the wheel directed a final narrow, almost knowing gaze at the youth, who cranked up the window, cutting off visual contact. The cruiser jerked away urgently, its blue light spiraling off into the storm.

2

There were many bars in the city that catered to young singles, but The Prophet was one of the few regular hang-outs for street people. Appropriately "far out," the dingy interior was splashed with colorful novelty posters, some of glowing green and scarlet psychedelic designs, or of nudes or cartoon characters in outrageous postures—Popeye mounting Olive, a cute blonde astride a grinning motorcy-cle freak, a naked, effeminate group of musicians coyly hiding their privates, a pregnant girlscout sticking out her belly. For variety there was an advertisement for "Cocaine" in an exact replica of the better known cola sign.

The auditory input was even more stimulating—a cre-scendo of rock music generated from the squat, shimmering juke box in a corner and amplified so many times that its steady, jack-hammer beat wore away the walls with deva-stating intensity, defying the mere physical impediments of wood and plaster, not to mention the less impregnable hu-man ear. The dead could wake to it, this pulsing, chanting, whining and wailing of voices and electric guitars, as though a strange, mystical cult was worshipping here in this dark temple of fire, calling up spirits with their frenzied drums and exhorting lost, imprisoned souls to be free. As for the youthful followers, they were at very best a motley look-ing lot, casually slouching, drinking and smoking, laughing, or just listening. Some couples danced through all the color and sound, moving their bodies naturally and spontaneous-ly to the undulating rhythm. And the entire crowd had a kind of cocky stage-presence, as though having just finished a well-rehearsed performance starting with the storming of the premises and finishing with the complete routing of all respectable patrons, who had fled either because of indig-nation or terror at the sight of this barbarous horde. From that moment of conquest, suits and ties were banned, as alien to their culture as the quiet rhythm of a fox-trot played by a big band. For this was the new order, a tribe garbed mostly in leather, bright shirts and denims, with hair flowing to the shoulders. Except for chin-whiskers and subtle body curves, the sexes were practically indistinguishable.

Fathered by the great war beyond their memory, they did not ask to come but history sent them anyway on a daring crusade to unseat the smug, button-down world of the sixties. Brash and rebellious, they descended, ran and shouted in the streets, trampled, heckled, and then were quelled by the forces of order. Their remnants collected into bands, safe among their own, where they stood disenchanted and despairing of the futureless present that held them like so many gnats caught in a lump of amber. It seemed impossible that the world around them, a world they had tried to save, could be so hostile, so ungrateful for their presence. Yet, unable to escape, they had to remain and find a place for themselves. They had to carry on as a new minority group, sharing the same hurt pride, miseries, and poverty of other minorities in their country, a common kinship of want and powerlessness.

The assembly of youths mumbled and drank, the music wailed and thudded and couples jerked seductively on the tiny dance floor. Most were here for pleasure, but one youth in particular looked tense and preoccupied. He perched soberly on a stool near the end of the bar, a little apart from the others, his eyes roving sharply about the room. In his mid-twenties, he had a long narrow face, a thin, aquiline nose and keen, sensitive eyes. A strong, well-formed chin lent a quality of ruggedness to an otherwise delicate appearance, also masked to some extent by a thick, Manchu mustache that curled defiantly around the corners of his mouth. His long black hair fell down to the shoulders, to the denim jacket he was wearing. Together with denim pants and leather boots he had the seedy look of someone out of another, wilder period of frontier living—that perhaps history had set him adrift in a sea of time to be washed up on this unlikely, desolate shore a century later.

And so he sipped his beer and looked around intently, his eyes never still. A girl paused beside him, brushed him lightly with her breast but he did not turn around. His thoughts were distracted elsewhere, to something remote.

He caught a signal all of a sudden, nodded quickly, slid off the barstool onto lanky legs. He left the club, vanished into the snowstorm. Minutes later he reappeared, slipped around in back of the club where he waited shivering in an alley. A shadow hurried up, short, thin, nervous, hands trembling, swiping at a sniffling nose.

"Where ya been? I'm sick as hell! Been out all day. . . ."

"Had to go back to my room."

"This your best?"

"Right."

They exchanged something, briefly, expertly, so that it was hardly noticeable to anyone who might be watching. Then they returned to the warmth of the bar, parting in silence. The tall youth perched on his barstool again, alert, stork-like. The shorter youth disappeared into the men's room. Some minutes later he emerged looking much calmer and more relaxed, even a bit dull. He did not linger but went out again, trudged back to the idling Volkswagen, and drove to a section of apartment houses where he abandoned the car. Like a frightened rodent seeking its burrow, he darted into one of the buildings. Solid and substantial from the outside, it was dreary and shabby within. His boots scraped on gritty, worn linoleum as he scuttled up two flights of stairs and down a dark hallway. The doorways were interspersed by only a few feet of cracked plaster. Once the rooms had been much larger but had long since been partitioned into tiny warrens, packed with more tenants than could comfortably fit or could easily get out in case of fire. Some did not get out of these human hives, foiled by blocked exits, sprinklers clogged with paint, or by malfunctioning alarm systems. And so they died like termites in a burning log, to be memorialized next morning in the papers.

The rent was inflated, yet cheap enough for low income tenants, most of them pensioners, students, or street people, to afford it. Slick did not care about the rent. He had not paid it in over two months. To him and Sherry, his girl-friend, the tiny rooms they shared were no more than a way-station, a jumping off point to another little place somewhere else, equally dirty and cheerless.

She greeted him at the door, almost sprang at him, her hands probing his pockets. "Slick, honey . . . I was wondering where you were! Did you cop?"

For the first time today he grinned, drew out two fist-sized bundles of small glassine packets. "Two bags a' this shit an' you'll be loaded," he bragged.

She resonated his triumph with a sigh of enormous relief mixed with gratitude. "I was climbing the walls," she admitted. "Couldn't keep anything down since this morning."

He fixed up for her, dumping one of the small packets of white powder amounting to a few pinches into the cooker, a bottle cap held by a bent bobby pin. He added several drops of water from the dripping tap and struck a match under it for a moment. Drawing the fluid through a piece of cotton into an eye dropper, he fitted on the needle. "This time don't drop it," he muttered, passing it carefully into her thin, quaking fingers.

She had already twisted a belt around one spindly arm, tapped and massaged her one good vein and inserted the needle. Releasing the rubber bulb, she drew blood into the eye dropper, mixed it gently with the fluid, then slowly squeezed the mixture into her arm.

"I'm gettin' off!" she said as her face brightened. A blissful smile turned up the corners of her mouth as she drew back more blood, mixed it with what was left in the dropper and squeezed it in. Then she withdrew the needle and leaned back with her head on Slick's chest to savor the brief rush and the prolonged, languid high. There was no other feeling like it in the world as far as she knew, like sex only far better. As always, she imagined herself floating up on a fluffy, pink cloud and drifting off slowly to someplace far away. "It is dynamite. . . ." she purred and snuggled into the gaunt ribs of her boyfriend.

They both stared contentedly with heavy-lidded eyes, heads nodding peacefully, oblivious of the shabbiness of their surroundings. There was no furniture except for the old mattress that they lay on, an ancient sofa, and a rickety kitchen table with two creaky straight back chairs. There was no food in the cupboards, but they did not mind that either. All the cramping pain, the shakiness, chills and nausea had flown from their bodies as if by magic. Nothing else mattered but this state of serenity. Now, and for as long as the dope lasted, life was worth living.

Slick found a cigarette, lit it, passed it to Sherry, and lit a second for himself. He was always a perfect gentleman when he was high, and she a mewing, cuddly kitten. They knew it was the dope that had kept them together for almost two years. Besides a lover, he played big brother as well, but most of all he copped for her. Slightly older than she, he was in his very early twenties but somehow looked old and uncouth with his long, stringy hair and wispy beard. Small of stature, he was almost gnome-like in appearance, agile and quick. As with his girl friend, his flesh had a bleached, artificial look of malnutrition. They were both underweight by fifteen pounds or more and in obviously bad health. His unwashed face was pocked with sores and set off by a cherry-red nose, a reaction to the quinine in the dope. He had not brushed his teeth in months and they were chalky and crumbling with decay. But there was something more unusual, something in the sharpness of the eyes. Like all creatures driven by a craving, the eyes shone with the intense energy of a predator, glittering and roving back and forth. Even when nodding out, he seemed constantly on the alert, poised and ready to pounce, to snatch at any opportunity.

Sherry was almost the twin of her boyfriend but even thinner and more pale, to the point of near transparency. Like an apparition she shrank into a small heap of bones huddled under the ankle length dress, almost without any life to them. The globular skull, too large for the body and sprouting locks of long, oily brown hair, looked similarly lifeless except for the occasional blinking of the sunken eyes and twitching of the thin lips drawn tightly over the teeth. Yet in the face as a whole, even though quite plain and listless, a fragile, unearthly beauty lurked, seen sometimes in the faces of the dying, or in young, sleeping children.

She stirred, yawned, shivered and came to life in the icy room, conscious that hours had passed since they last shot up. Arching her neck she blew provocatively into the ear of her sleeping boyfriend. "I wanna get off again," she breathed.

He awoke, pushed her off, got up and went into the bathroom to urinate. "We gotta make this last," he said irritably. "It's a hassle to. . . ." A knock at the door interrupted him and instantly he ran back into the living room, seized the cellophane packets and the works and flung them beneath the mattress. "Who's there!" he shouted. Pushing Sherry aside, he found his gun and hid that also. He had been expecting a bust for some weeks now and cursed himself for not moving out sooner.

A muffled, cheery voice seeped through the door. "It's me, Russ, man. Me an' Dee-dee."

They both relaxed. Slick should have known that Russ would show up just about now when they were getting high. He seemed to possess a special gift for divining just when others had something.

"Hey, baby, what's happenin'?" Russ said as he stepped in, working to conceal his delight at finding his friend at home. "Jus' passin' by. Cold in here—wow, what weather! Say, what's goin' on? You sounded pretty uptight when I knocked." He smiled jokingly at Slick.

"Nothin'." Slick replied with an answering, nervous grin.

A girl followed just behind Russ. She was pretty, high cheekboned, with striking green eyes, the long lashes lowered in a hint of embarrassment. She kept silent at first, only curving her small, full-lipped mouth delicately in an ironic smile.

"We were both asleep," Sherry explained dully.

The girl raised her long-lashed green eyes and gazed narrowly at Slick and Sherry, compressed her full lips slightly at the sight of their pinpoint pupils. "You both look high," she observed flatly, and frowned vaguely before resuming her former look of amused irony.

There was a pause. Everyone knew what was coming next. It was no more than a mere formality. Slick's predatory eye darted at Russ's smooth, amiable face. He shuffled with indecision, his nervous grin distorted now into a near snarl. "Yeah . . . ," he confessed at last. "Copped a couple bundles last night. . . ." His expression softened and he gave a shrug, decided he did not care much whether he had to share it or not. He still had the jewelry to get rid of, plus a little more cash left from the score on that rich couple. And again he thought how it was lucky he got his hands on the old lady when he did, because the old man almost shit and couldn't get the stuff fast enough. "Copped it from Dom," he went on. "It's dynamite."

"All right!" replied Russ, his round face crinkling up in splendid humor, appreciating that only a weak gesture of refusal was needed on his part for etiquette to be served. "Hey, but me an' Dee-dee only shoot dope just once in a-while, man. She don't 'zactly dig needles, if you know what I mean." He frowned and hesitated. ". . . Still, I ain't had much chance to cop, weather like it is. But we wouldn't wanna take all your stuff, neither, would we Dee-dee?" He glanced back at the girl, who looked down and smirked openly.

"You wouldn't be taking it all," Sherry interjected.

Russ broke into an apologetic grin and shrugged. "You sure now?"

"Sure," Slick asserted. "Try a couple bags."

Russ's coat was half off as he beamed gratefully at them. "Well, maybe jus' a couple bags, yeah! We ain't in no hurry, are we Dee-dee?" Before she could reply he was helping her off with her coat. "After I make this big connection in New York," he went on, "why, you can come over to my pad!" He laughed good naturedly, waiting to be seated by the host.

The storm blew all night and began to subside in the morning. The clouds broke up, dispersed in widening patches of pale blue, winter sky. The sun came slanting through the streets to brighten the new-fallen snow into pure, glaring rivers of white, ribboned with fresh tire tracks. The scrape of snow shovels could be heard below the apartment window, and the occasional, grinding roar of a passing plow. But the four young people sprawled in the chilly apartment heard and saw nothing. As they slept, the broad daylight etched their features clearly, heightening the serenity of their faces that were as calm as if struck from marble. The quiet dignity of this living yet inanimate beauty that shone from them contrasted vividly with the ordinary shabbiness of the decaying walls around them. Only the infinite expanse of the hushed snowfall outside could compare with it. They began to stir after a time, coming alive again in a world that lived, where snow was an inconvenience to be pushed and shoveled out of sight. Up till four in the morning, they had shot up nearly the whole two bundles. In fact, they were still so high that they did not need the customary "wakeup."

"Like I said, man," Russ began again as he tottered up. "Mos' dynamite stuff I ever done!" He had spent hours the night before singing praises of it, like a famished dinner guest devouring the main dish while flattering the cook. Russ did mostly cocaine, but this was such good junk that he indulged in spite of himself.

Dolores came out of the bathroom, still frowning for two reasons. First of all, she had missed work the previous evening because Russ was too high to take her home and she herself was too high to take a cab. Second, the tiny puncture marks in her arm where Russ had so obligingly shot up for her were turning a conspicuous black and blue. She liked dope but hated needles, especially when they left such visible marks. "Look at this!" she said to Russ and stuck out her arm. "What am I going to do? You should have been more careful! I don't work in long sleeves, you know!"

Russ met her snapping green eyes with his customary good humor. "Don't worry baby," he soothed. "Them dudes ain't lookin' at your arms nohow!" He grinned, tried to evoke a chuckle from Slick. He wanted to head Dolores off before she really started bellyaching, which he knew was in the offing. But Slick was disgruntled also. He had business to take care of, now that all his dope had been shot up. He had to sell the jewelry to a fence and go cop again before he and Sherry got sick, at least by this evening. Russ took a hint from Slick's unsmiling face. Yet, forever grateful, he was not the kind of guest to be hurried out the door. "Tell ya what, folks," he volunteered. "I'm hungry. How 'bout me goin' out an' bringin' back somethin' ta eat, some pizza maybe."

"Sounds neat!" Sherry echoed from the john. "Get me some candy bars!"

Russ cocked his head drolly. "Candy!" he declared. "Is that all a junkie goes for is sweets? No wonder you got such bad teeth, man! Now I got nice teeth!" He smiled widely at them.

"But you aren't a real junkie, neither," Dolores reminded him sullenly, resisting his bold attempt to humor her. She was no longer high, which also helped. "You're a coke head," she went on. "I oughta know, 'cause I support your habit. If it wasn't for me, you'd be out in the street hustling like everyone else!"

Russ slipped an appeasing arm around her. "Hey, woman, you do a little coke yourself!" he exclaimed. "Now, 'stead a arguin', let's go out an' get us a couple pizzas, like sausage and mushrooms, okay?

"Don't forget the chocolate bars!" Sherry called out again, and opened the door a crack to make sure he could hear.

When they returned with the food, another youth had arrived just in time to partake of nearly half of one of the hot, gooey, spicy pizzas. He ate silently, ravenously, while Slick and Sherry nibbled on candy. There were two things about Ramon that stood out to his friends. For one thing he never looked anyone in the eye longer than an instant, and for another, he was always alone. Like Slick he was busy, constantly on the move, for the simple reason that he also had a large habit. He needed at least a hundred a day just to stay straight and nearly two hundred to really get high. He shared the same alert, predatory eye, but, tough as he was, there was also a gentleness, a kind of latin poise in his manner that had reassured more than one of his numerous holdup victims.

"Where've you been hiding, Ray?" Dolores asked musically as they ate. "We haven't seen you in weeks." She enjoyed drawing out shy men. It was part of her job.

"Been out of town," he answered quietly with a slight

accent, and averted his eyes.

"Why? They got a warrant out on ya?" Slick asked, his mouth crammed with chocolate.

Ramon nodded. "Yeah, a friend told me. They think I pulled this stickup."

"You, pull a stickup? Get outa here, man!" Russ joked.

Sherry stood at the window, her thin figure silhouetted in the sunlight. "I think it's going to warm up," she observed. "Slick, you going out today?"

Dolores licked her greasy fingers, tugged at Russ's sleeve. "C'mon," she urged, "I've got to go get ready for work."

All were straight when Slick finally showed them out. "Come back later," he said to Russ quickly. "Ramon's got somethin'."

Dolores turned, jabbed a finger at Slick. "Don't you go getting my ol' man into trouble!" she warned. "He's been in enough as it is!"

"I never get into no trouble, baby, you know that," Russ quipped, knowing he had said the wrong thing.

3

Russ drove Dolores back to their apartment, located in the same rundown section of the city. Much more comfortable than the place where they had just spent an unplanned evening, a feminine hand was clearly in evidence. Her insistence on drapes, carpets, and decent furniture had converted plainess into relative luxury. Besides, it was necessary for business reasons.

She bathed and changed while he relaxed, sniffed a pinch of cocaine from the tiny, pearl handled gold coke spoon that he wore around his neck. Though preferring to shoot it by needle, he did not have time just now to get really high. So he held the tiny spoon under one nostril, closed the other and inhaled the pinch of white powder deeply. As much as he dug heroin, coke was a lot more fun, had more zip to it and did some other nice things, too. Dolores came out of the bathroom wrapped in a towel and finished dressing in front of him, her jet black hair flowing down over ivory skin and her generous figure scarcely contained in the tight bra and panties. He felt an erection rising, his excitement heightened by the cocaine as his eyes followed her ample buttocks. She sensing his interest, discouraged him by quickly wriggling into a tight, knit dress.

"I'm already late for work," she complained. "All because you had to get loaded last night. . . ."

He grinned, not minding her constant bitching. With a body like that she could call him every name in the book and he would enjoy it, especially with a few hits of coke to arouse him and the promise of having her close to him when he wanted her. But she believed in work before pleasure. So he stifled his impulses, found himself obediently driving her downtown to the Four-sixty Lounge, a seedy, overstuffed nightclub featuring go-go girls and expensive drinks. Dolores was one of the dancers and hustled besides. She made good money but got triple that turning tricks. And she watched every penny, or tried to, but found it awfully hard with an old man like Russ who was, after all, supposed to be managing the money.

"Now don't you blow everything on that damn coke, okay?" she cautioned. "Just cop me some methadone and stay out of trouble."

She kissed him quickly and stepped out of the car. To him it was a promising, reassuring kiss, asking him to miss her. Accordingly, he wheeled the Olds around and sped over to the home of a friend who attended a methadone clinic and saved part of his dose to sell for extra money. Fifty dollars bought five forty milligram wafers or "biscuits," enough to hold Dolores for two days. He did not care for it himself because the high from this slow-acting synthetic opiate was not as dramatic, lacked the "flash" of good heroin, or the rush of cocaine. Tragically, his friend also happened to have a few good dime spoons of coke on hand, but Russ had to turn down the offer mainly because he was broke. He managed to wheedle a "sample," snorted it, reveled in it, and with high praises for its quality, promised to return later and cop a few bags.

Driving off, he cruised at random through the city, alone and discomfited. He did not like to be broke. To him it was the same as running out of water in the middle of a desert, that is, a disaster. He knew that just as certain plants need more fertile soil in which to thrive and bloom, some people need more money in order to prosper and feel content. His dandified appearance suggested that he was not a plain, rugged species that could flourish under adverse conditions, but rather a sort of hothouse variety that needed a lot of care. The sleek, exotic look of colored suede and high-heeled lizard shoes matched his smooth, jaunty manner, exaggerated at times by a fixed, congenial smile on his round face. His eyes sparkled with polite enthusiasm, especially when he spoke, as though he were perpetually charmed by everyone around him. And yet, almost as if to counterbalance his studied charm he would break into an occasional little frown, or appear irked over trifles. His entire behavior, it seemed, was calculated to put others at ease, if not to disarm them.

In a few minutes, Russ found himself parking in front of Slick's apartment house. As a moth flutters into the flame, he bounded upstairs and eagerly rapped on the door. The flame, in this case, was the promise of some quick, easy money. Inside, Slick and Ramon were sitting amid the litter of candy wrappers and empty pizza boxes passing a joint, the pungent smell of the marihuana heavy in the room. Sherry lay asleep on the mattress, looking like a child curled in nest of dreams. They offered Russ a hit on the joint and kept talking.

"They got guards?" Slick was asking.

"No, man," Ramon reassured. "Just cameras."

Russ took a long tote on the joint and handed it back to Slick. "What's comin' down?" he asked.

Slick and Ramon turned as one smirking face, approving of his show of interest. "Wanna pull a holdup with us?" Slick asked nonchalantly. "We need someone to keep the peek."

Russ feigned mild surprise, as if he didn't know. "Huh? Where at?"

"This supermarket," Ramon answered. "It's a pushover, simple."

Russ accepted the joint, took another hit. "How much you 'spect to get?"

"Seven, maybe even ten grand. Who knows?" Ramon said.

Russ nodded. The marihuana began to relax him. It was strong, numbed his mind. The sunlit window grew brighter and a sweet, metallic taste came into his mouth. Now he felt carefree and unconcerned about everything. Pleasant notions flitted through his head as he thought about the money and the whole idea seemed not only logical, but perhaps willed by some ingenious, external power. He had a sense of unreality and unaccountability for his own actions. In a way he would be committing a crime but in a way he would not. After all, he was not a real criminal, simply someone in need who was acting on the advice of others. He smiled at them, felt his mouth stretch tight in unexplained gaiety.

"Sounds good," he said rapidly. "But . . . ," he paused, still smiling, "I wouldn't want no shootin', unnerstand?"

Ramon gave him a solemn, piercing look, then he too, grinned in spite of himself. "Don't worry, man, I'd run outa the place first."

Russ pondered a bit more. Still optimistic, he could not quite supress the awareness of several troublesome facts. If Dolores ever found out she would be shocked and very angry. Because armed robbery, especially masked, was a lot of time. Then they were intending to use real guns, not replicas, so someone might get shot. And it was only a matter of time before Ramon or Slick, with all their warrants, would be picked up. Maybe they would squeal on their partners to cut down the time. And he did not trust them, but then addicts seldom trust one another.

Sensing the reluctance of his friend, Slick spoke up. "Look, dope don't grow on trees, right? So we gotta steal. Now, ya in or ain't ya?"

"I sure wish it did grow on trees, man, 'cause it sure would be beautiful," Russ sighed.

"Hey, think what you could do with a few grand,"

Ramon said with a sly smile and Slick nodded in agreement.

Russ shrugged and grinned back at them. "Yeah, I could go down to New York an' invest it in a couple ounces of good coke, then sell it up here for five times what I paid for it." He felt drowsy from the marihuana and closed his eyes for a moment, vividly imagined all those fine, white crystals so easily converted into hard cash. One of these days he would be a big cocaine dealer, driving a big car, making money in the six figures as easily as snapping his fingers. And again that vague, slightly confused sense of warmth and abandon pervaded him and he yielded at last to their temptation.

"All's I got is a little .25," he said at last.

"That's all you need," said Slick. "I mean, you know, like we just want somebody to keep an eye on the door and drive for us. If the cops come, we run out the back . . . ."

"Easy, man," Ramon added, very coolly, as though this was something he did every day of the week. Casually he took a hit on the joint, passed it to Russ, who smiled and took it once more. It was good grass.

During the next few days the three of them cased the supermarket thoroughly, planning various strategies and alternate escape routes. And they studied the movements of any police in the area. Slick was flat broke by the middle of the following week, had blown all of the eight hundred from the jewelry on dope. He borrowed enough to stay straight from Ramon, who was also barely squeaking by. So they were more than ready at nine o'clock Friday morning when the supermarket opened. They had stolen a car the night before, hotwiring a dependable, four door sedan with a lot of power. When they arrived, a chill winter wind was pushing the clouds across a feeble sun, discouraging early shoppers and converting the parking lot into a vast, arctic wasteland of asphalt. Slick was dopesick, had popped some barbiturates to kill his sick but instead they made him drunk. Ramon had gone the other way by taking amphetamines to get his nerve up and became noticeably more talkative and irritable as they drew near.

Russ saw the change in his two comrades brought on by the pills and his belly tightened in fear. The closer they got to the supermarket, the more it seemed that he was the only sane one in the group. It was a terribly lonely feeling to have at such a fateful moment. "Oh, wow, is this stupid!" he thought, fighting a desperate urge to spin the car around and take off in the other direction. "They're bouncin' off the walls an' we ain't even started yet." He half turned and exhorted them aloud. "Play it cool, huh? If somethin' jumps up, let's split quick, even if we have to leave the money."

They disregarded him, busy slipping ski masks over their heads. The three of them spilled out of the car and entered the store. Ramon carried a sawed-off shotgun, Slick his chrome, .32 revolver, and Russ his tiny, pearl handled .25 Beretta, a favorite among addicts.

"This is a stickup! Nobody move!" yelled Ramon. He jabbed the shotgun at a petrified lady checker. "Where's the manager?"

She caught her breath, looked at the black muzzle of the shotgun. "He's . . . in back!"

"Go get 'im!" Ramon snapped, prodded her down the aisles of food to the rear, while Russ told the lone customer to lie down while keeping an eye on the parking lot outside. Slick tore out the phone, then herded another checker from one register to the next, ordering her to open them while he emptied the drawers of cash. Ramon returned a half minute later with the manager, a square-faced, efficient-looking man with a crew-cut, marching ahead of the shotgun beside the lady checker with his hands up.

"Open the safe! Quick!" ordered Ramon.

The manager hesitated, frowned and formed a word on his lips but was interrupted by a metallic click. Slick had cocked the hammer of his revolver and was pointing it at the man's temple. "Okay, sure . . . ," he mumbled.

They followed him into the office where the cashier stood, her hands up. "Hurry!" yelled Slick. He turned and glared at the frightened woman. "If you press that silent alarm, lady, you'll be sorry!" he growled.

"C'mon! C'mon!" Ramon shouted while the manager

crouched at the safe, hands shaking slightly as he twirled the knob backwards and forwards. He stopped, shook his head, cleared the lock and began turning it slowly again while everyone watched for what seemed an endless moment. Slick raised his gun, his thumb twitching at the cocked hammer, as the manager turned the handle and the safe door swung open. Ramon shoved the manager aside, tore out three canvas sacks of bills, tossed them to Slick, then hauled out two more sacks of coins, all he could carry with the shotgun.

"Stay down, everyone!" he warned loudly and backed out of the store together with Slick.

Russ was already behind the wheel when they scrambled into the car. All he could recall later was that Ramon had dropped one of the heavy canvas sacks of coins and stopped to pick it up, so that the car was moving slightly by the time he reached it and they had to help him in. This is why they did not see the police cruiser with its whirling blue light until it had swerved into the parking lot, stopping twenty yards away and blocking the entrance. Russ reacted an instant later by taking off with a wild skidding of tires and jumping the curb into the street, an alternate route of escape that they had planned on. As he hit the street he heard the siren whooping and caught sight of the cruiser looming up just behind them and to the right, trying to force them off the road. He cut the wheel and accelerated for a second, then realized he had to stop. At that instant, Ramon's sawed-off shotgun boomed out like a cannon, the two barrels going off almost simultaneously.

"Ya got 'im! Sonofabitch!" yelped Slick.

"Huh?" Russ exclaimed in disbelief, as he saw the cruiser fall behind and skid sideways.

"C'mon! Let's screw!" snapped Ramon. "Every cop in town's gonna be lookin' for us!"

They twisted briefly through a maze of side streets, followed an arterial out of the residential area into some woods where Russ had left his car. The ride had given him enough time to think. "A cop! They had . . . !" His emotion changed from astonishment to outrage. His premonition had been true, after all. He was the only sane person among them, but now it was too late. He began to sputter at them as they climbed out of the car. "What you cats doin', shootin' a cop! You gonna get us either killed or sent up for life, man! I thought I told you to . . . !"

"Aw cool it!" Slick sneered. "You think we coulda gotten away with a cop on our ass?"

"I had to do it, man," Ramon said calmly, his face quite pale, yet trying hard to speak with the air of a professional. He was breaking down the shotgun, wiping it clean, tossing the parts into the woods. He looked at Slick. "We'll divvy it up at your pad, huh? Gotta split up for now, though. Drop me in the subway."

"Yeah, then I gotta go cop," said Slick.

"Cop enough for me, too. I wanna do a whole bundle tonight," Ramon continued and a smile crossed briefly over his tense, pale face.

Shaking his head with woe, Russ warmed up the car while the other two loaded the gray, canvas sacks in the trunk and covered them snugly with a blanket. They drove out of the wooded area and dropped Ramon off at the nearest subway station, then went on to The Prophet. Slick opened the trunk a crack, groped around and dug out a couple of stacks of crisp, ten dollar bills. While Russ waited outside, he darted into the club, squinting along the bar and into the booths, probing every face with his glittering, ferret eyes. He asked the bartender a question, scowled at the answer, changed one of the crisp tens and went to a pay phone. He emerged looking genuinely troubled. Dom, purveyor of the best stuff available, was not around. Then he thought that Dom might be over at Joyce's. He went back and called her, but she had no idea where he was either.

Slick walked back to the bar, oblivious of the carefree atmosphere, the lively music, the pretty girls. A gray fog of oblivion and seething resentment had enveloped him completely, shutting out all reason. She had lied, he decided. They were balling together and that bitch didn't want to be disturbed. Besides, that damn guinea was worthless anyway and cared less whether you lived or died. His tormented mind struggled like a blind man groping through the angry fog and he wanted to rage and curse aloud, or slap or cut somebody, anybody. But instead he ordered a shot to steady himself. The barbs had worn off and his dopesickness was coming back even stronger, his hands shaking, his stomach churning. He downed the vodka, then bolted into the men's room and vomited, had watery diarrhea.

In this desperate condition a painful compromise was forced upon him in the form of Martin Shine, who had heaved his hulk into the men's room in order to get off. Martin was a dealer who had a huge habit, and therefore made it a practice to tap the bags, even burning unsuspecting people with talcum powder, flour, or baking soda. In his mid-forties, he was older by twenty years than most of the other addicts. Fat, amiable, balding with a salt-and-pepper goatee, his trademark was a pair of dark glasses that seemed welded to his face, the lenses nearly opaque. They reflected everything away and left him existing serenely in his own private universe of heroin and music. Like so many older addicts, he was a jazz musician.

Slick button-holed Martin just as he was fumbling a bag out of his pocket. "Hey, Marty, got anything? I'm lookin' for a couple bundles."

Shine gave him an enigmatic grin, tucked the cellophane bag back into his pocket, reached into another coat pocket and produced a fistfull of the same packets tied up with a rubber band. "All I got is one bundle right now. Hundred and a quarter, like always," he said.

Slick looked suspiciously at the bundle. "This stuff better be worth it!" he growled, passing him the bills.

The fat man fingered them, noted their crispness. Momentarily he directed the black discs of his lenses at Slick, as if taking brief notice of something important. He nodded and looked away. "That's as good as you can get anywhere right now," he replied thickly. "And I can get more. Do you want the other bundle?"

"I'll wait," Slick said with grating sarcasm. He had come close to killing Martin on more than one occasion because of his bad dope, but he never quite had the heart to hurt such an old man, who was probably pretty close to the end already.

4

Slick found Sherry waiting impatiently when he returned to the apartment, saw the same shivering, haggard creature he had known since the day they first met. It had always pleased him to see how his dope could transform her into another person entirely, smiling, sweet and cuddly. She got up and came to him as he closed the door, an urgent look in her wide, glittering eyes. She, too, awaited the transformation with eagerness.

"Did you score, honey?" she breathed. She hugged him, felt the bundle in his pocket and smiled. "Where'd you cop it?"

"From Marty," Slick grumbled.

She frowned. "Why from him?"

"'Cause he was the only one around."

She clung to him as if trying to communicate something desperate that she could not express easily. "I . . . I got the jones awful bad," she whimpered.

He shook her off. "Lemme try it first," he said. "It's probably garbage anyway."

His hands trembled as he emptied three of the packets into the bottle cap, though he knew perfectly well that it would take another three before he could really get off. He added a few drops of water and, holding the cooker by a bent bobby pin, heated the mixture with a match. It curdled rapidly into a thick jelly.

"Garbage! Sonofabitch!" he exclaimed, not quite willing to believe his eyes.

"Must be mostly talcum powder," Sherry observed disconsolately.

Slick went ahead and drew the viscid mixture laboriously through a piece of cotton into the eye dropper. Knotting a rubber tourniquet around his bicep he raised one of the small veins on the back of his hand by massaging it briefly, then with an expert aim, tapped in the needle.

Working the rubber bulb, that of a baby pacifier because of its larger capacity, he mixed the blood with the junk and squeezed it into his arm, waiting expectantly. He shook his head in disgust. "I don't feel nothin'!" he grumbled savagely. "This shit has everything but heroin in it! I shoulda gone down to Chinatown, goddamn it! Here, you try it!"

He threw some of the bags to Sherry, who snatched them up like a hungry monkey going after peanuts. She took the set of works, or "gimmicks," and fixed up quickly and expertly. Scarcely bothering to mix the blood and the dope, she shot up and waited in suspense.

"Gettin' off?" he asked.

She shook her head negatively, regarded him sadly. He stood up, his lip curled in an ugly snarl and flung the rest of the bundle across the room, scattering the packets on the floor. "That dirty motherfucker!" he yelled. "It's garbage! He beat me outa a hundred bucks! I'm gonna kill him this time!"

"Slick! What's the use!" Sherry argued. "They'll get you! It's not worth it!"

He calmed down after another round of cursing and they did eight more bags before they finally got high. They also felt a little sick and dizzy from the foreign matter in the junk, which in this case was close to ninety-nine percent. Even though the high was strictly second rate, it made them straight. Several hours later they did the rest, so that Ramon was quite upset when he arrived with a bad case of the jones and found no heroin left. A gentleman, he decided not to make an issue of it, realizing that it would not get him any dope but just cause the worst kind of trouble at this critical stage of their collaboration. His self-restraint was made easier when Russ showed up not long afterward. He was high on some of Dolores's methadone and sold Ramon a couple of forty milligram "biscuits," enough to keep him straight for awhile.

After wrapping the canvas sacks in blankets and bringing them upstairs, they emptied the contents into a huge pile and began dividing it three ways. Although jubilant at the sight of so much cash, they were also noticeably tense as they counted it, despite the soothing effect of the drugs in their systems. Even the total of nearly three thousand a-piece did not relax them and after a period of glum silence they began whispering to one another, trying not to let Sherry overhear.

"Heard anything on the news?" Russ mumbled, his eyes communicating a certain look of dread.

Ramon shrugged, his face frozen and impassive. "No," he replied.

"Don't get so uptight!" Slick hissed back to Russ. "We're okay! No sweat!"

Russ rolled his eyes and shook his head from side to side as he stuffed away his share of the money. He fairly oozed with fear and felt embarrassed in front of them, was afraid they would lose confidence in him if he started carrying on. So he left and headed over to a friend's house to pro-cure some of that highly prized cocaine he had been thirst-ing after. He copped everything Willie had, a whole ounce in ten fifty dollar bags. To celebrate, he and Willie shot up one of them practically on the spot, doing one hit and then another to stay high. They parted company in good spirits and Russ, bursting with the joy of cocaine, sped over to find Dolores. He wanted to tell her how much he loved her and buy her a present, then maybe get one from her. But the closer he got to the apartment, the more he was dis-couraged by the glimmering realization that all of these gestures of affection would only cause her to wonder where he got the money to get so high. And if she ever found out how he got it, and about the other unthinkable mishap, things would go hard for him. So at last his ardor was dampened by the rude prerogative of reality, and it was just as well. She was in an irritable mood and ready to quibble over trifles.

"Where've you been all this time?" she asked, and snapped her green eyes as though he had committed a capi-tal offense, which, in fact, could not have been far from the truth.

Russ balked and stared at her. Feeling "dynamite," he had come over to love her and now felt foolish, began grop-ing for excuses. He saw she was not in the mood, usually the case at midday. And he could not help envying the tricks who simply threw down twenty-five or fifty dollars or more and crawled into bed with her, just like that. And he, her old man . . . why he shouldn't have to. . . . He sighed, thought of an alternative. "Say baby, you know I been takin' care of business," he explained. "Now look, we oughta go over to Slick's. I owe him a few hits of this dynamite coke that I run into."

She almost asked him more questions, then compressed her lips in vexation. "All right. As long as I get to work on time. But don't you want any supper?"

Russ insisted they would eat later, and in ten minutes they arrived at Slick's. He and Sherry sat shrouded in smoke, the sweet odor of marihuana so heavy that it seemed possible to get high simply by breathing the air.

"We just got this today," Sherry boasted with the bright smile that she always wore after a good joint. "It's real gold, straight from Mexico."

"Where's Ramon?" Russ asked.

"He split," answered Slick. "Went to cop. He might be back in awhile."

They sat down, passed a joint around while Russ took out his works and disappeared into the bathroom. He banged some coke into his arm, careful not to miss, or "blow" the shot for fear of an abscess. Slick and Sherry, who were also *aficionados* of the needle, gratefully accepted his offer to share a bag, and quickly followed suit. Dolores sniffed a tiny but potent dime, or ten dollar spoon and soon everyone was humming.

Slick, who grins but almost never laughs, let out one of his rare chuckles and Russ asked him what it was.

"It's a joke," Slick replied. "we got all this money an' we can't even find one decent bag of dope. But when you ain't got nothin' to cop with, the stuff is everywhere!

"What money?" Dolores asked.

There was a tense pause.

"They hit a supermarket," Sherry said flatly.

Russ began to squirm as Dolores glanced coldly at him. The swell of jubilation from the cocaine subsided as quickly as it rose, leaving a dark trough of tension and suspicion.

"Is that what you came back here for that day?" she demanded. "I wondered where you got all that coke! And here I thought you'd smartened up! Can't I ever trust you?"

"Hey, hold it baby!" he crowed. "'Fore you get yourself all worked up over nothin', take a look at this!" He dug into his coat and pulled out a stack of crisp, twenty dollar bills while Slick grinned and Sherry puffed grandly on her joint. "Almost three grand! I got most of it stashed an' I ain't gonna touch it till I get down to New York to cop me the best coke I kin find! I'll have ten or fifteen grand by the time I'm through, dig? Then I kin start buyin' real weight, like that dude Cliff you used to work for. You can quit work an' jus' be my woman. How d'ya like that?" He slipped an arm around her, patted her curvy hip, but she was rigid, unresponding.

"Yes, Cliff made it big all right!" she retorted hotly. "Real big—with a couple of bullets in his head! And the same thing'll happen to you!" She looked at him, her accusing green eyes dulled, hardened into jade-cold doubt. "Now they'll be looking for you!" she went on. "It isn't worth it, don't you see? We've had enough trouble as it is . . . !"

Russ glanced at Slick and Sherry imploringly, as a defendant would turn to his lawyers. Sherry arched her eyebrows and huffed out the smoke in nonchalance while Slick reached for his works, his eye on the bag of cocaine. "Mind if I do another hit?" he asked absently.

"Sure, sure Slick," Russ said willingly. "You, too, Sher! Help yourself! Dee-dee, want another?" He smiled at them, seemed to regain his old self-assurance, and looked at Dolores now with earnestness. "I swear, baby, this is the last time, no lie!" You're right, what you say, it don't make a bit of sense to go gettin' into a lotta trouble over a few grand! His face sobered and he glanced quickly at Slick, then smiled again, tightened his arm around her waist.

She turned away in a huff, said she did not want to speak to him and started conversing with Sherry, exchanging feminine gossip that the men could not quite catch. Russ and Slick seemed preoccupied with their own thoughts and each looked troubled. Slick got up and paced about restlessly, wondering where Ramon was with the heroin, worrying that he could have been picked up, or perhaps had taken off with the money. Slick, who beat people regularly, realized that having put money into the hands of a dopesick junkie, he deserved to be beat himself. He moved over to the television and snapped it on. It was time for the news.

The story of the holdup came just after the first commercial, with pictures of the supermarket they robbed and the parked cruiser, its windshield peppered with buckshot. They tensed at the information that a patrolman was in critical condition at a local hospital.

Dolores reacted first, her voice cracked with dismay. "Oh, my God! Russ! Was that it? Was that the one? A cop! Oh, you didn't . . . !"

"I didn't shoot 'im!" Russ protested. "Least he ain't dead!"

"Who cares!" Slick scoffed. "Long as they don't know who did it."

Dolores clenched a fist, ready to explode, looked at Slick in disbelief. "Who cares? Is that all you have to say? Well . . . !"

Sherry interrupted with an upraised hand. She was trying to listen to the news, to one of the candidates running for mayor who was making a speech. A clean cut, youngish man standing behind a podium, he spoke in a righteous, indignant tone to a slightly intimidated audience of well-dressed matrons.

"I want to restate the very grave problem in this city of the rising crime rate which has been soaring in recent years to the point where crimes against property and persons are now considered commonplace, something that city dwellers must simply endure as best they can. . . ." There was a hushed silence, both in the audience of woman and in the shabby apartment, where the four young people watched the candidate intently, his angry face looming large on the television screen. "So I would want to appeal to the voters to examine this issue, and to consider what the present administration has or has not done in this area. How long can this shocking situation continue? It is clear that despite many promises, the people of this city are in greater danger of being victimized than ever before. I say that this will not continue if I am elected mayor!"

There was a burst of applause, cut short by an abrupt change of scene to a quiet office where two men were seated comfortably opposite one another. A young black reporter, his voice measured with respect, addressed a question to an older man, robust, with thick, silver hair. By the shrewd twinkling of his blue eyes, the older man seemed to be anticipating every word the reporter was saying and already had the answers in mind, answers to questions that were very old indeed.

"Mr. Mayor," began the reporter and paused as though a trifle embarrassed at what he had to say. "Do you have any comment on Attorney Loomis's statement about the rising crime rate in the city?"

The keen blue eyes narrowed and twinkled with a studied concern as they swung into the camera. "Rich, I'm glad you asked that question," replied the older man seriously. "Actually, ours is one of the safer cities in the United States, but, of course, I have no intention of glossing over a bad situation. As mayor, I have made every effort to combat rising crime, especially with regard to our police force, which is, as you know, undergoing a somewhat painful process of modernization. For one thing, we are striving to decentralize police field operations and increase response to calls." He paused for an instant. In response to the reporter's faint, ebony-carved frown his own face brightened, became more affable, more self-assured, the blue eyes twinkling more sharply. "Of course," he went on, "these and other measures will not end the problem. An elevated crime rate will be part of the urban as well as our suburban scene for some time to come. This is why crime prevention should be one of the personal duties of every private citizen. We must deputize ourselves as the eyes and ears of justice."

"Thank you, Mr. Mayor," said the young reporter and nodded into the camera. The picture vanished, replaced by a woman in her kitchen, holding up a box of macaroni.

"Wonder where Ramon is," Sherry whined, and got up,

yawned and tried to stretch the shivers out of her thin limbs. It had been almost eighteen hours and she, too, was getting sick. Yawning was one of the early signs. She looked at her boyfriend. "Maybe you should go out and try to find Dom."

"Yeah, maybe I can get a quarter piece and deal some of it myself," he grunted, reached nervously for his set of works.

Dolores looked at them askance as they started fixing up again. "How can you all just sit there like this when that cop may be dying in the hospital? Plus the mayor and everyone else is uptight! I mean, doesn't this even faze you?"

Russ shrugged. "Don't get me wrong! he consoled. "Sure I'm hassled! Why d'you think I been so high all this time?"

Slick tied off an arm, began hunting for a vein in the mass of scars and puncture marks. "Yeah, I hope the cop makes it" he remarked. "But he wouldn't give a shit about me if I was hurt, so why should I give a shit about him? Cops hate junkies anyway."

"Everyone hates junkies," Sherry agreed. "Maybe if people didn't hate us so much we wouldn't have to rob and steal to support our habits."

"Right on!" Russ declared, endorsing her reasoning and hoping Dolores would recognize the logic in it.

She only looked scornfully at them. "All the dope in the world isn't worth a life," she said solemnly.

Slick was just getting ready to shoot up, the tip of the needle hovering over a practically invisible vein. He thought how she was going to spoil his high and he did not get into this much good coke very often. He scowled at her. "Look, I'm too sick to worry about that shit," he muttered. "It was the cop's own fault. He shouldn't a' started shootin' at us. Ramon had no choice but to blow him away."

"I didn't want no shootin'!" Russ insisted. "I told 'em that from the start."

She shook her head. "It doesn't matter! You're in it with the others!" She sighed, dropped her eyes in resignation. She began thinking about how little control people have over their own lives, and that, as of this tragic moment, it was too late for the both of them. Not that she had ever had much hope as far back as she could remember. She, like so many women, had lived on empty promises, on dreams. She stood up, not wanting to see the truth anymore because it made everything look so meaningless— these people, the cocaine, and Russ even. "Get me my coat!" she ordered, then paused and looked at them contemptuously. "You're all soft, if you ask me!"

Slick had just finished banging the coke into his arm and grinned back at her. "You can say that if ya want, I don't care," he sneered. "I'm a dopefiend, see? Hustlin' an' gettin' high is all I give a fuck about."

"Me, too," Sherry echoed, then hesitated and frowned. "I wonder where that Ramon is?"

Russ gathered up the last of the cocaine. "Guess we'll be goin' home now, folks," he said, a little sadly. "If ya run into some good junk, gimme a call." He no longer felt like getting high, regretted the pain that Dolores felt and could only hope that time would somehow mend the fresh laceration that had just been opened between them.

5

Dom perched stork-like on his barstool, carefully following the crowd with a patient eye. Like a faded human tide, it ebbed and flowed to the upbeat and downbeat of the rock music careening off the walls. Each youthful face had a slack, washed-out appearance in the dim light that suggested early aging, the bewhiskered young men resembling old timers and the girls, crones. The common stamp of this young but old gathering was a look of apathy, of boredom and a lack of purpose that was to become the curse of their generation. Driven by insecurity and disillusionment, they had drifted like nomads into an urban desert, isolated and cut off, yet subsisting along with other minorities, with other peoples speaking different tongues. And the more barren their surroundings, the more cheerless and forbidding, the more they turned inward to discover another world, a giddy, fairyland of fascination. Like so many disparate groups down through the ages, they had discovered the forbidden world of drugs, a domain of altered consciousness, exquisite sensations, and bizzare thoughts and feelings. Perhaps it was only an illusory world, an artifact, but it held them in a kind of spell, piping a tune of enchantment that few could resist following. Dom looked again at their faces. He peddled that other world, offered it here in this busy marketplace of apathy.

He had been in The Prophet for hours waiting for the short, winter day to end. Finally, at four o'clock, he slipped on his leather coat and went back to his room a few blocks away. He got off on the last two bags of his personal dope, much better than anything he sold, and nodded. It was well after dark when he awoke, feeling hungry. He walked through the crisp, night air to a sub shop and ordered a meatball sub and a coffee. As he ate, a young blonde waited nearby and watched him intently. After he finished, she followed him outside and caught him by the sleeve.

"Dom!"

"Hello, Debbie."

She looked young, maybe eighteen, but at the same time, old like the others. Once she had been beautiful but now her face was sallow and drawn and her teeth were bad. Her eyes glittered and watered and her lips trembled as she tried to speak.

"Dom, I—I need just a couple of bags . . . I'm really desperate. . . !"

She had done this before, he recalled, and studied her coldly.

"I'm broke right now," she went on, "but I'll pay you tomorrow . . . honest . . . or I'll stay with you tonight if you like."

"Look, we went through this the last time," he said and tried to get away.

"Please!" she begged. "Didn't I spend the night with you? Remember? You said that anytime I . . . ."

"You know how I do business," he snapped, interrupting her.

She gave him an incredulous look, seized him with both hands. "But I'm sick, oh, Dom, please help me!"

He shoved her away and she fell against a parked car.

"Oooh! You dirty bastard!"

"Shut up and get outa here before the cops come!"

"You bastard!" she moaned.

Dom walked away quickly in the direction of the subway. He tried to avoid these incidents, yet they happened all too often and it distressed him. He did not like the idea of making people miserable, had not willed it but knew that it was a part of being a dealer. Ducking downstairs, he caught a train across town, got off in a quiet, rundown residential section. He walked a few blocks until he came to a bar, went in and ordered a beer. It was nearly an hour later, after glancing at the clock several times and seeing the hands poised exactly at five minutes of eight, that he went outside and stood waiting on the deserted corner. Even with a few beers under his belt he was wide awake now, shivering slightly in the damp, frosty night air. It had been nearly four hours since his last shot and the mellowness of it was ebbing out of his system as surely as sap running from a girdled tree, it dying by inches, leaving an inert, wooden stalk. He fought a powerful urge to fix up and get off again, then remembered he had nothing left.

A late model sedan caught his attention as it rounded the corner, slowed, then speeded up and circled the block twice, almost as a shark circles its prey. According to plan Dom walked to the next block and waited for ten minutes while the car sat at the corner, watching. He always dreaded the moment when it pulled up beside him and the door yawned open, even though he had been through it many times. As a dealer, he handled a lot of cash and knew a lot of names. If anyone ever killed him, not only the police but even the public would be grateful. But as in any business arrangement, he shared a mutual dependency with these men and therefore a necessary trust. A dealer-addict, he needed their heroin, and as distributors, they needed his trade. And he was even more valuable to them because he had never been arrested and was not well known to the police as were many dealers.

Spanky, the strong-arm man, usually sat alone in the back seat during these pickups. But tonight a second man had joined them. Dom had met the boss on only one other occasion, and as he slid into the rented sedan he found himself looking once more into the round, almost cherubic face with the inscrutable, heavy-lidded eyes. A short, stocky man, he was always well-dressed, wore a suit and tie, a fine, camel hair coat and a gray felt hat. And he was serious, so much so that whenever he spoke, everyone listened. He raised a hand, narrowed the puffy eyes, and his curiously high-pitched voice became harsh. Sometimes for emphasis he waggled his stubby finger or a cigar and concluded every remark with a sharp, convincing nod. Dom knew little about him except that he was the supplier of cut ounces, or "pieces," of heroin at one thousand dollars each. His runners usually dropped off a couple of pieces every week and came back later for the money from the week before. The boss used the name Motto and his men called him Tony. Dom did not know if this was his real name, or whom he was connected with. It was better that he did not know.

"How ya doin', kid?" he said sharply.

"Not bad," Dom replied, trying to hide his nervousness and wondering why Motto had come.

The boss waved a cigar at him. "Glad to hear it," he went on, clearing his throat. "Y'know, dope's gettin' tight. Might say there's a little panic startin' up. Elections are comin' up an' the feds are startin' to clamp down. Soon as they're over things'll ease up again, huh? But lately they grabbed a couple big shipments in France that we was expectin', so we had to make some other connections. His voice rose and he punched the cigar. "Of course . . . this stuff ain't like that other 'cause its been through a few more hands. Probably take one cut anyhow. Naturally, I don't know the difference, never used it in my life."

"Is it the same price?" asked Dom, relieved that this was all Motto had in mind.

"Yeah, sure!" Motto replied harshly. "Like I say, this stuff is tight now."

The car bumped down a gravel road and stopped. They got out, buttoned up their coats against the cold night and stood among the trees with naked limbs reaching mornfully into the frosty air. Joey, the driver, thin, silent, more a shadow than a man, glided around back, unlocked the trunk and jerked out a spare tire. He slashed it with a quick stroke of his knife, reached in and retrieved two softball-sized foil packages.

"Let us know how it is," Motto went on, his voice milder, as if apologizing for the inferior quality of the heroin and implying that it might not even take one cut to sell well. And then he nodded emphatically, dropping the subject.

They let Dom off at a taxi stand, he jumping out of the car with the two pieces of heroin bulging in his coat pocket. He crossed the street, hailed a cab, tried to look as inconspicuous as possible. It was another vulnerable time. People knew him and from now until he stashed the stuff he could be arrested by the police for possession or mugged by the addicts. The dealer, who preyed on human hunger, was in turn preyed upon by the converging forces of good and evil. He scurried into a cab, relaxed as it pulled away. But something gnawed at him, the awareness of a trap already sprung. Any dealer who handles large amounts of good dope for longer than a year develops a big habit. Motto, either knowingly or unknowingly, had provided only about one fourth the usual amount of heroin and then warned him to cut it conservatively. This meant that Dom was going to be sick, that he could get only a few bundles out of it for himself to last the whole week instead of the bundle a day that he was accustomed to. So he would have to cut down, or else cop the rest on his own. A wave of apprehension went through him, mixed with the chill of the cold night. By tomorrow he knew this would be replaced by the more gripping chill of heroin withdrawal, would have to be, for, as Motto said, dope was getting tight.

6

At six o'clock that same evening city hall was nearly deserted, most of the employees having gone home for the day. But the mayor was still upstairs, tied up in another meeting, the last of an endless agenda. He looked tired in his shirtsleeves, his youthful face creased with strain and appearing more aged now than when he took office three years ago. It was not easy for one man to run a large, sprawling city, a bubbling cauldron of racial crisis, of opposing interests, of big people versus little people, of partisan politics colliding and entwining with human need and want. His strength was in a personal charisma of youthful vigor that inspired confidence in the younger voters and in the people under him. But his weakness was becoming apparent, especially to long time residents and community groups, who were disturbed by soaring property taxes, a rising crime rate, and by residential neighborhoods deteriorating in the very shadow of high-rise, expensive urban renewal complexes.

Sitting opposite the mayor were two men, one heavy jowled and husky, in his sixties, and the other youthful, fortyish, his face smooth and sharp-featured, like that of a cadet. An aide was just ushering in a third man, tall, late thirties, with a trimmed, dark mustache.

"Mr. DiBona, this is Mayor Rowen," said the aide pleasantly.

"How do you do, sir. Steve DiBona, Bureau of Narcotics and Dangerous Drugs. Sorry, I'm a bit late."

The mayor smiled. "Shoppers' night, I know how it is," he replied. "I'm glad you could come. How about some coffee?"

The aide stepped out, reappeared with a braless secretary who poured out cups of coffee as the other men were introduced.

"This is Rich Caruso, our new police commissioner," said the mayor.

"How do you do. I've heard a lot about you," said Di-Bona, pumping the hand of the cadet.

"And our captain of the narcotics squad, Mike O'-Donnell."

"Pleased to meet you."

They all sat down, the mayor pausing politely, stirring his coffee, allowing the men to settle. He liked to make people comfortable and people in turn liked working for him. He turned to the federal agent. "Steve, I guess Mike talked to you already so you know how everyone's concerned about the upswing in crime in the city, especially as it's related to drugs," he said. He glanced at the two policemen who were looking very grave. "Of course, I realize this is a nationwide problem right now, especially in our cities. Now, the way it has been explained to me, the drug problem can't be licked on any one level but only through a team approach, that is, between city, state, and federal agencies."

"Certainly," the agent agreed, though he and the others in the room knew that the feds ran their own show.

"Too bad Lieutenant Colonel Lawton couldn't make it," interjected the commissioner, partly to relieve his own momentary tension.

"From State Police?" asked DiBona.

"Right."

"I've met him," DiBona went on. "Nice fellow. Very dedicated."

"A swell guy, he sure is," the captain agreed heartily, then began again, his voice gruff and authoritative, for he was the oldest man in the room. "Goin' back to what you said, sir, it certainly is a nationwide problem, all right. And even more, it's an international problem as well, wouldn't you say?"

The mayor nodded. "That's true, Mike. But when you have figures showing that fifty percent of property crimes in this city are drug related, most of them committed by youthful offenders, then it becomes a local problem."

"Right, sir," agreed the captain vigorously.

"Can't deny it," echoed the new commissioner, not about to be left out of the discussion. He had come from a job on a small, suburban force and knew that O'Donnell, his subordinate, considered him green in the narcotics field. "That's why we're cracking down on street peddlars," he went on firmly. "Unfortunately the courts are quite lenient at the present time and they are back out on the streets again in only a year or two, which. . . ."

"There's no place to put them except in jail with the real, hard-nosed crooks," O'Donnell rejoined, interrupting his younger superior, the object of his own secret contempt. "And at present there aren't any real good rehabilitation programs for these kids outside of jail."

"It's a knotty problem, all right," agreed the mayor, his voice conciliatory. "And it concerns our youth, which troubles me most of all because they are tomorrow's citizens. It could mean the decline of our cities as centers of our civilization." He paused, loosened his tie as if uncomfortably warm, though the office was rather cool. "Methadone maintenance is providing a temporary solution and crime has gone down a bit," he went on, frowning, "but now methadone itself is being abused more and more, so they tell me. So I suppose it's not really the final answer to the problem as we had hoped."

"Far from it," asserted Caruso.

"Right," DiBona agreed, at last feeling compelled to speak. "Methadone only complicates the picture because it keeps these addicts drug dependent and on the drug scene. No, there's only one thing they respect and I'm afraid that is strict law enforcement." The two policemen muttered their approval and the agent paused, then went on. "You have to strike at your distribution system. After all, most addicts prefer heroin to methadone if they can get it and if it is of sufficient quality. But with modern transportation over air, land, and sea routes from all parts of the globe, you can imagine the tremendous difficulties we're faced with."

The mayor sat with his hands folded, listening quietly, his blue eyes twinkling with interest, which DiBona took as an indication to continue. "Now, the strategy of the BNDD has been to try and locate the origin of heroin distribution, whereas Customs convoys it into the country in order to identify the major buyers and distributors. So occasionally they have been known to take some of our own undercover men into custody who were involved in tracing a shipment." The agent's face softened, as if recalling a joke, and he went on. "As you know, much of it has been originating in Turkey as raw opium, then is refined into heroin in Marseilles and shipped by boat to New York and then distributed from there, usually by air. But now that's been supressed to some extent and Asian stuff, both heroin and opium, is flooding in. Opium from Thailand, Laos, and Burma is refined into heroin in Cambodia and Vietnam, then shipped through Hong Kong by Chinese middlemen to Latin American middlemen, or else brought straight into this country by American servicemen. Of course, this is a much more difficult source to contend with because of the complicated political situation. And I'm afraid supplies are also increasing from Mexico and South America. As you know, in addition to our international efforts, we're also working locally to some extent. Now, we know of at least one major system of heroin traffic that involves this city in particular. Because they depended on French heroin, we believe now they're starting to feel the pinch and are shifting their operations to alternate sources, such as Latin American suppliers."

Commissioner Caruso nodded, his cadet's face attentive, almost obedient."Mm-hm!" he uttered. "That figures, because the quality of street heroin has gone down lately to around one percent."

"It's sort of like putting your finger in a dike, the way I see it," observed the mayor, unfolding his hands, and jabbed a finger at them. "Plug up one hole and the leak starts somewhere else."

"That's what I mean by an international problem," O'Donnell insisted.

There was a brief silence, the men thoughtfully acknowledging the senior captain's comment. After all, how could local officials be held responsible if the problem was worldwide in scope, they seemed to be saying to one another.

"Don't you think that this is a social problem also?" queried the aide, a young man with longish hair who had entered and was standing practically unnoticed near the door.

His question was ignored by all but the mayor, who directed a keen glance at his aide. "Oh course it is, certainly, Larry. It is that as well." He twirled his pen, fatigue deepening the lines in his face. After a brief pause, he turned back to the narcotics agent. "Say, have you identified any of the big dealers in this area?" he asked.

DiBona looked down quickly, as if put on the spot. Certainly, they could not expect him to name a list, he thought. After all, at least one of the major backers was also one of the mayor's largest political contributors in the last election campaign. "We have a few leads," he said at last, his voice crisp. "Most are not addicts, as you probably know. They stay pretty clean as far as the law is concerned. And some are reputable businessmen who provide mainly financial backing. These men in particular are very hard to prosecute, as I'm sure everyone is aware."

The two policemen looked disgruntled, while the mayor yawned and smiled affably. "If only we had more time to talk about this," he said. "But. . . ," he paused and nodded at his aide, "I've got to fly out of town for a speaking engagement." He stood up, the others rising also. "Well, gentlemen, thanks for coming. Steve, you've been a great help. You've clarified a lot of thinking I had on this." He smiled briskly and gave the agent's hand a warm squeeze.

"Thank you, Mr. Mayor. Glad I could be of help," the agent replied.

"And Commissioner Caruso and I, along with Captain O'Donnell, can assure you of our fullest cooperation," the mayor added over his shoulder and headed for the door.

7

Dom slumped in the taxi, watched the city lights stream

past the window like a milky way splashed with bright streaks of neon. He could have seen beauty in it, admired it with child-like fascination had he not been distracted with more immediate thoughts. They were troubling thoughts concerning a habit that was too large for the dope he carried in his pocket. The percentage of heroin in those two foil-wrapped packages complicated his life immeasurably, so that now there was very little chance of his enjoying anything. But when the taxi stopped in front of the ancient rooming house, his mind cleared, his senses snapping to the alert. He waited, had the driver circle the block and drop him at the corner. Again he watched, this time for several minutes. It was a bad place. Trees shut out the only street lamp and cast deep shadows that pooled in the dooryard. He advanced toward the entrance, felt a vague shiver running down the back of his neck, not from the cold this time, or from dopesickness, but from fear. His life as a dealer was nearly as hazardous now as it was in Vietnam almost three years ago. He felt the same prickle on the back of his neck then, especially on night patrol when something inside him sensed the waiting enemy. And yet, he was never more afraid than right now, here in his own country, standing at his own doorstep.

Acting on instinct, he did not enter through the front but circled quietly around back, lit a match, and descended to the cellar. Taking the two ounces of heroin out of his coat, he opened them, dumped about half of one into the other foil wrapping and shoved this high overhead, just under a joist. He pocketed the smaller packet and mounted the back stairs. The light of one naked bulb on the first floor left canyons of shadow yawning around him as he kept climbing, his footsteps the only audible sound. Then something struck him and he remembered nothing. The landlady, hearing the crash of something falling down the stairs and someone running out the front, waited timidly until all was quiet, then opened the door and peeped out. She saw one of her tenants sprawled semiconscious on the staircase, his head oozing blood.

Russ, Dolores, and another youth named Danny arrived at the city hospital late in the evening. Danny had been looking for Dom and got the news from the landlady. He was quite upset by her story and in turn got Russ and Dolores upset. A quiet youth of about twenty-six, he wore his long dark hair tied back in a pony tail, and his face was half hidden in a full beard. Small, wire-rim spectacles perched precariously on the bridge of his nose, giving him an aura of wisdom. His stoop-shouldered figure was lost in a pair of faded, baggy overalls decorated with military insignias and sunshine patches, set off by a necklace of amorphous black and brown beads. Such an appearance usually drew stares of indignation whenever he ventured outside of that part of the city frequented by street people. To straights he was a hippie, a non-American who never bathed and wanted to overthrow the government, someone contemptible who stood for all things obscene and indecent, like revolution and group sex. But they did not know Danny.

Shy and sensitive, there were two things he particularly abhorred—violence and women. All of his energies were invested in only one conviction, that his whole life was not time enough to unravel the puzzle of his existence. When he was not reading philosophy or religion, he expressed himself in hard-to-understand poetry. For relaxation he did yoga exercises and listened to music. And he was not above the use of certain mind-expanding drugs, such as LSD and mescaline, not to mention ordinary pot, to increase his self-awareness and enrich his life experience. Heroin addiction was something he had fallen into only lately, after speeding his way out of a long depression that he blamed on too much philosophy and not enough faith.

The three of them, the hippie, the black pimp and his white girl drew more than cursory glances as they walked across the hospital lobby and got directions to the overnight ward. By mistake they passed onto the accident floor where they were caught up in a melee of stricken patients, policemen, nurses, and harried interns. A clerk redirected them back through another gauntlet of wailing children, staring drunks, bloodied accident cases, and a heart attack gulping oxygen. At last they found the overnight ward, much quieter, a repository for those nebulous cases from the accident floor who were not quite sick enough to send upstairs but not well enough to send home.

A prim nurse stopped them. "DeCosta?" she repeated. "Yes, he's here, but visiting hours are almost over and I think he's sleeping."

There was a pause, the three of them looking at one another. "But I'm his sister," Dolores said at last.

The nurse looked at them suspiciously. "Wait and I'll ask the doctor," she replied.

A young intern appeared, pink-eyed, unchanged whites wrinkled from a long day of duty. "He had a bad head injury," he announced glibly. "Concussion and laceration of the scalp. But he should be all right in a few days. We may be transferring him upstairs, depending on the tests."

"Can't she see him now?" Danny asked.

The doctor eyed them with annoyance.

"Please?" begged Dolores, her face a picture of sorrow.

"All right, but only for a moment."

The nurse led them back to a bed behind a closed curtain. Brushing through they saw the tall youth, eyes shut, his head bandaged.

"He's asleep," whispered Russ. "Maybe we shouldn't bother him."

"Dom," said the nurse gently. "Your sister is here to see you."

He opened his eyes, stared vacantly at them for a moment, then his eyes flickered with recognition.

"How're you feeling?" Dolores asked with tenderness.

He opened his mouth. The words were slow in coming. "Got a real bad headache. . . ."

"What happened?" Danny asked. "Someone rip you off?"

Dom glanced at the nurse who stood listening. Conscious of intruding, she stepped out.

"Yeah . . . ," he replied finally.

"Wow! Y'know who it was?" Russ asked indignantly.

Dom closed his eyes. "Uh-uh."

"Could have been a lot of people," Danny suggested.

They looked around, heard the nurse a few feet away making up a bed, began to communicate in low whispers.

Dolores bent down, caressed his forehead. "Cops been around?" she asked softly.

"Not yet."

"They brought you here," said Danny. "The landlady found you lying in a pool of blood and called them."

There was a pause. The crucial subject had not yet been broached. "How much did they rip off?" Danny whispered at last.

"Only a half piece," Dom replied. "I got more stashed."

Danny sighed with relief. "Is it the same quality stuff?"

"No. You'll have to try it. I never got a chance. . . ." He winced. "Hey look," he went on, and touched Dolores's arm, "I need something now . . . bad. . . ."

"Ask for some morphine," Danny advised.

Dom shook his head feebly. "They won't give it to me, 'cause I got a head injury."

"That's silly," whispered Dolores. "Here, I'll give you some of my methadone. Sixty milligrams, that's all I have on me right now. But it should keep you straight through tomorrow. "Here. . . ." She opened her purse, wrapped the small white tablets in a tissue and slipped them into his palm. "Can you manage?"

He nodded.

"We'll bring you some more later, man," said Russ. "Too bad, with all the stuff they got in this place, you could stay high forever."

"When are you leaving?" asked Danny. "The doctor said in a few days."

Dom smiled weakly. "Can't stay here that long. Maybe tomorrow I'll split, even if I have to walk out."

The nurse returned and told them they had to leave because the doctors were coming through on rounds. Dolores gave Dom a sisterly kiss on the cheek and the three of them sauntered out, relieved that Dom was recovering.

"Dealing is a really rough business," Danny was saying. "I wouldn't want to get into it."

"I hope he finds out who ripped him off," Russ mused.

Dolores elbowed him. The nurse was right behind them as they quickened their step and departed.

8

Dom had slept badly that night in the hospital, and not because of the painful head wound. The methadone that Dolores had slipped into his hand lasted for only six hours and then the dopesickness began nagging him. By five o'clock in the morning it seemed the walls of the hospital were closing in around him as he lay awake, plagued by hot and cold sweats and muscle aches. He finally persuaded a gullible student nurse covering the ward to get a verbal order from the semi-somnolent intern by telephone. In this way Dom received some Demerol and fell into a fitful sleep for another hour or so. When he awoke it was barely dawn and just for a moment it seemed as though she were there beside him again, close in his arms, and he realized he had been dreaming about her.

He lay quietly, the sheets soaked with sweat, then began trembling from another wave of the chills and huddled into himself, conscious of the thinness of his body. Before, when he knew her and loved her, he had been a different person altogether. That day on the pitcher's mound five years ago had been the summit of his life, when the umpire jerked up his arm for the last time.

"Str-r-rike!" roared the ump, and a cheer rose from the bleachers as the batter walked away disconsolantly. Dom had just pitched his second straight no-hitter to win the high school championship. His teammates mobbed, hugged, pummeled him and the jubilant crowd swarmed out onto the diamond. In the midst of the crush he turned, shaded his eyes and saw her standing beside his parents, saw Brenda clapping her hands, laughing, bursting with joy. It was her greatest moment, too.

The coach trotted out, his usually stern face glowing with triumph, his mouth cracked in a wide grin, and gave Dom a hug. "Great work, boy!" he exclaimed. "That's some of the finest pitching I've ever seen!" The coach of the opposing team came over with some of the players to congratulate him, then his father appeared, beaming with pride. And Brenda was there suddenly to throw her arms around him and give him a kiss. Then his elated teammates lifted him onto their shoulders and, milling about and cheering, carried him into the dugout.

A tanned, middle-aged man waiting in the locker room grabbed his hand and shook it vigorously. "You've got a real future in professional baseball, son!" he boomed, then paused. "Say, what about the service? You 1-A?"

Because there was a war going on it was a practical question. "I'm 1-A," Dom replied, pulling off his jersey. He was waiting for this moment, knew that they had been scouting him for weeks.

The man handed him a business card. "Call us after graduation, son. We really want to talk to you. We can arrange things. Now, don't forget, will you?"

"No, sir, I sure won't," he promised.

His draft notice came three weeks later, just before graduation. He thought about the big leagues constantly and waged a long battle with his conscience. There was a war and his country needed him. As much as he liked baseball, he decided that his country came before a big league ball club. He called the scout, who understood and told him to contact the club as soon as he was discharged from the service. Next, he told Brenda about his decision. Curiously, he found himself apologizing to her.

"It happens to a lotta guys, sweetheart," he explained, putting his arm around her and kissing her gently. "I'll be back home before you know it. Only twelve months . . . ."

"I know, Dom, but oh, I'll miss you so much!" she said, unable to supress her sobs as she clung to him. After a moment or two she dried her eyes and smiled bravely. They sat apart, made an effort at rational discussion. But emotion came flooding back and once more they fell into each other's arms. They agreed to become engaged, unofficially for now. They would write, send snapshots, and the hated year of separation would pass quickly, like the mere jog of a minute hand on the clock of their young lives.

One of the more celebrated events in the history of

the DeCosta household was the farewell dinner for their only son on the eve of his departure for Vietnam. Like many leave-takings, the sadness was dispelled in a whirl of gaiety. The family made a great fuss over him in his smart new uniform as he moved, almost like a celebrity, among admiring glances and the pop of flash cubes. He had just come out of boot camp and looked the very picture of a clean-cut, American soldier, a boy any parent would be proud of. Brenda, equally impressive for her great beauty, stayed by his side. The family was proud of her, too, looked upon her as their own daughter.

Just before dinner his mother called him into the kitchen. She dried her hands on her apron and took him, pressing him to her soft figure that had carried the aroma of food for as long as he could remember, of oil, garlic, and seasoning. "You look so nice!" she cried. "Please promise me one thing, that you'll be careful! I know you'll do your duty, I'm not worried about that, but I just want you to be careful! Remember, you're still my little baby. . . !" Her voice broke and she hugged him again and he felt her face wet on his. Then she let him go and smiled. "And when you come back home I want you to go on to college. I've talked to poppa. Sure, he wants you to play baseball and that would be nice for awhile, but what's the future? You'll want to spend time with Brenda and the children. You were always interested in law school, remember? For a boy like you the world has an awful lot to offer. And you and Brenda can live here with us. You can have the whole upstairs. . . ."

He sat at the head of the table, erect and high shouldered in his uniform. Brenda sat on his right and then his parents, his sister, an aunt and uncle and two cousins, and finally Uncle Paul, who was a priest. He said the blessing, then added a special prayer for Dom's trip overseas. His mother literally threw the cookbook at them that night, serving a huge antepasto and minnestrone soup first, then deep dishes of lasagna, spaghetti, and veal parmesan. There was lots of Chianti, too, and it warmed them, kept the smiles on their faces. At last they turned off the lights and brought in a cake with one candle on it, especially decora-

ted with an American flag. It said, "Good Luck Dom."
The candle was Brenda's idea. It stood for one year.

9

The next morning, not long after Russ and Dolores had risen, Sherry knocked at the door. As she entered they noticed that beneath her Mexican blanket she wore an old pair of tennis shoes many sizes too large. Worn out and tattered, they flapped at every step. Because they were almost as big as she was, they exaggerated her thinness. She nearly tripped over them shuffling over to the sofa where she collapsed limply, like a burlesque rag doll.

"Why are you wearing those old sneakers?" Dolores asked sternly, while Russ tried unsuccessfully to stifle a guffaw.

Sherry curled up on the sofa, hid her face for a moment. "Slick took my good pair of boots while I was asleep," she whined. "Then he sold them for a bag of dope and told me to wear his old pair of sneakers. After that he split—I don't know where. I don't know when he's coming back, maybe after he does a score." She paused, angrily kicked off the old tennis shoes and curled her feet under her. "You know, we blew that three grand in about ten days. Since then we've both been real sick and, well, he's sold everything of mine—my ring, my coat, and now my only pair of shoes. Everything for dope. He'd rather see me freeze to death than get sick himself."

"That's sumpin' else," Russ observed, regaining his composure. "Why he'd sell the fillins' outa his grandmother's teeth just for a bag."

"It's incredible!" Dolores exploded. "I don't see why you put up with it! If he was my old man, I'd tell him where to get off!" Her green eyes snapped with anger, then softened with pity. She thought how truly pathetic and helpless Sherry was in her boyfriend's hands, and yet how desperate she was whenever he left her. She lost no time finding other company because she could not bear to be alone, not even for a single moment. The bleakness of her life and the barrenness of her imagination made idle time abhorrent to her, deprived her of any means of coping with it save the intoxicating escape of drugs or the diversions of other people, on whom she depended wholly. Dolores's natural impulse was to feed her, but Sherry refused food, asked for some grass instead. Except for heroin, marihuana helped her chronic depression more than anything else. As they passed the joint around, sucking the pungent smoke deep into their lungs, her lethargy changed to petulance and she became more animated. She complained raucously about Slick always running off and leaving her like this, without dope or money.

Russ sat listening nearby and almost unconsciously began comparing the two girls. Dolores, even though a confirmed prostitute, was clearly the better woman. She pulled her weight and more, working at her job, keeping up the apartment, plus hustling. Sherry on the other hand was a mere child, knowing only how to live off others, and to ball for dope. A lot of girls did it that way, which is why it was usually easier for them to support their habits than for the guys, who had to go out and steal. He did not mind her company when Slick was around because he usually had some good dope to make up for it. But now that he was away she became a definite nuisance. She constantly complained of the jones, of shivering and aches and pains and the rest, since like many addicts, she had a low threshold for pain, both physical and emotional. She was not a methadone user like Dolores, who only needed to pop a few ten milligram dolophines, or maybe one forty milligram biscuit, twice a day to get a moderate buzz and to stay straight. Sherry had to have that needle, which alone seemed to make her high, at least three or four times a day.

"Do you have something to hold me till Slick gets back?" he heard Sherry ask plaintively.

"When is he coming?" said Dolores.

"I said I don't know," came the whimpering response.

Russ sighed with exasperation, busied himself with a shot of cocaine. This would help lift his mood after the torpor of marihuana. He dissolved some of the pure crystals, or "snow," in water and banged it into his arm in the bathroom. Then, not to be stingy, he took the gold coke spoon from around his neck, filled it with a pinch of coke and passed it to Dolores, who sniffed it gracefully. And he let Sherry borrow his works for a hit. They all began to feel happy and elated. Suddenly things were not all that bad. Then momentarily the giddiness passed. Russ's mood blackened as he began to come down. He realized with a sense of panic that his supply of coke was nearly exhausted.

"Man, we gotta go cop!" he declared to Dolores. "We're almost outa coke! Only one bag left."

"What?" she cried. "You had two ounces just a few days ago, from all that blood money! You spent every nickel of it!"

Russ shook his head sadly. "'Fraid I put it all in my arm, baby."

"You're going to put us in the poorhouse with that habit of yours!" she scolded.

"What you sayin', woman? You get jus' as high on it as I do!"

"Yes, but I don't use as much."

"Cocaine?" Sherry laughed softly. "You must be jet setters or something to use that stuff all the time. What's wrong with heroin?"

Russ wrinkled his nose. "Fine for comin' down offa coke, but I don't like gettin' strung out behind it." He smiled at Dolores. "You dig it, baby? We gotta get some scratch, right now."

"I'm low on methadone, too," she replied. "Gave most of it to Dom. So we need at least a hundred extra tonight."

He looked slyly at her. "Then how's about beatin' a few tricks for some fast bread?" he suggested. "We ain't done it in a long time."

She frowned. "I haven't forgotten the last time that john almost killed me," she fretted. "You know that isn't my thing. I don't like to lose steady tricks on account of a bad reputation. Besides, its stealing."

Russ laughed at her hypocrisy. "Don't be stupid! It may not be your bag, but still, you're awful good at it. 'Sides, word ain't gonna get around. You know for sure them tricks won't go to the police."

She hesitated, thought how Russ's character left a lot to be desired at times. Then it occurred to her that if she beat a few tricks for some extra money tonight, it would give him enough for a few hits of coke and that would probably keep him out of trouble. Anyway, she liked the cocaine herself—it kept her going on a busy night. And then they would need something for both Sherry and, of course, poor Dom. "All right," she agreed at last. "I've got two steady tricks. Then we can do whatever you want."

10

As in any business, Dolores relied on steady customers, tricks that liked her company and came back on a regular basis. It had taken time to build up this kind of trade, now worth up to five hundred and very occasionally even a thousand a week. Take the six Chinamen who came together in one car every Sunday night, usually the busiest night of the week. They were on and off, quick as rabbits, at a modest twenty-five dollars apiece. Others paid more. One businessman came into town and spent seventy-five dollars for only an hour of her time.

But not all tricks wanted to go to bed. A man in his sixties paid fifty dollars just to have her undress and stand in the nude for forty-five minutes while he complained about his shrewish wife and business worries. That was all, and it seemed to be helping him because he kept it up regularly every week. Another man wanted her to whip him on his exposed buttocks, said it was worth every penny of the thirty dollars it cost him. Still another desired only that she squat and urinate in his face while he masturbated, which seemed to satisfy him more than anything else in the world. And many businessmen, especially the married types from out of town wanted nothing more than a dinner date, some female presence to relate to across the table. Whenever they came into the city they would always call, but seldom did they ever take her to bed.

Early in her career she learned to stay away from drunks, who were too slow and hard to handle, and kids, who were too rough and also hard to manage on occasion. She knew she was a quality whore as far as Russ was concerned, and knew also that he was glad to be her man. He did not have to intervene often in her affairs, only provided the apartment, took care of her if she got in a jam with a customer, and bailed her out if she was arrested. And he made love to her, real love every night to relax her after a long evening of continual stimulation without orgasm. As her old man, Russ was entitled to nearly all her earnings, which he spent liberally on whatever pleased him. Because she was his main heat he did not try to pull another whore. Once about a year ago when they were in another apartment, Russ did have another girl working for him. But that lasted only a few weeks. Dolores flew into a rage one night and drove the other girl out. Even though a whore, Dolores was a one-man woman.

It was after nine o'clock when Russ drove Sherry back to her place. She was content and kittenish now on some methadone they had given her. He returned to the apartment and lounged in the other room, shooting up the rest of the cocaine, while Dolores turned her last trick. He stayed out of sight, because the presence of a black pimp will scare off white tricks. Yet Russ was essentially non-violent, not at all the type of pimp that ripped tricks off, held them up, grabbed their pants, or mugged them in a dark hallway. The young junkies did this, but it was not his style. He was too sophisticated, preferred instead to use a good short game, like the Murphy.

Ten o'clock found the two of them dressed to the teeth in the lobby of a large, downtown hotel, patronized by itinerant businessmen. It was, in Russ's own words, the biggest overnight whorehouse in town, although most of the local citizenry were ignorant of the fact. Business was carried out not only in the rooms, but in the elevated parking lot next door, inside the tricks' well-cushioned cars.

Dolores, wearing a tight-fitting blouse and a miniskirt to show off her tempting figure, stationed herself in the lobby just outside one of the cocktail lounges while Russ went in, his eye on the patrons. He chose carefully, looking for men who seemed lonely and a little stiff. The combination was an easy one to find. Presently two men started out, their faces aglow. They spied Dolores across the hall and when she showed them some thigh, they stopped.

Russ intervened at that point. "You like her?" he asked politely.

They turned, eyed him with suspicion, then one of them smiled. "Hey, who wouldn't?" he replied.

"You can have her for twenty-five bucks apiece," Russ offered.

They both gazed hungrily at the tantalizing girl, captivated by her aggressive flirting. She could be theirs, it was clear, if they wanted to spend the money.

One of them winked at his friend. "Whaddaya say, Georgie-boy?"

The other shrugged. "Why not? I'm game. . . ."

"Okay, pay me here and then follow her upstairs," Russ said quietly. He nodded to Dolores and she smiled at them, walked away, switching her hips. The two men followed at a safe distance, after slipping Russ the money.

Ten minutes later, Dolores met Russ down the street in a barroom, a little out of breath. "I lose them on that elevator everytime," she laughed. "I hold up three fingers for the third floor, press two and three, and get off on two. While they're going up, I'm coming down the stairs."

Russ snickered. "It's true what they say, ain't it? A sucker is born every minute." His eye roved around the crowded room, again picking out the men who ogled her. "Try that dude over there, the one with the rug. He looks like a real sucker. You got the key?"

Dolores nodded and Russ sidled away. She caught the man's eye and began flirting actively with him. Well dressed, in his forties, and alone, he was soon over at the bar just next to her, obstensibly to order another drink. Gently she brushed him with her breast and he turned. "Can I buy you a drink?" he asked quickly.

They had a short conversation at his table over a second drink, then left the bar together. Outside Dolores turned and stopped him. "Honey, it's thirty-five dollars if you're in the mood. . . ." she said.

He smiled, put his arm around her. "Baby, I sure am! I'll even make it fifty if you can do a few things."

"Everything, honey. . . ." She slipped a hand down below his belt and squeezed.

"Let's go!" he muttered. "Where's your place?"

She opened her purse, took out a key. "Okay, honey, pay me now and I'll give you the key. I can't be seen goin' in with anyone. Cops, understand? It's that hotel over there, right down the street next to the theatre." She pointed to a shabby building, barely noticeable beside a glittering, X-rated movie house.

"Yeah, I see it." Hurriedly he drew out his wallet, gave her the money and accepted the key.

"Room 106, honey. Five minutes." She tucked the bills into her bosom and walked quickly down the street into the cheap hotel.

After a little more than two minutes the man followed, eagerly mounted the stairs, found the room and unlocked the door. Inside there was an old drunk passed out on the bed. He never saw the sexy young girl, or his fifty dollars, again.

Dolores met Russ in still another club a few blocks away. She gave him the money and he approached a friend of his, a dude named Ritchie who was a methadone user and a dealer. Russ bought thirty of the small white ten milligram dolophines, or "dollies" for sixty dollars. And from another friend he bought two fifty dollar bags of good cocaine.

11

Dom was too dopesick in the hospital to eat his breakfast but managed to hold down a few sips of hot tea.

"Are you all right?" asked a nurse, bustling by with a medication tray.

He wiped his watery eyes, nose, "Yeah."

She frowned. "Do you have a cold or something?"

"I guess so," he replied.

"Then tell the doctors," she advised. "They're starting rounds."

Ten minutes later three young men strode into the room. All were about his own age and uniformed in freshly starched whites. The youngest, a medical student who lugged an armload of charts, gawked owlishly at Dom through gold-rimmed spectacles, curious at this bizzare specimen from the streets. They knew little of his world, only what had been fed them in television, movies, or in best-sellers, where the streets were depicted as an alluring shangri-la of bright lights, vibrant music, and hip young people embarked on an eternal pleasure trip, where no one tasted of life but that they drank it to the dregs and threw away the cup.

On the other hand, the young doctors were aware, from the same mass media, that street life was brutal, a sordid exaggeration of their own world in which unscrupulousness was converted into power and greed into success. But they, having succeeded in medical school, had not the slightest need to escape into the limbo of the streets. They shunned it, wary of the violence, poverty, and despair that lurked there behind a facade of gaiety. Yet Dom would have startled them had he told them what he himself knew well, that these two worlds, his and theirs, were one and the same.

"This is the guy with the concussion," the medical student announced offhandedly.

The resident addressed Dom in a dry, almost artificial bedside manner. "How're you feeling?"

Dom grimaced. "Better, but I still got a lot of pain in my ribs. Musta got kicked. I could really use something for it. . . ."

The resident reached out, pressed his right side and he jumped. "It is tender," he observed. He yanked the chart out of the medical student's arm, flipped through it. "It appears that there's a possibility of heroin addiction here," he said drily. "Is that true?"

"No, 'fraid not," Dom mumbled.

The intern stooped down, squinted at his arm and smiled at his discovery. "Then what are those track marks doing there?" he asked.

Dom gawked at them. "Must have gotten them in here," he said. "They weren't there before."

"The police said they found a syringe in your pocket," noted the resident

"That's for my allergy shots."

"Allergy?"

"Hay fever and asthma."

There was a pause, the three of them scrutinizing him.

"Is that why your nose is running?" asked the student.

"Why are you shaking?" demanded the intern. "It must be heroin withdrawal. Why don't you tell us the truth?"

Dom shook his head negatively. "I always get like this just before an asthma attack. I take two shots a week for it right now, for the allergy, plus cortisone and epinephrine whenever I need it. I give it to myself."

They frowned, not at all convinced, yet the story was plausible.

"Who's your physician?" asked the resident, irked at the delay.

"Uh, Dr. Kurtz."

"Never heard of him, but you can really get into trouble with that stuff, fella. Better come back to our allergy clinic and get this thing checked out, if that's really what you have." He handed the chart back to the student, turned to the intern. "I think we can discharge him tomorrow."

The intern nodded at the student. "Discharge in a.m.,"

he said, and the student obediently jotted down the order.

"What about my ribs?" Dom insisted.

"Order an X-ray," the intern called to the student.

"But I need something for pain . . . I can hardly breathe."

"Darvon thirty-two, one q. six," the intern barked to the student, who was still busily writing the first order.

"Darvon's no good, and I'm allergic to codeine," Dom protested. "I got Demerol last night. . . ."

Immediately the intern flushed with anger. "So you were the one!" he exclaimed. "Boy, what a mistake that was! Well, I'm running this ward and I won't allow that! Wait till I see that student nurse . . . !"

The resident interrupted, his authority challenged. "I think you're over-reacting, Dick," he said mildly. "Actually, Demerol is not contraindicated here, considering his difficulty in ventilation due to pain. You could order, say, twenty-five q. eight hours, p.r.n."

The intern raised his eyebrows, let out his breath in dismay at the resident's poor judgment, especially unwise since it differed from his own. Yet, as a subordinate, he had to obey the house officer. "I wonder what Dr. Vogel would say about this, given the complete history," he countered doggedly.

"Ask him! Ask him by all means," replied the resident emphatically. "But for now, considering that adequate ventilatory excursion is essential for reasons that are self-evident, I think he should have it."

"Thank you, doctor," said Dom appreciatively.

The resident beamed. "Don't mention it, fella, and I hope you feel better."

The three of them moved on, the intern in a huff and not speaking to the other two. Sometime later, when they saw the X-rays, the resident was somewhat chagrined to find that the films were normal, and the intern was vindicated.

Dom got the Demerol as ordered but it was of little value in relieving his dopesickness. He had vainly hoped for morphine. Just before lunch, however, he was rescued by the arrival of Russ and Dolores. They were a welcome sight as he lay shivering, his bedsheets soaked with sweat.

Dolores bent over, kissed him, pressed a packet into his palm. "You look better, Dom," she was saying.

"Thanks, sis," he replied with humor. "Say, can you pour me a glass of water?" She filled a glass from a pitcher on his bedside table, while he slipped the two biscuits of methadone into his mouth, feeling a little disappointed. He had hoped for three. "You don't know how glad I am to see you people," he went on. "Real glad . . . ."

"I'll bet," said Russ, and smiled, glanced around at the three other patients watching them in the four bed room. His eyes sparkled and his face was suffused with the warmth of cocaine. "And when are they letting you go, man?" he asked.

"Tomorrow," Dom replied.

"Too bad," said Dolores. "This ward is a lot nicer than that old room of yours." Her eyes rested for a long moment on his. She habitually flirted with men, but this was more than flirting. Like most women, she found Dom very attractive, could not understand why he did not have a girl. Certainly he was not gay.

Dom lowered his eyes, remembered how chicks always get affectionate on dope, especially methadone. Not necessarily sexy, but cuddly. Like contented felines full of catnip, it made them want to roll over and be rubbed. And Dolores had that kittenish look right now. Then he saw Russ's arm slip around her waist to give her a timely squeeze.

"Give us a call when you're ready to leave, man," Russ was saying. "Then we can take care o' business." He smiled and drew her away.

Dom felt not only straight but even a bit high on the eighty milligrams of methadone, until it began to wear off toward evening. He never cared much for it, even though it was a potent drug and a first choice for many. For one thing he was never sure what it was doing to his body, since it was a synthetic compound developed by the Germans early in World War II for use as a substitute for the natural morphine, refined from imported opium. They named it "Adolphine," for Adolph Hitler, hence the nickname "Dolophine." Methadone acted more slowly and lasted longer than heroin. And in high doses it killed the craving for heroin. Unfortunately the withdrawal period went on for quite awhile, several weeks of acute discomfort for a large methadone habit. They say it gets into the bones and that is why they ache months later, long after the acute symptoms are gone. But Dom did not know. A week or two of kicking heroin cold turkey was not as bad, but bad enough.

The nurse on the evening shift became suspicious and refused to repeat his Demerol. Tired of finagling, he had no choice but to leave the hospital, which ironically was itself a treasure house of drugs, in order to return to his stash. He was about to call Russ for a lift when he had a visitor. It was Ramon, gliding onto the ward like a leopard, predatory eyes darting this way and that, alert as usual for any stray purses, valuables, or, most of all, drugs.

"Hey, man, so there you are," he greeted. "Been lookin' all over. You got ripped off, huh? Well, so did I, man, by two black chicks. We were havin' a party an . . . .."

Dom put a finger to his lips, glanced sideways at the other patients in the room. Ramon understood, waited till Dom got out of bed, put on a hospital robe. They walked down the hallway to the elevators.

"Know who did it?" Ramon kept asking, almost as if intending to exonerate himself.

Dom shook his head silently, studied Ramon who looked down. They both knew who it was.

"You got any left?" Ramon went on.

"Yeah, but I gotta get outa here first," Dom replied with vexation.

Ramon nodded, his eyes glittering with satisfaction. "Okay, that's all I need to know. Now, I'll go out and do a few things. Where and when can I find you, man?"

"I'm leaving here pretty quick," Dom assured him. "I should be back at my pad by suppertime. How much will you want this time so's I can bag it?"

"A bundle," said Ramon and turned to leave, in a hurry. "Gotta get goin'. . . ."

"Hey, seen Slick around?" Dom inquired innocently, almost as an afterthought.

Ramon stopped, his alert eyes darting at Dom for a split second, then darting away. He did not want to get involved. "No, man," he replied quickly. "He split somewheres. No one knows where. See you, huh?" His black-clothed figure slunk panther-like out of the room and disappeared.

12

As he slipped unobtrusively through the ward, Ramon was scarcely noticed in the clamor of activity. In addition to his other talents, he was an accomplished sneak thief. Pilfering was the first thing he had learned as a child in the Puerto Rican ghetto on New York's west side, where the family had nothing except what welfare gave them to subsist on. It was steal or go without, and so he stole. Because there were no good jobs or educational opportunities, petty crime became a way of life for him. It purchased the only escape he knew from his shabby existence. The escape was a carefree nod on heroin.

His sharp eyes found the medication room, but one of the nurses stood close by. He went a few steps further, slipped into the nurse's lounge for a half minute, emerged again unnoticed and left the ward. He had just gone through three purses, good for forty-five dollars in cash and some ID's. And he had taken a set of keys with a miniature license plate attached that led him now to the information desk in the lobby, where he asked for directions to the employee's parking lot. It took about fifteen minutes to locate the car, a late model sedan. He drove to a phone booth, found the number using the ID, and called. No answer. He smiled, hung up, and drove on about ten minutes to the apartment. He rang the buzzer. Still no answer. Satisfied no one was home he unlocked the door and went upstairs.

He locked the front door of the apartment behind him

and unlocked the back in the event of a quick escape. Then he searched hastily around for anything he could sell quickly. Apparently the apartment was shared by two working girls, but they did not have much, just a small, portable black and white television, a few cheap rings, an artificial pearl necklace and a wristwatch. The real choice items, like color TV's, stereos, cameras, typewriters, handguns, expensive jewelry, fine clothes, cash, and credit cards they did not have. Too bad nurses were not richer, he thought, as he picked through a drawerful of trinkets and jerked some clothing out of the bureau.

He took the television and locked the door behind him. So far he had made only about ten dollars. Disappointed, he decided to take a chance on another apartment in the building. In fact, he did not have much choice in the matter. His sick was just a few hours away and he had to steal enough to support his habit. He seldom failed, having broken into over one hundred homes in the past year and a half. Sometimes he got as much as two thousand dollars at a time, usually from jewelry and silver. He found another apartment that was quiet and knocked. No one answered. Quickly he went back out to the car, got the tire-iron out of the trunk, went upstairs and inserted the flat end between the door and the frame. He yanked and pried with all his might up and down the door until, putting a shoulder sharply against it and prying some more, the screws holding the latch gave way with a splintering snap. Once inside he shut the ruined door and latched it as best he could, thinking with satisfaction that locks were for honest people.

This was a much more affluent apartment, apparently inhabited by a fairly prosperous couple. In the bedroom he found a jewelry box containing a ladies' diamond watch, an emerald dinner ring, and some expensive looking gold earrings and a matching pin. In the closet he found a 35 mm. German camera and light meter. He threw all of these things into a pillowcase. The television in the front room was too large for him to carry but in the den he discovered a portable color TV and a portable electric typewriter. Also in this room he was pleased to encounter a stereo. Jubilant over this bonanza, he went right to work, ripping the speakers from the wall and moving everything to the back door, which he kept unlocked for a quick exit in case someone came in through the front. He pried open a strongbox but was displeased at the contents. No cash or credit cards, just some savings bonds, other securities, insurance policies, and miscellaneous documents. Then his eye gleamed as he found a book of travelers checks. Foiled in his efforts to find a set of matching ID's, he did not bother to look for personal checks. And he left the savings bonds—this was federal stuff and meant too much time if he was caught.

He checked the medicine cabinet for drugs and luckily found a few seconals. Just to settle his nerves, which were very raw from such hard work, he popped all of them on the spot and departed quickly, straight out the front, so that no one would think he was trying to sneak. Speed was vital in this operation and, straining his wiry but muscular frame to the limit, he had everything in the car in three quick trips while passers-by scarcely paid him any attention.

The fence he usually went to was a bookie who stored most of the stolen goods in the loft of a garage behind a tavern. At any one time he had the whole place filled with anything from hot TV's, cameras, tape decks, records, golf clubs and clothing, to new tires, batteries, air conditioners, furniture, and even children's toys. He also had guns, but only on request. He sold most of it to friends and their friends. Business was never better, for there was always a ready market for anything going at half price. He had never been prosecuted to Ramon's knowledge and was reputed to have bribed his way out of trouble on more than one occasion with varying quantities of these goods.

He was about forty-five, with a bland, pleasant face and a full head of neatly combed, silver-black hair. He wore loud yet comfortable clothes, usually a red or maroon knit jersey and checkered slacks, and smoked constantly. He spent most of his time in the barroom taking bets. Word was that he had a lot of friends on the force and often dropped their names to put new customers at ease. But such offhanded formalities were unnecessary with Ramon. The fence examined the goods with a casual flicker of interest, then looked closely at the jewelry and the camera. Ramon knew that the most he could get was, at best, one third of the retail price in cash. Yet, like most addicts he often had to settle for much less just for the sake of expedience.

"Most of this stuff is junk, kid," pronounced the man at last, with a bored, slightly put-upon expression, as though he were doing Ramon a great favor. "I'll give ya three bills for the lot."

Ramon said nothing. Both he and the fence knew he was being cheated blind. "Wanna buy these travelers checks?" Ramon asked after a pause, and displayed them.

"Got any ID's to go with 'em?"

"No, man. I'd use 'em myself if I did."

The man shrugged. "I don't fool with this stuff but I know guys who do. How many? Five hundred, huh? Hmm. Ten bucks."

"Want the hotbox?" Ramon pointed to the stolen car outside.

"Naw, too hard to get rid of," said the fence. "Guys who want 'em nowadays steal 'em themselves. Better get it outa here, though." He reached into his trouser pocket, retrieved a fat bankroll and peeled off the bills.

Ramon took the money and left without another word. He could have stripped the car of tires, battery and so forth, or sold it to someone who wanted to go to the trouble of either stripping it or changing the numbers, repainting it, and getting it re-registered, perhaps in another state. But he did not have the time or patience to find such a buyer. He left the car in an alley, not too many blocks away from The Prophet, and walked in the direction of the rooming house where Dom lived. In less than two hours he had made enough money to cop two and a half bundles of dope, good for as many days.

13

The sooty heaps of frozen snow piled along the city streets softened and shrank in the longer, brighter days of a dying winter. The numbing wind lost its bite, took on a promise of spring just weeks away. People stirred in their hide-aways, in cramped, row apartments and musty rooms, emerged like beetles crawling out into the soft glow of a returning sun. A current of excitement rippled through the patrons of The Prophet, enlivened their young faces with anticipation. Winter was an unwanted hardship for them that they had to endure, like so many pigeons huddled under the eaves with feathers fluffed uncomfortably against the cold. But a hint of sunshine sent them flocking into the streets to congregate happily on corners or in the parks. Bluebird weather was junkie weather, when hustling and copping were never so easy and the long, lazy days of summer left plenty of time to get high and to live the good life.

This excitement of good things to come, carrying an almost electric thrill of joy, throbbed among three young people one warm afternoon in late March. Dolores, Sherry and Jackie sat talking and smoking in Dolores's apartment. All of them single, the change in season meant something special. Brighter days quickened the blood and warmed the passions. Friendship thawed into romance and, as in Jackie's case, went on and flowered into adoration. In just two impossibly long weeks, she was to be married to the boy of her dreams.

"It's going to be a really dynamite wedding," she bubbled. "I've asked a couple of my girl friends to serve as bride's maids."

She took a short hit and handed the joint they were toting on to Sherry, who nodded a reply and passed it on to Dolores, also silent for the moment. It made sense to both of them that Jackie should prefer to have her gay friends in the wedding instead of themselves. But like all single

girls about to attend a wedding that was not their own,
they could not throw off a certain gnawing envy. The reason was not so much because of the inevitable, panic-buy-
ing that comes in seasonal bursts when eligible young men
are thought to be in precariously short supply and are
therefore snatched up as recklessly as marked-off garments
at a fire sale, and for no other reason than to avoid the
humiliation of empty handedness and the horror of being
considered an incurable old maid. In this case, it was more,
much more, because of the gall they tasted, an unexpected,
throbbing bitterness. As much as they were happy for
Jackie, they could not help wondering just how she could
have attracted a guy as good-looking as Rolf, someone
whom they themselves could never hope to find. They
both looked at Jackie once more, still puzzled. It was true
that since her plastic surgery a year ago she was much prettier, with a smooth, fine-featured, heart-shaped face and
flowing, bleach-blond hair. And her figure was certainly
passable, but only because of the hormone shots she had
been taking. But when it came to other, more basic female
components, the girls doubted that she had them, even
though they still accepted her as one of their own sex. Her
cup size, after all, was two sizes larger than Sherry's, thanks
to the shots.

"And where's it going to be held?" Dolores asked, handing the joint back to Jackie and smiling, partly because the
pot made her giggly, but partly to hide her moodiness.

Jackie flipped her long brassy hair, replied in a playful
lisp, sharpened by excitement. "Well, we tried to have it in
a regular church but the only one in the city that has them
is all booked up. So I have this friend who knows this fellow who'll let us have it at his place. It's right on the
beach."

Sherry's face brightened. "A summer cottage?"

"It'll be cold this time of year," Dolores observed dark-
ly, and snickered at her own gloom. "Why don't you wait
a few months?"

"We've already waited too long," said Jackie, showing
how she and Rolf were very much in love by the sparkle in
her blue eyes, a look which irked her two friends deeply.

"How many people do you expect?" Dolores went on cordially.

Jackie shrugged. "A lot, I hope. I've invited everyone. As long as it isn't the cops. . . ."

The two smiled at her laconic humor. "That would really be a bummer if the whole wedding party ended up in jail," Sherry teased, almost wishing it secretly, and the thought amused her. She and Dolores began tittering to one another.

"It could happen!" Dolores giggled.

"It won't! It better not or I'll really be pissed!" Jackie declared, tossing her bleached hair indignantly and taking a long, reassuring hit on the joint.

As predicted, it was a chilly, breezy day three weeks later, on the last Saturday of the month, when the wedding guests finally began arriving in an assortment of vehicles, from dented up old junkheaps to sports cars, shiny new Cadillacs, and a few big, chopped, chrome-laden motorcycles. Some of them, unused to the out-of-doors, sat on the porch overlooking the sea, watching the gulls skimming along the beach, their white wings drooping and blending with the salt foam of the rolling surf, or floating way out past the breakers like bright, boyant specks, bobbing, disappearing and reappearing in the choppy blue waters. Like gulls, the junkies were scavengers also, but not of the sea. They lived and roamed in the great cities, preying on the weak, the careless. All they knew or cared about the sea was that it floated great ships laden with kilos of precious heroin, cleverly concealed deep in the holds and ready to be smuggled into port cities, then distributed across the land. Yet the sea was a thing of beauty and they watched it serenely, smoking, chatting, sipping wine or beer, and taking in the keen salt air.

Most of the guests were in their late teens to middle twenties, though some were considerably older. The heroin addicts were dressed after the style of junkies—lots of leather, tight denims or bellbottoms, loud shirts—almost an offbeat, drugstore cowboy look. The gay people and the blacks went in for more flair—shiny leather suits or red cordouroy bell bottoms, so tight they displayed every bulge, gaudy silk shirts with puffed sleeves and high collars, high-heeled lizard or suede shoes, gold earrings, silver medallions, and jaunty felt caps or wide-brimmed hats with silver concho bands. For all appearances it looked like a gypsy wedding, more so with the frenzied dancing of some of the couples to a rhythmic, haunting refrain of rock music that emanated throughout.

When Dom and Danny arrived, they looked for, and found Rolf in the front room, his tall, Charles Atlas figure surrounded by admirers, both men and women. Rolf was in high spirits, laughing in his deep, jolly voice at the conversation. He had changed a lot, Dom recalled, from a year ago when he was strung out on dope. Dom avoided him then, as did the others, because of the disconcerting combination of Rolf's great strength together with his reputation for being a little crazy. But as time went on, Dom realized that Rolf's main problem was a painful inferiority complex and a maddening shyness that seemed to be aggravated rather than compensated by his handsomeness. So Dom became friendly with him, and heard all about his disappointments, his failure to make it into pro football and the loss of his girl because of it, a misfortune that Dom was in a good position to understand. So Rolf had turned to dope, as Dom had, and did inummerable B&E's to support his growing habit. Then he found an easier way, hustling at the better night spots in town, picking up well-heeled tricks, both male and female. The men, in their late thirties and forties on up, were usually bachelors, but some were married. The women, in about the same age range, were usually single, often widowed or divorced and very lonely. They wanted a man just to talk to, though few denied themselves his physical charms.

He would usually approach them with the hard-luck story of being a heroin addict who would get very sick unless he found money to obtain the drug. The women especially took pity on him and sometimes gave him as much as a hundred dollars in advance so that he could go out and cop. Once he was high he did not care what he had to do to earn it. Unlike many addicts who hustled homosexuals, he rarely beat a trick because of the trouble it caused. Gay people particularly can be extremely vindictive when crossed, and besides, Rolf was a gentleman.

"Hello, Rolf," said Dom, grabbing the strong hand and eyeing the broad, well-muscled shoulders, the tapering waist, and the rugged, princely face grinning with delight. Had Dom not known about the change that had taken place in his friend, he would never have suspected that Rolf had finally admitted to himself that he was indeed homosexual, had known it for certain after having fallen so deeply in love with Jackie, a transsexual.

"Good to see you, ol' pal!" Rolf boomed. "Going to watch us tie the old knot, huh? Ha-ha! Say. . . , want you to meet a buddy of mine. . . ." He turned to a square-faced, athletic looking youth standing beside him, his shoulders almost as broad as Rolf's but much shorter in height, dwarfed by Rolf's towering stature. "This is Sam. He's our host."

Sam smiled affably, extended his hand. "Nice to meet you," he said politely. "Make yourself at home. There's beer and a couple jugs of wine in the kitchen if you want anything."

"Terrific!" said Danny suddenly, stepping out from behind Dom and introducing himself. He glanced around through his thick wire-rims. "Wow, nice pad! Did I hear Rolf say you're the owner?"

Sam smiled again in a show of modesty. "Thanks, but I don't really own it. Belongs to the family."

Dom was studying Sam as he talked. Despite his mod, youth style look he did not have the aura of the streets about him. An honest, well-scrubbed look set him apart from the others. Dom himself had been straight once, had been an athlete and a soldier and at once sensed that they shared something in common. "You look kind of familiar," Dom said at last. "Have I seen you in The Prophet?"

The host nodded politely. "Right, I go in there now and then . . . ."

He was interrupted by a girl, conspicuous by her carefully bleached denims, every bit as snug below the waist as the sweaters of another era were above, and who staggered up as if drunk, stopping and staring at them with a glazed look. There was no odor of alcohol about her which meant she was stoned on pills, probably barbiturates.

"I'm Denise," she mumbled, her speech slurred. "When is the wedding gonna be?"

"Who knows?" replied Rolf. "Whenever the preacher gets here. Say, you going to catch the bouquet? Ha-ha!" He grinned good naturedly at the girl, who blinked, looked dully around the room.

"No thanks," she mouthed and moved closer to Dom. "What's your name?"

He edged back. She was somebody's personal property but he could not place her old man. "Gonna get something to drink," he announced, and excused himself. In the kitchen he found a bottle of Portugese rosé wine, uncorked it and poured a glassful. Never much of a juicer, alcohol in large amounts did funny things to him, made him aggressive. But he preferred booze over pills, despised the effect they had on people, the way that girl was bouncing off the walls, for example. She probably popped five or six seconals or tuinals and looked sloppier than if she had been drinking half the night.

He went back into the front room with the wine, lit a cigarette and sat down among the guests. For some reason he did not feel like getting high tonight. Instead, something inside inhibited him, signaled him to slow down and just watch. Keeping an eye on the host, he noticed that Sam seemed to be sizing everyone up by drawing them out, then listening and observing them as they talked. And he did so with a peculiar concentration, almost as if he were trying to memorize their faces. Again this set him apart from the others. The typical addict is very self-centered. He is a good listener only long enough to get his man cornered before opening up with his own harrangue, usually about himself, or his second love, drugs. He will dwell on the current size of his habit, on stealing, buying, and selling drugs, on strike-it-rich tales of drug bonanzas and binges. Or he will go on about his state of health, his love life or lack of one, his job or joblessness, or his ups and downs at home. Any comment or interruption from the listener, particularly a look of skepticism, boredom or even an accidental yawn, will prolong the conversation indefinitely. Now Dom saw that Sam let others do the talking, presently with two guests together. As expected, each one, sensing they had a considerate listener at bay, was trying to upstage the other with even wilder, more chilling tales of holdups, shootings, knifings, beatings, busts, car crashes, and OD's. And each claimed to be the sole survivor of a whole gang of departed friends, all of whom succumbed tragically to an overdose. It seemed that if every one of these dead comrades were still living, a city the size of New York would not be large enough to hold them all.

Sam simply nodded and smiled, went on scrutinizing. He did not have any stories to inflict on anyone. So Dom concluded that he was no junkie. And he also suspected that his name was not really Sam.

14

Slick zoomed into the yard of the beach house, throwing up a wake of sand behind his chopped Harley CH. Sherry sat on the back seat and clung to him expertly, so that the two riders moved as one on the machine. They climbed off, heavily bundled up against the cold, since it was still a little early for biking. Slipping the heavy chain from around his shoulders, Slick locked the bike to a porch railing. They removed their crash helmets but did not place them on the seat of the bike, knowing better than to leave articles unguarded among their own kind.

Inside they heard the loud hum of nearly fifty guests jammed into every corner of the small, Cape Cod cottage. Those who were tired of introducing themselves or hailing old friends had begun to get down to the serious business of getting high. There were knots of people quietly exchanging money and drugs, and a long line to get into the bathroom where they could get off in privacy. Those that

70

did not care to wait found a corner in the bedroom or went outside.

Slick found Russ sitting on the sofa, in the process of passing a bag of cocaine to Martin Shine, who sat beside him, occupying fully half of the sofa. Marty had agreed to cook up a few bags of his best heroin and then stir in the coke so that they could both "speedball." Dolores sat a little apart from them, looking disgruntled. Because she was on methadone and did not care that much for pills, coke was the only other thing she could get high on besides grass. It was for this reason that she did not like to see Russ passing it around like popcorn. Moreover, they just had a minor spat and Russ had said something that had aggravated her considerably.

"What could Rolf ever see in Jackie in the first place?" Dolores had complained sarcastically. "If you can figure it out then you're doing better than I can. After all, she's not even a real girl."

"He's a switch-hitter," Russ had whispered. "He digs both the guys and the gals."

"Well, if he likes both, then why is he marrying a drag queen?" she argued.

Russ shrugged. "'Cause, well, I guess Jackie's sorta everything all rolled into one," he replied thoughtfully.

"But she's not chick like me," Dolores persisted.

"Whaddaya mean? She uses the ladies' room, don't she?"

"Yes, but that doesn't mean . . . ."

"Huh? Why not?" Russ interrupted. "Why, since that face liftin' job she's as good lookin' as any ordinary chick."

"Ordinary!" Dolores repeated ruefully. "So that's it! You think I'm ordinary!" She turned away from him, unresponsive to his profuse apologies.

When Russ spotted Slick and Sherry he hailed them. "Hey folks, come on over! Say, change the music 'fore ya sit down! Over there, the radio! That bayou stuff is really gettin' to me!"

"Turn to VRN, why don't ya," added Marty sleepily.

Slick was not used to taking orders from anyone, but with an eye on Russ's cocaine he obliged, found the radio and twirled the knob.

"Hold it right there!" said Russ, smiling at the blaring upbeat of soul music. A bass player, he loved the rich chorus in rhythm and blues and as he listened his fingers twitched on imaginary strings.

Slick scowled inwardly. He had not wanted soul. He knew Russ and Dolores both dug it, but he went in for acid rock, which was big about the time he really got turned onto dope, near the tail end of the psychedelic era. It was in the late sixties when he was just eighteen, and he and his friends were coming down off of acid, doing more speed and looking for something new. Then came the flood of heroin in 1969.

Sherry said nothing, but after the manner of a girl who liked everything her boyfriend did, she shared his taste for the jumbled screeches and groans of acid rock. In fact, she had been a serious rock fan ever since the age of nine, just when the early rock n' roll was fading. She bought stacks of forty-fives and danced, shuffled, twisted, frugged, and otherwise leaped her way through puberty. Her favorite group was the Beatles, and when they made their big splash she was only thirteen, a shy little girl whose biggest thrill of the week was to go to a record hop with some girl friends on a Saturday night and twitter at the hopelessly awkward boys on the other side of the gym who had to be pushed out on the floor by a teacher and made to dance. These unwilling partners were frankly puzzled at being ordered to dance with such curious beings, who clutched at them with sweaty palms and had nothing interesting to say, and whose feet were always in the way. But that was before things changed, before an avalanche of commercialized erotica hit the young, closing their eyes to innocence and tempting them to embark on a campaign of sexual experimentation that saw Sherry and her friends grow old in just a few short years. Now, at twenty, she listened mostly to the bluesy stuff.

Martin sat immobile like a rotund Buddha, dark glasses lowered as he nodded and buzzed at the same time from the blend of heroin and cocaine. His fat fingers involuntarily drummed out another beat, the sparkling syncopation of jazz. He scarcely bothered his ears with rock—it was all the same commercial rhythm and blues to him, hardly worth his attention. It did not have the intricacies of jazz that he had spent years mastering, way back before rock began to take over. Oh, he still had a few gigs now and then but he was usually too strung out to play. Heroin slowed his beat. Instead, he lived back in another era, recalling his bandstand gigs of twenty-five years ago, when he was a young jazz drummer. He chipped on heroin some but never got strung out, and with so many contacts in the music world, things had looked very promising for him. But then he married a woman, a mantle-piece beauty with claws in her velvet paws. He fled from her into the arms of a second woman, a singer who worked in his band. Infuriated, his wife set about systematically to destroy him, filing for divorce and refusing to let him see his children. She poisoned them against him with stories of his dope addiction and had him jailed for nonsupport. He nearly abducted his two sons and daughter just to see them again, but lost courage at the last moment. The more they treated him like a stranger, the more he turned to heroin. It was good then, and cheap, so much so that eventually he was using nearly a quarter piece a day. From then on, his whole life went into his arm and inevitably he got involved in dealing to support his habit. Of course, many of his friends who were also jazz musicians had OD'd and were gone now. His life was even more lonely because of being despised by so many junkies for tapping his bags or burning the unwary with flour or baking soda. They certainly would have killed him long ago except that he was basically a genial man who meant little harm. He took a fatherly interest in "these kids" and gave them good personal advice, especially about women.

Russ mumbled something to Slick and Sherry and the three of them went outside with a glass of water. They returned a few minutes later, their faces brightened and cheered and their bodies warmed. Heroin and cocaine was the ultimate combination as far as Russ was concerned, and even Slick had fallen into a pleasant mood. Someone passed a hash pipe to them and they sucked on it, watched it travel around the group from mouth to mouth. Everyone liked hashish, the resin of marihuana, along with dope. It was stronger than most pot and boosted the high, prolonged the tranquility.

The hash made Sherry hungry and she got up, rummaged around in the kitchen, brought back some cheese and crackers and somebody's bottle of wine. She offered some to Danny, who did not even recognize what it was. He and Buddy and Tina, a married couple who took a big mongrel dog with them wherever they went, had been mixing LSD with dope and maybe some coke, and were out of their minds. The dog did not mind seeing his owners so wasted, and smiled a toothy canine smile at these supposedly more advanced creatures who could hardly walk and did not make the slightest sense when they spoke.

Suddenly a youth ran through the crowd yelling "Fire! Fire! The cops are burning the place down!" He dove into a broom closet, crashing into mops and buckets with a loud clatter. A brief panic followed, the guests jumping up and looking outside, but they saw no fire and no police.

"I know him. He's a speed freak," someone said. "He gets paranoid on the stuff."

They pulled him, wide-eyed and trembling, out of the closet. "Don't let them get me!" he kept pleading as three people held him down while a girl put a cold towel on his forehead. As they talked him down, he relaxed, began to babble gratefully, told them he had been speeding his brains out for almost two days on spoon after spoon of the best crystal methedrine he had ever banged. He buzzed for another hour or so, then crashed in the bedroom like a dead man and did not awaken until the next morning.

The preacher showed up at about nine o'clock on his motorcycle when everyone was almost too high to care. He was a slim, agreeable young man, balding, with a short, chestnut beard and dark glasses. He wore his collar, plus bell-bottomed denims. They turned off the music and people began to collect in the front room. Most of the gay crowd gathered to the left, presumably friends of the bride, but probably of the groom as well. The more heterosexual guests, including most of the junkies and their chicks, shifted to the right. The gay side was brighter, more festive. They habitually did more ups to give them a lift because of the discouragement that comes from being "different." Conversely, the other side was nodding out on downs, mainly heroin, the best escape they knew from the boredom of being straight.

There was quiet. Someone put on the wedding march and the minister stood at the front of the room. The bride and groom swept down an aisle through the crowd. Jackie was stunning in pink silk slacks and a white lace blouse. Her most striking feature, her naturally beautiful blue eyes with long lashes, were attractively tinted with iridescent violets and greens. Rolf nearly outshone her in a snappy red velvet suit, so tight it looked sprayed on. The ceremony was brief, followed by a kiss and congratualtions from all sides. Jackie cried with joy, threw her bouquet into the crowd and two girls leapt up and grasped it simultaneously, each insisting she had been the first to catch it. They poured the minister one drink and then another and offered him a joint, which he accepted. He got talkative, went on about how gratifying it was to unite two human beings in holy matrimony who were truly in love and not simply legalizing a sexual thing. And he insisted that real love was spiritual, not physical, and only then was it sacred.

The party shifted again to the newlyweds, who cut the wedding cake and passed pieces to the guests, although many were too stoned to recognize it. Coffee was served and by one o'clock people started coming down a bit, getting into serious rap sessions, going out and bringing back pizza, hamburgers, Chinese food, then drinking more and getting high again. Their numbers began to dwindle as they drifted away, the crowd thinning into small knots and lone couples. Rolf and Jackie departed amid a final hurrah, then the noise and clamor faded to distinct voices, interspersed now with pauses of stillness. It was the death of a party—people gathering at the front door with coats, jangling keys, saying goodbye. Others were sprawled asleep on the sofa, beds, carpet, while the survivors retreated into the kitchen for a determined last stand. A few got off again and crashed for the night. Sam made them breakfast the next day and graciously showed the last one out at four o'clock in the afternoon.

15

Slick roved the streets on a drizzly, spring day, his small, lithe body moving with the ease and grace of a predator as he sprang off a curb and darted through the traffic. A car almost struck him but he paid it no notice, was hardly aware of anything except his dopesickness and the uncomfortable reality of being broke. He knew he was the most dangerous at these times, both to others and to himself, but it was plain that he had no alternative but to do what must be done. It was almost as if he were at the mercy of the forces of nature. Like a rudderless ship spinning in a storm, his addiction lifted him high on a smooth swell of pleasure, then dashed him cruelly down into a trough of pain where he found himself struggling to survive. His powerlessness against it left him with a seething, inner contempt for his own weakness, and for the same weakness in others, and this overriding contempt drained him of any courage to oppose it.

He thought now, as he hastened through the glistening, wet streets, that Sherry was perhaps one of the few persons more worthy of scorn than he. Impetuously, he found himself resenting her even more than he resented himself. She, he decided, had a lot to do with his being out here today, in this place where he did not want to be, running along like a fool to do something that, if he had a choice, he did not want to do. Because of her, he had to steal every day, since she was next to helpless. Unlike a lot of the chicks who acted as partners for their dudes, even assisting in B&E's and stickups, Sherry did nothing but sit at home and complain. And because he stole every day, they both had big habits that required him to steal even more. He began to wonder why he had to produce two hundred dollars day in and day out just so they could get high together, so that she could snuggle against him like a grateful kitten. He knew that although he might be a dopefiend, he was no fool. He was getting tired of stealing, of worrying about being picked up by the police, and of being sick and in bad health. This time he had been strung out for almost nine months.

That was a long time for anyone, even for a young kid like himself. It meant getting out and hustling every day in any kind of weather, whether he felt like it or not. And he looked a sight, with his unbrushed teeth, shot through with decay from all the milk sugar he had been pouring into his system and from a diet of candy and frappes. He had to wear long-sleeved shirts and even gloves to cover up the mass of needle marks, scars, and abscesses pocking his arms and the backs of his hands. His normal weight had been around one-forty-five, but he had never gained back the fifteen pounds he lost during his last bout of serum hepatitis nearly six months ago. Of course, it was impossible for him to remember the dirty needle that he had contracted it from some months before the appearance of the usual symptoms of jaundice and fatigue. A doctor tested his blood and told him to stay in bed but he did not rest much, did not realize that hepatitis could become chronic and occasionally even fatal.

Aside from being physically unkempt, filthy and sick, his legal health was equally bad. He knew the police had at least two and maybe three warrants out on him for breaking and entering and for armed robbery. They were not going to bother to look for him just now because they knew sooner or later he would fall right into their laps. Slick knew it, too, knew that no junkie can stay strung out forever without getting caught. Once he was busted they could probably pin several other charges on him, since over the past four years he had done so many B&E's that he had lost count—maybe two hundred homes, stores, offices. Next to shoplifting and breaking into cars, it was the most practical hustle because if done properly it carried little risk.

He usually broke into private homes during daylight hours. A B&E in the nightime was a much more serious offense, considered a robbery because of the liklihood that someone might be at home. Sometimes he used a shortcut to find a house with no one home, simply by picking names out of a telephone directory and calling the number to see if anyone answered. But more often he roamed through a neighborhood looking for parked cars with tape decks inside, good for at least a "finner," or a set of golf clubs that might go for thirty dollars. At the same time he kept an eye peeled for homes that looked empty. He knocked or rang and when no one answered he tried the front door or went around back. It was amazing how many people left their houses unlocked. And even a locked door posed little challenge. Wood and screws gave and metal bent under his determined assault. But one thing he had to watch out for were alarm systems inside. He usually looked for a sticker on the front door that warned him of this, and steered clear if he saw one.

As in any business of this sort, he had his close calls. Once when he went into an unlocked home after ringing the bell and getting no answer, he heard someone upstairs. This did not deter him, since his dopesickness made him fearless. He went straight into the dining room, scouted around, and quietly rummaged through a chesterfield. By a stroke of luck he ran across a collection of gold coins mounted on a felt pad, took them and ran just as somebody came downstairs. He was lucky. Whoever it was could have had a gun. He knew of another youth, paralyzed from the waist down, who was shot in the back in just this way. Yet for Slick it had been worth the risk. The fence gave him a hundred dollars for the coins. Of course, this was only a small fraction of their actual value, but he was sick and had no time to pedal hot coins to buyers who could pay more. A junkie steals, cops, then shoots up.

Another time he had not been so lucky—the time he was caught. He and a partner had gone through an open garage and slipped the locked door with a strip of celluloid. Inside the house they found some silver bowls, a portable TV, and a movie camera. In less than ten minutes they had gone back out through the garage into the waiting arms of four policemen with drawn guns. It turned out that the residents of this prosperous neighborhood had been hit several times before and were well organized, had set up a system of surveillance.

He was twenty then. Besides a long juvenile record he already had been given a couple of two year suspended sentences for assault and larceny and was on probation at the time. So he went away to serve six months of a two year sentence in the county house of corrections. This lesson of incarceration made him very cautious indeed. The next time he knew it would be state prison, especially for armed robbery. And so he was worried now that the longer he hustled and stayed strung out, the bigger and more reckless would be his crimes. Five years ago when he started doing dope he could survive on fifty to seventy-five dollars a day, hustling it easily from shoplifting, mostly stealing records and peddling them to college kids. Then his habit increased both because of his growing tolerance for heroin and because he learned to be a better thief. He could hustle two or three hundred dollars a day now doing B&E's, stickups, muggings, and accordingly he developed a bigger habit. Whenever he made more money, he did an extra measure of dope, sometimes up to three thousand dollars' worth a week, a lot of it on cocaine.

He drew his collar up around his neck, put his cap low over his face, and walked into the bank. He would not stick up a bank because there was too much time involved for the money if he were caught. He was too smart for that. Instead he pretended to fill out a deposit slip. His hawk eye followed the nervous, sparrow-like movements of a little old lady as she cashed her social security check and stuffed away the bills. He waited until she hobbled out of the bank, then followed her up the street, hoping that she would not board a bus or catch a ride. He was lucky—she was thrifty enough to go on foot. He stayed a half-block behind for three blocks while dozens of shoppers passed with hardly a glance. As he quickened his step he found comfort in knowing that something could happen right under their very noses and they would hardly so much as bat an eyelash. It was this very unwillingness on the part of others to get involved that bolstered his courage and made it possible for him to operate openly, in broad daylight, in the heart of a large city. Like a fish in water, he negotiated best in a sea of apathy—a blind, sheep-like, herd instinct of individual self-preservation.

He passed a policeman casually directing traffic around a construction site. He had little fear of policemen, especially when they were more preoccupied with directing cars around ditches than with protecting the public from violent criminals like himself. Oh, they would come afterwards to ask a few questions and make out idle reports, but he would be long gone by then. In fact, he had learned that as long as he could handle himself, the police would not catch him at all, and even if they did he would be released on bail or on recognizance, to appear later in court, hopefully to beat the case. Or, he could simply default and not show up in court at all. But sooner or later, they would inevitably get lucky, be in the right place at the right time and grab him. For even if some cops are not very smart, they are always around. He had learned that for the first time at the age of seven.

He and the other boys were heaving rocks at the apartment window of an old man who kept shouting at them in Polish to go away. Slick hit the window and shattered it. As they ran off, a big, blue uniformed man jumped out of a car and collared him and another boy.

"Okay, you kids!" he roared. "So you're the ones, huh? Where d'you live?"

At first the boys were so terrified they could hardly speak. The policeman pushed them both into the car and took them home. He spoke to the other boy's father first. The father, pale with anger, apologized to the officer, then gave his son a slap and sent him inside. Next, Slick was driven to his home. His mother was out in the front yard clipping the hedge with sharp, decisive strokes. An attractive, buxom woman, her gardening outfit was the talk of the neighborhood back in those long summer days when Slick was a boy. She had always taken care of the yardwork because his father was rarely sober enough to do it.

"This your son?" the policeman asked, and pulled Slick out of the car.

Surprised, she straightened up, eyebrows arched, hands on her hips. "Yes!" she intoned. "What happened?"

"He an' some other kids were breakin' windows a couple blocks over," he explained. "We've had a lotta complaints lately on account of them, mostly broken windows and foul language."

His mother pulled up a strap of her sagging halter, directed her heavy breasts like twin cannon at the policeman. "How do you know he broke a window?" she retorted accusingly. "How do you know was the one?"

The policeman's face grew angry. "Because I saw him throw the rock, that's how!" he declared.

"But are you absolutely sure? Can you prove it?" she shot back.

"Sure I'm sure," he cried, almost said something more then caught himself. "Look, lady," he went on, "I ain't gonna stand here an' argue! The next time I catch him, you'll be comin' down to juvenile hall to pick him up, and that's that!" He took out a notebook, jotted down the name and address, then stalked away from the furious woman as discretely as possible.

"It may interest you to know that my uncle is a city councilman!" she shrilled after him.

Slick went on breaking windows for several more years and the neighbors went on complaining but he never went to juvenile hall. Now, more than ten years later, he was into bigger trouble. Nothing seemed too daring for him, and as the old woman hobbled stiffly up a hill and into a residential section, he closed in, pleased that the street was nearly deserted in the chilly weather. Suddenly, as if alerted by instinct, she turned and saw him behind her.

"Ya got the time?" he asked casually.

She hesitated, nervously fumbled at her sleeve, and at that instant he reached out, cat-like, and grabbed the purse. She uttered an anguished cry and held on. He smashed her in the face with his fist, once and then again and she fell hard on the sidewalk. Quickly he opened the purse. The money was not there. She had put it inside her coat. Bending down, he yanked at the coat, nearly tore it off the groaning, bleeding body, found the money and ran.

16

Born in the year nineteen-fifty, Slick was one of millions of human beings propagated in the comfortable postwar era. Christened Vincent Patrick Quinn, he was the youngest member of a family of five children. His father, a handsome but shiftless iron worker, had come down from Canada as a young man to seek work. Instead, he fell into a lucky marriage, at least materially speaking. His wife was not only a beauty, but an O'Hearn, and though there were many families in town by that name, hers had been intrenched in machine politics for two generations. Her own father had once been traffic commissioner and her uncle was later elected to the city council. A scandal implicating him and some others, including the mayor, in the diversion of city funds into the hands of certain favored no-bid contractors, brought no more than a mild wave of public indignation and he was reelected to a second term.

Slick's family lived in a lower-middle class neighborhood that had recently deteriorated into a working class section. Both the lace curtain and shanty Irish, as well as second generation Polish and Italian families found themselves jumbled together here in rows of ageing three story frame houses with a large family on each floor, lining narrow streets jammed with parked automobiles and teeming with children. They were everywhere, yelling, playing, shouting, getting out of the way of passing cars, and converging again in the streets to resume their games. But unlike many of these children, whose parents could barely afford to feed them, or who were already supported on welfare, Slick's family had enough money to send him to college. His mother had high hopes for him, wanted to see him become a lawyer and then maybe get into politics where he would have some connections. In fact, she was counting on him, since his older brother had surprised her by becoming a plumber. Two sisters had married before the age of twenty and a third was an honor student in high school who managed to win a scholarship to a good catholic college. Regrettably, it turned out that she was the only student in the family, for Slick never did more than below average work from the start. He had to repeat the fourth grade because of disruptive behavior and was nearly sent to a special class. Yet his IQ tested in the normal range. Tutoring, or other remedial work might have saved him but instead his case fell between the cracks of a hopelessly ingrown, politicized school system. By the time he reached high school he was chronically truant and in trouble with the police. He finally dropped out in the senior year, much to his mother's dissatisfaction.

Formidable obstacles prevented Slick from ever achieving his mother's expectations. Besides his low grades, there were family problems. His father drank and was always out of work. They could tell when he came home loaded because of the chip on his shoulder. And it seemed that at this delicate moment his mother could never resist giving her husband a verbal hotfoot, nagging him about one thing or another. Sometimes she liked to hold Slick up as an example, saying how much he had done for her, which in fact was very little, while his father was down at the pub. She would slip an arm around the boy, draw him to her and glare at the husky, red-faced man maneuvering his way through the door, that is, if she did not lock him out, which she often did.

"Well, what made *you* come home?" she would begin derisively.

His father would blink, then ignore her and shuffle into the front room to flop on the sofa.

"Vinnie helped me out while you were gone, took out all the barrels," she would go on. "He's almost too small to lift them—it's a man's job. But you were down at the pub as usual! And now look at you, coming in staggering like this . . . !"

"Aw, whyn't ya lay off, fer Chrissakes!" he would growl and look away.

"No I won't!" she would exclaim. "You can't stay sober for one minute! You should at least show a little interest in your children, to Vinnie, your own son, who never sees you except when you're this way! Today, now, he's been helping me while you're out throwin' your money away on drink! Or seein' one of your girl friends, perhaps? Who knows? I don't know what I'd do without Vinnie—why, he's the man of the house! He's ashamed of you, says I should throw you out!"

She stood scowling, hands on her hips. There was a long pause, his father staggering up, his face growing redder. That was the warning signal. It took time, like a boiler building up pressure. First came a few unintelligible curses, then the rushing attack and Slick would cover up as best he could. Usually he was slapped around, and always yelled loud enough for his mother to come to his defense. She was big enough to fight back. A tigress in her own right, she used her nails to good advantage. While she took a few bruising punches from her husband, she sometimes inflicted dreadful scratches on his face and neck. Now and then the police showed up, usually summoned by neighbors who could not stand the noise. Sometimes they would take his father for a ride in the cruiser for a half hour or so, listening to his side of the story and giving him a chance to sober up.

Slick never understood why his father acted so violently towards him. Other boys' fathers did not seem to hate their sons. Early in childhood he decided that there was something about him, some failing that he could not quite identify, that made him deserve this treatment. And he thought it had something to do with his deep attachment to his mother, an attachment so necessary to his survival and so powerful as to possess him completely. Only in later years did he come to resent the tyranny of this bond. His whole childhood was spent in self-pity and vindictiveness, bewildering because he could neither explain his feelings, nor avoid them. There seemed to be no escape until he reached the age of twelve and discovered glue.

He and his friends would steal tubes of model airplane glue from the supermarket, or buy cases of a dozen tubes each at the hobby shop, using the excuse that they were picking up supplies for a class at school. They spent the rest of the day truant, sitting on the rooftop of a housing project where no one could find them, squeezing globs of it into plastic bags and inhaling the fumes.

"Watch it fall!" one of them would exclaim as they kept inhaling and they would all focus their eyes on a distant church steeple. Slowly it would buckle and collapse, as if by some magical power they had willed it. The dizzying fumes had caused them to hallucinate, and each tube, inhaled one after another, carried them further into a strange, undreamed of world where nothing was impossible. Slick picked up a handfull of diamonds and fancied he had struck it rich, but the diamonds were only chunks of ice. Or his friends' faces would change to a deep green with noses a foot long.

"Hey, you're the jolly green giant!" he would laugh, not knowing how he must have looked to them.

He used to blow a tube of it and then walk into a long, dark tunnel. When he was halfway through a pink clown would jump out of the wall at him, laughing and dancing in front of him.

Soon he was using a case a day, and was never really happy without his favorite brand of glue. He sniffed it in his backyard, in the house, and in bed at night. He even kept a bagful in his coat, took whiffs unnoticed from his collar. When his mother questioned the odor he told her he was making model airplanes. She believed this for awhile, as she tended to believe everything he told her, until she began to wonder where the models were. Then she discovered a stash of glue and went to his father, a thing which she did only rarely. He guessed what it was for and whaled the daylights out of Slick, beating him so severely that he wet his pants, and it amazed him that he could take so much punishment and still get up and walk away. After that he was more careful, did not intend to risk losing the one thing that made him happy.

The gang switched to cough syrup when they were thirteen. It was easy to buy over the counter in those days and made them feel good if they gulped enough of it, mainly from the alcohol and the cough suppressants like dextromethorphan and codeine. At about fourteen they got turned onto marihuana. Not only did it boost the cough syrup but it made them really stoned, especially if they drank wine or beer on top of it. Acid was just coming in then and a few of the kids took it on a dare, then everyone in the gang had to do it to prove himself. Some of them developed a liking for it, for tripping in a fascinating, even frightening world of distortions and bewildering ideas, feelings. A few bummed out, had bad trips fraught with unbearable thoughts, emotions of terror, sadness, and had to be talked down by friends. Speed was another popular drug that was easy to get on the street, and some of the kids first popped it, then mainlined it. It was more destructive than acid but less bewildering. When Slick tried it he became talkative and aggressive, even felt superhuman. He had a girl friend who also tried it. She was ordinarily quite shy but on speed she acted like a queen bee and actually became hypersexed and very popular with the boys.

The "straight" kids only drank beer. But then they were mamby-pamby when it came to getting high. They wanted to preserve some remnant of their faculties, to retain their own identity for the most part. But Slick and his friends were really "hip," ready to obliterate their everyday thoughts and feelings, to literally blow their minds and identities on drugs. They had to be more than reckless to get so high; they had to be self-immolating, destroying their conscious beings as if in atonement for imaginary sins for which they stood accused. And then there was also the pleasure of losing oneself in another, more overpowering sensation. Sex and hard rock both shared a part in this and so were likewise considered "in," "groovy," and "far out." And, getting high was the way Slick's youth-oriented peer group proved their loyalty to one another, reaffirming their contempt and rebelliousness toward the adult world, from which they felt so excluded.

There was one trouble, though, in that drugs cost money. But even so, they were less expensive than alcohol.

A high on grass, speed, or acid was cheaper than the same high on beer or wine. On one two-dollar tab of good, orange sunshine a kid could trip all day, or he could speed for hours on a fifty-cent methedrine tablet. Even grass at ten dollars a "lid," or ounce, was good for dozens of joints. What money Slick and his gang needed they either earned doing odd jobs or stole from their parents. But when they could not get work, or when their parents got suspicious, they turned to shoplifting, rifling cars, and occasionally to mugging the elderly. They discovered how easy it was for two or three of them to snatch a purse or enter the home of an old woman and terrorize her into giving up her money.

Slick got very good at this sort of cowardly violence. He understood it, being physically small for his age and maltreated at home besides. He saw how life was made up of the strong and the weak, of predators and prey, and he was tired of playing victim. Now it was his turn to do the preying, perhaps if only to convince himself that he too was strong. He began to carry a knife, which made him feel nearly invincible. And it was gratifying to see how frightened his victims were when he brandished it, how quickly they were subdued by it. He began to collect knives and practice with them, with illegal push-button or legal clasp knives, became an expert at drawing them and snapping out the blade in one, lightning thrust. And because he was small and fast he instinctively learned how to maneuver a larger opponent off balance, then dart in unexpectedly for a stick or a slash and dart out again. After he cut a few people in this way, even the strongest bullies were afraid of him. Everyone said that he was slick with a knife. That is how he got his street name.

17

Danny had been very impressed by Sam Thornton, who not only had a summer cottage on the beach all to himself, but who just hosted one of the wildest, most successful parties anyone could remember. And the most amazing thing about it was that no one was arrested. There had been no cops on the scene whatsoever. Despite all the noise, not one complaint had been made by neighbors in the course of the entire night. Danny was quick to befriend Sam, and as his first gesture of good will, he invited this mysterious newcomer over to his house to smoke some good hash.

By some coincidence, Slick and Sherry had nothing else to do and also dropped by to visit Danny earlier the same evening. Just to be sociable, they offered Danny a bag or two of dope and all of them got off together. Soon they were quite high, with smug, languid faces and pinpoint pupils, and began passing the hash pipe. Slick just had time to hide his works when Sam rang the bell. He did not and could not trust any stranger and at first avoided speaking to Sam.

Sherry responded more warmly to the clean-cut, handsome youth, and made a special show of putting a fresh, pea-sized bead of hash into the pipe and handing it to him. "You light this one, Sam," she said indulgently, indicating that to do so was a great privilege. "It's great hash, and look at this pipe. Isn't it dynamite? The stone bowl improves the flavor."

"I got it from a friend in New York," Danny added, eager to remind his guest that, after all, it was his hash and his hash pipe they were smoking.

Sam grinned with his habitual friendliness as he struck a match and drew the flame down into the bowl, expanding his deep, broad chest to suck in the pungent smoke, then passed the pipe along. He paused, holding in the smoke, and nodded with approval. "Wow, this is potent!" he said. "I'm getting a buzz already!" He looked on with a smile while Slick drew at the pipe, then, as if sensing a coldness in Slick and wanting to dispel it, addressed him mildly, almost obsequiously. "Say, haven't I seen you someplace before?" he asked. "I thought I recognized you at the party. Did you do time in Eastborough about two years ago, say, December of sixty-eight?"

Slick held in the smoke, finally exhaled no more than a small remnant of it. "Yeah, how did you know?" he replied edgily.

"'Cause, that's when I was there and I remember you," Sam went on. "Don't you remember me?"

"Nope."

Slick's attitude was one of indifference, disdain almost, but Sam persisted. "Maybe we stayed in different blocks," he badgered. "I was in the old cell block, the one loaded with rats—the animal kind, that is." He smiled at this remark and continued. "I worked in the cement shop. Where were you?"

Slick paused before answering, then did so reluctantly as if to emphasize his mistrust of Sam. "I . . . worked in the boiler room mostly. . . ."

"What were you in for?" Sam asked.

"Ah . . . larceny? And you?"

"Possession. I was dealing keys of grass at the time and some cocaine and got busted in a hotbox that I didn't know was stolen."

"That's a real bummer charge," Danny interjected. "I know someone that happened to. He got probation, though."

Sherry had kept her eyes on Sam and had noticed already that he scarcely bothered to look at her. Impatiently, she turned his head with a question. "Do you do junk?" she asked insistently.

Sam shook his head. "I used to chip—just a few bags now and then, but it only made me sleepy, that's all. I like pills and speed better, or coke if I can find it. And I smoke a lot."

"I sure dig speed," Danny interrupted in a loud monotone. "But pills are not my thing. They make you too sloppy, especially barbs. And kicking barbs is supposed to be ten times worse than heroin. Those seizures—I couldn't take it. They can be fatal, right?"

"Yeah, barbs'll really waste you," said Slick with a note of great authority. "When you're strung out on 'em you're no good for nothin'."

Eager to shift the conversation away from himself, Sam turned back to Danny. "You into dope much?" he inquired.

Danny, squatting cross-legged on the floor and looking like a guru with his long pony tail and full beard, peered sphinx-like at Sam through his thick, wire-rim spectacles. Both Slick and Sherry knew what he was about to say because they had heard it a hundred times already. It took only one brief question of this sort to get him going.

"I don't really like smack that much," he began deliberately. "My thing was acid and mescaline. I did about ninety trips." He paused and they nodded with respect. All had tripped, but were not real "heads" like Danny, a fugitive from the psychedelic age. "But trouble was," he went on, his voice faint, puzzled, ". . . after awhile I . . . I sort of got, uh, these flashbacks, things I kept seeing that reminded me of when I was tripping, and I . . . got all tied up inside, real paranoid about it. So, I went to the hospital and saw this shrink who put me on thorazine."

He stopped, laughed a brief, toneless laugh, his expression curiously frozen. No matter what his mood, he seldom showed it either in his face or in his voice. He wore a peculiar, blank look and spoke in a hollow monotone that forced his listeners to concentrate on the words in order to get the particular import of what he was saying. Sometimes, as if to compensate for this lack of emotion in Danny, people would overreact to try to elicit something, expressing what he apparently could not express. But they only found themselves more disconcerted than before at the lack of any response beyond a slightly greater volume in the same, toneless voice, and a vague widening of the staring, carp-like eyes. Yet, everything he said made perfect sense, contained the studied logic of a disciplined intellect.

"So then . . . ," he recited methodically, "I got into speed and really did it a lot for awhile, but you know, it burns up your brain cells and you can't last. I used to speed for days and not eat or sleep or anything. Then I'd crash and wake up the next evening feeling ten years older. I felt like an old man after awhile, lost thirty pounds . . . so . . . ." He paused and stared through his spectacles. ". . . I did heroin to come down off the speed. It's sure beautiful but trouble is you get busted too easy with it. Like they even have a warrant out on me right now for selling it and I only sold one bag to a kid who was busted, and he ratted on me. . . ."

Slick laughed derisively. "Only one warrant? That's nothin'! I got at least three, maybe four, mostly for B&E's."

Sam puffed thoughtfully on the pipe, passed it on and exhaled. By the rapt expression on his square face he conveyed a fine appreciation for the hash. Not only was he a good host, he was a consummate guest as well. "Why don't you get into a self-help program or go to the state hospital and clean up where they won't bother you?" he suggested.

"Maybe I'll have to," Slick replied. "'Cause if they bag me I ain't got the bread for a good lawyer."

"You were in Project Comeback, right?" Danny asked.

Slick nodded. "Shit yeah, I been in there, I been to the program at Valley State Hospital, and a place down in New York. I been all over, man. He frowned with a vague, troubled look. "But ask any dopefiend. You shoot for a few months, get strung out, then you clean up for awhile 'cause you're sick and tired of hustling and 'fraid a' gettin' busted. But then you go right back on it again in no time. It don't matter what you do, it's no good. There's too much dope around an' you go back with the same friends who know where to find it. All's they have to say is 'Wanna cop some dynamite stuff?' and you're through, man."

"Right," Danny agreed. "Because a junkie wants to get off and off and off. He really digs the high so much he can't stay away from it. In other words, he's an addict."

The two of them were looking at Sam, whom they knew had not done much heroin. He was different, and by instructing him they brought out this difference and made Sam uncomfortable. Slick saw it and was reassured, felt now that he had the upper hand in his role of teacher, versus Sam's role of an uninitiated student.

"I need heroin just to stay straight," Slick went on, a bit dramatically, "'cause I'm mean as a motherfucker without dope, like sometimes I wanna waste people, cut 'em with my blade or blow 'em away with my piece. But on dope I'm gentle as a lamb. I—I don't think I could live very long without junk, man, 'cause it's everything to me, right?"

Sherry giggled at Slick's seriousness. "They should send us to the north pole or someplace like that where we could clean up once and for all," she joked.

"We'd still find it," scoffed Slick. "Even at the north pole. It's all over the world, man, no matter where you go."

Danny loaded a fresh bead into the hash pipe and relit it, nodding gravely, as if pondering an insoluable problem. "We should get into a methadone program," he tossed out. "Then at least we could get off the streets."

"I went once," Slick said with a sneer. "But they had a waiting list and you had to go through a buncha bullshit just to get your dose. 'Sides, you don't get as high on methadone, so why take it when you can do heroin? And methadone blocks the high from heroin so it costs a fortune just to get off every time. So why waste your money?"

"A lot of kids do nothing but methadone," said Sherry. "Like Dee-dee. She gets high on it. She doesn't like the needle, so it's good for her."

"Yeah? Well me, I'm a needle freak," said Slick. "Sometimes I think I get off just from putting a spike in my arm." He was looking at Sam with a cautious glitter in his eye, and paused. "You must not be a junkie, huh?" he chided, again to emphasize the incongruity of Sam's presence among them.

Sam smiled nervously and shrugged. "Right. But, everyone has their thing," he replied quickly. "Me, I don't want to start chipping and then get strung out, but I have a few friends who do it and get away with it. Hell, I figure I'm better off doing pills, bad as they are."

"Junkies do pills," Danny said didactically to Sam. "To keep down the sick and also to get high. And so they end up with a mixed habit a lotta times. But you must be kinda straight. They say if you strapped a straight person down on a table and shot heroin into his veins he wouldn't dig it at all."

"Not me," said Slick, grinning. "I'm just the opposite."

"Me, too," Sherry echoed. "I get too uptight otherwise. I couldn't cut it without junk."

Coming from someone who said so little, her comment seemed to cap the conversation. They finished the pipe and a silence fell over the four young people. Everyone was high and a little sleepy from the potent hashish. The light overhead shimmered and the furniture in the room warped oddly, as though built crooked by a prankish carpenter. They stared at one another, dumb immobile figures squatting like stone Buddhas in a temple. After a time they spoke, their voices coming from afar and with great effort.

"Where do you live?" Danny droned to Sam. "At your beach pad?"

"No, got a place here in town."

"You must have bread."

"Not really. It's just that I don't have a big habit to support," Sam replied and grinned, felt giddy and a little silly.

Danny nodded, his face remaining sober. "Wow, that's for sure. Like I'd be rich right now if it wasn't for junk. I used up my whole trust fund that my family had for me, about ten grand, in a little over a year on dope. And they thought I was using it for school. I had a really big habit then. It's funny, you know, the more bread you have the more dope you use."

"Coke is the worst that way," said Sherry.

"Right, the high only lasts a half hour so you have to keep bangin' it. When I was doing it, I used to shoot up five hundred to a thousand bucks a night to stay high...," Danny concluded.

There was another listless silence. Slick was watching Sam, more out of benign curiosity now than dark suspicion. That they had done time together went a long way to convince him that Sam was okay—that is, no more honest than the rest of them. But the realization still lurked in the back of his mind that undercover narcs often look up a person's record just to pretend they remember him from the joint. But even if this kid was a narc, Slick knew he had less to fear since he was not dealing. As it was, he shot up most of his junk and only sold a few bags now and then to teenagers. If he were ever busted they would mainly want information from him on who the big dealers were, and Slick could beat his case by ratting on them.

"How about some music?" Danny suggested tonelessly, aware that his friends were tired of talking. Sherry stirred, slowly came to life, rose and switched on the radio, fumbled the knob to some rock music. Danny nodded with approval, tapped the floor with his fingers. "I really used to like to get into music when I was doing acid," he mumbled, almost to himself.

The group listened quietly, lulled by the steady rhythm, almost a pulse beat, a heart drum, ageless as the thudding surf or pinetrees sighing in the wind. Like drugs it soothed them, eased the aching uncertainty of their lives.

18

It was Tuesday, Dolores's day off from dancing and hustling drinks at the Four-sixty Lounge. Like most of her days off, she was busy because she habitually put things off during the week until she had more than she could do. After all, the job took a lot out of her. For one thing, she disliked the people she worked for, who were gangsters, and went to a lot of effort to avoid them. She had discovered that the mob owned most of the clubs and bars in the bright lights district and that, curiously enough, the rest were owned by cops and politicians. But with the passage of time the distinction between these two classes of owners became altogether meaningless.

The patrons were likewise obnoxious, not for their male-
volence as much as for their phoniness. She had nothing
against them personally since they were good Joes for the
most part, but their shallow, over-familiarity turned her
off, their insistence on being someone they were not, as if
purposely hiding behind some slick facade. There was a
certain type of patron however, that she catered to, who
fascinated her in particular, probably because he had more
money. He was usually in the prime of life, hard driving,
successful, yet obviously lonely. After an initial pass at
Dolores and a lame attempt at ribaldry, he would most often bring up the subject of his wife who haunted him with
her own loneliness. He found this all the more vexing because nothing under the sun seemed to please the woman,
not jewelry, clothes, automobiles, or even a trip abroad. It
was as though they had both lost something along the way
that each one now expected the other to recover somehow.
And yet, curiously, they also sensed with some dread that
this missing thing, whatever it was, lay somewhere behind
them and that they would have to turn back the clock and
conduct an arduous search to recapture it. They would
have to be young again and frenetically seek it out, like a
lost treasure in some hidden cavern of the past. Their
searching often led them into the arms of others, or at
least into other mixed company. So he had come to the
Four-sixty Lounge to gaze upon Dolores's smooth, green-
eyed countenance as a pilgrim might behold the face of a
madonna. Dolores, in turn, looked pretty, and always listened. Sometimes, though less than half his age, she offered
reassurance, a word of feminine advice, and they enjoyed a
passing friendship. There was little more she could do unless he wanted to see her alone.

She did not mind stripping down to pasties and a G-
string in front of a whole roomful of these lonely men and
writhing suggestively to the pulsating music. She felt a
little sorry for them, and anyway she was too high to care
after popping a handful of dollies and maybe snorting a
spoon of cocaine. But when she came down off the high
she was very, very tired.

Now, on her day off she had a lot to do—clean up the

apartment, do the wash, have her hair done, send Russ to the store, make him supper, and then get ready for her first trick, the one who always took her out to dinner. She liked this gentleman, an older man-of-the-world type who enjoyed the company of pretty, conversant young women. He took her to the finest restaurants and was also very gentle in bed.

Just as Dolores began her work the phone rang. She thought at first it might be the trick, just arrived from out of town, but instead Sherry's voice came sighing over the wire.

"Ramon's OD'd and Slick's split 'cause he's afraid the cops'll get into it. . . ," she said, with an audible sniffle. "Oh, Dee-dee, I can't stand it here alone in this little place . . . . Can I come over?" There was another sniffle and a pause.

"I guess so," Dolores finally replied, trying to hide the edge in her voice. "I've got a lot to do, but come on over anyway and keep me company."

Exasperated, Dolores hung up. Another day off down the drain. Whenever Sherry was alone she called, and for some reason it was always on Tuesdays. Now she would have to feed both Sherry and Russ, and if he had extra coke or a few bags of dope Sherry would stay on through the evening getting off with Russ and his friends in one bedroom while she was seeing her tricks in the other in order to finance this merrymaking.

There was a soft knock at the door. Dolores opened it and Sherry entered, looking forlorn in a drab Mexican blanket that drooped about and nearly hid her frail body.

"My stomach's hurting again," she said weakly, and flopped down on the sofa. "Got any grass?"

Almost before Sherry finished, Dolores had gone to a drawer and taken out the papers and a nearly consumed nickel or five-dollar bag. She let Sherry dexterously roll the joint and soon the room was filled with the pungent, alfalfa-like odor of marihuana smoke. Sherry relaxed, even smiled a little. Her mind was numbed for a time against the fear of growing up in a world that held no promise for her, a wasteland of self-interested people stepping on one another in a crowded, polluted city to get ahead, little people absorbed in their own struggle with scarcely a thought for their neighbor. As far as she was concerned, only the simple things were safe anymore and could be counted on, like the bluesy sound of music, small talk, the flame of a candle, a glass of wine, something to munch on, and a good high.

"How did Ramon OD?" Dolores asked, not wanting to get Sherry started on her medical problems. "Dope, or was he barbed-out?"

"I dunno," Sherry replied, and let out a yawn. "He's always ODing. They just take him to the hospital and shoot him full of narcan and put an oxygen mask on his face and he starts breathing again."

Dolores bit her lip. "It's a wonder he hasn't gone out by now. It's bad enough to be strung out, even without ODing all the time. He should know better."

"If he doesn't OD on dope, he'll do it on barbs," said Sherry. "Funny, it's almost as if he wants to. . . ." She shuddered, took another long hit off the joint, burned it down to a tiny roach.

"Take the papers and roll another one," Dolores said. She passed the last of the nickel bag, hoping to get Sherry so high on grass that she would crash.

Sherry obliged, her thin, nimble fingers twisting the paper around the green flakes of dried weed. She lit it, smoked almost half the joint before passing it to Dolores, then brought up the subject she had wanted to talk about from the very start. "Slick and I had another fight last night . . . ," she began morosely. "First he slapped me after I dropped the cooker. The spoon just slipped out of my hand by accident. He said next time I did it he'd kill me. Then he accused me of tapping the bags behind his back while he was out hustling. He said I was a pain in the ass, dropping cookers all the time and sneaking dope, and he says he's fed up with me."

She sobbed openly now, wiping her eyes with a finger while Dolores looked on patiently, not knowing quite what to say. "But . . . I told him I wasn't a thief and if he thought so then maybe we should split for good," Sherry went on. "Like, I always told him when I needed an extra bag or two while he was gone, so you know what he said? He said, 'I'll kick your skinny little ass if you touch my stash, you sleazy bitch!' Can you imagine him saying that to me, his ol' lady? And then he said, 'I'll decide what junk you use!' You see how rotten he is?" She half-closed her eyes, the long lashes soaked with tears.

Dolores studied the frail girl huddled on the sofa, clutching her abdomen with one hand. "Well, did you tap the bags?" she asked.

"Only once," Sherry admitted with a sniffle. "I was so sick I couldn't stand it, and then Slick sold it to someone and they said he burned them. . . ." She looked at Dolores innocently. "I know it was wrong and stupid and all that, but at the time I couldn't help it."

Dolores was annoyed at the confession. She was resolved not to get caught between Slick's violent temper and Sherry's cringing helplessness that begged protection. "Maybe he had a bad day," she suggested. "I have them myself now and then and I'm sure you do, too. Now, excuse me, I have to get Russ out of bed."

She went into the bedroom where Russ was sleeping. Sherry heard a few words spoken between them and then several minutes of silence. At last Dolores emerged from the bedroom, looking a bit rumpled.

"Russ is awake," she announced breathlessly. "Here . . . ," She handed Sherry four little white tablets. "Here's forty milligrams. It's all I can spare right now but I know you'll need it sooner or later. It should hold you till Slick gets back."

Sherry accepted the tablets, grateful to Dolores for saving her the trouble of having to ask. After popping half of them straight away, she started talking about Slick again, rambling on endlessly about nothing. The methadone had loosened her tongue, a strange, dramatic effect in someone usually so quiet and mousey. Dolores was spared the role of polite listener by the appearance of Russ, looking bright and cheerful, the aura of cocaine about him. He offered some to Sherry but Dolores, seeing what was coming, put a stop to it by sitting them both down to breakfast. The marihuana gave Sherry an enormous appetite and she ate enough for two people, then went into the bedroom without another word and fell asleep.

"Well, guess that's the end of the party," Russ observed.

"It certainly is," Dolores replied and handed him a grocery list. She shoved him out the door and started her housework, careful not to disturb Sherry, her pale, smallish face with tiny features like that of a child, sweetest in sleep.

19

Sherry had not always been so thin. As a little girl she was quite plump but never very healthy according to her mother, a handsome, methodical woman who was herself a doctor, a busy pediatrician. Because her mother was able to stay home only until Sherry was six months old before returning to work at the clinics, the child was raised by a maternal grandmother, a kindly but stern Russian-born, Jewish woman. As if to reaffirm her own importance in the household, the old woman constantly fussed over the the children, sounding the alarm at any sign of illness. Clapping her hand on Sherry's forehead, she would often exclaim, "Don't ask me, but I think she's running a very high fever!"

Her mother would be summoned from the hospital to hover over the little girl taking the temp and eyeing the glittering column of mercury with appropriate clinical concern, as if the farenheit reading foretold the very life or death of her daughter. Any elevation of the temperature would result in a furious debate between both parents, for her father was also a physician, an eminent neurosurgeon. He was the same age as his wife but had an edge on her, being a full professor at the medical school while she was only an assistant professor.

A diminutive, sensitive man, he generally conveyed an air of great confidence and authority, but when his professional judgment was disputed, he became excitable and was given to shouting, especially in the operating room. The more his wife quibbled with him about Sherry's symptoms, and as a pediatrician she had more experience with children, the more upset he became.

"Don't forget! I have never missed a diagnosis in my life!" he would assert. "And I say it is nothing! A virus, perhaps, but no more! It will pass in twenty-four to forty-eight hours!"

"But you haven't even examined her!" her mother would argue. "So how can you be so sure? What about that cough? And the pallor? You can't rule out pneumonia, Gerald!"

"Then take her to the clinic and let them have a look at her!" he would snap back. "Remember, my dear, a doctor is never supposed to treat his or her own family! It's malpractice!"

The two of them would retire in a huff to opposite ends of the house while grandmother administered her famous remedy, chicken soup, which was scorned by the parents as a foolish bit of folk medicine. "Here, my darling! It's better than penicillin!" the old woman would cluck as she spooned it into the child's face.

Sherry would recover rapidly and a big meal generally followed, for grandmother constantly plied her with food, especially rich pastries. In order to gain so much attention, the little girl learned to manipulate the thermometer by rubbing it or shaking it the wrong way when no one was looking. Her mother nearly fainted one day when the mercury shot up to one hundred six degrees. Sherry was immediately sponged in an ice-cold bath for ten minutes. After that she was a bit more careful.

Her family lived in a large, elegant suburban home with rarely used tennis courts in the spacious backyard. She seldom saw her parents, both of whom were completely dedicated to their profession and spent long hours at the hospital, not to mention frequent medical conventions out of town. When they did stay home they acted more like overseers of a large estate, efficiently checking on affairs to see that all was in order. Sherry was taught never to bother them with trivial things because they were usually either very busy or very tired. She was allowed to say goodnight to her father in his study. Then her mother would dutifully read a bedtime story in a loud, rapid voice that permitted little chance for questions, after which she administered a firm and efficient kiss that never varied from year to year, and tucked the little girl into bed.

Every summer the family went away on weekends to their cottage on a lake up-country. It was a strange, lonely experience for Sherry, sitting next to her parents, her grandmother, and her older brother on their private strip of sand, watching a world at play swarming around them. She and her brother never went to the public beach because her mother considered it too unsanitary, a filthy place where strange children transmitted contagious diseases. Instead, they invited acquaintances, usually other doctors and their families, over for cook-outs, rather formal affairs, since Dr. Linsky was such a renowned surgeon as well as a full professor, and commanded considerable respect from his colleagues.

Her mother's and grandmother's preoccupation with Sherry's health pervaded all aspects of her life. The girl was kept home from school continually for minor ailments—runny noses, coughs, indigestion—things that the average mother would ignore. On her very first day of kindergarten, Sherry vomited because she was nervous and her mother, when called at the hospital, sent an ambulance to the school and had the child brought to the emergency room. Days later, when the little girl still had not returned to class, the teacher phoned her mother again, who said flatly, "I am a pediatrician and I will decide when my daughter is ready." The following day Sherry was sent back to kindergarten, escorted by her aging grandmother, who sat in the back of the room until the little girl was ready to leave, and this practice continued for almost a whole month.

The next year her first grade teacher observed that Sherry was extremely shy and withdrawn. The school counselor saw the girl and contacted her mother, who was indignant at first but reluctantly consented to have her daughter referred for psychological evaluation. Her name was placed on the waiting list of a local child guidance clinic and about three months later an appointment was received. The usual heated debate broke out between her parents as to whether or not she should keep the appointment. Finally her mother, who had made similar referrals for other children but never expected to see the day when a child of hers would have to be referred, dressed Sherry up and trundled her off to the clinic. There, she was surprised when a social worker wanted to see her privately while a psychologist saw Sherry alone in another room.

"I think I should stay with her, don't you?" her mother protested. "After all, I am her mother."

They reassured her at great length and finally simply had to insist that mother and daughter be seen separately. The social worker made very personal inquiries into Dr. Linsky's marriage, her family, her relationship with her own mother, father, and so forth, and a return appointment was made for the following week. When they got home, her mother was quite upset.

"You don't know what I had to go through at that place, Gerald!" she complained. "Why, I was so embarrassed. I said to myself, 'Who is the patient, anyway, me or her?' "

She did not keep the next appointment, or the next, and the case was dropped. As a pediatrician, she thought she knew as much about children as any social worker or psychologist. She was never aware of what had taken place during that first visit. It was one of the few times in the little girl's life when someone really cared about what was going on inside her. The psychologist, a relatively young, plain woman with a natural warmth for her small clients, had Sherry draw a picture of the family sitting in a house. Mother was a large, irregular figure with no arms and a crooked mouth. Father was thin, insect-like, off to one side. Grandmother was egg-shaped with a wide smile. Brother was tall and handsome, the only intact figure.

Then she drew a grotesque figure lying down without a face.

"And who is that?" asked the psychologist.

"A little girl," said Sherry. "She's sick."

20

Dom stared at the two shiny red capsules, then gulped them down, sat back and lit a cigarette with trembling hands. Barbiturates were no substitute for heroin but at least they helped keep down the sick. And they took his mind off of dope temporarily by dulling the craving, as well as the fear of getting sick, for it was the fear of dopesickness that was as bad if not worse than the flu-like syndrome itself. And as much as he detested them, he was using both barbs as well as the milder and more mellow valiums quite frequently now because of the trouble he was in.

Motto had warned him not to put more than one cut on the new batch of dope. But failing to reduce his habit accordingly, Dom had shot up half of it just to stay straight, and cut the other half four-in-one. This turned an already mediocre product into garbage that did not sell well, so he had to give the junkies a break on the price. In the end, he wound up four hundred dollars short on two deliveries. And word had also gotten back to Motto's runners that the dope was no good. Ordinarily they would expect it to be around five percent heroin, and no lower than three. But this stuff was around two percent or less. It was shit, and Motto and his runners were getting very suspicious.

Soon Dom grew very groggy on the barbs, almost sloppy, and hated the feeling. Blinking at his outstretched fingers, he saw they were still trembling, even after five seconals. He knew he was going to have to be dopesick, or else get strung out on barbs, sopors, valiums, doridens, or whatever, all of them downers. Then with a double habit of both heroin and downs, he would really be messed up. It was impossible to kick barbs without landing in a hospital because of the seizures. In fact, doing barbs was the main reason for his arrest a few weeks ago, which added to his difficulties considerably. He was simply too stoned, on top of the wine, to avoid the bust.

It happened of all places in a girl's apartment, where as far as Dom knew no one had done anything stronger than drink a few beers or smoke a couple of joints. Joyce was one of the regulars at The Prophet and he had known her for nearly a year, saw her off and on when he got lonely. She was a vivacious brunette who loved a good time. Her contagious sense of humor lifted him out of his frequent troughs of moodiness and depression, so that he naturally turned to her when dope ran low. After all, women were just another high, tantalizing and arousing him with their coyness, then yielding to his demands and setting off an explosion of desire inside him shook every nerve in his body. And, as with all such things, he found himself easily addicted to women. Yet, he would have preferred them to heroin, had he not discovered that the withdrawal was far more painful, neither bearable nor worth repeating. After Brenda, he could not get hooked on them again.

Joyce did not go in for drugs especially. Like many, she was more addicted to the permissive life-style and fell into that general, garbage-head category of varied drug experimentation. She did a little acid, speed, a few downs, smoked, and drank. She did what others did, for like most people who identified strongly with the youth culture, she wanted to belong, to be a part of something supposedly new and different and free from ordinary social constraints and pressures. One of her weaknesses, among other things, was grass and a few hits on a good joint made her giggle like a schoolgirl. In fact, she had been a co-ed not very long ago, with plans to be an art teacher. But to her way of thinking college was not the kind of opportunity to be lost on overzealous studies. Rather, it was an adventure, remote from the hidebound conservatism of her home town where she was free to try her wings as an individual.

She readily immersed herself in the frothy bath of campus social life—the parties and dances with wall-to-wall people rapping about new things, dropping the latest hip expressions. And there were all those exciting boys asking her out on dates. She had trouble fitting them into her schedule and finally found herself dating a very sophisticated, city boy who drove a Porsche.

All this social life took her mind off of studies so completely that she no longer cared very much about passing. When she failed at the end of her freshman year she was relieved, if anything, finding herself with more time for fun. An expensive abortion soon afterward caused her to argue and then break up with her boyfriend. She drifted into off-campus street life and found work as a cocktail waitress, first at a club for the young college set, which bored her, and then at The Prophet. This was more to her liking. There was something primitive and untamed about street people that appealed to her instincts as a woman, plus she got to know some slightly older men there whom she found exciting. With her looks she could have any of them practically at a wink. Dom was tall and handsome, and a junkie, which made him even more fascinating. It took only one play by another girl, a rival, for Joyce to move in and claim him.

Dom never shot dope around her for fear of turning her on. While not serious about her, he liked her well enough not to want to hurt her in any way. So instead of getting off together they did other things. They talked about life and about art. She made charcoal sketches of his lean, angular profile. And after the wine was gone and she was high on grass the discussion trailed off and they got down to the basics, for Joyce loved to ball. Just as when they were dancing, she liked the music turned up top-end when they were in bed, insisted it added to the ecstacy of the experience. This proved to be of considerable annoyance to her more immediate neighbors, who sometimes found themselves blasted out of a sound sleep by a roaring stereo at odd hours of the night. Frequently they shouted obscenities, or pounded firmly on the walls, and when this proved futile, as it usually did at such moments of inconvenience, they resorted to the police. A car would be sent over to investigate the matter, generally arriving long after the music had been turned down, the couple now engaged in quieter activities. But just this once Dom had picked the wrong night. For the last several days it so happened that the narcotics squad had staked out the apartment house because of reports of drug traffic on the premises. And it was equally unfortunate that the neighbors complained again that night, and that the call was answered by the same dectectives who had watched Dom enter the apartment.

In the middle of Joyce's ecstacy there was a loud knock on the door and when she finally got up to answer it, one plainclothes detective and three police officers swept past her with drawn guns and presented a John Doe warrant. Needless to say the couple was quite unprepared to receive them. Finding a few reds, four bags of dope, and a set of works in Dom's pockets, they dropped his hastily donned trousers and skin searched him, while he stood naked, feeling very foolish. Had he been thinking, he could have stuffed the dope and the pills into his mouth and excused himself to go flush them down the toilet. Then they would have him only for a set of works. As it was, the police were impressed by the heroin and also by a lid of marihuana and some speed they discovered in Joyce's dresser, plus a few plants in her kitchen window. Convinced they were on the trail of a really big stash, they handcuffed the pair and systematically proceeded to dismantle the apartment. In the living room they ripped up cushions, overturned furniture, pulled up the rug, and tore down the pictures from the walls. In the bedroom they pulled off the mattresses, and disemboweled dresser drawers and closets. Going into the kitchen, they looked inside the refrigerator right away since it was such a popular hiding place, dragging everything out. They were rewarded by a single tab of LSD wrapped in foil and tucked away in the butter tray. By now they had worked up quite an appetite and delved into some of the food. They polished off a roast chicken, tossing the bones on the floor, a half gallon of milk, and a half a loaf of bread.

Refreshed, it was time to get nasty. They slapped Dom around, pointed a cocked revolver at his head and demanded that he tell them where it was. But Dom was coming down out of his barbiturate haze and stubbornly kept insisting there was nothing more and that they were barking up the wrong tree. This infuriated the detective, who had invested considerable time and effort into the stake out.

"C'mon, let's go!" he snapped. "You're both under arrest!" And he quickly advised them of their rights.

"I didn't do anything!" Joyce screamed as they pulled at her. "Why don't you leave me alone!"

"Shaddup, ya cheap whore!" bellowed a sergeant. "We're takin' you in for possession and co-habitation!" He gave her a kick in the buttocks that propelled her out the door. When Dom objected to this treatment he was doubled over by a right to the belly, a favorite, paralyzing blow that leaves no mark.

They were both booked at the county jail. Then Joyce was taken into a separate room where the detective looked on while a matron had her strip off every stitch of clothing, spread her legs and jump up and down. This was a unique experience for her, but she was not really worried as long as she had no dope. She was clean and they released her on recognizance. Dom was locked up for the night, pending bail.

Motto's lawyer came down and bailed him out the next morning. The arraignment was held the following day and he was formally charged with possession of heroin. Joyce was there also to hear herself charged with possession of marihuana, LSD, and amphetamines, not nearly as serious a case as the possession of heroin or cocaine. And yet, as it worked out later, they each received identical sentences of two years' probation. The reason was that she did not have the kind of lawyer that Dom had.

The trial came up several month's after the arraignment. Dom considered himself lucky to have a man like Joe Donohue representing him. He was one of the best lawyers around, knew all the judges and clerks on a first name basis. A big, shambling man with his thick silver hair slicked down neatly, he wore a conservative business suit and striped tie. He had the look of a successful lawyer, a showy combination of flair and toughness, almost a stage-presence that hushed the courtroom after his first few words. He rose and addressed the presiding judge, a much older man and a close acquaintance of many years, who was invariably soft on negligent landlords or white collar crooks but hard on anything to do with drugs or street crime, usually crimes of the poor.

"Your honor," Attorney Donohue began, his voice ringing through the courtroom. "Let me point out first of all that the defendant...." He paused and gestured toward Dom who was sitting submissively behind him, wearing a borrowed suit. "... is a Vietnam veteran who served his country with honor and who received a purple heart and a bronze star in the line of duty. Now, I believe this young man plans to attend a school to study, uh, architectural engineering. So may I suggest to the court that in all fairness he deserves a chance to prove himself a worthy citizen who can contribute in a useful way to society."

The old judge was reading something, not really listening. He had heard variations of the same speech many times before. "Thank you, Mr. Donohue," he said, and glanced at the prosecutor who had testified that the defendant, a known heroin addict and probably a dealer, was arrested with heroin in his possession. Then he pronounced the verdict—the two years of probation.

With the bang of the gavel, Dom let out a breath, relieved to be free. But the fact that his freedom had been purchased at a price left him uneasy. It had cost Motto some money to get him off, probably a grand for the lawyer and maybe something for the judge, and this left Dom even more deeply indebted to his boss than before. His fears were confirmed after court when Mr. Donohue gave him a lift uptown. It was a cool, cloudy day for springtime and as they drove through the noontime traffic, the damp air streamed in through the car window and refreshed Dom. He settled back in the plush, leather bucket seat of the coupe-de-ville, relaxing with the solace that at least he did not have to worry about going away. Then he sensed by the lawyer's silence that he had something unpleasant to say. He glanced over at the older man, who responded with a quick, stern look before returning his eyes to the traffic ahead.

"I wouldn't get pinched again, if I were you," Donohue stated bluntly. "That was your first arrest but next time it won't be easy to get you off without a jail sentence."

"Don't worry," Dom replied. "I'll be careful, all right. Tell Mr. Motto I'm really grateful for his help and I'll make it back to him for sure."

The lawyer nodded. "He told me to tell you that he doesn't want to lose you. Apparently he thinks you're a pretty good kid and a hard worker. But he did say that you owe him some money, is that right?"

Dom swallowed and his stomach knotted. "Yes," he admitted, "but I'm going to pay it. . . ."

"I know, but they want the money when it's due, not at some later date. No one can run a business on credit. There are a lot of other payments involved, other investors who have put up a lot of money. So it's rather unwise for him to carry you indefinitely unless you can make the payments, wouldn't you agree?" Donohue looked back at the youth with mild condescension.

"Sure," Dom agreed. "If he's working for other people then. . . ." He paused, wanting the lawyer to go on, perhaps to drop some clue as to Motto's connections. But Donohue did not reply, and concentrated silently on the traffic.

21

Dom had spent the last of his money on one spoon of good heroin. He had cooked it up and was about to shoot it when all of a sudden the spoon slipped from his fingers

and clattered onto the floor, the shot splashing everywhere. In a panic he got up, began searching around the
room for more heroin. He looked in the stove and burned
his hand, jerked it back and then awoke. He sat staring
dully at his scorched fingers, and at the white blur of the
cigarette on the floor. It had already burned a hole in the
carpet when he finally stood up and stamped it out. He
reached for the pack but stopped, realizing he could not
trust himself to stay awake on the barbs. His heart was still
pounding from the dream, similar to dozens he was having
lately since he had been sick, and he went to the sink,
hoping cold water would revive him from his annoying
stupor.

His face cool and dripping wet, he raised the window
and looked out as his vision became clearer. An old oak
tree reached toward him, almost touching the wall of the
building with its freshly budded leaves. They were only
days old, still a delicate, tender green. It seemed only a
short while ago that he last saw it with its new leaves, and
yet he realized a whole year had slipped by with his hardly
knowing it. He tried to recall where he had been a year
ago, pictured only the same bewildering maze of vain
hopes and disappointments that he still found himself
caught in. Glancing again at the ancient tree with its
luxuriant, tiny leaves so tender that they drooped in the
sun, it occurred to him that whether he was there at the
window to look at it or not, it would go on budding and
leafing out year after year, transforming itself from gnarled
lifelessness to shimmering elegance through an endless
chain of seasons. And the constancy of it awed him, the
ever-flowing sap of life that oozed up from its roots and
which, by comparison, made his brief struggle with its
poignant vicissitudes seem paltry and insignificant. He
could live and die a thousand times while this tree only
bowed in the winds. But there had been a time when his
life was as green and as fresh with hope.

He remembered the summer of his seventh year, getting
up very early in the morning to water the garden. The dew
lay bright and thick on the lawn, catching the sparkle of
day as he brushed through it and he felt the coolness of it

bathing his bare feet. He picked up the hose, twisted the spigot, and sent the spray arching through the morning air. A rainbow appeared, dancing and clinging to the mist, dipping its iridescent colors toward the lush, green plants like the glistening wings of a fairy butterfly. And as he moved the spray the rainbow shifted, vanished and reappeared again, as if to beguile him.

His father would come out often before breakfast to stand beside his son and admire the thriving vegetables, perhaps stooping down to pull up an invading weed. As they stood together he talked about many things. One morning he praised the little boy.

"You're a fine son and a good worker," he said proudly. "You see how high the garden is growing? That's because you're out here working." He paused, his thoughts flying back in time. "Y'know, I had to work awful hard myself to get where I am. Like you in this garden, I had to make things grow. My father came over from Italy with nothing, worked in a shoe factory for three dollars and a half a week, lived in a company house. And they had nine children. He worked too hard—you know he died of TB when he was still a young man. So, I had to go to work in his place. When I was young like you I had to help support my mother and brothers and sisters. That was in the depression." He shook his head slowly, his face turning grim for just a moment. "None of the kids today'll ever know what we went through in them days. It was tough. I worked for fifty cents a day and was damn glad to get it. Then I met your mother. Oh, she was a pretty thing, and after we were married I started working two jobs. Went in the army in 'forty-one and came out in 'forty-five, went to school on a GI Bill. You were born while I was overseas and even when I was back goin' to school I never saw you much because you were always asleep while I was working late and going to school days. I studied construction engineering and that was tough, too, but I had faith in God that I would make it. Then I got a break. The family in Italy lent me a little money and I got more from the bank and started the business. And it was a good time for contracting—lotsa work around. After a couple years I got busy, and now I gotta nice little business, own my own home, car, and have a fine son an' a daughter, an' I'm puttin' a little away so that maybe mamma an' I won't have to worry when it comes time to retire. So, you see? Ya gotta work in this world to make it and nothin' comes easy. So mamma and I were thinking, why don't you get a paper route someday? You'll do good, like I did, make a little money, make things grow."

Beginning at the age of twelve, Dom spent every afternoon for the next two years delivering the local paper. He developed a perfect throw from a moving bicycle to a front porch thirty feet away. Only when the weather was bad did his mother drive him around in the car. He got so many new subscriptions that he was runner-up for the state-wide Carrier of the Year Award, and won a twenty-five dollar prize.

He was never the egghead type and neither was his younger sister. She studied harder, got better grades, and his father made a great fuss over her report cards. But he stole the limelight when, after a tireless campaign, he was elected student body president in the ninth grade and in high school, he emerged from the initial obscurity of the sophomore year to run for class senator, and won. Then in his senior year he was chosen "Outstanding Athlete" for his fine pitching. He and his girl Brenda were a perfect couple and the envy of the whole class. At graduation almost everyone asked to sign his yearbook and wanted him to sign theirs. One girl, a wallflower that he hardly knew, must have been a great admirer. She quietly penned a few words that stood out from all the rest when he read it later. She wrote, "To Dom with love. I'm super proud 'cause I can tell my children and grandchildren I knew you."

22

Slick and Ramon peered out of the car, their eyes keen with satisfaction. They had picked a perfect day, fair and warm, a shopper's delight. The streets of the downtown business section swarmed with mothers and their children, old folks, and office workers on their break, all jostling and maneuvering their way along the sidewalks and herding together on the corners, waiting to cross with the light, or else simply jay-walking in twos and threes between passing cars.

"You know where to park?" Slick asked the driver, a friend of Ramon's.

He nodded, spoke with an accent. "Yeah, I double-park here, like you showed Jimmy."

Then Ramon, high on amphetamines and irritable, snapped something in Spanish.

"What'd ya tell'im?" Slick demanded.

"Not to fuck up, man," Ramon replied. "If any cop cars come, to pull out quick, right?"

Slick was scanning the street, searching for a blue uniform. He saw none. "That cop just took his break!" he announced sharply. "Let's go!"

The car stopped and they got out, their hearts pounding with fear and excitement. Slick always felt this way before a score—high, almost as high as if he had banged a spoon of the best crystal meth. Ramon followed him, fidgeted with the sawed-off shotgun under his coat, hoping this time he would not have to use it.

"If we shoot, we'll hit someone for sure, man," Ramon muttered to his partner as they shouldered through the crowd of shoppers.

Slick reassured him with a taut, nervous grin. "Don't worry," he said. "Like Ernie told ya, if you don't shoot, they won't."

That was the beauty of the plan, as it was explained to them two weeks earlier, and they had bought it. After all, the man who proposed it was an undoubted authority and had guaranteed them at least fifteen or twenty grand for pulling it off.

"Use the crowd for protection," the man had said. "Cops won't shoot in a crowd. It's bad for police-community relations and they're big on that nowadays, real sensitive about their image 'cause they're a buncha knuckle-breakers and they know it."

Slick and Ramon knew him only by the name Ernie when they met him in a fancy, high-rise apartment out in the suburbs. Affable, balding, and early middle-aged, he told them he could not risk pulling the job himself because of being on parole on a life sentence. Their introduction had been arranged by Spanky, Motto's strong-arm man, who first approached Dom on the subject of a big score. Not that they wanted him to do it—they only wanted names, so Dom referred him to Ramon, who was just out of the hospital after ODing and flat broke. Naturally Ramon agreed and recruited Slick as his partner and two others as drivers. They went up to Ernie's apartment several times to study photos, floor plans, a map, and also went in town to case the store itself.

"It has to be fast," Ernie told them and lit another unfiltered cigarette. He was a chain smoker and drank scotch like water. "A crowd'll gather to watch. If you see cops, get behind the employees. That's why you want 'em all standing together. Now, don't shoot unless you have to, 'cause the beef for killing or wounding someone even accidentally can run up to life. I know, that's how I got my time—someone tried to be a hero. But nobody's a hero against two sawed-off shotguns. . . ."

The youths gave Ernie a look of uncertainty as he snapped his fingers, smiling, while Spanky poured a round of drinks. "So, no beefs, okay?" he went on, after tossing off the shot. "Just walk in, pull the heist, walk out. Safe as a church. Stay in the crowd and if any cop cars come, your boys'll pull out an' block 'em." He wiped his chin, chuckled. "Hell, I'd pull it myself but the cops know me so well they'd recognize me by the way I tie my shoelaces." He poured another shot, raised it. "Here's to a quick, clean job, and like I say, you get what's in that safe an' I promise you ten grand apiece, cash."

Slick grinned. "Sounds good. . . ." He did not drink the toast because he never cared much for alcohol, while Ramon swilled down his shot, remaining silent and impassive.

Spanky caught Ramon's stony, furtive expression. "You ain't gettin' cold feet, are ya, pal?" he muttered.

Ernie gave Ramon a fatherly squint, his high forehead with its receding hairline furrowed with benevolent wrinkles. "If you are, now's the time to say so, 'cause we don't want any slip-ups. It's either a hundred percent or nothin', that's how it's gotta be. Planning, sure, but most of all, teamwork. You gotta have confidence in the other guy and him in you. Otherwise you tighten up, get shaky, maybe do somethin' crazy."

Ramon smiled faintly. "You sound like a coach I used to know," he remarked.

Ernie chuckled. "Well, as a matter of fact, it's a compliment to hear that from a young fellow, 'cause I enjoy working with you guys. Matter a'fact, I did a little coaching at one time, a basketball team in the joint down in Missouri, but that was years ago."

After the pep talk Slick and Ramon left Ernie's place with an air of confidence. Both had been impressed by his level-headedness, his warmth and sincerity, and by a certain quality of bravado that criminals admire in one another. They were convinced that Ernie was right, that it would be a pushover.

Passers-by hardly noticed the two youths approaching the jewelry store wearing heavy coats, dark glasses, and hats pulled down low over their faces. Even as they entered, the clerks and customers paid them little notice until the sawed-off shotguns came out from under their coats and Slick yelled that this was a stickup. Everyone froze, then they were herded together and covered by Ramon, while Slick quickly prodded the manager into the back of the store and made him open the safe. A crowd of curious onlookers began gathering outside, peering through the glass, or backing away to clog the sidewalk. What they saw was a youth holding a shotgun on eight petrified people with their hands in the air. A foot patrolman appeared, then another, breaking through the crowd, their revolvers drawn. As they tried vainly to push back the onlookers, Ramon spotted them and ducked behind his hostages.

Slick reappeared, prodding the clerk ahead of him. He had stuffed everything from the safe that he could lay his hands on into a shopping bag and it fairly bulged. He did not stop to see what the items were, just scooped them out of drawers and boxes. He had been instructed not to bother with the less valuable merchandise out in the display cases.

As the officers tried to maneuver for an opening the crowd panicked, swept back as the two youths came through the front entrance pushing three of the employees ahead of them. Then they darted off into an alley at the side of the building. As they ran for daylight at the other end, they suddenly realized with horror that they had silhouetted themselves and were perfect targets. The alley, now without the protection of the crowd, was a shooting gallery and Slick and Ramon were the revolving ducks, a slight kink in Ernie's scheme that he had failed to mention. After a few awful seconds the bullets began whizzing past them, ricocheting off bricks and concrete as the officers tried their skill. They did not fire more than a few shots, afraid of hitting someone at the other end. At the last shot, Slick felt his leg go out from under him momentarily and in a flash he wondered if it had been broken, knowing that if it was, he was as good as bagged. But he recovered his stride a few steps from the corner and hobbled into the subway just behind Ramon. They had timed the trains in advance and knew that they did not have a second to lose. With Slick limping painfully they went through the turnstyles but missed the train they had planned to catch. Following an alternate plan they ran upstairs, moved with the crowd out onto another platform and boarded another car. The passengers only gawked at Slick as he applied pressure to his blood-soaked leg. A little old lady who was quite concerned got up and offered him her seat and with a taut grin on his pale face, he sat down.

They arrived at Ernie's apartment by cab an hour and a half later. Slick was a little weak and his leg had stiffened, but they went right upstairs. Ramon agreed to wait outside the door with a shotgun under his coat and to come in shooting if there was any trouble about getting the money. But Ernie, true to his word, did not pull any stunts. He was delighted, if not a little surprised that his plan had worked so well and inspected the fine jewelry triumphantly. Upwards of one hundred thousand dollars had just been thrown into his lap.

Grinning with satisfaction he went into another room and returned with a suitcase full of money, counted it out on a table and pushed it, a big heap of bills, over to Slick. "There ya go, ten grand apiece and a grand for each driver," he said, and frowned. "Hey, you're gettin' paler by the minute, kid. You better see a doc."

"I can't," said Slick.

"I know a man who'll look at you," Ernie insisted. "He worked for us. Want him to come down?"

Slick shook his head. "Naw, gotta go cop. Once I get off I won't feel nothin'."

"Maybe you can use some of this," Ernie said and reached for the bottle of scotch, uncorked it. He was very sanguine now, on the verge of celebrating. But he stopped for a moment and pointed a finger at the youth. "Maybe you should skip town and lay up somewheres till that leg mends," he suggested. "Remember, you're hotter than hell right now, especially if they got any kinda description. And if you're ever picked up, remember, better think twice about coppin' a plea, 'cause guys like that don't live too long in this business."

"Sure," Slick said with the taut grin appearing on his pale face, and his eyes glittered in a way that made Ernie draw back. "Don't worry, I ain't no rat." He studied the man for a silent moment with his sharp, reptilian eyes, then stuffed the money into his shopping bag and departed. In twenty minutes he and Ramon were down at The Prophet and within the hour they were high, enjoying the thing that they had both risked their lives for.

23

Russ and Dolores were on the brink of economic ruin in the face of his thriving cocaine habit of nearly two thousand dollars a week. On top of that, her business fell off sharply. First it was an unexpected heat wave in late May that caused the tricks to sit out in their backyards and sip gin and tonics. Then things took an even deeper plunge after the well-publicized news story of a big police raid netting a number of prostitutes, which caused the few tricks still on the prowl to take cover.

And so Russ sat in the apartment, fingering his empty coke spoon despondently, stung by the hard reality that they were barely getting by, scrimping just to support Dolores's moderate methadone habit with maybe enough left for a few blows of coke each day. So now at last he was forced to lower himself to doing pills. He copped a few biphetamines to go up, then tuinals to go down—sort of a poor man's coke high and he despised it because of the hangover. To get off of this he did some methadone, then popped valiums to boost it. He even got miserably drunk on a bottle of white port, a new low for a high-class addict like himself.

"I'm turnin' into a garbage head!" he complained to Dolores one morning as he lay in bed with glazed eyes watching her getting dressed. "I'm all pilled up an' all this shit is nothin' but a tease. When you gettin' paid, baby? We gotta really hustle today, y'know it? I gotta get me some good coke an' some skag, too. . . ."

"I wish you'd stop doing all them pills," she nagged. "You're no good for nothin' when you're loaded on them. I wanted you to love me this morning but look at you—all hung over and half-dead."

Indignantly he rose up in bed, propped himself on one elbow. "Hey, c'mon, baby, I'm ready!" he insisted.

She frowned, slipped on her blouse. "No, you're too wasted, and besides, I don't have all day. You know what pills do—you'd take forever." She smiled impishly at him, then reached over and pulled the sheet off the bed, leaving him exposed. "Now, c'mon," she coaxed. "If we want to hustle I've got to go now so I can get to work. I'd rather see you back on coke. At least you're ready when I am."

"Let's face it, baby," Russ said, hopping out of bed. "You miss coke as much as I do. . . ."

"No one digs it like you," she argued. "But I admit I go for a hit now and then. It helps me when I'm working."

Because poverty puts kinks in even the best of relationships, they left in sort of a huff and drove downtown without speaking. After parking they entered one of the big department stores and he gave her the hot card he paid fifty dollars for. She took it with reluctance. Being a woman she had been trained to do hustles like boosting, or shoplifting, using hot or phony credit cards, or passing bad checks and phony tens. But except for the phony tens, she disliked these hustles because of the risk. She had been pinched only once while boosting and got a ninety day suspended sentence. A second time she had a close scrape with a hot card that was too old, but insisted on speaking to the credit company over the telephone. She hung up on them and told the clerk they were checking something and would call back in a moment, which gave her a chance to walk out.

Another close call was in a bank when the teller told her to go see the manager about a check. She knew they were going to have her arrested on the spot so she made a hasty exit.

She and Russ found the escalator and went upstairs to women's coats, then split up. Russ stationed himself some distance away to keep an eye peeled for store detectives while Dolores went over to the rack to pick out something expensive. As she turned admiringly in front of the mirror a clerk came over and after a few words took the coat from Dolores and went to the register.

"Pure Kashmir," the clerk remarked. "Best thing for spring. Cash or charge?"

"My fiance is getting it for me," said Dolores and handed her the card.

"You have a very nice fiance, I would say," the clerk went on, looking at the card, and picked up the phone.

Dolores stood by tensely, ready to leave at any sign of hesitation or stalling. The clerk hung up the receiver, stamped the sales slip, and returned the card. She folded the coat, put it in a box and wrapped it.

"Thank you very much and have a nice day," she said, handing it to Dolores, then turning to wait on another customer.

They visited three other departments and Dolores bought sweaters, shoes, a leather handbag, and some expensive perfume. Then, because the card would not be good for very long, they visited two other stores and repeated the performance at each one, adding more purses, gloves, scarves, cosmetics and costume jewelry. Russ tried to buy a camera with it but was turned away partly because he was black and partly because he did not have matching ID's. But he managed to buy some records, a pair of shoes, and a cheap suit. Altogether they ended up with over fifteen hundred dollars worth of merchandise and had trouble getting all of it into the car.

"I want to keep that Kashmir coat," Dolores begged.

"You got a whole closet fulla coats," said Russ. "'Sides, it's hot. We gotta get rid of it. Don't look no good on ya nohow. . . ."

They drove across town and into the black ghetto where Russ had a lot of friends. He turned into an alley and pulled up behind a funeral home, got out and rang a buzzer. A face appeared at the window, then disappeared. The garage door went up and Russ drove in, parked beside a hearse and a gold El Dorado. A stocky, prosperous looking man appeared, wearing an ivory silk shirt, blue pin-striped bell bottoms, and black lizard shoes. A large diamond ring glittered on one fat finger. Another, younger man stood in the doorway, dressed in a maroon outfit with a wide-brimmed, black hat, and kept a hand in his pocket.

The fat man smiled, flashed a mouthful of gold teeth. "Hey, baby, what's happnin'?" he greeted.

"Need some bread, Daddy," said Russ, returning the smile. "Gotta whole shitload a' quality stuff for ya to look at."

The man wrinkled his brow and nodded while Russ took the garments out of the car and spread them out on a table. The two men examined them.

"Mmm. Nice coat."

"You ain't jivin'! Pure Kashmir wool. Jest looka that price tag."

"Two hundred and fifty dollars," the fat man noted. "Yeah, sure is quality, man." He displayed a glittering smile of approval, then shook his head sadly. "It's top shelf, but, thing is I'm loaded with this shit already, understand? Got all kinda coats I'm tryin' ta get rid of. . . ."

Russ shrugged. "Well, whatever you can give us, Daddy, 'cause we do need the bread for some coke an' a few other things."

"Hey, dig it!" the man laughed pleasantly and peeled some bills off a thick bankroll. "How 'bout five, an' I'll give ya a break on some dynamite coke I jus' got up from New York."

"Five hundred? Is that all?" complained Dolores from the car.

The fat man turned to her with a grin, his voice intoning an apology. "Hey honey, don't forget I'm takin' a chance jus' keepin' this shit!" Before she could reply he gestured to his assistant. "Moss, go git the coke!"

"I want four fifty-dollar bags an' some good skag, if ya got it, maybe six bags," Russ requested.

"Don't forget the methadone!" Dolores cried.

"Got any dollies? We need about twenty," Russ added.

The man winked at Dolores. "Sure do! How ya been, baby?"

"All right," she said, and smiled her special smile reserved for admirers.

He nudged Russ, took him aside. "Tell ya what, man," he breathed. "I could sure use some a' that! Lemme see her an' I'll give you a couple extra bags a' coke like you never done!" His voice communicated a special promise of ecstacy from one who was a connoiseur of cocaine.

"Wow, dig it!" Russ exclaimed. "Dee-dee, honey, come on! Daddy wants to see ya for just a minute, okay?"

The older man took Dolores into the funeral home while Russ and the bodyguard snorted coke and chuckled over a joke or two. A short time later she reappeared, looking as neat and bright as ever, and clutching the bags in one hand.

"Is everything cool?" Russ asked, eyeing the coke.

She nodded and got back into the car.

"Hey, take care now," Russ said to the two men, closing her door, then walking around and sliding in behind the wheel. "Dee-dee, I'm hungry," he went on, as the garage door went up, and they drove out in the crumbling ghetto neighborhood, the place of his boyhood.

24

Russ pushed the fork away, closed his eyes and made a face. His mother sighed with frustration. "C'mon now, baby, eat. . . ." Five years old and he refused to open his mouth. He hated beans. Chicken was his favorite and his mother had been promising it for days. "We'll have chicken tomorrow, honey, honest," she went on. "Now you eat what's on your plate, hear?"

"I don't want no beans!" he cried.

His mother put the fork down. "Lord, you sure take after your father!" she declared, and pointed at the three girls, the oldest fifteen, and a brother, twelve. "See now? They ate everything, so now why can't you? C'mon . . .!"

He always remembered her rich, pleading voice, gentle even when she was upset. And he still remembered that row of faces around the table, his sisters and brother staring at him with round, wondrous eyes, fascinated at the stubborness of their little brother and awed by the thought that he might starve to death at any second if he did not eat.

The family lived on the second floor of a ramshackle, three-family house, the weathered shingles warped and screaming for paint and the rotting timbers of the porch sagging in a state of near collapse. It was a place better suited for vermin than for human beings and accordingly, rats and roaches thrived. The absentee landlord had flatly refused to make any repairs, yet raised the rent year after year until it ate up nearly their whole welfare check. Russ's mother had applied for a place in the equally squalid but cheaper housing project a half mile away and her name was placed on an interminable waiting list.

Under these conditions his father did not last more than a few years. The bickering drove him out, incessant tongue-lashings by his wife over his chronic joblessness. He had many jobs but could never seem to get ahead of the bills. His longest spell of employment was fourteen months as a laborer in a nursery, but when some money was found missing from the office he was arrested and questioned. Advised to plead guilty to a lesser charge, he spent three months in the county jail. Russ was four then and never saw his father after he went to jail. There was no need for him to return because his mother had found another man. His name was Jake—big Jake they called him, a tall, powerful man who was good to Russ's mother and always seemed to have money. No one knew where he got it and no one asked. He would go away for a few days or a week and come back again with money. He drove a white Lincoln Continental, wore nice clothes, and bought Russ's mother nice things. He did not care that much about the children because they were not his, but then he never bothered them, either.

And now as Little Russ sat at the table refusing to eat, the deep voice came booming through the house once more, so loud it even scared the cat. "Alma, baby! You c'mon, hear? Your daddy's waitin'. . . !"

His mother stood up, sighed, patted Russ on the cheek, looked at the oldest girl, "Now y'all try an' get somethin' in him, hear? I'll get some money from Jake and send you to the market. And don't you kids bother me, none, or I'll bat you 'side the head!"

His oldest sister, second in command, rose and took the fork while their mother went out, unbuttoning her dress in the hallway, then disappearing into the gloom of the bedroom.

Jake stayed with them off and on until Russ was eleven, then he too vanished to parts unknown. Word had it that the law was looking for him and detectives came to the house, searched it and asked his mother a lot of questions. Russ was never sure what Jake had done and no one ever told him.

The family was again thrown into the jaws of poverty. His mother went to work as a home health aid and Russ had to shift for himself, working at odd jobs wherever he could. In his twelfth year, around Christmas time, he went around to all of the neighborhood stores looking for work. Business was good, shoppers caught in the last minute holiday rush were buying everything in sight. He tried the local hardware store first because it was close to his house. The clerk said no, there was nothing, but then had second thoughts and shouted into the back office. The owner stuck his head out, a disgruntled, heavy-jowled man with thick, horn-rimmed glasses.

"Do I got what?" he grumbled.

The clerk pointed to Russ. "Says he wants a job. . . ."

The boss peered at him with disapproval. "Listen," he said loudly, "the last colored kid I had tried to walk off with everything that wasn't nailed down! How do I know you won't?"

"Try me, mister!" pleaded Russ.

There was a pause, the man frowning through the thick glasses. "Okay, c'mon back," he said.

Russ followed him through the cramped aisles between high shelves crammed with boxes of merchandise. They stopped at the restroom. The owner pointed to the stained toilet. The tiny room reeked with the odor of urine.

"This place is gettin' pretty bad," he said. "Clean it up an' I'll give ya half a buck."

It was one of Russ's first adventures with paid employment. He did a good job. "Want the floor swept, mister?" he said when he was finished, and the owner told him to do it. So he made a dollar that very day. Encouraged, he trooped into all the stores along the avenue and wound up with two steady jobs sweeping and snow-shoveling. Then came a day that winter when the weather was very cold, a Saturday, and he and a few friends were huddled in the stairwell of a housing project, smoking cigarettes and trying to stay warm. Two older boys, about fourteen or fifteen, approached them.

"Hey, kid, wanna make a buck?" said one. He appeared slightly sleepy, a slack, apathetic look about him.

"Sure, you bet!" Russ agreed.

The youth handed him a twenty dollar bill. "You go on over 'cross the avenue to Lawndale Street, number forty, knock on the door an' ask for Louis. That's Louis, understan'? Nobody else. Give 'im the bread an' tell 'im Marcus sent ya, understan'? Bring back what he gives ya, dig? An' if ya don't show up in half an hour we'll whup yo ass good!"

Russ was gone with the money, scampering and skidding down the icy sidewalks along the bleak, gray avenue lined with decaying, boarded-up stores. Louis turned out to be a surprisingly grown-up young man with dark glasses. He eyed Russ, looked all around and up and down the street, then disappeared, returned with a couple of foil packets and took the money. "Put 'em in your pocket, man," he instructed, "so's you won't lose 'em."

Russ knew what it was. He had seen it before many times. He ran back to the stairwell, delivered the two bags, and the youth gave him a dollar. He split it up among his friends and they all went to the store and bought snacks and some soda pop. It was the easiest dollar he ever made.

25

There is one thing that man seeks in life more than riches, and that is the raw experience of pleasure. Ironically, a part of it already exists within him, a system built in at birth, lying dormant until a sudden stimulation of the senses awakens it. A substance is released, triggers that part of the mind that knows pleasure, and he becomes a captive of his own senses, unable and unwilling to escape. Elusive and fleeting, pleasure begs a long pursuit, yet inevitably flies to meet its opposite, suffering. The two lie entwined in the depths of every soul, now nourishing the roots of life, now withering them, now warming the heart with joy, now burying it in ashes. Man is crucified, for to know pleasure he must know pain.

Russ and Dolores lay resting in spent passion, their bodies still locked in an embrace. And as the love-spell wore off they opened their eyes, saw again the drab room, breathed the closeness of the air. They felt the stiffness of their limbs, and the aching burden of their emotions, knew hunger, thirst, and the need to excrete. Reflexively they fled back into the refuge of pleasure. Russ reached for his works, did a bang of coke for a "wakeup", while Dolores popped her methadone and sniffed a pinch of coke from Russ's gold spoon. To prolong his ecstacy, Russ slid down off of his cocaine high with a bag of heroin. Again they revived their world of enchantment, if only for a time, staving off the corruption of their flesh and halting the hourglass of their lives for as long as the high lasted.

"Wow, I ain't got but two bags a' doojie left," he remarked, putting away the cellophane packets.

Dolores bounced out of bed, wrapped her pendulous breasts in a robe. "I wish you'd quit saying that," she fretted. "It sounds so funny. . . ."

"It's French," said Russ soothingly. "Don't know what it is in English but the black people in New York use it all the time. It means 'heroin'."

"I know," Dolores sighed grumpily. Obviously her nerves were on edge even after the methadone, which was supposed to relax her. "Remember, I've been around, too. I had a trick from Harlem, a rich one, tell me that when you're high on doojie, even the rats are beautiful."

"Sure 'nuff," Russ agreed with an ironic smile, and paused. "And I ain't never said you haven't been around, baby, 'cause I know you have."

"What? I know, that's what I said," she argued.

He looked at her, read the narrow green eyes with concern. "Hey, baby, what's the matter?" he asked. "Why you so uptight this mornin'? Hell, the day ain't even started yet."

She turned away abruptly. "I'll be all right. . . ." she murmured with a note of distress, as though not quite willing to let him drop the subject of her health.

"Maybe you been workin' too hard, need a rest," he suggested and reflected for several moments, then smiled and snapped his fingers. "I know, why not cut out the tricks for a while an' do some checks instead? Easier money, know what I mean?"

Dolores pouted, then turned around and glared at him. "What's the difference?" she snapped. "I do all the work and you go an' coke it up in a week's time!"

"Aw c'mon, baby, take it easy," he pleaded, recognizing her line of attack. "You chip too, dig it, every day you do!" He grinned uneasily, sensed a major squabble in the offing unless he acted. "Hey, I got it!" he exclaimed. "I'll go out an' hustle up some money m'self! I'll show you what I can do!"

"You? Hustle? Oh, Russ, come on now, you're kidding!" she said and laughed faintly.

He nodded, almost bobbed his head for emphasis. "I ain't jokin', no sir! I'll do some noting and a few other hustles, enough for three or four hundred bucks! Then I'll go over to Richard's and see if he got any stolen checks he'll sell me, and borrow his check-writing machine. I'll take you to a picture ID place, the same one as last time. They'll make up a card and I'll get some matching ID's to go with it, maybe one a' them social security cards. Then you practice the signature and open an account, you know, like we did before. No sweat!"

Dolores compressed her lips in exasperation. "There you go again!" she scolded. "I said I don't like it! I'm afraid of getting jammed! Remember the last time when they told me to go see the manager? I had to run out of the bank!"

"I know, baby," he crowed. "But that was my fault. Using that fake savings account number was no good 'cause it was a branch bank an' they checked it. I'll admit they are gettin' a lot tighter, but we'll be more careful an' do everything right this time, understand?"

Dolores fell silent, apparently too tired to argue further, which was unlike her and this worried Russ as he got dressed and left the apartment. She told him to be careful but the warning was unnecessary. He was already careful, a clever, shrewd young man brimming with self-confidence and style. He evaded trouble, which seemed to swirl about him but left him unmarked.

Starting with only twenty dollars, he stopped in a pawnshop in the ghetto where he bought two watches and a set of rings, all cheap imitations of much higher priced items. He pocketed these, drove downtown to the business section, parked and stationed himself on a side street lined with banks and multistory office buildings. He chose his victims carefully, knowing from experience who to approach.

"Pardon me, sir," he said politely, addressing a prosperous, fortyish businessman, and flashed the watches. The man looked and hurried on, but a second man stopped. "Wanna buy a hunnerd dollar watch for twenty dollars?" came the offer.

The gentleman picked one up, looking slightly amused as though he enjoyed examining hot goods. "It's Swiss, all right," he remarked. "Seventeen jewels, huh? Where'd you get it?"

"A friend," Russ replied quickly. "But I need the cash, if you know what I mean."

"Sure, sure. Twenty, huh? Don't see how I could lose at that price." With a smug look, he paid Russ, pocketed the watch and walked swiftly off.

After several more tries, Russ sold the other watch but the rings were more of a challenge. "Hey, mister," he said to a carefully chosen, stylishly dressed bachelor-type. "Wanna buy a set a' rings worth six hunnerd for seventy-five bucks?"

The man stopped, eyed the glittering paste with interest. "Are they hot?" he asked innocently.

"Wouldn't know," said Russ. "I'm just sellin' 'em. Maybe you got a lady friend who might want 'em."

"Lemme see 'em," the young man asked, took the paste, turned it over and over, watched it catch the light. "How do I know this isn't just a cheap copy?" he added cynically.

"They're real," Russ insisted.

The stranger snorted, not intending to be taken in. "Well, then, are you willing to let me take it to a jeweler's up the street and have it appraised?"

"Look," Russ said, acting in a hurry, "I wouldn't mind, heck no, but I gotta go 'cause I'm late to get someplace an' I don't have no time. If ya want, you can take 'em now, gimme what you have, an' meet me here tomorrow with the rest."

The man hesitated, a faint smile flickering over his face. "Well. . . ." he drawled. "Okay, why not. I can give you, uh, thirty bucks right now."

"Make it thirty-five an' you can take 'em. I can get the other forty from you tomorrow, right here, same time, okay?"

"Fair enough," the stranger agreed, slipping a few bills out of his wallet and looking around as he paid Russ. "See you tomorrow."

The bachelor hurried off, the rings safe in his pocket. Of course, Russ knew the man had no intention of ever coming back, thinking he had taken Russ for a pigeon. That was the game, the crux of every flim-flam, to appeal to the victim's inner sense of larceny—make him think he is taking advantage of someone else, or getting something for nothing, and he will fall for it every time. This alone explains why a sucker is born every minute.

Russ had enough money now to do some noting—a dynamite hustle that he used whenever he needed quick cash. Working with a fifty, he could expect about twenty dollars a sting. He changed his money for a fifty at the bank, then headed for a street lined with retail stores, entered a busy discount drugstore staffed with a couple of young cashiers. Picking out a one dollar bottle of shaving lotion he chose the youngest of the two cashiers, a girl of no more than seventeen, and laid down the fifty.

She hesitated. "Is this the smallest you have?" she asked.

"Yes it is," he replied, began looking around, then walked off a few steps.

"Sir, your change!"

"Oh, sorry." He came back and accepted the twenty, two tens, a five, three ones and nearly a dollar in loose change. Stepping back again, he pocketed the two tens, then returned to the counter, laid down the twenty. "Could you change a twenty for me?" he requested.

The girl nodded, began counting out the change.

"How much is this gum?" he went on.

"Ten cents."

"I'll take two packs."

"Do you want me to take it out of this?" she asked.

He nodded and she dipped into the change, put down nineteen dollars and eighty cents on the counter. Russ reached for it, then hesitated, shook his head with a frown. "Say, that's an awful lot of small bills. Can I get back the fifty I gave you? I don't wanna take all your change like this."

"I don't mind," she said, looking past him at the growing line of customers.

"Here," he offered, counting from the change she had just given him. ". . . Ten, eleven, twelve, thirteen, fourteen. . . ." Then he took some more small bills out of his pocket. ". . . Fifteen, and two fives are twenty-five, twenty-six, seven, eight, nine, thirty. . . ." He shoved the pile across the counter. ". . . And the twenty I just gave you is fifty."

Perplexed, she looked at the twenty she had placed in the cash drawer, then again at the thirty dollars in change on the counter. She paused, smiled nervously.

"Where's the toothpaste anyhow?" he asked, looking away.

"Uh, over there. Wait. . . ." Quickly she scooped the pile of bills from the counter and handed him back the fifty.

Less the bottle of shaving lotion and the gum, it was about a nineteen dollar sting. In the midst of all the distractions she had forgotten about the two tens she had first handed him in change, which he had tucked away in his pocket. Later, when the register was found short she would be unable to recall exactly what happened. Even if he were caught in the act, as he once was, she would make a poor witness and it would be her word against his. He actually beat a case this way one time when two police detectives witnessed him noting and arrested him on the spot. In court their testimony was too weak to convict him.

He went to two other stores, hit the first for twenty but lost the fifty in the second. He went back to the bank, got a hundred dollar bill and hit two more stores for forty dollars apiece. He quit after that, satisfied to have used psychology to convert twenty dollars into almost two hundred dollars in less than four hours, and with practically no risk. Now he had enough money to buy some stolen checks and phony ID's. Then he would really take care of business.

26

The winds of fortune blew more favorably when the heat wave died down and Dolores's business picked up again. Even though she was still tired, she made money. Beyond her regular salary as a dancer, she hustled as many drinks as she could, worth a dollar apiece, for an extra ten to thirty dollars a night. And in the course of meeting new patrons she picked up a lot of good johns. But this was only the beginning of a great new era of prosperity for them both. On Friday Dolores opened a checking account and on the following Monday she cashed eight forged paychecks at different branch banks, each for about three hundred and fifty dollars, though they varied slightly in amount. For the sake of credibility she deposited twenty to forty dollars in her checking account each time. Then within three working days, which was the time it took for the fake checks to clear, she closed out her account. Suddenly they were nearly three thousand dollars richer.

"Wham-o!" cried Russ jubilantly. "We really killed 'em this time! They won't cash no more checks made out to Rona Appelbaum for awhile, that's for sure, an' Electron, Inc. is gonna hafta stop payment on all of its checks an' reopen its account."

"Now, please, honey, let's hang onto this money," Dolores begged. "And just to make sure, I'm putting it away for safe keeping."

"Huh? What you talking' 'bout?" Russ exclaimed, astonished. He had his own plans for the money. "I don' 'low that shit, an' you know it! I'm the boss!"

"Well, I don't allow you coking up every cent we make, neither!" she retorted and faced him angrily. "Remember, I'm not one of your black whores that you can treat like a piece of shit, uh-uh! You're lucky to be my man and you know it!" Her green eyes snapped with scorn, then she smiled, tossed her black hair. "Why, if I ever got fed up I could just find me someone else or work without a man, I wouldn't care! I'd sure have more money!"

Russ hung his head. This sudden flareup was unexpected. He loved her too much to let money come between them, yet he needed it for cocaine. "That ain't too cool," he muttered ruefully. "It's sumpin' else, why. . . ." He began to sulk and she came over, put her arms around his neck.

"Oh, calm down, for Godsake," she said, her voice soft now, musical. "I've got some good news for you. One of the owners is throwing a stag party and they want a couple of girls to do an act for two hundred apiece and maybe see some tricks afterward."

Russ's frown gave way to a smile at the thought of enough extra money coming in to smooth things over. "Hey, wow, all right!" he exclaimed. "Maybe it'll be worth three, four bills 'fore the night is over, right?" He paused, went on earnestly. "Hey, why don't I take some of the money now an' we'll replace it with what you make at the function. How does that sound, honey?"

Before she could reply he gave her a quick squeeze, stilling her objections with more talk, his voice louder and more persuasive. ". . . Then I can go on down to New York an' take care a' business . . . cop me a couple ounces a' pure cocaine an' then sell it! Hey, we'll really get it together, baby, can ya dig it? Shit, I'll make thousands off the deal an' that's only a start! Why, one of these days real soon you won't hafta turn no more tricks 'cause your daddy's goin' to see to that! He's really gonna get it on, understand? Baby, you're cool an' I dig ya the most, honest!" He gave her a kiss. ". . . An' I sure 'preciate it! I ain't uptight neither, baby, 'cause I love ya an' I wanna be your man always, you know that!"

Slightly befuddled by his show of sincerety she smiled and moved close to him. "Of course, I know it," she replied. "An' you know I love you too, honey."

They embraced tightly and impulsively went to the sofa and made love, as eagerly and passionately as first lovers. And she never missed the money he took.

On Wednesday night Dolores approached another dancer at the club about taking part in the stag party. She wanted someone who knew how to dance, someone experienced and attractive. Sylvia was a journeyman stripper, a blonde, about twenty-four, with a widely-touted bust. She wore fine clothes, drove a big car and lived in a plush, high-rise apartment. And to finance her high living, plus her very moderate practice of sniffing dime spoons of cocaine between acts, she danced, hustled drinks, and sold her body at top price. The main professional difference between Sylvia and Dolores was that Sylvia did not really belong to the drug scene, did not have a real habit, and did not work for a pimp who copped for her. Instead, because of her reputation as a stripper, Sylvia went strictly for quality tricks, working out of a ring of two-hundred-dollar-a-night call girls. This meant that she had to spend more time waiting for the phone to ring than did Dolores who, with her bargain basement trade, could count on a larger but less prosperous clientele from day to day, and therefore a steadier income for drugs.

Sylvia was a natural born hussy, one of those rare showpieces of womanhood. Brassy and sensuous, her figure had more curves than a pretzel and more power than a charge of TNT. Her notable endowments were already in evidence at the age of ten when she was made a woman by her stepfather. As she continued to develop, a seduction by an eighth grade teacher caused her to drop out of school at the age of fourteen to get an abortion. At fifteen she began earning extra money as a prostitute, until she met an older woman in one of the clubs who took her in tow. Because her own mother had abandoned her when she was young, Sylvia, had been raised by her stepfather and his several sisters, all close to her own age. So the girl had never had a real, understanding mother and started looking on this woman as such. Like any good mother, the woman wanted to point the girl in the right direction. She gave her advice, such as not to just give herself away, because she would not last long in this world if she did. And the woman sensed talent in the girl, taught her the fine art of exotic dancing. It paid off and they became first a "mother-daughter" team and then the woman became her agent. Sylvia danced up the ladder the hard way, through smoke-filled dives, skid row girly shows, and carnivals until at last she made a modest name for herself.

Since she and Dolores were both dancers, it was natural for them to put something to music and to make a sort of production out of it. Their style was exotic dancing to rhythm and blues, and for the sake of the party they would appear *au naturel*. They chose a romantic theme and ended up with a fairly contemporary version of rock ballet.

"We'll come out together," Sylvia chirped brightly, sitting with Dolores at the end of the bar, dangling her shapely legs off the stool. It was early evening, around seven o'clock, so things were slow and they had time to talk. "We'll start out with the slow twirls, bumping and grinding, you know."

Dolores nodded. "Yes, right at the first. Then what?" she asked.

"Oh, we'll do the whole bit. We'll get them all excited, don't worry," Sylvia replied confidently. "The bump and grind first, then you follow my lead and we start the strip. Same bit, you know, just for openers."

Uh-huh," Dolores agreed. "And how long do we strip? We'll have to make it quick. . . ."

Sylvia was distracted for a moment, flirting with a likely-looking customer who might be good for a few drinks. She slouched a bit, let the cleavage of her bosom show to its utmost. "Just go along with the rhythm and follow my lead, like I say," she said, a little impatiently. "I should know. After all, I've been through it enough. Main thing is to drag it out almost to the end, 'cause it's the tease they're after. Once you're undressed they start to yawn. Funny, a guy told me one time that when you've seen one girl bareass, you've seen 'em all."

"So, we'll dance," said Dolores. "They won't be bored. But then what, after we've stripped?"

"Same thing only with our clothes off," Sylvia responded, and turned back to Dolores, her big blue eyes smiling playfully. "And after that we really get passionate. We touch each other, kiss, really act aroused. Don't forget, I've done enough of these shows to know what they like."

Dolores raised her eyebrows quizzically. "I guess we'll just ad lib that part of it, huh?"

"Right, you do what I do and vice versa. Sort of like that. But then I'll pretend I'm balling you," Sylvia went on. "They get a charge out of that. You know, guys are animals. . . ."

"Well, yes some are," Dolores agreed. "Some are certainly gross, but others are a lot more modest than women, so. . . ."

"But these are the animal kind," Sylvia insisted. "Or they wouldn't pay good money to see us. It's just a certain type of guy. I agree, they aren't all like that. Some wouldn't come on a bet. But we don't care about them, anymore than they would care about us. We never see them in these places."

"I never see them," Dolores admitted ruefully. "We don't cater to that type. He's out fishing, or with his family, his children. . . ." Her voice trailed away and there was a pause, both girls staring glumly at the handful of flashy, male customers in the club, leering back at them with slack, suffused faces.

Sylvia produced a cigarette, tamped it sharply on the bar, lit it and offered the pack to Dolores. She blew out the smoke with an audible sigh. "Like I said, we'll really be sexy," she began again, clearing her throat. "We'll really turn them on and they'll be as horny as barn rats by the time we're finished. Then maybe we'll get a few johns, who knows? I hope so, 'cause some of these guys are really rich." She winked at Dolores, who could not help giggling.

The night of the party Dolores got a mysterious headache and almost bowed out. But when Sylvia reminded her of the easy money she came around. The party was held in a dimly lit, smoke-filled function room in the rear of the Four-sixty Club. The place was packed, and the deep, throaty guffaws, laughter, and cheering of the men as they watched the films reverberated back down the hallway and into the dressing room where the girls were waiting. Sylvia was tittering uncontrollably, obviously flying on cocaine. Dolores had done two forty milligram wafers of methadone and felt warm and cozy, ready to do her best.

The movies ended and there was a lull, filled with the clinking of ice cubes, coughing, and the bass hum of male chatter. Then their act was announced, the clamor dying away as a spot played on the floor up front.

"Boys," shouted the host. "Now for our feature of the evening! I'd like to introduce a couple a' real swingin' playmates. . . ." Whistles from the audience. ". . . Who've come all the way from Chicago to present their version of spin the bottle, an' I don't mean Old Grandad." Loud chuckles. ". . . May I present, Gigi and Kiki! Come on out, girls!"

The applause and whistling was deafening as the two attractive young women appeared, the audience obviously delighted at the prospect of their stripping down to nothing. The girls stood smiling awkwardly for a moment while someone fumbled around with the stereo and finally got the music playing. The girls began to move in unison with the rhythm, swaying, bumping, grinding. The men stared impassively, then grew restless, buzzing and guffawing. Even when the girls began the strip they were noisy, lit smokes, ordered drinks. Dolores, already down to her G-string, was disappointed with the response so far, thought angrily how those movies the men just saw must have really been something. Dramatically, Sylvia flung off her pasties and Dolores did the same, to draw only a few stray wolf-whistles. The girls bumped around in front of the roomful of jaded, sneering faces, feeling a little foolish. Then they discarded their G-strings, still without any reaction beyond a few drunken catcalls. More drinks were ordered and the men started talking again.

Sylvia came over and embraced Dolores at that point and the faces of the audience turned as one to view them fondling and kissing. They sank to the floor of the now hushed room, Sylvia taking the lead, biting, tonguing her partner in a great show of passion. Digital manipulation and an awkward gesture at cunnilingus brought the men to their feet, crowding forward to see it, some whooping with approval, which made Sylvia ham it up even more. Anxious to get it over with, Dolores threw her head back, hands spread around her thighs, a signal for Sylvia to fall upon that spot and bump crazily to finish the act in a final display of lust. Sylvia, a rather heavy, solid girl, responded by driving her hips relentlessly with practiced ease, while Dolores lay half-crushed and nearly exhausted.

"Don't stop!" Sylvia panted in her ear, and Dolores only gasped while the audience kept up an enthusiastic round of shouts, whistles, and applause.

"Encore! Encore!" the men yelled in their deep, resounding male voices. The host, obviously pleased by it all, came over as they got up and took both girls by the hand. "Any you guys game?" he quipped with a broad grin and they answered with affirmative shouts and whistles.

The two girls circulated among the tables, still in the nude, accepting a drink and letting a few of the men pinch and pet them. Sylvia had to slap more than one hand, shaking her finger saucily at whoever it was for being so fresh. Then she persuaded one man to fold up a one dollar bill and hold it out, whereupon she deftly snatched it away between her thighs, a gambit she had learned years ago. He joked that this was an example of inflation putting a squeeze on profits, and everyone got a good laugh. She did it again with a silver dollar, which the original trick called for back in the days when these were still in circulation. She kept on doing it until she had snatched a whole fistful of ones and even a few fives, demonstrating how much truth there was to the name for her anatomy. Meanwhile, Dolores was perched on the lap of a prosperous looking gentleman whom she wanted for a trick, maybe worth fifty or a hundred dollars if she were lucky, and by the feel of it he was interested.

"I've got a place close by," Sylvia suggested, with her sugary smile. "If you boys want to come down after the show and have some fun. . . ."

Happily the girls netted a party of about fifteen merry men, who drove them in a caravan of sleek, late model cars to Sylvia's apartment. There they both disrobed once more and took turns in the bedroom while the others sat in the front room drinking. The men consumed three fifths of whisky and two fifths of scotch in the course of a few hours. Near the end everyone was so drunk they sat around in a stupor, unable to perform with the girls beyond laborious, clumsy attempts. So they both got sore and quit. Most of the customers crawled or reeled to their cars, somehow managing to unlock them and drive off. A few stayed the night and the girls charged them an extra fifty dollars the next morning, insisting that they had slept with them. Sylvia was heavily tipped by an older man who swore she had given him the best head in years. When it was all over the girls were tired, but richer by twelve hundred dollars.

27

Dolores was used to being around greedy, self-indulgent people. Both her mother and father were alcoholics. Her father left home when she was six and all she remembered of him then was a hairy hulk reeking with sweat, lolling on the sofa in his underwear, his face blackened with stubble, yelling at her mother. All they ever seemed to do was drink and quarrel, usually over money.

A thin woman with a somewhat puffy, tragic face, her mother made the usual preparations for an argument by clinking a fresh ice cube into her glass, filling it to the brim with gin, and lighting a cigarette. After a few defiant puffs she would take up a position across the room from her father, who habitually watched sports events on television, and utter the challenge.

"Excuse me, Jack, I hate to interrupt," she would begin with exaggerated courtesy. "I know how important the game is, but would you mind telling me where this week's check went? You said you'd give it to me on Friday, remember?" She finished on a note of open contempt.

"Huh?" her father grunted, rolled over to regard his wife with bleary eyes.

"You know what I'm talking about," she went on deliberately. "The check, Jack. . . ."

He took one gulp of beer, then another and guffawed. "Ha! You'd just piss it away if I gave it to yuh. . . ."

She interrupted him sharply. "You call it pissing money away to buy food for your family, for your three kids? You expect me to run the house on nothing? Come on now, Jack!"

Aroused, he sat up, drained the beer, tossed the empty can down clattering against the others on the floor. He reached for a fresh one, snapped off the top and drank. It was only eleven o'clock in the morning and the day would be a long one.

"Did you hear me?" she grated.

"Yeah, I heard you. . . ." He took another long drink from the can. "An' I'm tellin' you that you'll run the house on what I give yuh an' that's that!"

She puffed furiously on her cigarette, short, indignant puffs. "You—you're drinking and gambling away practically every penny and you know it! Why don't you come out and admit it for once!"

"Shut up!" he spat. "Take a look at yourself, why don't ya! You're half in the bag every time I come home! Can't even hit the floor with your hat, fer Chrissake! I seen all them empties out back—smashin' 'em up don't help. . . .!"

"Well, well. . . ," fumed her mother and her thin hands trembled as she lit a fresh cigarette. ". . . At least I care about the kids and the house! But you, you don't care about anybody but yourself!"

He leaned forward and bellowed so loudly the neighbors could hear. "You-you-you! You sound like a goddamn cracked record the way yer always bitchin' at me! I said, why don't ya take a look at yourself for a change! A cheap goddamn washed-out barroom whore like you shouldn't even have kids, or a home, or a husband in the first place an' you know it! Sonofabitch, when I come home you don't even know what time a' day it is you're so soused! Talk about me! An' here you expect me ta give you my check?"

"That's right, Jack!" she blared, still in the same raucous tone, as though she had scarcely heard his comment beyond what she needed for a riposte and wanted to continue simply for the sake of arguing rather than to settle any differences. For never, as far as anyone knew, did she admit to the slightest fault and was positively insulted whenever anyone, including her husband, accused her of any. "Yes, go ahead!" she went on. "Blame me like you always do! That's right, it's all my fault, by God! But you haven't answered my question! The check, Jack! Where is it?"

She regarded her husband with her tragic eyes, wide with indignation, as he scowled and fumbled at his beer, then drank deeply. She knew he did not have the check, that he had already gambled and drunk away a good part of it. What remained, she usually had to steal out of his pocket at night, causing a loud tiff the next morning. Of the money she took, she laid aside enough for a few quarts of cheap gin for herself, and the rest went for food. Miraculously, even though the children were poorly clothed and fed and the apartment in a woeful state, the family never went on welfare. Dolores's father held a steady job with the city transit system for years. But he was eased out of his position on the trains at the age of forty-four by a younger man and placed in a change booth at the turnstiles. He hated this job and after a holdup in which he was beaten by two youths he began drinking even more heavily and popping a few pills. As a result, and perhaps also from the severe blows on the head, though this was never proven, he became unreliable and was laid off. Now unable to fully support his family, his wife saw no reason to put up with him any longer and filed for a separation and got a restraining order. She went on welfare and he went to live with his mother, seldom returning to the house to see the children.

Dolores's later childhood was spent doing housework and cooking for her younger sister and brother while her mother looked after business in the local tavern, where she had become first a steady customer and later a small-time, local prostitute. The other residents on the delapidated block did not approve of her activities, but being poor themselves they recognized that it was probably an economic necessity for the family. Business declined after a few years when her mother's limited charms began to fade as an unhappy result of premature aging. This caused some trouble between her and Dolores, who was at that time blooming into a beautiful young woman.

The rivalry defined itself more cruelly in the presence of her mother's male friends who could readily appreciate the difference between the two of them and were not bashful about expressing themselves. And, as hard as she tried to resist, Dolores could not help flirting with them, enjoyed the little thrill it gave her, a sensation of pleasurable excitement at being admired as a woman. When she went to look for her mother in the barroom as she sometimes did, they were always there, gawking at her and making little wisecracks and she would look back at them provocatively, enchanting them with her pretty green eyes. After all, they were harmless, these regular patrons and friends of her mother. They passed their evenings and weekends hobnobbing and joking, playing the same sentimental tunes again and again on the jukebox, and most of all, drinking. Sometimes they danced, the couples doing an awkward shuffle with a dip and a hint of the twist in a modest, almost apologetic imitation of a younger generation. The women all looked pretty much alike. Years of smoke, bad air and alcohol had withered their faces. The mask of rouge that they wore, with heavy makeup, garish lipstick, and flamboyantly tinted hair gave them an appearance quite the opposite from what they intended, for they resembled macabre, painted dolls rather than living human beings. They perched together at the bar with their gentleman friends beside them, cracking the latest off-color jokes and otherwise carrying on. They could often count on the men for more than a few drinks. And though they never drained their glasses completely for the sake of appearance, they could imbibe as much or more alcohol in the course of an evening than most of the men.

The first sign of Dolores's entrance would be the heads of the men jerking around, and as usual her mother reacted with irritation. "Dolores, didn't I tell you not to come in here?" she squawked one evening.

"But mamma, you said you would be home for supper," she answered and looked provocatively into the hungry faces of the men who were staring at her.

Her mother turned to a broken man at her elbow, let out a reedy, scornful laugh. "Y'see, Georgie?" she said. "This is what I've come to! I'm a woman without a man, got three kids without a father, and my daughter has to help me out of the barrom every night? What d'ya think of that?"

"Sounds like a helluva note," said the unshaven man in work clothes.

"Whaddaya want us ta do, Ellie, cry in our beer?" crowed another.

Tell you what," said the first man, jerking his thumb at Dolores. "If she ain't got no father, then I'll be her ol' man, whaddaya say, sweetie?" He winked at the girl and she smiled almost involuntarily. "Hey, you ever been kissed?" he went on and broke into fit of laughter. He swilled down his drink, bug-eyed, to relieve a coughing spell.

"I'll wait for you at home, mamma," said Dolores, smiling nervously and moving toward the door. She sensed that they were testing her, they way men will do, to see how easily she could be embarrassed. Suddenly she found one of them standing in her way, grinning. He grabbed her quickly and before she could pull away he planted a one hundred proof kiss directly on her mouth and she felt the scratch of his stubble and the stink of his tobacco breath as she pulled away, embarrassed and annoyed.

"Well, she has now!" he laughed, and stepped back with a foolish grin.

The bartender came down, amused, but not happy about having a minor on the premises. "Hell, Al," he joked. "Since when did you start robbin' the cradle? Better let her go home where she belongs."

"Fer Chrissake, leave my daughter alone, Al, you ol' lecher!" her mother rasped loudly. "Now come over here!" Al stepped over reluctantly and she embraced him and kissed him with a great show of passion. "Mmm! Try that one on for size, honey, and you know there's more where that came from!" she declared.

"Whoee! Don't fight it Al!" they joked.

"There's more where that came from, too!" one of them remarked, grinning at Dolores, and again she could not help returning his smile and feeling that little thrill at the man's attention, despite his unattractiveness.

Her mother slanted her pencilled eyebrows into a frown. "Now you get home, Dee-dee and I'll be along in jus' a little while. . . ."

Dolores could hear them carrying on about her as she left, and it pleased her to think she could cause such a stir. Certainly, it was proof that she was pretty, if nothing else.

"Don't break her in too fast, Ellie," the bartender was saying.

"This ain't the best place for a little dish like that," remarked one of the women. "You'd better go home and tuck her in bed, Ella, before ol' Al does it for you."

"Al knows who he can tuck in and who he can't," her mother kidded, and the men guffawed. They liked Ella because she was always good for a couple of laughs.

28

Unfortunately Dolores's mother was not always in the best of health. More than once her liver failed from heavy drinking, the first time when Dolores was about thirteen. It was in the wintertime, when the children usually saw their mother only in the half light of early morning while they were getting ready for school. They went in to wake her and she groaned, turned over and blinked at them dully, smelling of drink, and they noticed that her face was darker than usual, and bloated. Later, in succeeding days and in better light they saw that her skin had a definite yellowish-bronze cast and that the same color stained the whites of her eyes. And the darker the color, the more she seemed to stumble around in a daze. She stayed at home more now, drank alone instead of at the tavern, and kept muttering little remarks that bewildered Dolores and her sister and brother.

"Dolores," she would fret in a shaky, halting voice. "Did you kids go to school today?"

"Yes, mamma. We said goodbye to you this morning."

"Don't you remember?" piped her little sister. "You told us to do the wash when we got home."

Their mother returned with a tremulous smile. "Oh, yes ... and I want those sheets done, too, all of them in the basket. ..."

"But the sheets are clean," said Dolores. "I washed them yesterday after you told me to do it, remember?"

Their mother ignored them, lit a cigarette with wavering hands, got up and shuffled unsteadily across the room, then put down the cigarette in an ash tray with the half-dozen others resting there untouched, some a finger of ash, burnt down to the filter. "Girls, take that money . . . that five dollars and go buy a pound of hamburg for supper."

"You only gave me a dollar, mamma," said Dolores. "We spent it for lunch."

"What's the matter mommy?" asked her little brother, trying not to stare. "You said the yellow color would go away but it's getting worse."

"And you can't remember a thing!" Dolores added, showing her alarm.

She leered at them with her muddied eyes. "Nothing is the matter with me . . . now, if . . . what was I saying. . . ?"

"The hamburger for tonight," said the brother.

". . . Let's see, did you take that?"

"What?"

"What? That money. . . ."

"What money?"

"That five dollars—I have it here, uh, wait . . . where's that. . . ."

She shuffled unsteadily to a drawer, nearly lost her balance and fell, then fumbled through it, pulling out odds and ends, papers, recipes, wads of string. ". . . That check. . . ," she mumbled.

"It doesn't some till Friday," said Dolores. "It's only Tuesday."

"Oh . . . it should . . . tomorrow then . . . just have to wait awhile and. . . ." She sank into a chair, lit another cigarette and closed her eyes, seemed to sink into a deep sleep. She stayed this way for several hours and the children could hardly rouse her. They got a neighbor who tried to wake her with a cold towel but she only muttered incoherently.

"She looks very bad," said the neighbor. "I'm no doctor, but I know she has to go to the hospital. I think she has the yellow jaundice. You go over and stay with my kids while I call my husband."

Just as the neighbor predicted, their mother was admitted to the hospital and the children spent the night alone. The following afternoon a smartly dressed young woman with dark glasses the size of saucers and a lot of brass bracelets jangling on her wrist paid them a visit. The children asked if they could go visit their mother.

"Of course you can. I'll take you," said the woman briskly as she surveyed the cluttered flat, saw the ash trays piled with butts, the half empty glasses and bottles. There was hardly any food in the kitchen. "How would you children like to stay at someone else's home until your mother gets well?" she added.

They did not want to leave their apartment but the lady insisted and drove them across town to a private home in a respectable, middle class neighborhood. Mrs. Beeson, a widow, took in foster children for the Division of Child Guardianship. The agency had known about Dolores's family for a long while because of a report made by a teacher a few years previously. She had noticed that the children wore ragged, dirty clothing and had head lice. At that time the teacher on her own initiative, made a home visit, saw the conditions, and reported them to the welfare department. Welfare sent out a social worker to make regular home visits. But unfortunately both of these young women married and left their jobs within the year. The case was reassigned to an already overloaded male social worker who let it fall between the cracks. It mattered little—all the understaffed agency had to offer for the most part was temporary foster home placement for a few weeks or months. Only rarely were these children ever placed permanently in healthier families, and not because of a lack of willing foster parents. The process was complicated—the courts seldom separated children from their natural parents unless they were unusually cruel or negligent.

A large, efficient woman in her late forties, Mrs. Beeson had two grown sons of her own and was kind to the children. But she preferred them well-scrubbed and obedient and let them know it when they were not. Dolores's sister, Debra, was spanked when she refused to go to bed, and Gary, their eight year old brother, was put in his room for quite awhile after he broke a vase while roughhousing. Yet they ate well, took fluorinated vitamins, slept on fresh linens and wore clean clothes. And how that woman carried on about tooth brushing.

From time to time they went to the hospital to visit their mother, where the doctor said she was improving gradually. Of course he insisted that she not drink at all, and she promised she would not. Six weeks later their mother was discharged from an extended care facility and the family was reunited. But she went right back to drinking again, her liver failing several more times even while Dolores was in her teens. Each time she became jaundiced and was sent back to the hospital for treatment, which consisted largely of vitamins and abstinence from alcohol, and each time she came home in an improved condition, swearing to everyone that she would never touch another drop as long as she lived.

29

Slick called his mother and told her he quit his job and was coming home for a few days while he looked for work. But the truth of it was that he and Sherry had been evicted from their tiny apartment because they owed three months' back rent. He knew it was risky to go home now because of the warants out on him, but he decided his mother's cooking and accommodations were worth it. He would bring Sherry along and introduce her as his fiancee. Her presence would curb his father's violent temper if he happened to be at home.

They were also broke for the moment, having shot up almost the entire ten grand from the last holdup at the rate of three hundred dollars a day with the help of a few friends. The rest they blew on a plush hotel room where they lived like royalty for nearly a week, enjoying the best food and drink money could buy, provided by a heavily tipped room service that looked askance at the disheveled, glassy-eyed young people but asked no questions. Ramon had joined them with Angel, one of the drivers from the holdup. And since Slick had his girl in tow, they hired two call girls through the hotel management to keep their half of the party going. Unfortunately the young men were too wrecked to enjoy the girls, who soon felt neglected and managed to sneak away almost unnoticed. Besides, the only bed, a queen-size, made conditions too close for comfort.

After the party was over, Slick had just enough money left for cabfare to his folks' house. He took along a bundle of dope he had saved and also copped about fifty seconals to help them withdraw, for he knew he had to clean up soon or get busted. He expected a cool reception for the reason that Slick had never really been on his parents' good side since he had done six months in the county house of corrections two years ago. He had gotten off parole only last year.

The jail sentence had surprised no one. After all, he had been in constant trouble with the law since his early teens. Even then his father was always going down to the station to claim him after the gang had been picked up for drinking on a corner and harrassing passers-by, even police officers. Now and then members of the gang were also arrested for slashing tires or joyriding in stolen cars, provided they were unlucky enough to get caught. The police might slap them around at times, especially Slick who was particularly insolent, and his enraged father would give him far worse when they got home. But it never seemed to do any good.

And then his mother was always going up to the school, stubborn woman that she was, to try to explain his one hundred days of truancy in the eighth grade. She conveniently threw the blame back on the school and quoted her son as saying he wasn't learning anything and that the place was a zoo. Her three daughters had said nearly the same thing but one of them managed to finish with high marks in spite of it. Slick, on the other hand, was not in the college preparatory courses like his sister. He hated to study and could not sit still long enough to do his homework. So he hooked, said it made more sense to clown around and smoke dope down on the corner than to do it in class like some of the other kids.

The growing seriousness of his delinquency could be seen neatly chronicled in the local police and juvenile court records, beginning with his first arrest at the age of thirteen for unauthorized use of a motor vehicle, for which he received one year of probation. At fifteen he was arrested again for petty larceny when he and some friends entered a neighbor's garage, stole a set of tools and sold them to get money for drugs. His parents hired a very good lawyer and his case was filed on the grounds that he was not one of the leaders of the gang and was present only during the illegal entry but not as an accessory.

His mother and father were beginning to smart with embarrassment from repeated court appearances, trips to station seven, and to the school. His father thought the boy should be punished more severely, and gave him regular beatings, and his mother tried pleading openly with her son.

"Vinnie, please, how can you do these awful things?" she intoned one day, looking at him earnestly. "Don't you know that you're only hurting yourself?"

He shrugged and looked down at the floor, as he always did, bringing a sigh of exasperation from her.

"I just don't understand it!" she went on. "Why, you come from a respectable family, except for your father of course! Surely you don't mean to act like this, do you?"

"I dunno. . . ." he mumbled, and grinned at her insolently.

"What's so funny?" she responded, genuinely aggravated, voice becoming shrill. "Wipe that silly grin off your face this instant, Vincent! Honestly, I wish you'd amount to something! You're just like your father who has done next to nothing all of his life! Bob, or Kathy, or Denise—they would never think of doing any of the things you do!"

"Yeah?" Slick sneered. "Kathy got pregnant, didn't she?" He liked to say things to upset her, and he knew that this was her Achilles heel, something that she had never recovered from inside.

She bit her lip ruefully. "Well, that was your father's fault!" she shot back. "He never paid the slightest attention to that girl and look what happened! In fact, this whole mess is his fault, if you ask me! If only he was a decent man, but no, he's far, far from it and I have to pay the price!"

She did not let the matter of her son's misconduct rest, but carried on about it late at night, after he was in bed. Lying awake listening, partly to escape the fearful nightmares and terrors he suffered from since childhood, he gleefully heard his mother hurling shrill accusations at his father, who resisted with weak, petulant denials.

"You never give him a moment of your time, you're so busy up at the pub!" she complained one night. "I don't think you even know you have a son! And now look what's happening to him—he's turning into a young crook!"

"C'mon, c'mon, cool off, Maureen," his father said appeasingly. "You're too easy on him, that's the whole trouble. You always stick up for him no matter what he does, so he runs to you. Honest, he does, Maureen, I see it."

"Oh, you do, do you?" she retorted, working herself up into a kind of semi-hysterical state in which she spoke so rapidly that her words were sometimes incoherent. "You don't know what you're talking about, Mr. Know-it-all! You're so ossified half the time you—why you never even know what's going on in your own home! Why your own daughter was seven months pregnant before you even noticed, and then you— you thought she was overweight!"

"Look," he sighed. "Can I help it if the girl got hot pants?"

"Don't you say that about her!"

"But Maureen!" he insisted, trying to make sense to his wife. "You let her stay out practically all night with that, excuse the expression, asshole, an' look what happened!

'Let her use her own judgment,' you kept sayin' an' you let her stay out night after night with that jerk! Then you went and conveniently buried your head in the sand. But me, I knew what was goin' on! I ain't stupid, Maureen, but no, you wouldn't listen to me, and the chickens came home to roost, didn't they?"

There was an uncomfortable pause.

"Why don't you get out!" she snapped.

"Hey, wait," he protested. "What kinda talk is that. . . !"

"Because I'm fed up! Sick of listening to all your excuses! Can't you see how irrational you are! And now I see that same thing in Vinnie! More and more he's getting to be like you—shiftless, a failure, a stew-bum that never amounted to anything and never will!"

By now she was shrieking at him so savagely that to be heard at all he had to shout even louder. "Oh yeah?" he bellowed. "Well it's a wonder I ain't balmy. Look, you'd drive a man to drink, by God! Vinnie this an' Vinnie that! Blah, blah, blah! Well, if ya ask me he's nothin' but a punk an' always will be, just like the rest a' them kids he hangs with! Now, when I say he stays in, it ain't fer you ta let 'im go out, no matter what kinda stink he puts up, an' that's all I got to say!"

There was another pause and the snap-hiss of a fresh beer as his father grabbed another cold one, hoping that this might also serve to cool down their discussion, but in vain.

"I said I want you out of here by tomorrow!" she repeated, quietly and deliberately.

"Look, will ya shut up and leave me alone?" he growled. "This is my house as much as it is yours! Now I'm goin' . . ."

He was interrupted by a loud crash and screeching. She was throwing things at him, Slick knew that. Sometimes there would be nothing to eat off of the next day after one of these sessions. There followed another long tirade of insults from both sides, scarcely intelligible now amid the crashing and the dull smack of his hands on her flesh and her screeching again. No one ever won these contests—it was as if both sides had lost. His father had to make a fool out himself by ripping out the phone and then wiring it up again the next day, and his mother had to back down on her ultimatum and spend the next morning cleaning up the broken china and other debris. The only winner in a way was Slick because the whole thing was quite a show and he got a kind of perverse bang out of it, felt almost like Jack-the-Giant-Killer to have been the cause of these two titans battling it out over him.

All this emotional turbulence in his family sent Slick flying out of control, his destructive impulses aroused like an angry swarm of hornets. It was as though he was driven by an unbearable anxiety to prove himself powerful and terrible, lest he be exposed as the weak little impostor that he really was. Therefore he could be honored and respected only by being hated. So he set out, roving around the neighborhood looking for drugs to settle his nerves, and for trouble in general. He was the modern-day equivalent of the gunslinger folk hero who orders a shot of whisky and then shoots up the barroom just because somebody smiled. He had seen this hundreds of times on television, so he knew that when you made trouble, or waved a gun or a knife, everybody respected you and even the town marshall quivered in his boots. In fact, Slick was a product of this video, celluloid culture.

Passing through the glue-sniffing stage at thirteen and cough syrup the next year, he began using marihuana and alcohol by the end of his fourteenth year, the hallucinogens—LSD, mescaline, and THC, at fifteen, speed at sixteen. He found that each successive step involved him more deeply in drug use, made him more dependent on drugs to maintain his equilibrium and to narcotize himself in his suicidal, banzai charge through life. And since each step was more expensive, he and his partners were committing more crime, misdemeanors at first and then felonies as time went on.

Not that drugs were the answer to his problems by any means. He bummed out on acid twice. The first time he saw police uniforms on his friends and thought he could read their minds, that they wanted to kill him. His friends talked him down after he pulled a knife. The second time, after two tabs of the best orange sunshine, he heard God telling him to jump out the window and actually tried to but again his friends intervened and restrained him. His later trips were smoother, as he learned to handle himself on acid, to slow down and not take things so seriously. And after awhile even tripping grew monotonous. He got used to the twelve hour scene of illusory, sensory paraphernalia, distorted sights and sounds, rapid, bizzare thoughts and feelings, and an eerie, extra-keen self-awareness, so that he felt almost like another person whom he was getting to know for the first time and yet already knew profoundly. But like so much in life that was alluring, the novelty wore off. And in the course of tripping he discovered something that unsettled him, gave him a curious glimpse of himself as someone possessed, guided by a kind of demon inside him that he could not cast out, something goading him unmercifully toward a tragic end. Unfortunately, this simply increased his sense of fatalism, a feeling that he was not answerable for what he was.

If the course of time had changed acid from a pleasure to an imposition, a burden now on an already troubled mind, speed was a new thrill. He not only liked popping the tiny, white "cross-roads" by mouth, which made him giddy, but found that nothing he knew could surpass the swift exhilaration of shooting by vein a spoon of good crystal methedrine. This was the first time he had used the needle regularly, although he shot acid once or twice before. The minor discomfort was more than compensated by a superlative high. He could almost see his heart bulge in and out under his shirt as he experienced a tremendous rush, then weightlessness and exhilaration. He greeted perfect strangers like long lost friends and even got along well with his father on speed. Then one day after speeding on and off for about a month, he got the idea that the FBI was following him. He waited in an alley for them to come by so that he could count the number of agents. He counted four of them and went to borrow a gun from a friend, who saw how excited he was, sweating and trembling, with pupils dilated. The friend warned him he was on a paranoid trip from speed. Slick crashed soon afterward and woke up almost a day later feeling completely wasted. He had lost twenty pounds and was suspicious of everyone. His friends told him to cut out speed, that it was burning up his brain cells. Fortunately acid and mescaline went out of vogue for awhile and the supply of speed dried up temporarily. So the gang switched to pills—"ups", one of which was speed, but mainly diet pills made up of other amphetamines, such as benzedrine and dexedrine, and "downs", barbiturates and non-barbiturate sleeping pills plus some minor tranquilizers. A kindly "croaker", a willing physician, wrote them prescriptions for amphetamines at ten dollars a visit and these were filled by their friendly, neighborhood pharmacist.

Slick never forgot the first time he went to the doctor's office. He knew he was in the right place when he looked around the waiting room and saw two hippies, three plump housewives, a drag queen, and a black dude, all waiting patiently for their prescriptions. He was even more encouraged when the office nurse called him in after twenty minutes or so and the doctor, who was actually an osteopath, fortyish with a thick mustache and longish black hair, looked up and asked, "Want diet pills eh?" Now Slick was as thin as a pretzel from doing speed, and even his parents were worried about his emaciated condition. Yet the doctor simply reached over, pinched his gaunt ribs, and instructed him to follow a high protein, low calorie diet. He also wrote out a script for thirty of what turned out to be elongated blue and white speckled pills. They were not the classic proprietary biphetamines, or "beauties" in the shiny black capsule, or the yellow and blue desbutals or "bombers", a potent barbiturate-amphetamine combination, or the greenish dexamyl caps, or "Christmas trees", or one of the many others he knew of, but two or three of them worked well enough to keep him on cloud nine for the rest of the day.

"Downs", mainly barbiturates but also non-barbiturate sleeping pills and minor tranquilizers, gave the kids a different experience from the "ups". The high was not brilliant and racy, but more easy and heavy like alcohol, erasing their sensitivity and leaving them "stoned". Downs seemed to come into the neighborhood illegally in large batches and at these times could easily be purchased from the right people for around fifty cents apiece. The bright red capsules of seconal, called "reds", were the most common, then the blue and pink tuinals, or "rainbows". Nembutals, or "yellows", were widely sought by discriminating down freaks because they cooked up well and could be shot intravenously.

But as drug-wise as he was becoming, Slick was still relatively innocent. He had yet to be turned onto "hard" drugs, the opiates and cocaine. Opiates were downs but in a special class by themselves because of the euphoria, a surprisingly pleasant feeling of satisfaction that went along with the calmative effect. But it was not long before Slick was to lose that innocence. The same kindly doctor who supplied him with the amphetamines wrote one of the gang a prescription for "blues", or Numorphan tablets. They skin-popped it first, then mainlined it, discovering a truly new high, an orgasmic flash of ecstacy giving way to a delicious glowing warmth spreading through the entire body, followed by hours of dream-like repose. Cares and worries, unpleasant thoughts and violent urges were dispelled as if by magic, replaced by a sense of tranquility and well-being. It was the Cadillac of highs, everyone agreed, as it had been for untold millions of addicts down through the centuries. Soon the whole gang was cashing scripts for numorphans and dilaudids, either getting them from the "right" doctors or stealing prescriptions and forging them. But such prescriptions, especially when written out to long-haired youths, excite the suspicion of forgery. One of the gang was finally picked up for passing phony scripts after an alert pharmacist called the police. So the rest of them turned to heroin. At ten dollars a bag it was more expensive and less pure than "dillies" or "blues", but it was readily available on the street. Slick cooked up his first bag, shot it up and got a satisfactory rush. He did two more and nodded out contentedly. In discovering opiates, he found the love of his life at only seventeen.

30

The heroin high is a veritable luxury, surpassed in cost only by cocaine. Like the illegal British and American opium trade in China in the nineteenth century, the traffic of heroin is an infamous tribute to the economic genius of man. Not really expensive to produce, it is a derivative of natural opium that comes from the white, purple, or red opium poppy. Tincture of opium is a medicinal drug that has been prescribed as an analgesic, antitussive, antispasmodic, and sedative for innumerable ailments, especially hypochondriacal and other nervous conditions, since the days of the renaissance. Heroin, which, like morphine, is a derivative of opium, first made its appearance in this country around the turn of the century in cough medicines. Along with cocaine, it was highly touted as a cure for the epidemic of morphine addiction, or "morphinism", rampant after the introduction of morphine by needle during the Civil War. But heroin fell out of favor in the early nineteen-hundreds when tens of thousands of ordinary citizens became addicted to the drug, especially because it was so widely distributed as an additive in cough syrups and many other remedies, including patent medicines. Most of these unfortunate addicts had to kick "cold turkey" when, in 1914, passage of the Harrison Narcotics Act drove the narcotics trade underground. Doctors tried to ease the problem at first by continuing to prescribe it to addicted patients, but raids by G-men shut down these illegal clinics and over three thousand doctors were jailed. From then on the illegal drug market took over.

Up until the Second World War the people who used heroin were chiefly in entertainment or in the underworld.

After a five year lapse because of the war interrupting trade routes, the market expanded with the migration of large, poverty-stricken populations of blacks and Puerto Ricans to northern cities looking for work, but more often finding only despair and disillusionment. Still a tiny capsule of heroin went for only a dollar apiece and four people could "get down on a cap" by snorting their share through a "quill", a rolled up dollar bill. Since it did not cost much to get high, no one worried about the next fix and addicts were friendly and protective toward one another, many supporting their habits by working. Then in the nineteen-fifties, young, white gangs began to get turned onto it and the price started rising. These kids resorted to crime to pay their way and heroin addiction became a community concern. This caused the syndicate as a whole to back away from it so as not to endanger their more solid activities, such as gambling, loan sharking, and prostitution, but it still afforded quick money for some independent operators. Next, what is known as the "panic" hit New York in 1961, when heroin supplies dried up for only a few weeks, but long enough for the price to double and triple. Dealers discovered that heavily adulterated heroin sold as easily for an even greater profit, and cutting, as well as "short counts", or selling less than the stated weight, became standard practice. Further, smaller panics each year kept the price up and addicts found themselves caught in a desperate struggle for heroin. They had to go out and hustle ten times the money and then shoot the "junk" intravenously just to get high. Finally the demand peaked in the late sixties when an epidemic of heroin addiction spread among young, middle class whites. In 1969, dope was very abundant, though costly, but two years later saw the beginning of another panic. Again the junk became poor and hard to find and more expensive than before.

In those two decades of relative scarcity, addicts grew disinclined to help one another, tended more than ever to drift apart, to work alone or with a partner. They quit trusting their own kind or the world for that matter, finding themselves in the unique and unenviable position of being addicted to a substance infinitely more precious than gold. But this was only because they, like all little consumers, were caught at the bottom of the distribution chain and had to buy it on the street from the lowliest vendor. Yet, as with so many commodities sold far from their point of origin, the production cost was only a tiny fraction of the final selling price. In fact, heroin marketing and distribution is a classic story of the middleman.

One kilogram, or 2.2 pounds, of raw opium selling for $350 in the Near East doubles in price when refined to morphine base. But its value really begins to soar after being processed into pure heroin in France, Italy, or other parts of Southern Europe, or elsewhere. Through a courier, an importer in the United States can buy a kilo of 80% heroin for $5,000. Usually never seeing the heroin, he sells it through an intermediary for $25,000 to highly trusted customers known as "kilo connections". The kilo melts rapidly now, adulterated two to four times the original weight with varying blends of milk sugar, or lactose, for weight, quinine for the "rush", and mannite, a fluffy product of the ash tree sold as a mild laxative, for bulk, although mannitol, or even talcum powder may also be used. The kilo connection sells it now in half or quarter kilos for a gross of between $40,000 and $80,000 to the next level, the "ounce man". The ounce man cuts it again perhaps to double the weight, then breaks it down into "short" or underweight ounces and sells them for $700 to $1,000 each to the next link in the chain, the "weight dealers" for a new aggregate value of around $175,000 for the original kilo.

Whereas the links above are less vulnerable to arrest, the weight dealer is the man who takes chances in the business. His name is kicked around on the street and if caught and convicted, he can expect a lot of time. Motto was at this level, constantly worrying about the time, and busy paying off the right people or backing the right politicians, like the others above him, to stay above the law. Yet, if danger is any measure of profit, then the risk was well worth it. Reducing the aggregate weight of the short ounce even further and hitting it with a three-in-one cut, he got four

158

or five "cut ounces", or "pieces", measuring about twenty teaspoons in volume, though a few years earlier it was thirty. He sold each piece for anywhere from $500 to $1,500, depending on the demand and the location, for a new aggregate value for the original kilo of up to $500,000.

Street dealers, users like Dom who were frequently arrested, bought the pieces and cut and bagged them into eight or ten "bundles", each of twenty-five "bags", small pinches of the white powder in glassine, paper, or foil packets. Or sometimes they sold it in "spoons", or in "grams", usually uncut and of higher quality, often Chinese or Mexican in origin. They shot up a good portion themselves, but hopefully not more than half or they would be unable to sell enough to pay the weight dealer, known as their "man". So they sold it to the junkies for between $75 and $150 a bundle, or by the bag for as little as $5 to $7 in New York, where dope is cheaper, and $10 elsewhere. The junkies themselves would also sell individual bags to their cohorts. But at this point addicts were not "copping", or buying real heroin anymore, or not very much of it. Instead it was "street dope", "junk", "smack", "skag", or "horse", maybe three to six percent heroin in each bag, and sometimes as little as one percent, sifted in with an unappetizing conglomeration of assorted powders that were never intended to be injected wholesale into the human bloodstream. The original $5,000 kilogram had reached the bottom of the chain, now sifted far and wide from its starting point overseas. And though cheapened in quality, it was immeasurably more valuable in price, finally worth over $1,000,000.

The story does not end here. It leaves a boy like Slick with the irresistible compulsion to re-experience the heroin high again and again, and having to commit ever more serious crimes in order to procure this outrageously adulterated and expensive product to accommodate his growing habit. He and his partners began by stealing from homes, including their own, from neighborhood stores, and from automobiles. Then they apprenticed themselves in the fine art of breaking and entering and in the coarser art of mugging. And the better they got, the more dope they could afford and the bigger their habits became.

It was dopesickness in Slick's sixteenth year that drove him to stab an old man one day for his pocketbook containing four dollars and thirty cents. Unfortunately the victim identified him. They picked him up, searched him and the knife was discovered. Naturally very apprehensive, his family hired the same good lawyer who succeeded in getting Slick off the last time. But Mr. Lee, his juvenile officer, was piqued by his two previous arrests plus other complaints from the neighborhood and had the judge remand him to a youth facility.

It was there that Slick first discovered who his real enemies, his tormentors were. They were not necessarily his parents or his teachers, or the local police. They were the faceless members of society who went happily about their daily lives while he was locked up half-naked in a bare metal room wearing an oversized pair of white socks, the sun pouring in through an unshaded window to transform the cell into an oven. His enemies were all those people who paid the hired goons to come in three at a time, tossing him around like a sack of flour, beating him when he cursed them. His enemies were all those who ate good food while he ate slop, who were clean while he reeked with urine, who slept in beds while he slept on a pallet on the floor. Oh, but he hated them, these nameless, faceless enemies, when he got out six months later. Some of the guards had tried to beat this hatred out of him but succeeded only in beating it in more deeply.

Released on two years' probation, this "correctional" experience had little effect on his continued pursuit of drugs through crime. It only taught him to be more careful, to do his work more quickly and cleanly. Eight months later at the age of seventeen he was picked up for questioning for stolen scripts but released. Then when he was almost eighteen he was arrested as a passenger in a stolen car but the case was continued on the insistence of Mr. Lee, who assured the judge that he was meeting with the boy regularly, wanted to get him a job, and that the boy had plans to go to night school to take the high school equivalency test.

"I think he's learned his lesson," Mr. Lee concluded sincerely. He was a tall, earnest man with thick, neatly combed white hair, and wanted more than anything to help these boys.

Mrs. Quinn wrote Mr. Lee a letter of thanks, praising him for having such great faith in her son who was after all a good boy at heart. Unfortunately it was not long afterward that Slick was arrested and fined for speeding and a month later got involved in an accident. Rumor had it that he was stoned on barbiturates at the time. In any case he managed to change seats with a girl friend before the driver of the other car, who was injured, could identify him. When the police showed up and searched the car they found a nickel bag of marihuana under the seat. Both Slick and the girl were booked on possession, and again his parents had to come down and bail him out. Several months later in court he was blessed with the same good lawyer and understanding judge. His case was filed, but his driver's license was suspended.

He ended his juvenile career at age eighteen with another arrest for breaking and entering the home of a neighbor, who identified him as he walked out with her color television. This time the judge wanted to send him away but again the lawyer, plus other family connections, got him off, and rumor had it that the court was befriended with a certain sum of money. The sentence was reduced and he was placed back on probation and ordered into a drug treatment program. He stayed in one month and kicked his habit, then dropped out to get high again. After all, dope was easy to find.

Methadone began showing up on the streets about this time, much of it leaking out of the early, very loosely supervised maintenance programs, and a lot of Slick's friends got turned onto it, favoring it over heroin. There were no needles to contend with and it was much cheaper. Small, white ten milligram tablets of dolophine, or "dollies", went for two dollars each and the chewable, forty milligram orange wafers, or "biscuits", scored into four quarters, sold for ten dollars. Methadone got them plenty high and these kids could swing a sizable habit for only twenty to forty dollars a day. But Slick spurned methadone, preferred the spectacular "flash" and the soaring high of heroin. And like many addicts he prided himself on a he-man image of the tough, ruthless junkie, cold-blooded to the point of not giving a shit about anything except putting a spike in his arm. People respected him, even feared him because they knew he was a dopefiend. Of course his family could not easily face up to the truth of the matter, that their son was a criminal and an addict. And when they did, one parent heaped blame on the other, his mother accusing his father of heavy-handed abuse and his father accusing his mother of over-protection. They continued to quarrel furiously, expending all of their energy in attacking one another for the sole purpose of defending themselves.

A lot of the other kids in Slick's peer group were more fortunate. With or without the help of their parents, they got tired of the drug scene, outgrew it so to speak, and went to work, finished school, got married, or joined the service. Because of the war, even Slick might have been drafted had the local board not gotten wind of his criminal record and history of drug dependency, and reclassified him. No one, least of all Uncle Sam, wanted a junkie.

31

Maureen Quinn heard the roar of her son's bike and went to the back door. "Vinnie's here!" she cried and stood out on the porch eyeing her son nervously as he clambered up the steps with Sherry trailing behind. "Vinnie, you look so thin!" she declared with a disapproving frown. "Where've you been the past few weeks? We haven't even had a phone call from you! At least you could have called to tell me you were all right! I worry about you! I'm getting those awful cramps again and the doctor says you're half the cause of it! What do you say to that! And your father, of course, is the other half!"

She blocked the entrance for a moment awaiting his explanation, if not an apology for her suffering, but Slick ignored her, pushing his way into the house. His father, having successfully defended his squatter's rights, was still at home, comfortably settled in the living room watching the game. He sat up as they entered and Sherry saw him for the first time, a fiftyish man, dressed for loafing in wrinkled paint-spattered work clothes. He was heavy, a beer belly protruding over his belt that seemed ready to push the baggy trousers down at any moment. He held a cigarette in nicotine-stained fingers and emitted faint, juicy coughs, almost as a reminder that he was not quite well, while gulping air in little puffs, his slack cheeks working like bellows. He had not shaved for several days, not since going down to the yard in a futile search for work, and finding none, had returned home again to numb himself with alcohol against not only the days of boredom, but the razor-sharp tongue of his wife. Now, surprisingly, he took the trouble to greet his son, not with any degree of enthusiasm, but more out of curiosity. He warped his suffused, cherry-red face into the suggestion of a sardonic grin and regarded them with protruding, frog eyes that, in their bulging, seemed to express a kind of perpetual, baffled amazement.

"Well, hello stranger!" he wheezed, and stared.

Every addict, including the alcoholic, sees himself in every other addict, and Mr. Quinn had been noticing more and more of himself, or at least that part of him that wanted a drink, in his son. He watched now, his bleary eyes straining to pick out the discolored needle marks, faint and tiny, but visible on the backs of the hands. Of course it was not obvious, but then shameful things like this seldom were—flaws that people are not very proud of and tend to conceal from others who would condemn them. And yet, perhaps almost intentionally, these same flaws are never hidden completely. Just enough hangs out to give them away so that a basic kind of honesty is maintained.

For no matter how hard people may try to be otherwise, they usually remain true to themselves in every sense of the word. As an alcoholic, Mr. Quinn knew well this art of deceptive non-deception, of the shoddy coverup serving both frailty and candor at the same time, the one excusing the other. He knew all the double talk, half-truths, memory slips, stout denials, and even forthrightness for the sake of false penitence. All this to be free again and again to indulge, to perpetuate the humiliating enslavement of one's own will under the tyranny of pleasure.

"How long you goin' to be with us this time?" he wheezed once more, gulping air.

"Oh, be quiet, Pete!" snapped his mother, coming in behind them. "It's a wonder he came home at all." She looked at Sherry. "And who's this?"

"This is Sherry, ma." said Slick with an innocent grin. "We're engaged."

There was a shocked pause.

"You're engaged?" his mother repeated, and her face fell imperceptibly as she turned to the girl. "What was your name?"

"Sherry. Sherry Linsky. . . ," the girl said with shyness.

His mother flinched, gave one her charming smiles that usually meant the opposite of a smile. "How do you do?" she replied formally. "I'm Vinnie's mother." She turned back to her son and the smile faded quickly. "Really, Vinnie, I didn't know you were engaged. . . ."

"Look, ma," he said nervously, "we wanna stay for a few days, okay?"

She hesitated, glanced questioningly at his father.

"Sure, why not!" his father declared with an edge of sarcasm in his voice. "After all, they're engaged, ain't they? Who knows, someday they may even get married!" He broke into a rasping fit of coughing, then with sudden, unexpected charm, for he was a ladies' man once, he addressed the wide-eyed girl. "Nice ta meet ya, Sherry. I'm Pete, Vinnie's dad."

"Hello," she replied, again with her shy smile.

On seeing her husband's old charm shine through at this young girl Slick's mother intervened and shooed the two young people into the kitchen. She made them supper, then for the sake of etiquette, offered Sherry the guest room. Slick waited for his parents to go to bed before rejoining Sherry, and the two of them got off on a couple of bags, talked, did some reds, balled, then crashed.

They stayed for about a week, working on what was left of the dope. Slick's parents could only speculate as to why they kept to themselves so much, were so quiet and withdrawn and took so long in the bathroom. Slick sensed their vigilance and took care to hide the dope in a plastic bag in the bottom of his mother's flour tin, a place he had often used before, and nearly foolproof because whenever she scooped out some flour he would simply add more. The rest of the dope he kept behind a picture, another favorite hiding place.

The big event of their stay came one evening when his parents stepped out together on one of their rare excursions, this time to play beano at the local church. While they did not go to mass regularly, they belonged to the social set in the parish that did, and Mrs. Quinn's own cousin was a priest at that very church. After they had gone, Slick called up Russ and he, Dolores and Danny came over with some cocaine. They all shot or sniffed dime and quarter spoons and enjoyed the brief, exhilharating highs again and again, almost like scooting up and down on a roller coaster except that the ride was a bit more expensive. Then they put the brakes on gently with the King of Downs, Boss Heroin, who sent them gliding smoothly earthward like a swanboat skimming over a glassy sea.

Predictably, after the feast was over, famine set in. The dope was exhausted. Zero hour had arrived—it was time to kick because they had no money to cop, and because Slick intended to suspend his hustling activities for the time being to keep from being arrested. They were already a little sick, having cut down their habits for the past few days to under ten bags. They copped enough methadone from Dolores to help carry them through another few days, then scrounged up some percodans from another friend, just to avoid staying on the methadone. They were afraid of methadone because it took twice as long to kick compared to heroin. Still they suffered with the growing insomnia, chills and sweats, nausea, sneezing and coughing, and muscle aches, almost like an acute attack of the flu though never fatal. Then there was the nervous shock, the psychological disorientation of being sick and doing without something vital to their sense of well-being. The night they ran out of percodans, Sherry broke down and cried. She begged for dope and Slick had to break out the downs—quaaludes, or sopors, plus some reds and valiums. A few of these afforded them several hours of sleep. Again, they were careful not to get hooked.

Just when they were really beginning to wonder if they could stand it, Martin Shine, the consummate street pusher, paid them a visit along with Sam Thornton, who wore his usual polite smile. Martin had heard they were trying to kick and was determined not to lose two old customers. He fixed up and got off on a bag right in front of them, then offered them a couple of free bags.

"Take it," he urged, grinning like a Cheshire cat. "I hate to see you kids so sick when I got some of the best stuff I've seen in a long time."

Slick refused the offer with a snarl. "You gotta a lotta balls comin' out here with dope when you know we're tryin' to kick! But sure as hell, if we were strung out and wanted a bag you'd burn us for it! Now screw, you sleazy motherfucker!"

Martin left without a sale, looking appropriately chagrined and apologizing as he went, insisting he did not know. Sam, who had said little, followed him, still smiling. That was another reason why Slick did not consider copping even one bag, because he did not trust Sam and wondered why all of a sudden this outsider was so chummy with Martin, who was ordinarily a loner.

32

The next day Slick called a self-help program and he and Sherry were accepted. They left the house that morning to go in town to the familiar, ancient brick building where he had kicked once before. Like birds of a feather, the two of them felt very much at home there among the other addicts. Actually it was still the drug scene, the same almost carnival atmosphere of gregarious, long-haired young people provocatively clad in T-shirts and tight denims and surrounded by the usual novelty posters of nudes, musicians, and bikies. Some listened to the usual rock hits blaring from transistor radios, or strummed out a rendition of their own on the guitar. But there was an important exception, that they were one step removed from the streets, a quantum jump out of the mainstream of drug traffic.

Rolando, the director, greeted them with his usual aggressive charm, the firm, thumbgrip handshake and shoulder clap. He was a fine front man for the organization, a real tough addict-type with a goatee, tattoos, scars, and a polite insolence that captivated civic groups and even recalcitrant bureaucrats. He boasted of a golden touch because everything he did turned into money, into grants or gifts from a wide variety of sources. He knew Slick from before and realized he was taking a chance admitting the two of them. But continued federal funding of his and all other types of drug treatment programs, including methadone maintenance, depended on dragging those clients in by the heels if necessary to keep the census up. And the longer they stayed, that is, the longer it took for these patients to get well, the better it was for the staff who were worried about keeping their jobs and about the grant that funded them.

"No problem, Slickie," he agreed, "as long as you've already started to kick and as long as you and your chick go by the rules. But remember, everyone's gotta vote on whether or not we wanna keep ya."

"Don't worry, we've kicked," Slick replied, sniffling and trembling convincingly. "We ain't had nothin' for two days, honest."

Rolando, who had already checked their pupils and found them dilated, assented with a faint smile.

The whole staff at Project Comeback were ex-addicts, which explained why the rules were so strict, since only junkies can truly appreciate the tyranny of their weakness and the awesome price it exacts. So new members have it rough in the beginning, a kind of initiation and probationary period. Slick and Sherry were not to see one another privately for any reason. Sexual contact was taboo and dating among the patients could be grounds for dismissal. No passes were permitted without the counselor's approval. Newcomers were assigned the most menial chores in order to humble them and to give them something to work up from. And they had to attend mandatory groups. Of course, any use of drugs meant automatic probation or expulsion.

First, as was the policy for all incoming males, they shaved Slick's head, denuding him completely of his long, brown hair that hung nearly to his shoulders. Then to make their hell a little busier, Slick and Sherry were given the job of cleaning out the lavatories for nearly twelve hours a day. From then on, they did not see much of one another except at group or at mealtimes. They knew better than to meet secretly because everyone had an eye on them.

Slick got into a little trouble on the second day for badmouthing a counselor who made him scrub out a perfectly clean toilet. The penalty for his insolence was to wear a dunce cap and sit on a footstool without moving for two hours. Several times he nearly stood up and cursed, throwing off the dunce cap and walking out, but thoughts about the "heat" outside discouraged him.

He met Sherry in the hallway alone on the third day. Not nearly as sick, the worst was over for both of them, but they still had considerable trouble sleeping. She looked pale, drawn, and unhappy.

"I can't stand it," she whined. "All this work! I just may go home for awhile."

Slick nearly slapped her across the face. "Listen," he muttered, "you're crazy to split now! We've almost kicked! You gotta hang in there! This work is s'posed to keep your mind off the sick, right? Pretty soon they'll ease up an' put us out in the kitchen or somethin'. But if you split now, you know what'll happen. . . !"

She frowned, shook her head emphatically, as though irritated at hearing a question that she had anticipated and had already weighed very carefully in her mind. "Without you to cop for me I doubt it," she said flatly and looked down, avoiding his eyes.

Slick sneered with rage. "So that's it! No dope, no Sherry, huh? Why, you stupid bitch! If you left me you'd just go find another sucker to support your habit! Why don't you try to get it together just for once!" Again he fought the urge to strike her and walked away, disgusted with her spineless betrayal and incensed at the suggestion that he was to blame for her weakness.

They did not meet again until that afternoon in group. Because their spat turned into more than either of them had intended, they sat down together, almost in a gesture of reconciliation, though a noticeable degree of tension still remained between them. There were ten others in the group, six men and four women. One of the young men, about twenty-four, complete with tattoos and a Manchu mustache, was a counselor and supposedly the group leader. The others were in their late teens and early twenties except for a beatnik-type man with a shaggy goatee and very long hair in his early thirties. Since Slick and Sherry were relatively new members, having just been voted into the group the day before, the tension between them was noticed immediately by all and it seemed to spread around the circle. Everyone sat for the most part in chairs or on a divan, a few seated cross-legged on the floor. The room was very quiet at first, people fidgeting, lighting cigarettes and glancing furtively at one another or staring at the floor. Finally Rona, a large, black girl of about twenty-two with an Afro hairdo, spoke up loudly.

"Has everyone here had a chance to meet the two new people?" she asked, just to be saying something, for she knew that everyone had.

It broke the ice. The others glanced stiffly at Slick and Sherry and a few nodded at them. Roger, a gangling youth with frizzy red hair and a downy mustache, pointed a finger at Sherry.

"Hey, don't I know you from someplace?" he blurted. "Yeah, I remember! Did you use ta live on the hill, a couple a' years ago?"

"No...," said Sherry after a pause, smiling her shy, inviting smile.

"You sure?" he demanded.

She shrugged. "I've visited friends there. Maybe you saw me then."

"Well, don't you remember me?" he went on. "I'm sure I saw you." He gazed at her expectantly. When she did not reply immediately he continued in the same, eager, hurried voice. "Did you know a kid named Mike and another by the name of Scottie? The three of us used ta hang together up there."

She nodded. "I knew someone named Mike. Tall, sort of blondish hair?"

"Yeah! Yeah!" Roger exclaimed, jerking his head affirmatively. "Tall, right, but his hair isn't blond, it's dark, like...."

"She probably don't know 'im," Slick interrupted, irked.

"Probably someone else...," a few of them murmured.

Roger paused, then burst out once more. "Hey, I know! Tell me some a' the kids you know on the hill an' I'll tell ya if I know 'em, 'cause like I knew every kid that used to hang there!"

Sherry huddled next to her boyfriend under Roger's aggressive gawking and finger pointing. "I—I can't think of anyone right now," she said softly.

With a look of amused contempt, Rona interjected. "Hey, how come you always do that, Roger?"

"Do what?"

"Try to act like you know everybody," she declared, smiling at the others and they in turn smirking while he glared at her in defiance.

"It's no act!" he insisted and jabbed his finger at Sherry again. "I do know her, but it's weird . . . she doesn't remember me!"

Sheery smiled at him politely. "Maybe I met you, but. . . ." She shrugged with embarrassment.

"See?" Rona went on scornfully. "She don't even know you!"

"It's an act, all right!" growled Vic, the thirtyish beatnik, his expression inscrutable behind dark glasses. "A put-on, man, that's your bag, ain't it—tryin' ta put us on all the time!"

"I think maybe Rog wants us to feel that he's somebody important," suggested the counselor in a hasty gesture of diplomacy. "As important as anyone else in the group."

Rona stubbed out a cigarette, annoyed that they were going to talk about him again today, the way the group had done continuously since he came back two weeks ago. "Yeah, we're sure impressed with you, Roger. You're real cool," she chided and burst into a squeaky laugh.

"Yeah, outa sight," Vic agreed with sarcasm.

"Oh yeah? Well you should talk, Vic!" Roger shot back. "You an' your freaky poems!"

"Hey, shut about my poetry, man. . . !"

"Some of his poems happen to be very good," said Paula, a fat girl of about twenty with bad skin and wearing a loose, ruffled blouse embroidered with flowers.

"Thanks," Vic responded with appreciation, and was about to go on when the counselor interrupted.

"But it's natural for all of us to wanted to feel accepted and liked," he explained.

"Uh-huh," Rona agreed. "We all do. Love is what makes the world go round."

Roger was waving his arms for attention. "Love! Right! Like I want someone. . . !" He gestured at Slick and Sherry. "Like them—they got each other! But me, I'm . . .

what have I got, right? I'm alone all the time, even in a crowd! I'm always lonely!" He looked around at the group longingly.

"You're jivin' us, man," scoffed Sonny, a taciturn black youth with a nervous smile. "All we do is sit an' listen to you. So, how can you be lonely?"

"Misery loves company," laughed Rona. "I guess that's why we're all here, to. . . ."

"To make each other miserable, that's why!" Vic broke in angrily. "Well, fuck that! I'd rather be miserable all by my lonesome! I got enough shit on my mind already without gettin' all hung up with somebody else's shit, know what I mean? I tell ya, people really get to me at times, man, I mean they burn my guts! So I don't give a shit about anybody, see? I think frankly that's the reason I got into dope like I did, to forget about humanity!"

"What do you mean?" asked the counselor. "That you can't face the world unless you're high?"

Vic compressed his lips and started pulling on his shaggy goatee. "Yeah . . . you might say that," he replied thoughtfully. "If I was stoned, why this cat Roger could talk all night long an' it wouldn't even faze me, see?" He looked around at the group sullenly. "Look, I know where you people are coming from. Like we all got our hangups, right? So, I'm not the only one. Now, if I could do something about my hangups, I wouldn't be shootin' dope, dig it? I wouldn't be a dopefiend." There was a respectful pause as Vic stared at the floor, still inscrutable behind his shades.

"You're too hard on yourself, man," Sonny consoled. "It ain't too cool to just give up an' say, 'I'm a dopefiend and that's all there is to it, so I can't do nothin' about it', dig?"

"Sometimes other people can help," observed Paula gently, "If you let them. . . ."

Vic laughed silently, fumbled for a cigarette. Then everyone began lighting cigarettes and the atmosphere became heavy, almost gloomy. A sensitive area had been broached and the group members grew silent. The counselor was tempted to probe more deeply but decided to let it go by for now.

Resuming her role of informal leader, Rona spoke up again, changing the subject by addressing Slick and Sherry with a pleasant warmth. "You come from around here?" she asked, indicating that they should tell more about themselves.

"Yeah," Slick replied curtly. "This is my second time here."

"I been here two weeks already!" interrupted Roger excitedly. The faces of the group turned toward him and, caught in the limelight, he jumped nimbly up on his chair, flipped his long reddish hair out of his eyes with a haughty toss of his head, and pointed a trembling finger at the counselor. "An' this guy won't even lemme have a weekend pass to go home an' see my folks!" he shouted dramatically.

"You had passes," the counselor replied with coolness. "Why don't you tell the rest of the story?"

"Just because my folks called the cops," Roger went on. "I mean like, wow, that's almost a reason!"

"Sit down!" snapped Rona.

"Yeah, man, cool it!" said Vic.

"And the longer I stay here the more they don't want me back home again! They want to get rid of me!" Roger shouted in anguish. "I can't get my shit together in here, man! No one understands the hassles I have with my folks!" He stood towering above them on the chair, breathing heavily, his fists clenched in defiance, while the group gaped at him uneasily.

A few of the members began to snicker. One of them was Sonny. "Must be real heavy," he sympathized, flashing a grin. "But, hey, we all go through that thing, Roger. Like it's just part of growin' up."

"Everyone here thinks I'm just an asshole who doesn't know what the fuck life is all about!" Roger objected, somewhat subdued now that he had gained the attention he was seeking, and he stepped off of his chair and sat down.

"Not really," Paula consoled. "But I guess you must think that of yourself, right? Or else you wouldn't say it in the first place."

"Don't blame us for your problems," Vic broke in sourly. "And don't tell me what I think because you don't know what I think! I don't even know what I think sometimes!"

"Everyone has problems and needs help at times," the counselor explained. "Take me—I was hassled for years with two different chicks and then dope. And I wound up in the gutter before I finally realized what I was doing to myself. Now I'm straight."

"It was the same with me," said Margaret, brushing her long, straight black hair out of her eyes and huffing out a self-conscious stream of smoke that matched the color of her complexion. She held her cigarette in front of her as she spoke, like a conductor with an upraised baton, commanding attention. "First I did mescaline because it was a real body high," she went on. "Like I was extra sensitive to everything around me and it was easy to speak what was on my mind, so I used to like to get high on it with friends." She paused, stared blankly at the group, brushed back a strand of hair from her forehead. "Then I got wasted on speed, and that was the easiest thing I ever did, easier than to look at what was going down. Like, when I wasted myself I didn't want to kill my daughter."

"Aw come off it!" said Vic. "You wouldn't do a thing like that anyhow! We told ya that before! Why blame your kid? If you're a junkie mother, that's your trip, your thing you're into, not your kid's!"

"Let up on me, will you Vic?" Margaret replied with a hurt look.

"Why should we?" Rona chimed in.

"Let it hang out, baby!" Vic prodded. "Don't just sit there like a blob!"

"If you have feelings, you can go ahead and express them," the counselor advised. "That is, instead of making excuses for yourself, the way you've been doing, why not stand up for yourself. Defend yourself as a feeling person."

"I can't," replied the girl, "If I copped what I really felt, they'd blow me away."

"Stand up for yourself!" Rona urged. "Tell Vic where to go!"

"How do you feel right now?" demanded the counselor.

Margaret compressed her lips, her face growing paler. "You want me to get up and scream and get radical," she said evenly to the counselor. "But what does that prove? It doesn't change anything. The subject doesn't end there, so. . . ."

"You're copping out!" Vic charged.

"I won't get radical unless I feel it's justified," she replied stubbornly.

The counselor leaned forward, prompting her. "You shouldn't be afraid to express your feelings, as long as you don't act on them. You don't have to act on your feelings, get the point?"

"It's better to look at what's going down than to waste yourself," Paula advised in her soothing voice.

Margaret only nodded and her eyes where shiny with tears. Vic sneered and almost said something, then buttoned his lip, and there was an uncomfortable silence for a moment.

"Dope is a big hassle," Sherry volunteered suddenly, speaking directly to the counselor, while Slick looked at the floor.

"Dope, man, is a bummer," Vic agreed. "When I was using I felt great but I guess I was really just running away from things, from my boss, my wife, my kids, my folks . . . I just couldn't face life. I didn't want to at the time."

"Yeah, yeah," Slick uttered with a grin. "That's me—I'm running away. I'm copping out on dope. Everything else really sucks, right? Why get uptight about it when, like she said, you can get wrecked on drugs an' then you don't give a shit, right?" Obviously he had said the wrong thing at the wrong time, but he could not help it. He was a renegade, even among his fellow users, and gazed at them insolently.

"That's not what my probation officer says," countered Bill, a slight, long-haired youth who had remained silent, smoking and listening attentively. "I used to think like you did. Like dope cured my stutter, and I had bad skin and it cleared that up. I thought it was the greatest thing ever. Heroin, I mean. But my probation officer put some sense into my head, gave me another chance. He says you can't get it together on dope, man. Like you gotta be straight to hold a job. When I get outa here he's gonna get me a dynamite job where I'll learn carpentry an' get paid at the same time, no lie."

"Where's this?" Roger asked.

"I'll tell ya later," Bill said softly, as though willing to share this important secret in private only.

There was a pause interlaced with yawns. The time was nearly up and the group was waiting for their leader, the counselor, to recite the daily liturgy denouncing heroin and all other drugs, which as their luck would have it, was just about the only thing that had ever really made them happy. And because things bountiful in pleasure are also rich with the venom of pain, the group wanted to pluck up their courage together in order to renounce it, for alone they were weak and subject to the tyranny of the senses.

Attuned to their mood, the leader solemnly spoke. "Anybody who goes back to doing dope when they have a chance to stay straight is a fuck-up! They're a fuck-up because they're pulling the wool over their eyes and letting the world know that they're losers, that they can't get it on. And so naturally people look down on someone who is a user because it keeps them from having to look at themselves. 'Here's a dopefiend,' they say. 'I'm better than he is.' You see what I mean?"

There was an appropriate, cowed silence, then Frank, another youth, large and flabby with short hair who had scarcely said a word, raised his hand. "But . . . when I'm off dope, that's when I do fuck up," he said haltingly with a tone of apology. "I mean, I can't keep a steady job or nothin'. I feel better when I'm doin' dope, honest."

"Naw, ya don't!" Vic said with a sneer. "You just think ya do! But all the time you could be dyin', like with hepatitis, an' never even know it."

"You know somethin'?" Roger shouted. "If people accepted junkies as human beings, man, like they wouldn't need dope, right? But bein' a junkie is worse than. . . !"

"Don't say it," said Rona.

"A junkie is worse that shit," Slick interjected with a stiff, half-grin. "I know, 'cause that's what my ol' man keeps sayin' all the time. An' in a way he's right, 'cause when I'm dopesick I'm like an animal, man, an' I don't give a shit, not even about myself."

"That's why you're here, so you won't have to be that way," suggested Rona. "An' not because of what your ol' man says, I hope! He sounds like a real winner!"

"Yeah, really good for the ego, like my ol' man," Vic echoed.

"That's why we're all here, to improve ourselves," the counselor reminded them.

"Right" Roger burst out. "An I really like to rap about my problems in these groups! Like I think I'm even startin' to get my head back together again, right Dave?" He smiled at the counselor, then reflected for a moment and his expression changed to sadness.

"But . . . sometimes I'm afraid . . . afraid I won't make it. . . !" he whimpered.

"Oh, I felt that way too when I was in the gutter," the counselor said reassuringly. "But you've got to fight your way up. I talked out all my feelings down in New York just the way you are now and it helped me get it together after awhile."

"But my folks don't understand me!" Roger prostested. "They think I'm no good, that I'm a criminal or something, and it's true! I am no good. . . !"

"My parents don't even know I'm an addict," said Margaret, her face almost expressionless. "They'd die if they knew."

The counselor frowned, "It's true that people don't understand. They just don't understand the problems junkies have inside. So that's why we have to help ourselves, help one another."

Marie, a shy, pretty girl who had remained silent up to now, spoke out earnestly. "That's right, you know it? Like I've done everything—turned tricks, boosted, stole off my parents, and it was all because my mother refused to take me back after I got pregnant and my father went along with her. They never understood me at all, never even realized how much I needed them, so I started doing dope, maybe to get back at them in a way. But here, like in this group, people care, and that's what counts, I guess, for people to care. . . ."

The circle nodded in agreement, heartened by her testimony.

"So why can't I go home?" Roger began again after a pause. looking around the group imploringly. "Tell Dave I should go home. . . ."

They discussed the matter briefly, finally persuading the counselor to give Roger one more pass. "Everyone deserves a chance to make good," Rona concluded.

The group broke up after about an hour. The members all looked bouyant and inspired. They were, in fact, high, exhilarated by the intimacy, the emotional catharsis, the intense experience of sharing one another's feelings, doubts, insecurities, and of voicing their own frustrations. This was a different kind of high, a human high that came from people caring.

33

Despite Slick's threats and intimidations, Sherry left the self-help group the next day. Not even the director could get through to her and persuade her to postpone her decision and to discuss her feelings at group. "I'm going home," she said simply. A quiet girl, she was never much for words.

She packed up, stood ready to leave, clutching a paper sack full of her belongings, facing Slick.

"If you split I'll never give you another bag of dope, so help me God," he muttered. "Even if you come crawling back on your hands and knees!"

"We'll see each other again, Slick," she replied meekly. "I'm just going home for a visit. My parents haven't seen me in awhile."

If she had examined her motives more carefully before departing she would have seen through her self-deception.

But like most addicts she did not dare look at herself too closely. She had actually persuaded herself that she was leaving in order to visit her parents, who no doubt missed her terribly. Getting a fix was only incidental to her visit, to stay straight so that they would not notice her sick. But of course this did not mean that she was going back on dope, not at all—she was just doing it this one time, so it did not really count. Besides, anyone who took the trouble to go all the way home to visit her parents deserved to get something extra special, if only for a short while. Entwining all of these little deceptions and excuses together, she spun a web so tight that it shut out every glimmer of truth and common sense, leaving her mind and even her very soul immersed in a gloom of self-delusion.

The morning was made for hitching. A portrait of an early northern summer, it was already warm outside with a haze of humidity hanging around the trees. Puffs of cloud admitted, then obscured the sun, climbing like a bright copper penny into the pale blue sky. Sherry had no trouble thumbing a ride into the downtown area, all the while thinking so intensely that the driver scarcely heard a peep from her. Distracted by plans for her first move, she got out of the car without a word of thanks and slid through the huge revolving doors into a large department store. Locating men's furnishings, she prudently checked for watchful employees, then stuffed a half-dozen fine silk ties into her underwear. Shifting next to the cosmetics counter, she asked to see some expensive perfumes and the clerk brought out several bottles for her to sniff at. She stalled, told the clerk she was waiting for her boyfriend to come and give his opinion. As soon as the clerk turned away, she filched a bottle and departed. In twenty minutes she had thumbed her way across town to Dom's rooming house, but found him not at home, nor was he in The Prophet. Finally, after considerable effort, she tracked down Martin Shine hunkered in the booth of a nearby diner having his usual late breakfast.

"I don't like to trade dope for hot stuff," he rasped apologetically, buttering his toast and eying the ties with indifference. " 'Cause I can't get rid of it, dig? But . . .

realizing the difficult position you're in right now, what the hell, I'll give you a bag. . . ."

"One bag! Oh, please, give me at least three or four!" she pleaded. "Your stuff isn't that good anyway!"

He shrugged, looked around apprehensively, hoping they had not been overheard. "You're right," he admitted with a low grunt. "So, come back to my room with me an' I'll make it six."

"I don't have time," she replied impatiently.

He hung his head and sighed, then shoveled a forkful of omelet into his mouth, talking as he ate. "That's . . . what they all say, but then . . . I'm too old anyway. . . ." He smiled faintly, as if recalling something long ago. "Okay, three bags, but only for you. Wanna cup a coffee?"

This she accepted, but only after hurriedly borrowing his works, disappearing into the ladies' room and getting off on the three bags he had just passed her. Immediately she got a fairly decent rush owing mainly to the fact that, having just kicked, her tolerance was way down. What little had remained of her sick vanished in a flood of warmth. Now she felt whole again, invulnerable to any and all hurt. She was ready to go home at last. But as she stood outside thumbing again, it occurred to her that the three bags would not hold her for more than about six or eight hours and that she would need something else for that night at least. Then she planned to kick again, slowly, over a week or so, cutting down very gradually.

She arrived at Slick's parents' house an hour later. The place was empty. His father, who had been out of work for nearly a year, was in the pub drinking up the last of his unemployment check, and his mother was down at city hall where she worked in the office of her uncle, the city councilman. Sherry knew where the key was hidden and went to get it. Slick's mother had given them little handouts now and then during their stay and the girl had taken care to observe where the money was kept, just as she did in her own home. She found it after rummaging around in the bureau, seventy dollars in cash rolled up in an empty cold cream jar. She took forty dollars, hoping they would not miss it right away.

She slipped out of the house, hopefully unnoticed, for if Slick found out he would all but kill her. She thumbed back into town, to the area where she and Slick had lived together. She did not particularly care for methadone, but knew of a clinic nearby where doctors and nurses gave it out each day to addicts who were patients there. She waited near the entrance and followed several of the youths as they came out.

"I need to cop some methadone," she said, looking at them urgently. "The dope is nothing now. . . ."

"Don't have ta tell us," one youth replied. "That's why we're here. Only way ta get high nowadays." He looked at her placidly with glazed, pinpoint pupils, his face exuding the affable glow of opiates.

"Yeah, dope nowadays is garbage," agreed another. "Why don't you get in this program? They give you enough methadone to keep you straight at first, then you can build up your dose."

"How long do you have to wait?" she asked. "Can I get something today?"

"Maybe," said the first youth. "Just tell 'em ya wanna detox an' they'll always switch ya to maintenance later. Might hafta wait around, though, till the doc comes back. He ain't in half the time."

She shook her head. "I need something right now. Can you spare anything?"

They hesitated. "Hey, we can't sell much, 'cause it's our take-home dose," said the second youth. "But I'll sell ya a couple wafers for ten bucks apiece. That's eighty milligrams. An' you're gettin' a good deal. Over at the other clinics it's mixed up with Tang an' you don't know what you're gettin'."

"I know," she said. "A friend of mine bought some over there and he got burned. That's why I came here. But I wouldn't care what they mixed it with, as long as it made me straight."

She slipped him twenty dollars after checking to see that no one was watching, and he handed her the two wafers, slipping them into her fingers unobtrusively. They had to be careful because even though selling methadone was commonplace, it was strictly forbidden both by the clinic rules and by law. But like any other unenforced statute, it was more honored in the breach than in the observance.

"Uh, what's yer name?" he asked amiably as she was about to leave.

"Sherry Linsky. My boyfriend is Slick, You know him?" she replied with a faint smile.

The youth returned her smile with an ironic twist. "Yeah, heavy dude. . . ."

"Real hardnosed dopefiend," said the other. "What's he doin' now?"

"He's in Project Comeback. I was there too, but I left."

"Comeback!" he sneered. "That place sucks! All they do there is shave yer head an' call you an asshole! You oughta try this place. No hassle, just get yer dose an' that's that. Maybe a little counseling, like 'hello and goodbye' once in awhile, but that's no sweat, really."

"Maybe I will sometime," she said. "Thanks an awful lot."

They grinned at her for some reason that she did not understand as she hurried on. She did not want to draw too much attention, and moved out of the area quickly. By now it was almost four o'clock and she had twenty dollars left. She was hungry enough to thumb down the avenue to a roast beef sandwich shop where she bought the special and a chocolate frappe, plus a twenty-five cent chocolate-dipped cone. Standing on the avenue licking the cone she began thumbing again, her hip thrown slightly out in the suggestion of a temptress. She accepted a short ride through town to the main route, got out, and resumed thumbing as the long summer day, though far from over, began to darken under a thickening layer of cloud. The fresh breeze of impending rain was stirring her long brown hair when someone finally stopped to pick her up, the typical young straight in a Volkswagen who thought he was rescuing a wayward girl. Like most, he tried to start a conversation but she discouraged it. It seemed to her that his world was so remote from her own that hardly a syllable of meaningful communication was possible between them.

"Looks like it's going to rain," he persisted.

"Umm."

"Where do you live?"

"Newsome Heights."

"Out on the great suburban desert, eh?" he quipped.

"Um, well my parents live there."

"It is a nice area. . . ." He gave her a sidelong glance, no doubt curious how a girl from a fashionable suburb could wear such an outlandish getup—faded, patched dungarees that in fact had been carefully bleached, an old, wrinkled, tie-dyed T-shirt, and sandals. She looked more like a vagabond or a street urchin than a suburbanite. He turned back to watch the road and fell silent, not pretending to understand the ways of this next-youngest generation, so opposite from his own.

As the car spun along, Sherry thought about the self-help group she had left that morning. It had shaken her sense of individualism to be reminded again of all the other young addicts in her predicament, disillusioned and alienated from the system, at odds with the stodgy, traditionalism of their parents, and having to depend on drugs instead of on real life for some kind of vital experience. They were substituting chemical happiness for the joy of living, considering the latter to be no more than an elusive platitude reserved for either the old and reconciled or the very rich. But she and the other young addicts were just setting out on life's journey and felt a gnawing dread of where it would lead them. Tarrying now to share the empty frivolity of drugs seemed the better choice. There were supposed to be ten thousand of them in the city at this very moment, all child-addicts gone astray in the trek through their lives.

"This is good enough," she said to the driver suddenly.

"Here?" he asked with uncertainty, slowing and stopping beside an iron fence. "Kinda creepy, huh?"

"Thanks a lot," she murmured, climbing out and rewarding him with a smile.

"Good luck," he returned, and sped off, leaving her alone, wandering near the gate.

The clouds had settled into a gray canopy by now, masking the sun almost completely so that it shone only as a dull hot glow from time to time in the darkening sky. The cool breeze whipped into a gust that swirled the clean smell of rain into her nostrils as she passed through the gate and followed a gravel path, looking from side to side. The trees round about were full and green, leaves fluttering violently in the wind, so different from the naked branches she had seen clutching the bleak winter sky the last time she had come. She picked her way carefully now, stopping often to get her bearings. It was odd not to be able to find it right away, like searching for a familiar face among a crowd of strangers. She frightened a squirrel and it scrabbled up a tree, looked down in alarm as she passed. Then the rain came down in scattered drops, one pelting her, then another. She went ahead, lost her way, retraced her steps hurriedly and continued. It was harder to see now, the sky overhead turning an opaque, leaden gray as the rain quickened. Then she found it, not as big as she had remembered it, but the name was there and the date. She knelt down and touched it, felt the dark, water-stained granite, cold and wet on her fingertips.

"I'm sorry, granma...," she sobbed. "...I'm sorry...."

Abruptly she stood up, lingered for a moment at the gravestone, regretting that she had not brought flowers. Her clothes soaked, and knowing it would have worried the old woman, she went back to the road.

34

Sherry's trouble with drugs began back in her early teens, that critical stage when frolicking little girls undergo a metamorphosis into proper young ladies. Although her overworked parents expected this process to come about naturally without a great deal of involvement on their part, she surprised them. She ran away from home at the age of fourteen, the same year her grandmother suffered a stroke and was sent to a nursing home. The girl's behavior took the entire household by surprise, for although her parents had noticed her growing moodiness, they did not make a great deal of it. More surprising, even shocking, was her sudden involvement not only with marihuana, but with other young people who smoked it. This led to her being picked up with several others for possession. Her parents were called and her father had to tear himself away from his medical journals and papers in order to appear at the station where he extricated his daughter as discretely as possible.

"Sherry," he stated as they drove home. "I prohibit you from seeing any more of these new friends of yours. Now, if you promise to stay at home, I will double your allowance and I promise you'll get a new car when you're sixteen. How does that sound?"

She did not answer.

"Did you hear me?" he asserted, and still getting no response from his daughter, began shouting at her in spite of himself. "Wait until your mother gets home then, you can talk to her! I am simply too busy, young lady, to quibble with you!" An important man, he was unaccustomed to being defied.

Though informed by telephone of her daughter's whereabouts, Sherry's mother did not arrive home until eleven o'clock that evening, having had a number of responsibilities to attend to at the hospital. As usual, no matter how hard she worked, she never looked tired and wore that same characteristic expression of sober efficiency, her face serious and unsmiling, her jaw set firmly. Her look did not change in the slightest as she regarded her teenaged daughter huddled in a chair with her head in her arms. It was a curiously cold, scientific kind of scrutiny that always made the girl uncomfortable, despite her lifelong attempt to adjust to it and to be, in fact, whatever those questioning, glacial eyes of her mother's wanted her to be, so that they might admire rather than study her.

"You are still up?" her mother observed tersely. She had long ago fallen into the habit of stating the obvious with great authority, and for reasons that were and always would be unclear to her daughter, except that it invited complete agreement and left no room for any doubt whatsoever.

Sherry looked up with her arms folded, her lips unmoving, then looked down again.

"She isn't talking, Susan!" came her father's voice from the study. "As soon as I mentioned these friends of hers she just stopped listening. I offered her an allowance and even a car when she was older if she agreed to stay home. . . ."

"I don't want anything, father!" Sherry burst out suddenly, keeping her face hidden.

Her mother removed her coat and sat down opposite her daughter, let out an impatient sigh. "Of course you do!" she declared. "You can't refuse your parents! We want you to have whatever you need! But you simply cannot see these so-called friends, definitely not! Now why don't you go to bed, dear! I have to be up at six o'clock myself for a cesarean section!"

"You'd better get some sleep, Susan," came her father's voice again. "You've been overdoing it lately."

Her parents never seemed to tire of their hectic schedule of clinics, conferences, rounds, scientific papers, and research projects. This left them very little time for leisure, or for the precious, fleeting moments of child-rearing. Besides, they saw little need to babysit a fourteen year old girl, who was nearly full-grown already and should learn to think for herself. Like many very superior people who overestimate not only themselves but everyone around them, they did not consider it necessary to indoctrinate their daughter with a practical philosophy of life, or with a love of truth and a respect for honesty and sincerity, toward herself as well as others. These precious legacies were never bestowed on the young girl. Instead they were to remain inaccessible behind a wall of dry pretense and profound scientific wisdom, with its indisputable inter-pretation of proven fact. So, though showered with material things, she remained forever poor, deprived of these priceless treasures that she hungered for so desperately, and which could have belonged to her but for that awesome, impenetrable wall.

Gradually she began to strike out on her own. She searched elsewhere along with other seekers of her own age who became her friends. Together they experimented with life itself by trial and error. In high school she was frequently truant, and left home again for nearly a week in her sophomore year after her older brother was accepted at Yale. The police picked her up with three youths after a high speed chase in a sports car, and the driver was booked for being under the influence. The group she hung with was using marihuana heavily by the end of the sophomore year and in the junior year they were experimenting with LSD, mescaline, angel dust, and speed. Sherry became so ill from angel dust that she was afraid to try acid at first until a boy she knew insisted she pop a half tab.

The acid was quite different from what she had expected. For one thing, she had never been so high in her whole life. And it fascinated her, being fun, yet almost too much so, like a carnival ride that starts out enjoyably but gets too wild and crazy to be really pleasant. She was left confused and disconcerted, her mind racing like a computer gone wild, sorting through a limitless array of impressions, jumping from one thought to the next, and then getting off the track to muddle around in pure nonsense. She felt exaggerated emotions varying from the deepest gloom and despair to the utmost hilarity, often weeping or laughing over something absurd. At other times her mind burrowed rodent-like into any subject at all and explored its every ramification in minute detail, the whole range of thoughts and ideas bursting out in her mind's eye in an elaborate design, like the intricate pattern in a kaleidoscope. And it took concentrated effort to switch her thoughts from one subject to another, so that unless she was careful she went on and on in just one line of thinking.

One night she learned never to translate these crazy thoughts or impulses into action. She and the boy she was with suddenly had the urge to get on their feet and move about while tripping on two hits of mescaline apiece. Once they started walking they just kept going, for almost ten miles as they found out later. When Sherry saw the same gas station on both sides of the road she knew it was time to quit. They lay on a roadside with sore feet in the middle of the night wondering what they were doing there. Close to the airport, they spent the rest of the night coming down slowly on the mescaline, watching the big jets swooping in to land like metallic dragons roaring and belching fire and skimming onto a twinkling sea of blue lights.

That such a freaky, alternate world existed, so different but not really any crazier than her own, intrigued her. This, she reasoned, was the forbidden paradise that had been denied her, a refuge from her depression, from her hunger to really feel. And she could escape there almost by magic, simply by blowing her mind on a tab of good mesc or acid. So she went on a lot of trips, until the kids soured on acid after word got around that a youth had taken a fatal leap off a bridge while tripping, shouting just before he jumped that he was no good and that angels were telling him to destroy himself.

Sherry discovered something about herself in the course of tripping as everyone does on acid. Once she was high she became naked and vulnerable—all of the everyday conceits and little self-deceptions she employed to protect her ego were suddenly stripped away. It was like stepping through a mirror and looking back at herself for just a second with great awareness. Free now to think and feel, to see the truth, the reality behind appearances, she saw a sulking child, unwilling to reach out to others, yet stubbornly resentful unless others reached out to her. She saw her own life, and the lives of her parents, as devoted to getting for oneself, for the self was the infant who wanted all. She saw that she got her own way by pouting and whining, forcing others to give in to her. And for the first time she also saw how she had taken advantage of the one kind person in her life who had really given of herself, her grandmother, who at that time had just suffered a stroke.

Sherry then reasoned that she had only two choices open to her—either to make amends, or to kill herself. Because she knew her suicide would hurt her family, she decided on the former. She began visiting her grandmother daily at the nursing home, bringing little gifts and staying by the hour. She showered all kinds of little attentions on the old woman, who was by now quite unable to respond coherently but was none-the-less overwhelmed with joy.

It was about that time that she discovered a new high that completely distracted her from her humanitarian crusade. The boy that turned her onto acid took her to a rock concert one night and they got stoned on grass and wine. Afterward they went back to his house and started their usual session of cuddling and petting. Then he was telling her that sex was something she should really try. He knew what he was talking about because he balled his last girl friend for over a year, and all the other guys were doing it with their girl friends. Of course she knew this, but hesitated. The combination of wine and marihuana numbed her inhibitions so that she wanted only to enjoy, to feel good. Of course, she had wanted it for a long time, but the fear of pregnancy, the awareness of girls being whisked away for abortions, had inhibited her. Now this rose into her consciousness for only a moment before evaporating in the haze of intoxication. She smiled at him and her body ached with desire. Closing her eyes, she let him undress her and do everything he wanted. He was right—she did enjoy it, and wanted to have that feeling again, often. They did it a lot after that, for she could not resist it. But even though he was "careful", she finally missed a period. They talked briefly about getting engaged or something of the sort but realized they were both too young. Then when her parents found out about it through the grape vine and began giving him stony glances whenever he showed up, he stopped seeing her and took up with another girl. Heartbroken, Sherry had to face her shocked and indignant parents. They arranged a legal abortion at a local hospital after paying a psychiatrist fifty dollars to sign a statement that the pregnancy would endanger the emotional health of the mother.

After her D&C, Sherry refused to eat at the supper table and spent the better part of two weeks sulking in her room. She grieved at having lost something that was not only a part of her, but a living thing that, had it survived, could have been the object of her own, very special love. And her parents, after an initial display of consternation at their daughter's unthinkable behavior, also fell silent and said almost nothing to one another for days. Then late one night they quarrelled in the study, her father shouting out his frustration. The next morning her mother came into Sherry's bedroom, her jaw set in that business-like, clinical expression, as if she were about to administer some especially bitter but essential medicine.

"On the advice of the psychiatrist, we're sending you away in the fall to a private school in upstate New York," she said crisply. "We feel it will be good for you and, moreover, it will get you away from all of these so-called friends of yours."

"It's expensive," added her father, standing behind his wife in the doorway. "But of course money is no object. We'll send you whatever you need so you'll have everything." He paused, his voice growing milder. "And, if you do well, why your grandfather will give you a sports car. He's getting Larry a Porsche, you know."

"Of course, he deserves it," remarked his mother. "He's worked very hard."

At their ultimatum, Sherry's lower lip curled out hurtfully in the habitual pouting of the little girl. She saw it as nothing more than a plot on their part to get rid of her. "I don't want to go away, and I don't want a sports car, either," she whimpered and turned her face to the wall.

35

After weeks of sulking to no avail, Sherry took a different tack. She repented for the rest of the summer, apologizing and asking her parents' forgiveness. She even had a brief flirtation with religion at the local Unitarian Church. In fact, she was so good that at last her mother was persuaded, against her better judgement, to let Sherry stay at home and return to her old high school. That fall, as a junior, she met another boy and soon began seeing him almost every night. This time her mother asked her outright if she was "having intercourse," as she termed it, and Sherry finally admitted she was. After a long, angry phone call to the psychiatrist and another shouting match with her husband, who kept exclaiming, "You see? I told you so!", she was referred to a gynecologist and put on the pill.

Avoiding one disaster seemed to invite another. This boy had a lot in common with Sherry. They were both thin, shy, and somewhat socially withdrawn. He became convinced from listening to others that speed would be a mind expanding thing for both of them. They tried it and indeed it enlivened them, made them supersexed. And now they were more outgoing and even popular with the kids who had scarcely noticed them before. Sherry and her boyfriend went speeding every weekend, first popping "crossroads", or dexidrines at fifty cents apiece, then switching to crystal methedrine by needle at ten dollars a spoon for a better high. But her parents, with their medical training, grew suspicious at their daughter's sudden talkativeness, irritability, dry mouth, dilated pupils, and lack of appetite.

"I tell you she's emaciated and cachectic," declared her father to his wife and colleague. "And it's not from the pill!"

Her mother agreed, and proceeded to make the diagnosis by forcing Sherry to urinate into a container and having the specimen analyzed at the hospital. The test was positive for amphetamines. Her mother told the girl to stop taking the drug or be committed to an institution for treatment.

Sherry stopped, but for a different reason. Her boy friend had some buddies who were experimenting with hard drugs, mostly heroin and dilaudids, skin popping it at first. Then the pusher, an older boy about twenty, showed them how to mainline it and it felt so great that they started doing it that way, whenever they could get hold of a few bags.

"I tried it and it's really dynamite," her boyfriend reported back to her one day, his eyes shining with unusual enthusiasm. "It's kinda like when you're balling for the first time. All you think is, 'Wow, I wanna do that again!' "

"If it's that good, then how do you know you won't get hooked on it?" she asked, curious but wary.

"Oh, no, I'm careful!" he insisted. "I just do it now and then when I feel like gettin' high. You oughta try it— you'd really like it! It's the best way to come down offa speed, honest! You don't feel wasted anymore at all!"

She shook her head emphatically. "I'm scared to. I don't want to get strung out like Freddie and those other kids he hangs with."

"Aw, that's just 'cause they're crazy anyway," he scoffed. "You gotta watch it, that's all. Jus' chip, use a bag now an' then. That way ya won't get hooked. All the kids I know do it that way. Freddie's an exception."

Unfortunately her boyfriend forgot his own advice a few weeks later. Depressed over bad grades and trouble at home, he stayed high for a few days. The morning after he ran out of dope he noticed back pains and a trembling, sweaty feeling. At first he thought it was a mild flu but then it got worse. He copped a few more bags from his friend the pusher and it took the sick right away. And so he acquired a light habit of four to six bags a day. But after several months he needed more to get high and increased his habit accordingly. He had no time for Sherry now, would see her only occasionally and spent most of his time either hustling or getting off at home alone, a sure sign that he was strung out. He was up to ten or twelve bags a day now and had little interest even in having sex with her.

Neglected, she decided at this point that he would like her better and take her more seriously if she did dope also. One night when he was fixing up he offered her a skin pop.

She accepted it and he shot up the rest of the fix. While he went into a nod, she sat there feeling dreamy and relaxed. It was the same delicious, sensuous pleasure that she had known in sex, only much more tranquil and peaceful. It was at that moment, in fact, that she forgot all about sex. In her eternal quest for gratification, she had found something even better. Just as her boyfriend had said, all she wanted to do was to repeat the experience again as soon as possible. She took three more skin pops that very night but the next week, after her tolerance had increased, it only made her sleepy. A friend of theirs, a user, said, "You oughta mainline it. Otherwise you don't really get off."

"Hey," protested her boyfriend, "she'll get strung out, like we are!"

The friend sneered. "She's goin' to anyway just bein' around you, so what the hell, may as well let her go ahead an' enjoy it!"

Her boyfriend was nodding out and did not care much one way or the other, only wanted to savor his high. After his eyes were closed, his friend dumped a bag into the cooker, drew the fix through the cotton into the syringe. "Come on," he beckoned. "Swear to God, you'll never want to skin pop it again."

She let him tie her off and find a vein. He inserted the needle, drew a few drops of blood and mixed it with the dope, then squeezed slowly, watching her. "Wow . . . I'm getting really high," she said weakly as he withdrew the spike and skin popped the rest into her arm. "I'm—I'm really getting a buzz off this stuff. . . ." She began to scratch, and suddenly vomited. "Whatsa matter. . . ?" she asked groggily. "How come I itch?"

"You'll get over it!" he laughed. "That's just from the quinine in the dope. An' pukin' means you're really gettin' off on some dynamite stuff! Now sit back an' enjoy it!"

She never forgot the orgasmic rush and the blissful nod. Junkies never do forget that first time, that first big "flash". They lose their innocence and are forever changed. From then on they must struggle with a new urge, a new craving, a new weakness. Later she discovered that heroin did something else besides getting her high. It relaxed her. She worried less about life in general and got along better with her parents. She agreed to whatever they said. It was no bother anymore to hear her mother fuss about her appearance, her hair, skin, teeth, bowel habits, menses. And they seemed to like her better, so that in a way everyone was happier. Certainly, as physicians they should have suspected something from her docility, should have noticed the faint but clearly visible needle marks on her arms, or the pinpoint pupils. But like many a calamity, the nearer it was, the harder it was to see. Only her brother knew for certain that she was using something. He had seen it at school. But he too kept silent, afraid of being blamed for telling his parents their business.

One thing Sherry did not like about heroin was the withdrawal reaction. Like many who become addicts, she had a poor tolerance for pain and discomfort of any kind, physical or mental. The insomnia, nightmares, muscle aches, hot and cold sweats, nausea, and diarrhea were almost unbearable for her and she grew to dread dope-sickness, so much so that even the very thought of it made her ill. She found the only thing that could prevent it was more heroin, or some other potent opiate such as dilaudid, numorphan, morphine, or maybe percodan. Thus, the only antidote for her condition was more of the same poison. She began doing five or six bags a day, two in the morning for a "wake-up", two at about four o'clock, and another one or two in the evening. But as the months went by it seemed that she and her boyfriend needed more and more just to stay straight.

"The dope's no good anymore," he said disgustedly. "I need six bags in the cooker just to get off. An' I'm sick as hell on ten bags a day, so fifty bucks for a half load doesn't do shit."

"I'm sick, too," Sherry said. "And I'm up to eight bags. Are you sure it's the dope?"

He shrugged. "I dunno. Bobby always has the best. He swears he isn't tapping the bags. I asked him."

They did a few more bags a day to get the same high and to stay straight, and as their habits grew, so did another problem—money. At first Sherry supported her light habit by petty theft, by stealing from her mother's purse, or by shoplifting. Her boyfriend worked at odd jobs and shoplifted also. But now they needed nearly a bundle a day between them, or well over a hundred dollars. They spent less time in class and more time hustling, she doing more shoplifting, he ransacking cars for tape decks, golf clubs, or anything else of value. And he went into people's homes, looking for the usual items he could get rid of quickly. Then one night she and her boyfriend were picked up in a stolen car that he had bought from a friend for twenty-five dollars to use in a burglary. They were both booked for larceny and her parents, shocked at their daughter's recidivism, hired the best lawyer they could find. When her case came to court some months later it was continued, not only because it was her first offense but because she was attending school. What no one knew at the time was that she only checked into homeroom each morning, spending the remainder of the day on the streets. She also forged her report cards, smiling shyly at her parents' praise over her straight A average. Naturally they were very surprised when the school informed them of their daughter's failing marks at the end of the semester. They were now forced to take notice of some money that had been missing from the house on several occasions, plus several mysterious checks made out for cash that had not been entered in the checkbook. And at last they saw her pupils and looked at her arms, and were alarmed.

"It's high time we stopped kidding ourselves about Sherry, don't you think?" her father said one night. His wife was having another one of her migraine headaches, the kind he blamed on nervous exhaustion. Yet he had to broach the matter, and waited for her opinion, which secretly he took great stock in.

She had expected it, that they would both have to face some kind of terrible truth about their daughter that up till now they had succeeded marvelously in ignoring. "Obviously the child is . . . well, ill," she murmured from the sofa where she lay, very still, eyes closed and head somewhat elevated. Any movement, bright light, or loud noise aggravated her condition.

"Yes...," he replied slowly, and looking at the supine figure of his wife on the sofa, he was struck by her obvious incapacity to do anything about it. He realized that, in fact, neither one of them could, and for the first time in his career as a physician, he felt lost. There were no easy solutions, nothing to be removed or repaired by the facile turn of his scalpel. He was out of his depth at last. He knew little about drug addiction beyond the popular stereotype of the vicious criminal addict running amok in society until arrested, that is, if he did not die first of an overdose. Surely his own quiet little daughter could not fit into this category. As a surgeon, he naturally believed in drastic cures for drastic illness. It was time to cut out the cancer, taking an arm, a leg with it if necessary. He could not handle it himself, would need a lot of help. Psychiatrists? He did not trust them, never got a straight answer out of one yet. He rose from his chair, quietly went into his study and picked up the telephone.

The following evening Sherry and her boyfriend were out cashing stolen checks at supermarkets with a phony ID. Because the pusher did not show up till late with the two bundles he had promised, it was nearly midnight by the time she got home. Two gentlemen were waiting in the living room with her parents.

"Sherry, these men are detectives," her father announced calmly. "They want to talk to you for a moment."

"May I see your purse, Miss?" one of them asked politely, almost with a note of apology.

She froze with astonishment at first, then turned to run upstairs where she could get rid of everything. But she ran straight into the arms of the other detective, who gently restrained her.

"Sir, ma'am, I'm afraid she's an addict all right," the first detective informed them sternly after they had discovered the heroin and the set of works. "I'm afraid we're going to have to book her for possession, and maybe stolen checks, we don't know."

Even before Sherry had arrived to face arrest, a plan had been worked out between her parents and the police. She was to be sent immediately to a resident drug treatment program after posting bail. Her commitment to the state hospital, where the program was located, would be confirmed by letter at the time of her arraignment for the charges against her. When she came to trial later on, it was probable that her case would be continued, as her last one was, and that she would remain on probation as she was at the present time, provided that she stayed in treatment. Acting on the advice of their attorney, her parents dutifully cooperated with the authorities, first by urging her to identify the pusher, which the detectives said would mitigate her case considerably. This she steadfastly refused to do, did not even name her accomplice in cashing the bad checks, though her parents gave the detectives her boyfriend's name.

She went into treatment, stayed in the hospital worrying and despairing, sitting glumly in group therapy and hardly saying a word, until her case came to court months later. Even though several supermarkets had identified her from her photo on the phony ID, and even though heroin possession was a serious charge, she did not have to worry about going to jail. As the other kids in the treatment program kept telling her, no one with her money and family prestige ever went to jail. She would almost have to kill someone—something like that—and even then her folks could get her off by putting up enough money for an insanity plea. And the kids were right. With her excellent attorney, Sherry got a two year suspended sentence. She was placed on probation for that period of time on condition that she stay in some kind of treatment, either inpatient or outpatient, depending on the judgement of her psychiatrists. Her parents were required to make restitution for the eight hundred dollars in checks she had cashed at various supermarkets, and this was quietly arranged through their attorney.

36

As kind as Russ was to himself, he was kind to others also and to every living thing. He did not believe in suffering, did not accept its inevitability. Instead, he sought to undo it whenever he could. At the age of seven he took in a stray kitten that had been played with too roughly by some other children until it dragged one leg. He put it in a box, fed it, and took care of it. It died and left him feeling very sad.

"Don't fret," his mother consoled, "You got it in you." She patted him on the head with affection mixed with admiration. "You like to take care o' sickness. . . ."

She told a neighbor, an older woman known locally for her wisdom who agreed with a polite smile. "Uh-huh! He'd make a fine doctor, sure enough! An' he be smart fo' his age, too! 'Course, you got to have a lotta schoolin' for it!" she advised.

From that day on whenever the old woman saw the boy she would remark, "There goes the doctor," and she spread it through the whole neighborhood so that by the time Russ was thirteen he had earned the name "Doc". To live up to his title, he provided free consultation for a wide range of clientele, from puppies with warm, dry noses to little children with skinned-up knees. He did so well that his mother urged him to work hard at his lessons so that he could make the necessary grades for college, and then hopefully enter medical school. But in a two bedroom flat inhabited by five children and their playmates and pets, it is hard to do homework. His mother could read but not well and could hardly understand the work her son was assigned, so she was in no position to help him when he got stuck. And he was stuck often. Russ asked the teacher for help now and then but the classroom in the public school he attended was so noisy that he could barely hear what she was saying. And anyway she did not really seem to care very much whether he learned the lessons or not, so preoccupied was she with just keeping order in the room. All the class did for the most part was tell jokes, gossip, pass notes, shout, and throw things. In gym they snapped towels, and in wood shop they sawed big blocks into little ones and made them into nic-nacs. Noontime was a free-for-all down in the cafeteria, a riot of yelling, screaming, and tossing empty milk cartons into barrels at thirty feet. The lavatory was a haven for smoking, drug-using, fist fights, and writing on the walls. And when they were not engaged in any of these activities they were sitting down in the principal's office because of having done them.

Near the end of the ninth grade the teacher passed out booklets in homeroom one day and announced that everyone would spend two hours filling in the answers. No, it was not a test but they had to do it just the same. The class opened the pages, saw questions on spelling, math, little puzzle-like problems, and all kinds of other riddles. "Start," said the teacher, glancing at the clock on the wall. "You have until three-thirty." Then every twenty minutes she would say, "Even if you have not finished, stop, turn the page and go on to the next part." Russ went through it as best he could. He had never seen half the material—some of it was complete nonsense to him. "Stop, put your pencils down, close your booklets and pass them to the front of the room," he heard the teacher say. Almost before he knew it the time was up and he had not finished.

The next fall, in high school, Russ and practically everyone else from his junior high school, which was nearly one hundred percent black, were placed in a "dumbell" class. The college preparatory classes were filled mostly with white kids from the better neighborhoods. Russ's mother complained to the principal, who told her he had not done well enough on the scholastic aptitude tests he had taken the year before. Russ himself went down to see his counselor several times during the first semester because he did not like his courses— woodshop, gym, everyday math, history, and social studies. "This is the same stuff I took in junior high," he complained. "I wanna take algebra an' biology. I gotta go to college 'cause I plan to be a doctor."

The counselor, a thin, bothered-looking man wearing a fixed expression of annoyance mingled with boredom, squinted down his nose at the black youth as though he could hardly believe his ears. "I'm afraid you will have to change your mind about that," he said drily. "Because, well. . . . you're just not smart enough to be a doctor."

This remark caused a great deal of turmoil in Russ's household. His mother made indignant phone calls to the principal, who sympathized and explained that if Russ were to score adequately on certain qualifying examinations they would be glad to place him in the college preparatory class, but that considering his poor performance the preceeding year, it was doubtful that further testing would be worthwhile. And so his course was set, marking him for disillusionment as long as he stayed in school. Rather than vying for academic success, he began working to develop his musical abilities. He took up the bass fiddle, practiced hard and was placed in the school dance band at the beginning of his junior year. He had already been working on the electric bass guitar and that year joined a local group called the "Del Rays". As the group improved they got occasional bookings at parties and in small clubs, mostly in the ghetto or around the colleges. He decided to drop out of high school in his senior year to play full time.

"I can't see no point in school," he announced to his mother. She was very disappointed.

But the group broke up some months later when two of the members got into drugs. Russ was even experimenting with cocaine for awhile but could not afford enough of it to develop a habit. He did it more or less because the others were doing it. Now, without the income from the group, he was forced to do odd jobs. He soon learned that high school dropouts sit at the bottom of the list as far as employment opportunities are concerned. He worked in parking lots, warehouses, laundries, and even in a hospital around real doctors and nurses, but always at minimum wage or less and with little or no fringe benefits. He spent nearly everything he made just to keep a shirt on his back and a meal in his stomach. The rest he gave to his mother. Other boys he knew did as well on unemployment.

A big break came at last in a large restaurant where he was doing kitchen work, when the chef, an old Jamaican, began to take notice of him and teach him a little cooking. He was a wizard, this fellow, when it came to seafood, especially shrimp dishes—casseroles, creole, baked-stuffed, cocktails and salads. Russ admired all these as works of art, impressed by the skill it took to prepare them.

"You really are the greatest," he said to the old man. "This food is the best lookin', best tastin' ever."

The old chef nodded, actually agreeing. "It take me very many years to learn all these things," he explained in broken English. "Don't got no recipe . . . jus' feel it, thas' all. If you wan' you learn . . . maybe two, three year you can cook all these things."

Russ jumped at the offer. And his mother and sisters were very pleased. "A good chef can get work anyplace," they said. "And it pays real good."

At the old Jamaican's urging, the owner of the restaurant agreed to elevate Russ to cook's helper, a job that paid minimum wage. He had to come in at five-thirty in the morning with the baker, assist him with the dough, then start slicing vegetables. He had to put the meat and fish out to thaw, cut it up for stews, soup, and so forth. He had to put things on the stove and in the oven, then start the salads. The chef oversaw him and the two other helpers and added the finishing touches. He impressed everyone as a bright, capable worker, a young man who was surely going to learn how to cook and do it well. Soon he mastered the soups and some sauces, the art of roasting meat and a few special desserts. He was noted for his good memory, never seemed to forget the directions and picked up everything very quickly. And he began to see cooking not only as an art but as an exciting discipline nearly as rigorous as any science, with basic laws, variations, constants.

About this time the owner retired and handed the business over to his son, a college graduate in business administration. The son analyzed the gross, the profit margin, and so on and concluded that changes had to be made to offset rising taxes, food prices, and minimum wage. He decided to invest considerable capital into modernizing and automating the kitchen so as to reduce the work force by one half. A sleek new automatic dishwasher eliminated two men, and a peeler, slicer, blender, new roasting oven and a fryer eliminated two more.

"You can stay on as busboy," said the new boss. "But that's all I've got for you right now."

"But I'm learning to cook," Russ reminded him.

The man regarded him with the cold eye of an entrepreneur who has a sizable investment at stake, a man with visions of expanding and opening new restaurants, or even starting a food line or a franchise, the only avenue to big money nowadays. And he could not let altruism stand in his way. According to the textbooks, Russ was an expendable unit of labor, nothing more. "I'm sorry," he said, "but you gotta understand that I'm running a restaurant business, not a cooking school, okay?"

Russ stayed one week as busboy, got tired of looking at dirty dishes and quit, much to the sorrow of the old chef, who had himself decided to retire.

37

Drifting around the city, Russ kept looking for work but found nothing. It was summertime and jobs were scarce because of the students. So he went on unemployment and collected eighty-five dollars every two weeks, just enough to keep body and soul together. One day because of his relatively impecunious situation he decided to appropriate two twelve dollar pairs of slacks from a clothing store. He had them rolled up in his coat pocket and was about to leave when he was arrested by a store detective and turned over to the police. To his surprise and anger they pushed him around down at the station, took away not only the slacks but his good leather coat for "evidence", and relieved him of the money he had in his wallet. He was locked up and the next morning bail was set at thirty dollars.

His sister promised to come down and bail him out as soon as she could get up the required cash. He was more fortunate than the homeless man in the next cell with no friends or relatives, who could not put up money to the bondsman and had been in jail for nearly a whole month awaiting trial. But Russ's cellmate, a muscular, good natured man in his thirties who called himself Lightfoot, was a different case altogether. He was being held without bail, having been picked up on two counts of grand larceny, plus suspicion of assault with intent to commit murder. He took a liking to Russ right away.

"Hey, baby," Lightfoot whispered. "How's about gettin' high with me tonight on some junk, man. . . ."

"In jail?" Russ half-whispered in astonishment. He looked around, fearful they would be overheard. "Look," he went on. "I don't do no dope, see? Besides, I'm gettin' outa here tomorrow."

Lightfoot pulled out a roll of bills and chuckled. "So what if we in jail? Man, that don't mean nothin'! See this bread? That's all you need! Like I pay this screw twenty-five dollars an' the cat brings me my dope, an' anything else I want—cigarettes, whisky, you name it, I got it!" He chuckled again in a triumphant falsetto.

Russ nodded, duly impressed. "I ain't never shot junk," he said reluctantly. "Just snorted it couple times. Made me sleepy, that's all, but look, I. . . ."

"Hey, outa sight!" Lightfoot interrupted. "Why this jail, bad as it is, ain't never looked so good behind dope, y' understand? We gonna get high tonight man, no shit! Ain't no brother been in the jail 'th ol' Lightfoot gonna refuse my junk, ya dig?"

Russ had been placed in an awkward position as the guest who had to accept the hospitality of his host or be considered rude at the very least. And since by nature he did not like to offend people, he accepted the invitation. That evening he took a skin pop and the golden high made him forget all about jail. He did not even care about leaving as long as it lasted, about an hour. But when Lightfoot insisted he mainline it, he declined, having all but fallen asleep as it was.

His sister borrowed the thirty dollars in cash to post bail and Russ was released and told to appear that morning for his arraignment on a charge of petty theft. He found that inquiries as to the whereabouts of his coat and money were futile, but he did not press the issue, satisfied at being released from the grimy, uncomfortable confines of his cell.

Bad luck with the law continued to haunt him when only two weeks later he bought a ten dollar spoon of cocaine from a friend in order to relieve his depression brought on by being arrested, jailed, and losing his coat on top of that. Just as he was walking off with the cocaine in his pocket, two bearded, long-haired young men approached and also purchased some cocaine, then promptly arrested the dealer while a third man, disguised as a gardener clipping a hedge, arrested Russ. They identified themselves as narcotics agents from the Drug Control Unit of the city police. Russ was booked and released on recognizance, since he could not possibly post bail, while the dealer was locked up pending a much larger bail. Apparently they had been after Russ's friend for months, had staked out his house and so on, so that Russ simply walked into the trap without realizing it.

The following morning he returned for his arraignment on a charge of possession of cocaine, and another felony of presence at the sale of narcotics. The public defender, a short, nattily dressed young man who appeared harried and pressed for time, listened with passing interest to Russ's side of the story, that he was actually not present at the time of the actual sale, although he admitted having just purchased a small amount of cocaine prior to his arrest. The counsel did not ask for details, since the police had already given him the particulars at the indictment proceedings, held just prior to the arraignment, where Russ had not been present. "Look," said the PD officiously after Russ had heard the charges and had protested to the judge. "This kid you were with is a big dealer. Now, if you can give them some other names, people he might be working for, I'm sure it'll help your case an awful lot. I can probably get your petty larceny charge dropped, for one thing." He glanced at Russ with the matter-of-fact expression of someone who knew an addict when he saw one.

"But I didn't have nothin' to do with that kid," Russ argued. "An I wasn't at no sale. I jus' copped a spoon an' took off."

His counsel shrugged. "The agents say that you witnessed the sale, but I'll see what I can do, okay?"

Russ stood trial for petty larceny three months later and drew a ninety day suspended sentence and was placed on probation. A full seven months after that, seven months of sleepless nights spent worrying about going away, he went back to court again for his narcotics case.

The PD took him aside before the trial, looking about as usual as if expecting someone important to happen along whom he should not miss recognizing. "Look, fella, I've got it all set," he declared, exuding an oily confidence as though about to share some special inside tip with his client. "The best thing you can do is plead guilty. I can get you off with no more than two years, so you'll probably have to do only six months, maybe seven at the most."

"Huh? Plead guilty!" Russ exclaimed.

The PD was busily scribbling on a piece of paper, then pushed it over to the youth. "Sign this and we'll be all set."

Russ read it, a statement declaring that he would agree to plead guilty in return for a sentence of two years. The charge of presence would be dropped, so his only charge would be possession.

"Heck, it's the best I can do," the PD replied. "I know the judge and as I said it'll mean only six months of actual time. But if you don't sign, you could get five years or better on two counts of felony, possession and presence, don't you see?" He sighed, looked up as if glancing at an imaginary clock on the wall racing ahead of his lagging agenda. "To tell you the truth," he went on earnestly, "we're so backlogged right now that we've simply got to hear these cases as quickly as possible, so that's why you're getting off so easy."

Against his better judgment Russ agreed to sign. After all, he had to trust his legal counsel but he deeply regretted not having the money for a really good lawyer who could probably get him off with probation. The courtroom was so jammed with people that they were standing along both walls as case after case was heard, so Russ had to wait for some time. He saw the defendants being led in and out sullenly, some in handcuffs, while attorneys exchanged hurried comments with the judge. Everyone seemed rushed, working under great pressure as the morning wore on. It was almost noontime when Russ was called. His case was no exception—things went so quickly that they seemed pre-rehearsed. The prosecutor read the charge while the judge was still writing on the last case. The defense rested, then the judge looked up from his work long enough to hear the plea of guilty as charged. Russ had not said a word, had not demanded jury trial as he could have done and could not appeal the case anyway because of the plea. He reappeared for sentencing a few days later and was given two years in the county house of correction. They took him away to the island right afterward, to do six months of time for the man.

38

Russ met Lightfoot again a year later in the ghetto, driving a big yellow Cadillac. "I beat that case, man," he announced with a sly grin. "They didn't have enough evidence an' so when I appealed it I got off. Now I'm really into somethin' that's outa sight—payin' off dudes to fake hijacks, give the drivers, say ten percent of whatever we can get for the cargo. Made seven grand last week! Gonna hit a couple warehouses next, peel the roof, see? Somebody from the mob got it all set up an' we're still lookin' for another man if you're hep to it." Lightfoot grinned again and Russ saw how happy he was, saw the fine clothes he was wearing and the big car he was driving. But with the experience of prison still fresh in his mind, Russ was unimpressed.

"Sounds real good," Russ admitted tactfully, "but me, I got a year of parole left an' I ain't takin' no chances. I just want to get a job an' make a good week's pay. All I'm lookin' for is a break, get into somethin' steady, you know what I mean?"

Lightfoot responded with hilarious laughter and started the Cadillac. "Man, that ain't too cool!" he exclaimed. "You ain't never gonna get nothin' wukkin' fo' the man! You gotta make your own breaks in this world, y' understan'?"

Russ did not argue the point, knew Lightfoot had a case but also that he needed a lot of money for dope. For his own part, Russ was not doing any more cocaine and had not done heroin since they had been in the county jail together. He realized that heroin was dangerous, even though he had been exposed to it often enough in the past, having snorted it every now and then since he was twelve. As he had told Lightfoot, he meant to go straight. He had taken a job washing and jockeying cars in a used car lot, hoping eventually to become a salesman. But as time went on it became obvious that like all of his other goals, this too was out of reach. He could work around there for a lifetime and never be anything more than what he was the day he started, and if he did not like it, he could always quit and go do the same thing somewhere else.

"Hey, go check the number on that '67 Plymouth for me, will ya kid!" said the boss one day. He was a heavy, sedate man who rarely got up from his chair and left any leg work, no matter how trivial, to his employees.

Russ did not go out to check it, only paused for a moment to think. "It's A57-379," he replied.

The boss looked up. "How d'you know?"

"I know all the numbers," said Russ simply. "I never forget a number. Like, I keep every phone number I ever knew right inside my head."

The boss frowned with skepticism and in one of his rare attempts at physical effort, heaved his hulk out of the chair and waddled outside, returned breathless and red faced, clutching a note pad in his plump fist. "Okay, what's the number on that '66 Rambler?" he wheezed, lowering himself back into his seat.

Russ hesitated, then recited it, missing only the first letter.

"By Jesus," the boss grunted excitedly. "You must have good eyes, too! Try this. . . ." He took out several sets of keys, each bearing a long serial number. "I'm going to show you one of these keys for just a second. See if you can remember the number." He flashed a key. Russ could barely make out the small, stamped numbers. "Got it?" Russ nodded. The boss waited for several minutes, talked about the ball game, tossing out scores as if deliberately trying to confuse him. "Okay, what was that number?" he asked finally.

"Uh . . . S365175R."

The man squinted at the key, "S . . . what was that again?" Russ repeated it and the boss nodded, tossed the key on the desk and looked at the youth sharply. "You got a new job, kid," he declared. "If you want it, that is. And it'll make what you're getting now look like peanuts."

The way he described it, the thing sounded fairly simple and relatively safe. Russ recalled again the words of Lightfoot, his cynicism and derision at the very thought of succeeding honestly in a basically dishonest system of dog-eat-dog, and at the same time, recalled his contentment behind the wheel of his new Cadillac. Impulsively, almost recklessly, Russ agreed to give it a try, reasoned that if he had to steal, he minded less stealing from those who could afford it.

After a few days of training he was dressed up in a brand new suit and dropped off at a new car dealer. He entered the showroom, looking business-like and prosperous. "Excuse me," he said politely. "I'd like to look at a model that's roomy and holds the road good. I'm taking a long trip down south."

"Certainly," said the salesman, eyeing him with reservation. "And what price range were you. . . ."

"The best," said Russ. "Mainly it depends if I care fot it. I'm paying cash."

The salesman gave an involuntary grin and waggled his head approvingly. "In that case, we have a lot of models to choose from," he replied in a much more familiar tone of voice. "Step right this way and I'll show you our big luxury line first, that one over there. A very fine automobile, as you can see."

Russ looked admiringly at the long, sleek sedan, highly polished, sitting like a huge, semiprecious gem on the showroom floor. The salesman opened a door, the new lock clicking cleanly, letting out the fresh, brand new car scent of vinyl upholstery. Russ marveled at the elaborate interior, the carpeting, the beautifully designed padded dash. It was truly a luxury car, almost a yacht on wheels.

"Can I test drive it?" Russ asked.

"Of course," said the salesman. He explained all the magnificent and equally expensive extras, then went into the office, fetched a set of keys and they went outside to an identical car parked in the lot. "A nice interior," he went on. "And these are power seats, adjustable four ways for the last word in driving comfort. . . ." He turned the key and the engine purred to life, a huge brawny beast rippling its muscles under the hood. "Two hundred eighty horsepower. It's automatic, of course. Go ahead and try it."

Russ declined to drive it any further than around the block. He turned off the ignition, asked a question about the seat belt and while the salesman was demonstrating it, and quickly read the number on the key. Repeating it in his head, he passed the keys to the salesman. "I'll go home and talk it over with my wife," he said. "Then I'll let you know. It's the best thing I've seen so far, just about what I had in mind."

"Fine, come back anytime," the salesman urged, almost insisted, anxious not to lose the sale. "You might want to bring the wife in and let her test drive it if she's interested. By the way, where're you going on your trip?"

"Florida."

"Oh, great place. Yes, well, this is just the model for a road trip like that. Nothing but comfort the whole way. Remember, we're open till nine six nights a week, so drop back and see us."

Russ did, about one hour later. It took that long for the man parked a block away to jot down the number Russ gave him and drive off, then return with a newly cut, duplicate key. After checking to see that he was unnoticed, Russ unlocked the car, got in and started the engine. With a surge of power he drove straight over the cement curb and into the street, surprised at how smoothly the big car handled. He followed another car a half mile or so, stopped and turned it over to two men who put on new plates and whipped it away to a garage somewhere, to be altered sufficiently for re-registration in another state. They gave him one hundred dollars per car. In six months' time, working three different cities, he made nearly eight thousand dollars. Then the operation ceased for awhile because word had it that they were stepping on someone else's toes higher up in the syndicate. Russ was glad to quit. He was starting to worry too much about getting caught and had a couple of close calls, like the time he had to abandon a car and run for it when he ran out of gas only two blocks from the dealer.

Now he had enough money to do some of the things he always wanted to do. He paid off his mother's hospital bills and bought her a new set of teeth. He sent his sister to secretarial school and hired a good lawyer to get his older brother out of an assault case. And finally, he got himself some nice clothes, a new car, and a girl, one of the prettiest in the neighborhood whom he had been afraid to ask out up till now. She had expensive tastes and especially liked banging good cocaine and then coming down from it on heroin. She turned Russ onto this and they had a wonderful time together until his money ran out and she took up with someone else. But she left one legacy with Russ, a deep appreciation for the pleasures of cocaine, and after he lost her he turned to it as a consolation.

39

It was a warm day in May when the sun comes down hot enough to soak into the earth and make things come alive, when plants explode and splash the dead, gray hills with a dainty, fresh green. Even in the traffic-choked city the onslaught of spring was irrepressible. Dom felt the warmth of sunshine on the back of his neck and caught the glare of it lancing into his eyes from the concrete underfoot. A new season had brightened the land, yet he could only blink stupidly, still stuck somewhere back in winter, in a gloom without end.

He had more than the usual worries. He owed his man several hundred dollars, even after he had been warned repeatedly, and still he did not have the money. On top of that he was out of dope and sick, had gone on putting too much of it into his arm instead of selling it as he was supposed to do. It seemed he could not control his habit, but that it controlled him instead and was intent on destroying him. He knew what would happen if he did not have the money for them tomorrow. First he would be beaten, then later, their patience exhausted, he might be maimed or even killed. He had to struggle to try and save himself now, before it was too late, and the first step was to get the money now.

Taking along a coat, unusual for such a warm day, he walked several blocks to a shopping center, went into a men's clothing store. He glanced around quickly to estimate where he would be partly hidden from the mirrors, then avoiding the clerks, went to the coat rack and removed four coats, one by one. He draped them over his arm and covered them with his own coat, and walked out. Quickly he hid his merchandise in an alley, returned to the hardware store and made off with a toaster, again under his coat. He hid this also, then went into a stationary store, poked at the typewriters. As soon as the clerk turned away he threw his coat over a portable, picked it up and moved toward the door.

"Wait a minute, fella!" someone shouted. It was a man in the rear of the store, who ran up, blocking the door. "Put it back!"

"Huh?"

"That typewriter! There, under that coat!" He turned to the clerk. "Hey Margie, call the cops!"

"Wait," said Dom. "I was going to pay for it!"

"Sure, sure, kid. . . ! Hey, Jack!"

Dom saw a husky man come out of the rear of the store. He put the machine down, instinctively checked for the knife in his pocket. "Look," he said indignantly, "If you want to call me a thief, then go ahead! I'll take my business somewhere else!" He raised his voice excitedly, as the second man came toward him. "So just lemme alone, okay? Get away from me!"

Customers and employees alike stared as Dom edged toward the door, wide-eyed and trembling. The owner, non-plussed, let him go. It was one of many successful gambits to get out of a tight spot that Dom had picked up from his addict friends. Like many shoplifters, he had been caught but not arrested, had talked his way out of the pinch. He picked up the coats and toaster and moved out of the area quickly, keenly disappointed that he had not gotten the typewriter, worth double what he was carrying. He cut down a side street until he came to a neighborhood tavern, rang at the back entrance. The dank, moldy smell of refrigeration and accumulated filth greeted him as the door opened and a heavy, sallow-faced man in his sixties with thick white hair leaned out.

" 'Lo there," he said thickly.

"Got something for you to see," said Dom.

"Yeah?"

"Here, it's all brand new," said Dom, sweeping off his coat to unveil the merchandise.

"What're them coats? 'Bout fifty bucks?" the old man asked, tottering down the cracked cement steps to inspect the tags, turning them over with trembling, pudgy hands. He started to say something but broke into a coughing fit, expectorated a large wad of yellow phlegm and regained his breath. ". . . Give ya . . . thirty for them coats . . . five for the toaster. Thirty-five."

Dom flushed. "Thirty-five bucks for two hundred plus worth of stuff?"

"Look, pal," said the bartender, shrewdly noticing Dom's slight shakiness and runny nose. "Take it or leave it. Remember, I'm lucky to get half price for it."

Dom took the cash with a sense of defeat mixed with desperation. He needed hundreds more, and now. He returned to his room, got the long screwdriver and walked nearly a half mile to a neighborhood where the mail had just been delivered. Quickly he began prying at mailboxes, searching for checks, all the while lamenting about how low he was stooping. He had never considered himself a criminal, did not get any pleasure from stealing the way many junkies did. Yet he was doing it, despite all of his inner qualms. By his thoughts he might be a contrite, basically honest person, but by his actions he was a common thief, no better or no worse than all the other thieves whom he had looked down upon, considering himself to be of better character. They were the more honest for admitting what they were, he decided. With a shudder of anxiety he realized that, even if he saved his own life by stealing, he would irrevocably lose something much more precious, the last remnants of his pride. It had been trampled on and badly wounded these last few years but he had clung to it with the fierceness of a cornered beast. Yet now he was degrading himself again, digging like a madman at a mailbox with his screwdriver, taunting himself, the disgust of it all burning away at his insides. He was a coward—he had to live.

In the course of two hours of hard searching, he found only two checks. One was a federal check for $180 to a Mildred S. Donovan, and the other a paycheck for $132 to a Donald P. Ellis. He knew, as he headed out of the neighborhood, that his next task of cashing the stolen checks would be difficult, especially since he was an amateur, not a hard-nosed junkie who knew the ins and outs of doing checks. But he had picked up a few tricks from being around these people for nearly three years, and he was at least as smart as they were. Arriving at a bank, he entered with a noticeable limp. He endorsed the federal check with the woman's name in blue ink from a borrowed pen, made it payable to a second, fictitious name signed in black ink. He eyed the two tellers to pick out the one that looked the most gullible, chose a young woman in her twenties who smiled at every customer. He limped up to the window, passed the check.

"Hi," he said with a disarming grin. "Good thing it's nice out. Took me forever to walk six blocks. . . ."

Her pleasant eyes shifted to Dom and grew serious. "Oh?"

"Yeah, I'm a Vietnam veteran. Stepped on a mine. Actually I'm lucky to be alive."

"Gosh, what a shame," she replied earnestly, glancing down through the bullet proof glass at his stiffened leg.

He shrugged. "That's life, I guess. I'm not good for much right now, though. Thank God Mrs. Donovan hired me to take care of her yard and do errands. She's real old, crippled almost as bad as me with arthritis."

The teller had flipped the check over and was scrutinizing the signatures. Other people began to crowd into line behind him.

"Want me to get out my ID?" he asked.

"Yes, please."

With difficulty he fumbled at his pocket, grimaced, grabbed hold of the counter with one hand for support.

"Never mind," the teller went on after waiting a few moments. "Does she have an account here?"

"Yes, she sent me here," Dom replied.

The teller hesitated, then pressed the changer, counted out the bills hastily. After all, it was a federal check and negotiable. "Hope you feel better," she said, as he nodded his thanks and limped away.

Out on the street he counted the money again with mixed feelings—further proof, he decided, that he really was a dyed-in-the-wool thief. He had no real compunction that poor Mrs. Donovan would not get her check this month and would probably starve because of it. Again, like a true criminal, the only thing that concerned him was whether or not he might get caught. There were cameras in the bank and federal checks were a federal beef. The U.S. courts were the toughest in the land and most of his check-passing friends never touched federal stuff for this very reason. The payroll check was not as bad as far as time was involved if he were convicted, but it would be harder to cash. He hurried to a supermarket, decided to sacrifice some of the money on a food purchase since he did not have the proper ID's. He picked out a basket full of food, some meat, a carton of cigarettes, and tossed in some baby food, powder, laundry detergent and sanitary napkins to throw off the checker. He arrived at the counter with a list in hand, glancing at it now and then as he emptied his basket.

"Twenty-three-o-nine," said the checker, tearing off the slip.

Dom took out some bills, counted them. "Gosh, all I have is eleven bucks!" he said. "Can I cash my paycheck here?"

"You'll have to see the manager," the checker replied, and called to someone.

The manager arrived, asked the usual questions after scrutinizing the check. "Do you have a customer card with us?" he asked crisply. "Got any ID's?"

"I—I don't have my billfold with me," Dom answered, feigning embarrassment. "I can call my wife and she can bring it down. . . ."

Exasperated, the manager eyed the purchase, shaking khis head. "If you're gonna shop here regularly you'll have to get a customer card in order to cash checks," he grumbled. "Do you want to make one out now?"

Again, Dom had no choice. "Sure," he said.

They took his picture and issued the card. He was as good as nailed now because they stamped the check with it. He got his money, though by now it was hardly worth it. Disgusted and a little firghtened, he tossed away all of the items except for some of the food and the cigarettes. The dopesickness was coming on stronger now and he could not delay his next task—copping. There was only one problem. He was used to dealer's dope, some of it almost twenty-five percent heroin. But he was out of that and had no intention of wasting his hard-earned money on the garbage that most street pushers had to offer at ten dollars a bag. There was a much cheaper and more sensible alternative, yet one that required a little more effort. He hitched across town to an address he had memorized some months ago. It was the office of a physician who was known to be very kind to people in need of prescriptions for controlled drugs, especially narcotics.

Since Dom handled and used some of the best heroin around, it was logical now that he would turn to the equally potent synthetic morphine products—Dilaudid and Numorphan. They were both very popular with addicts because, unlike methadone, they cooked up just like heroin for shooting by vein and provided the same, dramatic high. Methadone, on the other hand, was not that water soluable and addicts had to "cold shake" it with enough water to dissolve it, so that the volume could be several syringe-fulls for one fix rather than just a tea-spoonful. Dilaudid was the favorite, very pure and potent, with no hangover. It came in the small, white two and four milligram tablets and sixteen milligram "footballs", as well as injectable powder. One four milligram tablet was equivalent to nearly a bag of average street dope and cost as little as fifteen cents apiece by prescription, but sold for about five dollars on the street. The footballs went for ten or fifteen dollars on the streets. Numorphans were just as potent but not quite as pure as dilauded and produced a mild hangover. Each large, pale blue ten milligram tablet was as good as about two to four bags of good street heroin and was priced as low as twenty cents apiece by prescription, but went for anywhere from ten to twenty dollars on the street.

Dom sat in the waiting room for almost an hour, the sick gripping him now, cramping his back and leg muscles, roiling his stomach, prickling his skin. He tried not to shake and fought the urge to vomit. He had to have something soon.

"Next, please," said the nurse, watching him as he rose stiffly. "Did you have an appointment?"

He winced. "No, ma'am, I just need something for pain. I'm going to the hospital to have surgery on Thursday and my prescription ran out. Kidney stone. . . ."

"Of course," she replied absently and filled out a card, ushered him into the doctor's office.

He was an older man, well past middle age, with thick, horn-rimmed glasses and a prominent double chin. Pictures of grandchildren sat on an ancient, oaken desk cluttered with varied nic-nacs serving as paperweights on a pile of receipts, notes, bills, and so on. A dusty book case crammed with faded volumes stood in one corner and an antique examining table sat against the wall. The only relatively new objects in the office were medical journals heaped in disarray, drug brochures, and a red plastic, cutaway model of a human heart imprinted in gold lettering with the brand name of a medication for heart ailments.

The doctor raised his head, seemed almost to look past Dom, who sensed that just as with his addict-patients, something had broken this man also. "What can I do for you, son?" he asked hoarsely.

No wonder they called them "croakers", thought Dom, because many of these physicians who wrote prescriptions for controlled drugs were older men in declining health, their practices shrinking in the face of modern assembly line medicine in clinics and hospitals.

"I've got a kidney stone and I'm having surgery for it as soon as they get a bed," he replied, and tried to conceal his trembling hands. "My doctor gave me some little white pills but I ran out. . . ."

"Dilaudids?" said the doctor and raised his eyebrows knowingly.

Dom nodded. "Yeah, that's what they were. Four milligrams ... they really work. I can't sleep without 'em."

"How many do you need?"

"Uh. . . ."

"Here's a script for twenty. That ought to hold you for now," the doctor rasped, his voice a bit stern, as though disapproving of this illegal act that he was obliged to perform for humanitarian reasons. He jotted on a prescription pad, added his narcotics number on the bottom. "That'll be ten dollars."

Dom handed him the money, genuinely grateful. "Thank you, doctor," he said. "I certainly appreciate it."

"That's quite all right, my boy. If you need more, come back in a couple of weeks," the doctor said, getting up from his desk and solemnly watching Dom leave the office before admitting his next patient, another seedy-looking youth from the streets.

40

Dom stood near the corner in a little patch of shade that scarcely cooled him on this sweltering afternoon. The humidity clung to him doggedly like a hot-breathed beast, choking him and robbing him of his precious, inner strength. And it was one of those times when he needed to be on his toes, a time of fear. He dreaded this rendezvous, hoped that the rented car would never appear. But it did, right on schedule as always, cruising by, coming around again and stopping a half block behind him. They waited, the men in the car and the man on the corner, waited and sweated in the close, sultry air. When they pulled up at last, Dom could tell right away that things were not good. He caught the leer on Spanky's face and his stomach tightened as he got into the car. Then block after block of run-down, frame houses slipped by, and the blur of traffic and exhaust haze as they turned out onto the expressway. Dom handed Spanky a roll of bills, watched him count them.

"I still owe two hundred," he said taughtly before the strong-arm man finished counting. "Next week I'll have it for you. . . ."

His voice trailed off as Spanky's small, pig's eyes blinked in the large, fleshy face, regarding him not so much with anger but with an ominous look of pity, as one sees in the eyes of a jailer beholding a condemned man. "I got news for ya, kid," he growled, yet speaking distinctly so that Dom would not misunderstand. "Tony says from now on, no money, no dope. He ain't gonna front yous no more. Now, he put himself out, see, gettin' yous outa jail, helpin' yous to beat that case. An' he's a helluva'n honest guy, but he don't like bein' made a sucker, see? Now he says, that he is very unhappy but he's gonna give yous one last chance ta do good. Go down ta New York an' make a connection for him an' he'll forget about the money. Whaddaya say?"

Dom smiled faintly, trying to hide his relief. He had expected a beating. "Sure, I'll do it," he said.

The strong-arm man smiled, exposed missing teeth. His face was a mass of scars. "Dope's gettin' real tight. Feds grabbed a couple big shipments in New York and there's a lotta heat in Marseilles, so we gotta go to the chinks an' the Puerto Ricans for some stuff till things cool off." He reached under the seat, yanked out an attache case. "Tomorrow when we take you to the airport, there's gonna be ten grand in here. Tony wants half a pound a' heroin with no more'n two cuts on it. The deal's already been made through a middleman, so all yous got to do is call him an' make the connection. These're the Puerto Ricans so y' gotta watch out, don't let the middleman pick up the stuff 'cause he'll cut it before he delivers an' how yous gonna explain that to Tony?"

Dom nodded. "So I pick it up myself, right?"

"Right, let him take you over and yous can give him a couple C-notes for his trouble. He may try ta shake ya down for more but...," The goon paused, as though considering something that was his specialty. "Like I said, y' gotta watch out. But don't try an' fight 'em or they'll cut ya inta little pieces. Remember that. An' I wouldn't screw up, neither, 'cause we got ways a makin' it kinda unpleasant, too, see?"

"When do I leave?" Dom asked, ignoring the threat.

"Like I said, tomorrow evening," Spanky replied. "Meet us same spot at five sharp. Call the middleman from La Guardia airport in New York an' he'll pick yous up. Here's the name an' the number. He's expectin' ya at around seven-thirty or eight." Spanky handed him a folded piece of paper, paused while Dom memorized it, then continued. "Then when yous get back it should be around midnight, one o'clock. Call us an' we'll pick yous up—not at the airport—we'll tell ya where, okay, kid?"

They drove him back through the run-down neighborhood, dropped him on the same corner. People as old as the houses were stirring on the rickety porches or poking around in cramped, overgrown dooryards. Children flocked together, playing, running in the narrow streets and some of them called to the tall youth. He smiled and waved to them. He liked children, liked the way they made him smile.

Going upstairs to his room, he lay down, conscious of the fear stirring inside him. It was a way of life, just as it had been in Vietnam. Over there he had discovered that real fear was the threat of death or mutilation at any moment, no longer imaginary or abstract, but real. In combat it ate at him day and night, sat on his back and dug its claws into his flesh, distracted him from even the basic functions of eating and sleeping. But there was one thing that had brought relief because it stood for something positive in his life, something to struggle for in this bombed-out hell he had come into, and that was his love for Brenda that glowed so warmly within him and the joy at knowing that it was mutual. And when he wrote her it was as though he were whispering into her very ear once more and feeling the softness of her hair on his face.

He wrote often, every day when he was not on patrol, and though the real message in his letters was his love for her, he had to fill them somehow, with comments about the weather, the countryside, or about his buddies. He tried to strike a note of optimism and confidence about his tour of duty overseas and said things like, "I think what we're doing here is right because it will help end the war", or, "The South Vietnamese need our help because they're up against a tough enemy who wants to take over their country". Like many GI's he did not write about things that might upset the people back home—details of combat, of civilian air strike victims, body counts, of American casualties, some from fragging incidents or from accidents with friendly bombs and artillery. He did not go into the squalor of war-torn cities filled with homeless refugees living in packing crates, the streets teeming with young prostitutes and war orphans, some disfigured, hobbling on crutches. Nor did he mention how many of the people resented foreign troops on their soil and while some responded with courtesy, others retaliated with violence, using a surprising assortment of weapons ranging from modern armaments to homemade booby traps loaded with scrap metal and human excrement, or pits of manure bristling with spikes. And he also omitted the bitter reprisals of the American troops against this aggression. Dom was a hero at home and so wrote hero's letters. He did not write of the horrors of war.

As often as he waited to die, hugging the dirt in his bunker, the earth trembling from mortar blasts, or prowling the night jungle on patrol, the enemy lying somewhere near, he thought of going home. It would be just as it was then, during his last visit after boot camp when he had only a few days to spend before going overseas. Lean, tanned, and in top shape, he cut the very figure of a combat infantryman. They all admired him more than ever, especially Brenda. She stayed the night at his house after another elaborate dinner. The family, sensing that the two young people wanted to be alone, had retired early. Brenda's room was downstairs and so the two of them were not disturbed.

They clung to one another the whole night. Between lovemaking they talked drowsily, their cheeks pressed close, then drifted into a semi-sleep for a few moments before reawakening. Toward dawn she had cried, not briefly as she sometimes did during intense moments of desire, but wept silently, her cheeks wet on his. "Dom. . . ," she murmured, "I love you so much! I don't know what I'll do when you go. . . !"

"Remember what your mother said," he went on. "Absence makes the heart grow fonder. While I'm gone our love will grow. I'll write every day. It'll be almost as though I'm right at your side every minute."

"I'll wait!" she exclaimed. "I won't be able to stand it without you ... oh, Dom!" She buried her head in his shoulder and sobbed.

"You'll be all right," he consoled. "Think of all the other girls that go through the same thing. What about the Second World War? Guys were gone four and five years. But we're young, sweetheart, we've got plenty of time."

She kissed him again and again, many times, as though trying to get in all of those kisses that she would miss over the next year. And a woman in love is really something beautiful, he thought as he held her, and she was in love with him—he was the lucky guy.

At the airport he kissed his whole family goodbye and hugged the weeping girl for one last eternal second before going up the ramp into the plane. He turned, saw his father waving proudly, his mother trying to hold back her emotions, and Brenda, her dark eyes still shining with tears. And he saw that she was not so brave, but so very beautiful and he was never more heartsick to leave her than at that moment. Even months later, the thought of lying close to the girl he loved and feeling her softness, her lips, and sharing her passion, was almost more than he could bear.

Perhaps that is why he was drawn to a little boy he met in Vietnam, scraping about in a rubbish heap near a bombed-out village. Himself loved, Dom could reach out to others, could share his love. He gave the boy a chocolate, watched him claw at the wrapper and look up with grateful, dark eyes, her eyes almost. Through an interpreter the boy said he was five years old. His family had disappeared after the bombs fell. He was very hungry and wanted food. Like a puppy he followed the patrol back to the firebase. Since he was too young to pose any threat to security, Dom was allowed to take him inside. Again he fed him and again saw the wide, dark eyes thanking him. And he fell in love with this boy.

By the end of the week the whole company had adopted him. He followed Dom wherever he went, sat in his lap and ate from his plate, even slept beside him. Dom read him stories from comic books and the boy pointed at the pictures and laughed, babbled in Vietnamese. His first word in English was "Dom", so they named him "Little Dom". He made all of their lives fuller, this little boy, and Dom wanted to keep him. He wanted to start the paperwork for adoption. It took a great deal of time and red tape, but if approved he could take the boy home with him when he left. He wrote Brenda about the child, sent snapshots of the two of them together. She replied that it was a wonderful thing to do but that she should talk it over with her parents.

41

Because Dom had never done anything badly, and because he believed in himself and in his country, he became a good soldier. And he had to be in order to survive. He was the best point man in the company and also the longest-lived, with an unusual twenty-seven days on point to his credit. His company trusted him and even when he was not on point the CO would send him crawling ahead to size up the situation.

"I don't like it up there, sir," he said to the lieutenant one steamy, tropical afternoon. "It's too quiet and you can see signs, like the grass trampled down in places."

Lieutenant Foley, a young, eager ROTC graduate just out of boot camp, lifted his helmet, wiped his smooth, perspiring face with his sleeve, and turned to the sergeant. "Whaddaya think, sarge?"

"I go along with DeCosta," the veteran soldier replied uneasily. "I think we oughta follow the ridge over there instead, go through the bush instead of followin' this trail. This is suicide. . . ."

"Look!" the lieutenant snapped nervously and glanced again at his watch. "It's already fifteen hundred hours! Now that's way out of our way to go up there! It'll take us another hour just to get over to Hill 34!" He pointed to the convoluted rings on a contour map he drew from a hip pocket, then jerked his head at a shell-pocked summit devoid of trees, looming out of the jungle two miles distant like a scorched, scrofulous skull. "Now we've got a job to do and it's to reconnoitre our objective and get back to battalion, and we can't do it by laying down here on our backs like a buncha broads!"

"But sir. . . !"

"That's an order—we move out!"

The sergeant sullenly wiped the sweat from his eyes, gazed at the young officer and then at Dom with disbelief. "Yes, sir. . . ," he mumbled.

The patrol moved out and was well into the saddle in the ridge when they were hit. Two men dropped in their tracks, the others diving for cover and returning the fire. A soldier rolled over, reached for a clip of ammo in his back pocket and a burst from an AK-47 severed his arm neatly at the shoulder. Bullets smacked into the dirt and mortars and grenades crashed in among the dozen men sprawled in the elephant grass. Another man was hit and the lieutenant scrambled for the radio pack, called for air support.

"Spread out! Go after 'em!" yelled the sergeant, firing his grenade launcher into the trees.

Dom crawled a few feet, raised his M-16 rifle and got off another clip at ground level, then saw the machine gunner slump dead over his weapon. He crawled over, pushed the body to one side and began firing the M-60 machine gun into the tree line, raking the jungle with long bursts. Then he was aware of an impact lifting him up bodily and hurling him backwards. He lay stunned, paralyzed, looking up at the sun. It blazed down on him with blinding intensity and he felt small and helpless under it, like a child. The fighting, though all around him, seemed far away now. There was only this solitary, burning globe in the pale blue sky that bathed him with its eternal brightness, lulled him with its gentle warmth even at the moment of his death, and with the message, as though spoken from on high, that all of the small tragedies of mankind came to nothing under this proud brilliance that would survive forever, shining through an eternity.

Then he became aware of the gunfire thundering around him and knew that he was still alive. He tried to move, finally rolled over, noticed blood oozing out of his sleeve. He saw his M-16 rifle and clutched at it but could not fire it because his arm would not obey him.

The hostile fire slackened as survivors of the patrol spread out to lob grenades and fire burst after burst into the jungle. Then came a break in the firing and all was silent. Dom saw the blood running over his hand, drenching his entire sleeve from the shoulder down. Flies crawled on the fresh blood and he shooed them off. Dimly he remembered it was his pitching arm but did not dwell on it. At least he was alive. A gunship arrived a few minutes later, made a pass over them while the sergeant fired a red smoke grenade into the tree line. Like a great bird swooping down after its prey, it came in low and riddled the area with .50 caliber fire, the big slugs tearing the trees into splinters. Then they heard the throbbing drone of a second chopper, the medevac with its red cross clearly visible on the fuselage. It hovered, then settled down with the gunship covering. Two medics ran out, took on three badly wounded men, one of them the young officer.

"I'm hit, too!" Dom yelled to the medic, holding his blood soaked arm and attempting to rise.

"Better get on, then," said the sergeant, helping him to his feet and supporting him until he reached the chopper.

Even before they landed at the hospital fifteen minutes away, a medic had taken a morphine syrette out of his treatment bag. Holding it against Dom's leg, he pressed the button on the end of the syrette and Dom felt the jab of the spring-driven needle. Then the throbbing, knife-like pain in his arm and shoulder started to wane. He had a strangely pleasant feeling of mild drowsiness and composure in the midst of groaning, dying men.

The medevac chopper slanted toward a broad scar in the jungle, one of the larger firebases in the division area, and settled into a sprawling array of tents pitched well within the perimeter, their red crosses clearly visible. This was a MASH unit, or Mobile Army Surgical Hospital, a tiny island of mercy, of life, in a dark sea of pain and death. Dom climbed out unaided to give the medics more room to unload litter cases. He waited inside the triage tent for forty minutes while two medical officers examined the more serious casualties, deciding whether or not to operate. A chest wound was rushed to surgery, followed by a perforating abdominal wound. A head wound, considered more grave but less treatable, was evacuated by chopper to a field hospital many miles to the south.

"Shrapnel in the arm and shoulder, eh?" observed one of the young doctors as a medic snipped off his shirt. "You were lucky. . . ." He probed and poked, then nodded. "Doesn't look like a fracture. We'll check it by Xray. Feel this-this-this? Move the hand up, down, make a fist. Open. Uh-huh, nerves are intact. You were lucky, soldier."

"A million dollar wound," quipped the medic.

"Not exactly," retorted the captain. "It's a helluva nuisance to carry shrapnel around in your arm for the rest of your life."

The Xray showed that a bone had been chipped and over a dozen tiny metal fragments were scattered through the soft tissues of the right arm and shoulder. Two hours later, in the operating room, they numbed the arm with a local nerve block and cleaned out the puncture wounds, picking out bits of cloth and metal if they could find them, irrigating the holes with sterile saline solution. Then they applied a bulky dressing and immobilized the arm in a sling.

"We'll send you back to the field hospital for a rest," said the medical officer. "Just as soon as we're sure there isn't any serious infection."

They gave him a bed and he undressed, lay down, had some supper. As the local anesthesia wore off the throbbing pain returned. And he began to worry now if he would be able to pitch. Then something unexpected happened—he cried briefly, cried about his arm, and about the other men groaning in the tent because he knew some of them were dying. A medic appeared, stood like a shadow at the bedside.

"Have any pain?" he asked.

"Yeah, it's keepin' me awake," Dom replied.

He felt the wet alcohol on his arm and the jab of a needle. The same pleasant sensation flooded through him again and the pain faded. He felt less despair now, thought how he was lucky after all, how things could have been much worse. And he would pitch again, no matter what it took. He drifted into a restless sleep but was soon awakened by the noise in the tent, the groaning of the wounded, someone crying for a medic, the movements and low conversation of the doctors and medics checking the patients, taking blood pressures, setting up pints of blood. One man stopped groaning and his bunk was soon surrounded with personnel attempting to revive him by thumping and shoving at his chest. Then they gave up and called in a chaplain, who muttered a few words of prayer before they caried him out. The bed remained empty for only a few minutes before a new casualty was brought in from surgery, slowly awakening from the anesthesia to lie groaning like the man before him. Soon Dom himself joined the chorus of piteous cries, calling again for more morphine to quell the pain that gnawed at his arm and shoulder like a thousand knives. He received three more shots of morphine that night, each one spreading a soft gauze of warmth over him, the pain melting into a dull ache for two or three hours while he dozed back into a fitful, dreamlike state halfway between sleep and wakefulness.

He found himself caught in a deeply troubling dream filled with grief and sadness, in which he heard not only the groans of the wounded but the throbbing roar of choppers arriving and leaving and the distant rumble of bombs and artillery, with an occasional explosion quite near and shaking the earth under the tent. And this was war, he kept saying to himself over and over, where people were trying their hardest to kill one another, as though it were proper and even necessary. For it seemed somehow that everything bright and joyous in life cast its equivalent shadow of darkness, so that wherever there was happiness there had to be suffering. Having known heaven, Dom had arrived in hell, a perpetual night of slaughter, a place filled with demons bent on destroying one another.

The next morning, he learned that the man who had died during the night was his young commanding officer, Lieutenant Foley. Dom waited until the medical officer had finished their rounds, then he asked a sergeant if it could be arranged for him to return to his unit as quickly as possible. The sergeant conferred with one of the captains, who came over to the bedside.

"If you leave now, I can't guarantee that you won't have complications," the captain said sternly.

"I'll be all right," Dom insisted, intent on leaving because he was worried about Little Dom. "Just give me some morphine to kill the pain. I'll get the company medic to check it and change the dressing."

The medical officer shrugged impatiently to the sergeant. Both of them badly overworked, they had no time to quibble with soldiers who wanted to go back into action. Usually it was the other way around, where they had to argue with those who had very minor wounds and who wanted to stay for a prolonged convalescence. It was their objective to keep as many soldiers fighting as was humanly possible, and so they consented to his leaving after giving him instructions to see his battalion surgeon as soon as he arrived. And the sergeant handed him a box. "You'll need this," he said. It contained a dozen morphine syrettes.

42

The medevac chopper streaked low over the jungle to avoid enemy fire, ferrying Dom and two other minor casualties back to the firebase. They spotted it in the distance, a vulnerable bald spot atop one of the misty, shell-pocked hills.

"It's a good thing Charlie ain't got air cover," drawled one of the men as they banked toward the firebase.

"With them mortars an' rockets they don't need none," remarked another.

Even before they landed they could see unusual activity. Everyone was up out of the bunkers, loading trucks, hitching up guns. "Battalion's goin' on a search an' destroy mission," one of the medics informed them as they climbed out of the aircraft and ran out from under the whirling rotors. Dom went into his bunker, found it empty except for his pack and field gear. Searching for Little Dom, he discovered him standing next to the mess truck. The child tried to run away at first and hid his eyes, but Dom caught him up, laughing, and kissed him, and the child hugged him around the neck.

"Dom! Dom!" the little boy chattered excitedly and went on in Vietnamese, pointing at the cooks.

One of them, a young private, grinned. "He's been talkin' 'bout you ever minute since you left," he said. "We had to keep his mouth full just to shut 'im up. 'Course we can't understand 'im er nothin' but I think he wondered if you was maybe kilt er somethin!"

Dom smiled at the child. "I'm okay," he said. "Okay...."

"Okay...," echoed the child and bubbled with laughter, and the sound of it was as pure and delightful as anything Dom had ever heard. He put the child down and they walked off together, holding hands.

The first sergeant saw them and called out. "How's your arm, DeCosta?"

"Shrapnel. They said I'd be all right."

The sergeant eyed the sling with skepticism, then the little boy. "You can't take him on this sweep, y'know that. We expect to make contact with that North Vietnamese regiment to the west of us. Matter a' fact, you shouldn't even be goin' yourself."

"I'll have to take him along," said Dom. "He's mine."

The NCO reflected for a moment. "In that case, I got a better idea," he continued. "They're detailin' a few of our guys to go TDY as advisors to one a' them fortified hamlets. From what I hear it'll be rough but I think you got the experience and the guts to qualify. And you can find someone there to take care of the kid."

"I'll take it," Dom agreed without a moment's hesitation.

He wheedled another dozen morphine syrettes from the medical supply sergeant in headquarters company, after the battalion surgeon supervised the changing of his dressing. So far there was no sign of infection, though the arm was very stiff and painful. That evening he said goodbye to his buddies, some of whom he knew he would never see again. At 0500h the next morning the battalion of eight hundred infantrymen moved out, the gunships churning up the dust and the convoy of trucks, jeeps, and armored personnel carriers growling down the mountain, winking their pale orange, cat eye lights in the gray dawn. Pack-laden troops marched on either side of the vehicles in a shadowy single file, five yards apart.

Dom met the other two men assigned as advisors. Lt. Trager, their CO, was a pudgy, quiet, round-faced first lieutenant from North Carolina. Spec-4 James, a radioman, was the opposite—a tall, gangling, voluble black youth from Detroit.

They waited until eleven hundred hours, when a lone chopper arrived from division with newly cut orders to pick them up. They went aboard with their gear, Dom holding the child in his arms. The turbojet engine whined to a high pitch, lifted them up into a bright tropical morning, the jungle a dull emerald blur sliding beneath them. After forty minutes they veered down over a village of about two hundred huts surrounded by a wide expanse of flooded rice paddy. The rusty, sheet metal roofs of the huts blended with the clay streets teeming with the inhabitants and their animals, some moving busily out through the main gate into the fields. A wall of fortifications surrounded the entire village, a barrier of sandbags, trenches, and barbed wire.

"Loc Nan," announced the crew chief. "I'll tell you right now, no matter what they say, this place is lousy with gooks. We take hits flyin' through here all the time and they say this hamlet gets somethin' almost every night."

"Thanks for the encouragement," drawled Trager. "I 'magine we'll find out for ourselves soon enough."

After they landed the three of them were officially welcomed by a Mr. Vien. He was the village chief, an ebullient, high cheekboned man of early middle age who had the restless, haunted look of someone high on the Vietcong assasination list.

"I very happy American soldah come," the headman said rapidly in broken English and pointed anxiously to an ancient drum tower standing in the middle of the village with half its roof in shambles. "Last night makee mohtah attack. . . ." His hands flitted up in the motion of an explosion. "Two die."

They also met Major Huong, commander of the ARVN company garrisoned in the village. He was a short, stocky man, impeccably dressed with a field cap, dark glasses, and a pair of binoculars slung around his neck. He courteously introduced Captain Trung, commander of the small local militia. Very proper and gracious, the captain was somewhat older, with white hair and a Ho Chi Minh beard. He limped noticeably from an old wound, explaining in sing-song French that he fought with that army before Dien Bien Phu.

After settling into their bunkers and inspecting the perimeter, the Americans, except for James who was told to man his radio, were invited to dine with the village chief and the officers. At dinner, Mr. Vien did all the talking and mainly seemed interested in practicing his pidgin English.

But he made it a point to address his servants in excellent French. His family, he explained, was once very well-to-do, of aristocratic origin, and still owned much of the land around the village. He was convinced that the Americans would help the government save the country from the Vietcong and from the North. He despised the northerners as invaders and felt that the Vietcong, many of whom were southerners, were traitors who thought nothing of killing or maiming their own people to get their way. "We fight till last communist dead!" he exclaimed, shaking a tight, bony fist.

Dom had arranged through the chief to have Little Dom cared for by a *mamma san,* a spry old Vietnamese woman with a sharp twinkle in her eye. She spoke rapidly in Vietnamese with emphatic gestures, apparently easily ruffled over trifles. Yes, she would be glad to take him in. There were so many like him and it would cost only fifteen American dollars a month. And then the interpreter laughed and refused to translate what else the old woman was saying. Dom prompted him and the interpreter broke into a toothy grin, pointed to a nubile girl standing in the doorway.

"She say she have nice granddaughtah," the interpreter explained. "Make nice wife fo' soldah. You take her to you house tonight . . . she say you like very much."

Dom glanced at the girl who looked down bashfully with graceful, dark eyes, the loose pajamas almost concealing the voluptuous curves of her hips and budding breasts. He guessed her age at about fourteen, possibly a virgin. He could not help imagining the smoothness of her skin, so very soft against his, and thought about how long it was since he had been with a woman. Yet the inevitable complications of such a union deterred him, for he suspected he would be asked to marry the girl. And besides, he wanted most of all to stay faithful to Brenda.

He smiled politely to the old woman, bowed ever so slightly. "Thank you," he said. "Your granddaughter is very pretty. I am sure she will make a good wife. But I must do my job to defend your village against enemy attack."

The reply impressed the old woman but brought a flash of hurt into the girl's eyes and she disappeared into the house.

The village was hit the second night they were there. Dom had just stood watch in the sandbagged tower and had used a morphine syrette in order to get some sleep, but the pain woke him up again around two o'clock. He was just about to break out a second syrette when a round whooshed in and erupted in a yellow flash. The deafening roar was followed by bits of shrapnel and debris rattling off the tower. Villagers began yelling and screaming as they scurried into underground bunkers. More rounds came in and the South Vietnamese troops, some of whom had just returned from patrol, opened up blindly with mortars and automatic weapons. Someone fired a magnesium flare to illuminate the periphery and it burst brilliantly in the night sky, drifting slowly earthward like a falling star, casting a faint, eerie light across the paddies and onto the forested hillside. The garrison now concentrated their fire on suspicious shadows. The machine gunner in the tower opened up just beside Dom, sending streaks of orange tracers out into the night.

"No, no!" Dom yelled to Captain Trung. "He'll draw fire!"

A hail of bullets struck the tower, spintered the wood and whacked into sandbags as they sprawled belly down on the floor. A militiaman dropped his ancient French rifle and collapsed, holding his face, as Dom cranked the radio and contacted his CO. "Bravo to Xray! Taking heavy fire from hillside northwest corner, range about two hundred fifty yards, over!"

Trager crackled a reply and redirected the fire onto the hillside, laying down an awesome barrage of tracers, mortars, and artillery. It was answered from the surrounding forest, mortars and rockets whooshing in one after another and crashing into the village with bright flashes. Moments later Dom fired a flare out over the periphery behind them and as it hovered and glowed, he saw the shapes of men running across the paddies below.

"Sappers!" he cried to Captain Trung and pointed with his grenade launcher. Trung pushed aside the young militiaman at the machinegun, turned it around and raked the field with fire, while Dom loaded and fired grenades as best he could with one arm. Then the flare died out, covered the enemy in a protective blanket of darkness. Another flare was fired and several men were seen throwing bamboo mats over the concertina of barbed wire and running on toward the sandbagged trenches. Then several more flares went up and in the phosphorescent light now nearly as bright as day, Dom could see the faces of these men as he and the entire garrison began firing at them. All but two went down, collapsing like miniature rag dolls. The survivors made it to the trenches, tossing grenade after grenade before they died.

Captain Trung's face wrinkled into a triumphant smile. *"Voila!"* he exclaimed. *"Ce fortresse est formidable, non? Vive les Americains!"*

They surveyed the damage at sunrise. Besides the militiaman killed in the tower, two ARVN soldiers died in the grenade attack and three more were wounded, one gravely. One villager died in the mortar barrage, an old woman, and four others were injured when a round barely missed their bunker, yet they were lucky because a direct hit would have killed them all. Medevac choppers busily droned back and forth, ferrying out the wounded, while people picked through the debris, salvaging what they could.

An ARVN patrol sallied out to recover four enemy bodies in the paddies, triumphantly bringing them in slung upside down on long poles. A battle report and official body count was radioed to division. The corpses of the two ARVN soldiers were flown out with the wounded while those of the militiaman and the old woman were prepared for burial. Their wreath-covered coffins were mourned and wept over for a whole day by the families and then interred to the solemn chanting of Buddhist prayer.

43

By the end of the week following the attack on the village, Dom and Specialist-4 James were tired and worn out from constant patrols. They requested permission from Lieutenant Trager to take a jeep ride over to An Khe, a much larger, neighboring village of several thousand, fortified like their own village and therefore considered secure.

Trager grinned at the request. "Sure," he said. "Been thinkin' 'bout goin' over m'self. Check out the hooches an' broads over there an' lemme know what gives."

Despite the morphine he had taken that morning, Dom felt considerable pain in his arm, partly because he had used it during the attack a few nights ago, and because the jeep bounced dangerously over the rough dirt road, deeply rutted by trucks and armored vehicles. They had less fear of ambush in daylight because the area was heavily patrolled by ARVN and American forces. By the peaceful rural surroundings, the grazing water buffalo, women working in rice paddies, and farmers driving bullock carts to market, they might never have known a war was going on, a violent conflict that set one village, one countryman against another and drew intricate lines between family, class, education, property, and religion. But if by day the land was comparatively peaceful, by night it was torn with fire and soaked with blood.

There was a second reason why neither of them was too concerned about an ambush. Dom was just coming down off a high from morphine and James was smoking marihuana. In fact, the radioman's main purpose in going to An Khe was to buy some more. Like many troops in this unorthodox war, he had discovered that the very potent domestic cannabis steadied his nerves against the ever-present fear of sudden mutilation or death.

An Khe was large enough to have a main street with shops and even a few bars, or "hooches", as they were called by the GI's. These were patronized mostly by

ARVN soldiers, though one was inhabited by Americans. And there was even a touch of Saigon here, with teenaged streetwalkers loitering in doorways and prosperous civilian youths barrelling around on motorbikes. They parked and the Vietnamese driver stayed with the jeep while they went inside one of the hooches to ask for some marihuana. James located an old woman who made the sale, two packs of reefers rolled up to look just like regular cigarettes in Lucky Strike packs for one dollar apiece in military script.

"Hey, man," said James, tucking the roll of script back into his pocket. "It's still early. 'Stead a' gettin' all boozed up, wanna do some opium? That stuff is really outa sight, man! There oughta be a den around here somewheres."

"Better count me out," said Dom.

"Huh, what you sayin'? Why, man, that morphine's 'xactly same as opium, only this is the gum that they make from the milk that comes directly from the poppy itself, unnderstan'? Now c'mon, we wastin' time jus' standin' here jivin'." James laughed good-naturedly and propelled Dom out of the hooch.

By using the Vietnamese driver as an interpreter and offering him a small bribe, they were eventually directed to a second hooch next to a Buddhist temple and shown down a flight of stairs, through a series of cluttered storerooms filled with burlap sacks of rice. They mounted another staircase and found themselves in a dimly lit room with elaborate mandalas painted on the walls and a polished statue of Buddha himself visible through a distant doorway. An elderly monk approached the two soldiers with a cordial smile.

"Smoke?" James asked, making the appropriate gesture.

The monk nodded. "*Fumer? Oui,* smo-king! Come, sit down, please. . . ."

They sat down on a bamboo mat and as their eyes became accustomed to the gloom they saw three or four other people stretched out on mats. Momentarily the monk brought back a large bowlful of smoldering opium resin with tubes running from it fitted with mouthpieces. James paid him the equivalent of fifty cents in military script.

"We can smoke all day if we want," he said happily as he took a deep drag and held it in.

"We better not stay too long," said Dom, "or we'll end up like that guy over there. . . ." He pointed into a corner where an emaciated old man lay like a somnolent skeleton on a mat. As they watched, wondering whether he was dead or alive, he groped for his opium bowl, slipped the tubing between his lips and with eyes dreamily closed, he puffed the fragrant smoke blissfully.

"Wow, he's really wasted on the stuff," murmured James.

"He must be too stoned even to eat," observed Dom.

As they smoked from the smoldering bowl between them Dom felt the same tantalizing euphoria that he had with the morphine, and again his pain was eased. And the opium took care of something else he had been feeling lately, an uncomfortable stiffness in his muscles, sweating, shakiness, and diarrhea that came on after the morphine had worn off. He had rightly guessed it was a withdrawal reaction and noticed that now, as he got high on the opium, all this disappeared and there was not even the tiniest pain or trace of discomfort in his entire body.

"I'm really gettin' a buzz," James gloated. "Wow, man, how 'bout you?"

"I feel high, but it's not too different from the morphine," Dom said.

"Keep smokin', man, an' you'll be spaced. Me, I'm gonna roll a joint. Wanna hit?"

Dom did not ordinarily smoke marihuana because it made him dopey and sluggish, but now he shared the joint with James and found it augmented the effect of the opium. They both felt peaceful and far removed from the war and the constant fear of booby traps and ambushes.

"Man, I dig bein' stoned," James was saying. "That way you got a better chance a' comin' outa this thing alive than if you're straight. Now looka me, man, been point man, been in a couple ambushes where practically every cat took hits, but me, I ain't gotta scratch on my beautiful body. . . ."

"I can see what you mean, in a way," Dom admitted. "You're more relaxed, more at ease."

The conversation shifted to women. James's old lady had a kid by him but he had refused to marry her and had joined the service instead. Dom spoke of his engagement and showed pictures of his girl. Yet for the first time, even as James admired her beauty, Dom looked at Brenda's smiling face with a sense of detachment, as though she were something abstract, part of another world obscured now by the immediacy of war, by the ordeal of survival here in this tropical land, in this hell of human suffering and pain. And if women were meant to give comfort, they served no purpose here where animal guts and the will to go on were all that mattered. He and James did not need or want them when the opium could deaden their senses.

Dom did not realize how high he really was until he tried to stand up an hour later. The two of them could hardly walk. They staggered upstairs out of the opium den, the old monk escorting them, and finally arrived back in the hooch.

"Hey, I'm really fucked up good on this shit, man," James was mumbling. His face had a slack, mask-like expression with tiny, pinpoint pupils. Dom guessed he looked the same way, certainly not as American soldiers on or off duty ought to look.

"I'm gonna cop me some dynamite smack while we're here." the radioman went on thickly. "But don't say nothin' to Trager 'cause he won't unnerstan', see? Like one of the reasons I came to Nam is 'cause the dope here is the most. It's pure an' like it grows on trees just about. But squares like Trager are in this bag of winnin' a buncha medals an' gittin' all us black people killed doin' it, an' that ain't too cool, but like that's where his head is comin' from, unnerstan'?"

James found the old *mamma san* who ran the hooch and asked her a question, held his thumb and forefinger against his arm as if pressing a syringe. She nodded, said something in sing-song Vietnamese and a small boy ran out of the hooch. They sat down, had a watery Vietnamese beer. James was telling Dom how he had been using heroin off

238

and on back in Detroit since he was ten, and that his
mother was in jail at the present time serving a long
sentence for dealing. Presently the boy returned, handed a
small vial filled with white powder to the *mamma san.*

"Fi-dollah," she demanded shrilly and James gave it to
her in military script.

"Is that really heroin?" Dom asked.

"Um-hm! This is pure dope!" James replied proudly.
"All you need is a tiny pinch or you'll OD. 'Course me, I
could do half of it an' still be okay. You don't even have
to cook it. It jus' dissolves, it's so pure." James tucked it
carefully into his pocket and smiled. "Why, back in
Detroit this would be worth five hundred dollars on the
street."

They climbed back into the jeep and woke the sleeping
driver. Then they in turn fell asleep on the bumpy trip
back to the village. When they woke up they had arrived in
Loc Nan. They were surprised when the driver pointed to
several bullet holes in the vehicle that they had taken
about three miles back. He explained in pidgin English that
he floored it and sped away when he heard the shots.

James grinned sleepily. "See what I mean, man?" he
chuckled, "In this war, you're better off high!"

44

Dom lay in his room smoking a cigarette, watching the
window shade burn yellow and then slowly grow dim in
the summer evening. He lived the life of a shut-in as a
dealer, going out only to sell or to make his connections.
He shunned humanity because basically he had no friends,
only customers who hounded him day and night. He alone
possessed their heart's desire, something that they were
willing to degrade themselves, to commit crime for. So he
could never really trust them as friends, could never turn
his back on them.

He gazed again at the dimming shade, wondering whether it had been drawn against the world outside by his own hand or by the hand of fate. He felt trapped and powerless, burdened by the agony of the uncontrollable compulsion of his addiction, by the pain of having to submit to it and to suffer the inevitable consequences. He pondered what it would mean for his "man" to place ten thousand dollars in cash in his hands at a time when he would be dopesick. Perhaps he would not be able to help himself and would cop with some of the money and later try to beat someone to recover the difference. He did not know, and was afraid.

He got up and dressed, stiff all over from the growing dopesickness. Out of dope, he had to go out and cop now like a common street addict. Reluctantly, he called up Martin Shine.

"I'm flattered," said Martin, his sarcastic, gravelly voice sounding much older over the phone. "Meet me over at Danny's in about an hour. A few of us are getting together for pizza and to watch a little TV. And who knows, we may even get high."

"Save a few bags for me, goddammit," Dom muttered.

Danny lived at home with his parents in a respectable, middle class neighborhood. They were not natives of the area but had moved up from New Jersey several years ago in order to get their son away from his addict friends. They were very concerned about him, especially his mother, who had heard how dopefiends have to steal and get mugged and robbed by other dopefiends. So for his own protection she gave him enough money out of her purse to support his habit. Then he would not have to steal or otherwise risk his life. And she even drove him around to his connections and waited nearby while he copped in relative safety.

Occasionally this well-intentioned woman would get it into her head that Danny should stop using. She would refuse to give him the money, but without fail it sent her ordinarily docile son into one of his surprisingly violent tantrums. Screaming and shouting, he would smash chairs against the walls, throw things, and otherwise terrify his shocked parents. Not even his father could control him then and finally, short of calling the police, they always gave in. Yet, in talking to his several therapists, they never admitted their role as accomplices in their son's addiction, carrying on instead about the hopelessness of his condition and how they had suffered so on account of it.

Dom rang the doorbell of the neat, single family home and a flustered, dumpy woman with a vague look of nervous apprehension answered the door.

"Why, hello! Come on in!" she managed to say, after an initial period of befuddlement, and gave an uncertain smile. "Danny and the others are in the den watching TV. It's nice to know that he has so many nice friends who come and visit him like this, don't you think? And what is your name?"

"Dom. . . ."

"Dom? That's a nice name. It's short for Dominick, isn't it?"

"Yes."

"This is Danny's father," she went on, gesturing toward the living room.

A newspaper in one corner collapsed with a loud rattle to reveal a wiry, pessimistic looking man with a thin mustache, who eyed Dom sharply. "Hello," he said disagreeably and hoisted the paper again, almost as if to shut out the world around him and Dom recalled the dimming window shade in his room screening his own view of the world.

Entering the den he was surprised to find nearly the entire ingroup that hung in The Prophet—Danny, Russ and Dolores, Jackie and Rolf, Martin Shine, and even Sam, the joiner. Hard rock welled up from a stereo in the corner and a television glimmered in the shadows against the wall, its sound barely audible beneath the thumping music. The only other source of light came from a large blue, decorative candle flickering on a low table in the center of the room, and dimly illuminating the faces of the guests as eerie, grinning masks.

"Hey, Dom baby, how ya feelin?" Russ crowed.

" 'Lo, Dom," said Danny. "Sit down and relax.

"Hello there," offered Sam, and smiled mechanically.

Dom squatted on the floor, crossed his long legs stiffly. By the trembling of his hands and the staring look in his eyes they sensed he was sick. Dolores was the first to make a gesture of sympathy.

"Want to try some good grass?" she asked attentively, and offered him a joint.

He took a long hit and after a moment the candle grew brighter and the people seemed to slow down and freeze in their places, almost like grotesque puppets smirking impishly at him. He always felt a little uncomfortable on strong grass for some reason, stiff and wooden, himself a puppet in the hands of this hallucinogenic drug. He grinned back, feeling a little ridiculous as they kept passing the joint around until it was reduced to a tiny glowing roach, discarded at last when it scorched the lips of the smokers.

Dolores yielded to a powerful urge to eat and delved into the potato chips with a loud crackle.

"Got the munchies?" Jackie piped up. "It is good grass."

"Sure it isn't treated?" asked Rolf in his deep, sonorous voice, asking this delicate question in an amiable rather than disdainful manner, for he was always the gentleman.

"I don't think so," Danny asserted loudly. "It's just good grass, real Alcapulco Gold. I bought a whole lid of it."

"Can I have some of the seeds?" Jackie asked.

"Sure."

There was a pause, everyone regarding one another with a spritely playfulness.

"I'm spaced," someone said.

"Me, too. Wow, that candle looks weird. . . ," said another.

"You all look weird, you know it?" said Jackie.

"You do, too," said Martin.

With a cat-ate-the-canary grin, Jackie turned to Dom, an obvious outsider. "I'll bet you don't know something," she teased.

"What?"

"We're all tripping . . . can't you tell?"

"On acid?" he replied. "So that's why everyone looks so freaked out."

"Yup. Marty has some. Wanna try it? It's smo-o-o-oth!" she purred contendly, like a connoisseur who has discovered excellence after a long search.

"No thanks," Dom said absently. "I came to see Martin. . . ."

Shine rolled over and sat up like a chubby, mischievous jack-in-the-box. "I've got some good mescaline, too," he croaked, "and some of that THC the kids're doing. It's kind of like acid in a way."

"I never was much of an acid head," Dom said tiredly, addressing the fat man. "What I need is a half load of your best if you've got it." He paused, turned to Dolores. "And I could use a few of your dollies if you have any extras, just in case I get stuck somewhere."

"Are you taking a trip?" Danny interrupted, guessing that his friend had something weighing on his mind.

Dom nodded, unsmiling. "I have to go down to New York tomorrow night, so. . . ." He caught himself, looked at Sam, who dropped his eyes.

"Dope's gettin' tight around here, that's for sure," Russ observed with seriousness. "Makin' a connection?"

"You're own or Motto's?" Shine asked drily.

Dom flinched. "I. . . ."

"Sure. . . ," Shine added apologetically, understanding his not wanting to talk.

"Well, I hope you bring back some quality stuff," Russ jabbered on, in a lame attempt to cover up Shine's deliberate slip.

Shine grinned. " 'S all right, Russ ol' pal. But it's true, things are tight. Feds must've grabbed some real weight down in New York, 'cause they say a two dollar bag down there has gone up to three and a five dollar bag is seven nowadays." He shoved a pudgy hand into his pocket and pulled out some glassine packets. "How many?"

"A half load."

"For you that's only sixty bucks."

"Thanks." Dom handed Martin the money, then turned to Sam, who was watching them. "You do dope?" he said ironically.

"You asked me that at Jackie's wedding," Sam replied politely, his eyes steady. "I do mostly downers. . . ."

Dom ignored the reply, as though nothing Sam could say would change a certain preconceived notion that Dom had of him. Abruptly, he excused himself and went into the bathroom where he dumped four of the bags into his cooker, added a few drops of water, struck a match under the bottle cap. Tying himself off, he drew the already curdled sludge laboriously through a cotton and booted it into his old, calloused vein. He waited and then cursed—it was garbage. Stuffing his works back into his pocket, he emerged from the bathroom in a silent rage.

"This stuff has everything but dope in it, including the kitchen sink," he grumbled.

"That's 'cause you've been shootin' dealer's dope," Shine argued. "So naturally you don't feel it."

"I did four bags!" Dom yelled suddenly, losing his temper. "Now gimme my money back, before I. . . !"

"Hey, take it easy!" Rolf intervened. "Marty doesn't mean any harm. Marty, why don't you give him back the money if he isn't satisfied."

"Look, a deal's a deal!" Shine insisted stubbornly. "Dom, ol' pal, if I was sellin' dealer's dope I'd have to charge thirty bucks a bag for it, you know that? So let's be reasonable."

"Why don't you take some of my methadone," said Dolores, again with her special gentleness that she reserved for him alone. "At least, you know what you're getting."

Still shaking from the jones, he bought thirty ten milligram dolophines from Dolores for only forty dollars, a giveaway, because she obviously liked him and wanted to show it in front of the others, her boyfriend included. He popped ten of them on the spot and after about twenty minutes felt a buzz—not like the rush he was used to on heroin, but a gathering warmth inside him that he knew would go on glowing for twelve hours or more. As he relaxed the group did also. Danny opened another bottle of wine and they lit a joint, began passing it around. Martin lay back on the floor, unruffled at Dom's flare of temper, and dozed off.

"He's been shootin' all day," said Jackie.

They studied him, envious of his blissful state. All of them knew about his twenty year history of using heroin, up to a quarter piece a day back when the dope was really good, when it took two weeks to kick a habit instead of two days. He still had a taste for the best, which was why he sold garbage to young junkies who, unless they were Vietnam veterans, did not know what good dope was and never would know. Even with a thirty year sentence hanging over his head if he was ever busted again, he kept right on dealing and shooting. He hardly worried about it when he was high, which was most of the time. The main thing he brooded about was his lack of good veins. His arms had burned out long ago, pocked with scars from the quinine in the heroin, from paregoric, where he had missed the hit, or from abscesses. He had taken to shooting into his jugular or into the veins under his tongue on occasion, but now, despite the danger of blood clots from phlebitis, he shot mainly into his legs. They were covered with so many tracks from the knees down that it looked as though he had run back and forth through a cactus patch. He said sadly that the only good vein left anywhere on his body was the one on his penis, but as much as he was tempted, he never used it. He was afraid that if he ever OD'd he would not be able to untie in time, and once the circulation was shut off, he would forfeit his manhood.

They kept watching his flaccid hulk, respiring peacefully on the floor, snoring softly.

"He's happier 'n a pig in shit," Jackie observed.

"I wish I was that happy," Danny sighed.

"Hope he don't OD," Russ said and nervously tapped out the syncopated beat of the rock music with his fingers. "I sure like that group," he went on. "Terrific sound, man. Makes me want to get back to playin' again. That's the only time I was really happy, when I was playin'."

"You'd have to get off coke, first," said Dolores emphatically. "I hear Slick is cleaning up, and Sherry too.

They're both in Comeback. He had a big habit, a bundle a day."

"Who?" asked Sam, leaning forward quizzically.

"You remember him—short, brown hair, kinda smiles all the time," she added.

"A real hard-nosed dopefiend," Russ spoke up. "An' I'll bet he's in there for the same reason the rest of 'em are, to stay outa jail."

"But he wasn't sent by the court," Dolores argued.

"No, but he has a lotta warrants out on him," said Danny. He took a sip of wine and stared at the candle. "Slick's different from the rest of us. He. . . ."

"I know what you mean," Dom interjected. "He'll rip anybody off."

"Most junkies have soft hearts," Danny continued. "They wouldn't hurt a fly if they could help it. All they want is dope. But him, he's something else."

There was a pause, no one disagreeing.

"The acid's wearing off," Rolf boomed out at last. "Jackie said so."

"I did not!" she said playfully.

"It is," Dolores agreed. "I'm starting to come down."

"A half tab isn't really enough," said Russ. "Wanna do a whole hit?"

"We'd be here all night," Sam remarked.

Dom stood up, feeling tired and not enjoying himself. He stared briefly at this circle of people. They were intoxicated with hallucinogens and looked ludicrous, even phony and affected in this artificial state of consciousness. He would have joined them in their never-never fairyland of illusion, but the thought of his own face grinning as idiotically as theirs, and his actions approaching the same height of absurdity, repelled him.

"Gotta get some sleep," he said. "I'm really beat. Thanks a lot for everything."

"Hey, be careful," Sam warned. "The junkies down in New York are like animals."

"Yeah? I thought you weren't into dope," Dom remarked with a wry smile.

Sam grinned sheepishly, gave a shrug. "Right, but I have a lot of friends who are."

"Well, I'll be back tomorrow night, sometime after midnight. See you people later," Dom said and waved as he left them.

In the living room Danny's mother popped up from her chair in front of the television, looking puzzled at his sudden reappearance. "Are you leaving?" she intoned. "Oh well, I hope you come back again. Danny is always glad to have visitors. . . ." She turned to her husband. "Benny, say goodbye to the boy."

" 'Bye," grumbled her husband without turning his head.

The woman showed Dom out, eyeing him with vigilance as he descended the front steps, checking warily for any sign of difficulty, as though watching the uncertain progress of an invalid. Dom had the feeling that she would have helped him across the street if he had given her his arm, and that as Danny's friend he was getting the same kind of worried attention that she lavished on her own son.

45

Slick did not intend to go back on dope so soon. It was just that another patient had a connection with one of the counselors for some really good junk. The kid got off on it right in front of Slick in the lavatory. After puking once, he grinned and said, "See, I told you it was dynamite! Wow! One bag an' I'm loaded! Try some!"

No junkie will pass up good dope if he can get his hands on it, even if he has kicked a hundred times over. The kid was right. It was dynamite, and Slick had a genuine nod sitting on the hopper for an hour. Naturally the other patients know what it means when one of their own tarries in the head for longer than a quarter of an hour, and so

Slick was caught with the set of works and pinned pupils. To avoid the indignity of immediate expulsion, or of having to remain and scrub out the same toilet all day long, or of otherwise sitting on a stool wearing a dunce cap and a sign around his neck saying "Fuckup", he discreetly ratted on the other patient, and on the counselor, too.

The accused staff member, who also happened to be one of the leaders of the program, vigorously denied the charge. "You sleazy dopefiend!" he shouted in a rage. "Tryin' to set me up, huh?" He pointed at a full length mirror on the wall, shoved Slick over in front of it. "Just look at yourself! Yeah, we're gonna get at ya! We're really gonna get at ya, man! Go ahead, look!"

Slick regarded the diminutive, haggard figure with thin brown whiskers grinning like a weasel in the mirror. "You're right," he said. "I am a sleazy dopefiend. So what?"

Rolando called a special meeting of the staff to decide on Slick's punishment. But before they could decide, he left, taking a transistor radio, a watch, ten dollars from someone's pocket book, and one of the girls. Her name was Mary, a quiet, nineteen-year-old who had her eye on Slick from the time he arrived, the type who cannot resist tempting a guy away from another girl. And because many addicts who turn off on dope get turned onto sex, the two of them had only one thing on their minds when they left. She took him back to her pad and after they ate, they balled for two hours. They rested, ate and balled again and then went out to sell the watch and radio. They got rid of them for twenty dollars. The next stop was The Prophet, where they hoped to find Dom. Inside they met Danny, sipping a beer.

"Dom's gone down to New York to make a connection," Danny explained. "He'll be back tonight, sometime after midnight."

"Seen Ramon?"

"Not for days."

"Any dope around?"

"Marty has some," Danny replied softly, looking around.

"Shit!" Slick cursed under his breath. He sat down and brooded, ordered a whisky and a beer, and a glass of wine for Mary. He did not like alcohol because it made him wild, but right now it was the only convenient thing around. He was gassed after the first round. It did not take much because he seldom drank. As he sat listening to the music and watching Mary's plain, sallow face, deeply lined and prematurely old from her excesses, his mind wandered back nearly two years to jail. There every night for six months he listened to the very same music in his five-by-twelve foot cell from 7:30 till 10:00 at night. Only then there were no women to look at and the music was amplified a hundred times, a bewildering cacophony of radios, tape decks, and stereos reverberating through the cell block. Then the lights went out at ten and there was silence except for men coughing, stirring, and the occasional pacing of the guards or the resounding crash of a steel door. And in thinking back, he remembered how jail had saved him, yet had changed his life.

It had come at a time when, if allowed to run loose for very much longer, he would have destroyed himself. Sent up on a two year sentence for grand larceny, he thought he was pretty tough coming to the county house of correction at the age of only nineteen. But like most beginners he was in for a surprise. Getting into the system was not easy.

The first few weeks inside the dreary brick walls were the hardest, especially trying to figure out where he belonged. After some observing, he noticed that the prisoners hung in cliques—the armed robbers stayed in one corner of the yard, the junkies in another, the embezzlers in still another, and so on. And each group passed a good part of the day bragging. Murderers boasted of the number of victims to their credit, or of the best techniques of killing, and robbers talked about their biggest jobs, or of pulling the ideal holdup. Muggers did the same, while embezzlers bragged about all the money they had made off with before getting caught. Junkies went on and on about the size of their habits, or their best hustles. And when the inmates grew tired of hearing each other's war stories, they talked of women, or complained about the guards or the food, or discussed the perfect escape.

The leadership of the addicts was split between two men, white and black. Vic was in his late twenties, of Italo-American descent and with mob connections. Bubba was a powerful black man, influential among most of the blacks in prison. Since the two factions stayed pretty much apart, Slick joined Vic's band, along with Jeff, another newcomer, a slim, smooth-faced youth of the same age who had been sent up for dealing marihuana. The group, averaging about twenty-one years of age but ranging from nineteen all the way up to the mid-forties, looked the two of them over for a day or so. Some of the older, tougher men seemed to be particularly interested in Jeff, who was quite a comely lad with delicate features and pale, creamy skin. Teddy, a big bruiser covered with tattoos, a professional hit man on the outside, began trailing Jeff around, talking to him in private. The boy welcomed any companionship because he was lonely and it was his first time in prison. One day when Slick came up to them, Teddy scowled at the unwelcome intrusion.

What's cookin', junior?" he sneered insultingly.

The men all turned and waited.

"Answer me, ya little punk!" he roared. "Or I'll kick ya so hard yer balls'll hang outa yer mouth!"

He shoved Slick, who was frightened to death of anyone this big. Yet it was this very fear that made him dangerous. Without warning he lashed out with one hand and gashed the man's throat with a piece of broken glass he had kept hidden in his pocket. Because he inflicted only a deep scratch, his adversary was not stopped but simply enraged further. He beat the tar out of Slick, knocking him down, kicking him in the groin and face until he was senseless. The guards watched from some distance away but did not intervene. Even though it took him a week to recover from the beating, Slick was never offered out after that. The men respected his viciousness and he had earned their acceptance.

Jeff met a different fate. When he got shoved around he chickened out and let Teddy come to his defense. From then on it was clear to everyone—he belonged to Teddy, who became his old man. Teddy brought Jeff presents of candy and cigarettes, and their trysts in the lavoratory were frequent. Teddy had a lot of fights with others who also wanted to know the flaxen-haired boy. Jeff, for his part, seemed willing to stick with the admirer who offered him the most status, security, and money, and this was Teddy, to whom he was largely faithful. He grew to resemble the gentler sex in other ways, wearing his hair longer, with bangs because the other queens had them. And he became obsessed with his physical attractiveness and flirted a lot.

"He's Teddy's pussy boy now," an inmate remarked to Slick. "Happens a lot in here, but even more up in state prison, 'cause them guys're in fer life. Good thing you put up a fight that day or they'da turned you out, too."

Slick asked Jeff about it and he shrugged coyly. "Heck, I ain't really faggot," he insisted. "Just once in a while. Teddy'll take good care of me as long as I'm here. Anything I want, he gives me. . . ."

Indeed, Jeff was so well cared for that he had little time to spend with Slick, who turned his attention elsewhere. He got to know a lot of inmates and listened to their stories. Because just about every one of them considered himself the greatest criminal ever born, they were always showing off their knowledge, expounding on not only the basics but on special tricks of the trade. And they enjoyed talking to a novice like Slick who was easy to impress. Thus began his formal education in crime. The faculty was made up of accomplished professionals. With great expertise they covered such key subjects as murder, armed robbery, lockpicking, safecracking, introduction to alarm systems, car theft, pickpocketing, forgery, mugging, and the do's and don'ts of beating a case. And when they were not discussing techniques, they were actually making preparations to employ them, lining up connections and laying plans.

Slick listened in awe to a clique of armed robbers engineering a bank job. Photographs and maps were smuggled in and they spent weeks discussing the best alternatives. They made the necessary contacts through other specialists in the prison for rental of weapons, stolen plates, and for getting rid of the money.

"This one can't miss," one of them said to Slick. "Take it from me. I know all the angles to banks. The main thing is speed—get in, get the money, and get out fast. Naturally they gotta silent alarm, naturally they got them cameras, an' guards. But so what? You're gone, see? Gone before the cops come. An' if the guard gives ya any trouble ya can't hesitate, gotta blow 'im away or he'll spoil it, 'cause once the cops get there an' pin ya down, unless ya got machine guns ta hold 'em at bay, yer all through. An' now they're usin' snipers, an' those boys shoot to kill. So if ya ain't shot tryin' to get outa there and they take ya alive, why it's back to the joint fer fifteen to twenty."

Slick remarked that he was learning an awful lot here in jail. The inmate surprised him with his reply.

"Hey, this ain't nothin'," he scoffed. "We're in the minor leagues compared to state prison. Hell, this is only boot camp down here. Up there you run into the really tough guys, the real pros. Some're too crazy to let out, so they've got a lotta time an' that make's 'em even meaner. It's dangerous as hell up there, guys gettin' stabbed all the time. But you make some awful big connections in state prison, or in the federal pen. I should know, kid, I spent half my life in one prison or another."

This was a real jailbird, Slick thought, as he nodded at the man, saw how his belly bulged comfortably under baggy prison clothes, his sluggish, heavy-lidded eyes blinking almost without expression from his pallid, bloated face. Here was a man who sold himself down the river for three square meals a day and a roof over his head, to a place where the painful choices of everyday life could not haunt him. He was safe from a society that had defeated him. In fact, he was never very happy on the outside and admitted it freely. It seemed that no one wanted an ex-con. But Slick shuddered at the thought of being institutionalized like this, growing fat and sassy on starchy, prison food. It might not be such a bad life for some, but he was young and yearned for so much more. As the novelty of prison began to wear off and the same routine crept on from day to day, he grew more conscious of the burden of time weighing on him and stifling his youth. He ached to be free and chafed for his release. Yet he had to adjust to this structured way of life in order to survive. He grew accustomed to eating at the appointed times and to coming and going on schedule. But he seethed under the constant harrassment of the guards, which he and the other inmates responded to with cursing, rock throwing, spitting, or throwing feces from the upper tiers. Most of all, he hated the twelve hour stretch of confinement in his tiny cell. It had a strange effect on him, made him feel more vicious inside than he had ever felt before, like a caged animal waiting to break loose and run wild.

His day started at the crash of the guards opening the steel, cell block doors at 6:00 a.m. He washed up in the basin in his cell. He rarely used the small toilet because there was a rumor that if you sat down the sewer rats would pop up inside and bite your testicles. At seven o'clock they opened the cell doors and after the lineup, the inmates went to the dining hall for breakfast at 7:30. Then came the work details. They did not assign him to the hospital as he requested because as an addict they knew he would expend all his energy beating the patients out of their medications. Instead they sent him to the boiler room. It was a hot, sweaty job. Rarely having done a day's work, he hated swabbing floors, changing filters, and polishing pipes. He worked till eleven, lined up for the noon meal, went to work again until four, had supper at 4:30. He killed the early evening hours watching television, playing cards or checkers with the other inmates, shooting the breeze, flipping through comic books, or playing basketball. Some of the boys liked to box, but because he was smaller than most of them he shied away, having already had enough beatings for one lifetime from his father. After the evening lineup they locked him up again at 7:30 p.m.

In no time he became so bored and depressed that he felt like getting high. Happily he did not have to look very far to find drugs. Whatever he wanted was available. Vic, among others, had them smuggled in by his wife in large amounts. It was easy for him because he had money on the outside, money to buy the drugs and then money to pay off certain friendly guards that looked the other way during their visits out in the yard. Because of his money, Vic had almost everything else he wanted in prison. His cell looked like an apartment, with a television, a rug, pictures on the walls, curtains, nice blankets, a good mattress on his cot, and even an aquarium. He also had a special locker to put things into, like food and cigarettes, which were worth far more than money in jail.

"You want some speed? Acid? You name it, kid," he offered. "Heroin? No problem only come up with somethin' ta pay for it, huh? My stuff ain't fer free, ya know."

For days Slick tried to figure out how to get up the price of a bag—in money, twenty dollars in the joint. But then money was rarely used. Barter was the rule, so he began to look around for something to trade with. He had noticed that almost every prisoner kept a homemade knife hidden somewhere. These crude but lethal weapons were in great demand and were used not only in self-defense, but to settle a grudge, such as in a jealous quarrel between homosexuals, or to silence a rat—the human kind.

The boiler room where he worked was next to the plumbing shop, which was equipped with a grinding wheel and steel brush to clean up pipe. Slick expressed a strong interest in helping the plumber cut pipe and make fittings. To do this he had to work in the plumbing shop and use the grinding wheel occasionally. They watched him closely for a few weeks whenever he went near the grinder, then grew to trust him. Meanwhile he obtained a couple of table knives from someone in the kitchen in return for a carton of cigarettes that his mother had brought him. He hid these in the shop and one day when the foreman was out and the guard had just passed through, he quickly ground them into stiletto-like weapons.

Vic was more than delighted. "Them shanks're worth two cartons apiece!" he gloated. "Look, I'll see that ya get the table knives an' you keep makin' 'em whenever ya get the chance, okay? An' I'll give yous two bags fer each one."

Slick traded a couple of bags for a needle and syringe from someone who worked in the hospital. He shot as little as a bag a day, but because he was clean at the time, he really got loaded. And when he could not afford heroin he shot speed, and even LSD. His life improved after that. He was part of the system now, a cog in the prison economy. He had learned how to con the other inmates and work the angles, and in so doing had mastered the art of survival on the inside.

Then one day he got into trouble. He had not started it, and was guilty more of being in the wrong place at the wrong time. He and Jeff happened to walk into a lavatory one noon break and were shocked to see someone slumped on a toilet with his throat cut, the blood spurting from a severed artery. Right away they had a pretty good idea who had done it and accordingly they did the wisest thing—walked away as though nothing had happened. But two guards entered behind them to search the lavatory because the inmate had been missing from lineup. Finding the victim still alive but in severe shock, they sped him by ambulance to the nearest hospital where he died in surgery an hour later.

Slick was the first to be questioned by the warden, a beetle-browed, sallow-faced man with a lantern jaw. He had a surprisingly mild voice but a very hard look as he addressed the short youth standing in front of the old-fashioned oak desk in the paneled office. And as Slick studied him he pictured this man in prison clothes, and was struck by how much he resembled most of the inmates. Momentarily, the warden surprised him by emptying out the contents of a manila envelope—a set of works, a bag of heroin, and some speed, yet only the works belonged to him.

"We found this in your cell, Quinn," the warden said casually. "Now we know that the guy who was killed hung out with your group. And we also know that he was probably involved in an escape plan because we found a grappling hook in our shakedown of the machine shop where he worked. Now you're guilty of possession of heroin in a prison, you know that? And that's pretty serious, son." He paused, looked at Slick, his gray, expressionless eyes like chips of stone. "But we'll let it go if you tell us everything you know. . . ."

Slick grinned nervously at the warden's unwavering gaze. "But sir, that's like a death sentence," he said.

"Not at all," assured the warden. "We'll place you in protective custody and then parole you as soon as possible."

The youth shook his head. "PC? I don't want that, sir. They'd get me anyway."

"Well, goddam it, you'll go to the can if you don't cooperate!" rasped the warden, his beetle brows bending into an angry scowl. "Now which is it?"

Slick grinned again. "I'll take the can."

As for Jeff, he was sent to the hospital for treatment of anal gonorrhea. The warden told him that after he was treated, he too would be put in the can until he talked. That was all it took. Jeff sang and was mysteriously paroled the next day, with good reason. His story led to the discovery of hidden guard uniforms, dummy guns, and a zip gun, all intended for use in an escape. Shortly afterward, Vic and a few others were transferred to the maximum security block.

As Slick discovered, the can was bad enough, but the trip to the can was even worse, a notorious punishment that he had already heard about from the other inmates. Three guards poked and beat him with clubs as they pushed him ahead, throwing him bodily into the cottage. Things got much worse when he took a swing at one of the guards and connected. He was rewarded with another transfer, this time to the hole.

The hole was something unique in his experience, one of those singular events in life after which one is never the same. He gained a new perspective on existence, discovered how low he could sink and still survive. What made it so unpleasant was not the dampness, or the cold cement floor and stone walls, or the ceiling only four feet high so that he could not stand up. It was not the single pot provided for relieving himself, or the identical pot thrown in twice a day full of slop. He anticipated these things. What he did not expect was the almost total darkness.

He once a human form leaping and running in the sunlight, now a blind, torpid newt squirming in a black chasm in the earth, in a place where he existed scarcely more than the stones themselves, they mocking him with cold silence as he groped at them. And cruelest of all was the miniscule shaft of light penetrating the chamber for nearly an hour each day, the taunting reminder of a world still bright and alive outside, a world that had banished him. And in a faintly lit corner the youth caught sight of his only visitor, a tiny mouse appearing as a sprightly shadow, darting about in search of crumbs. He left scraps for it and watched gleefully as it nibbled and nibbled. Then as the light dimmed he could not tell if it had gone or not and would reach out to try to touch it, but felt only the cold, damp roughness of the stones. It had disappeared, to come back each day with a new ray of light.

Slick and the guards got along badly. They learned how to needle him so that he would react violently. "Hey punk!" one would sneer. "I'm fuckin' my ol' lady tonight! Who're you goin' ta fuck, yer buddy next door? Ha-ha-ha!"

"Stick it up yer ass, you sick fuckin' screw!" Slick would curse.

They retaliated by spitting in his food. This went on for almost two weeks, although he was not sure of the exact time. Then one day they let him out and returned him to his regular cell. Later he was surprised to learn that there were some men who stayed down in the hole for months at a stretch.

He changed after that, never said a lot or took much interest in his surroundings. Because he had become so quiet and withdrawn, the parole board granted him a release after seven months. In their eyes he was ready to return to society. He did not dare tell any of the other inmates the exact date of his release. The three-to-fivers or more would pick a fight with him to ruin his parole. The final day arrived safely and the officials presented him with an old, double-breasted suit to wear and fifty dollars to get home on.

"Don't worry, you'll be back in no time," a guard taunted as they unlocked the steel door at the main gate.

Slick stepped through it into the airy vastness outside. Everything looked strange and alien. For a moment he wanted to go back inside, to retreat behind the safety of those weathered brick walls. Then, like a wild creature obeying an age-old instinct to be free but not knowing quite where to run, he crept hesitantly forward. He glanced back one last time at the yawning steel door, and turned and darted into the waiting car.

46

The next eighteen months saw a remarkable change in Slick. He forsook street life, with its excitement and bawdiness, and even abstained from the pleasures of heroin. He exchanged all this for the phlegmatic routine of working in an auto body shop for two dollars an hour, a job obtained through his parole officer. Not that he was that fascinated with auto body work, although he found himself developing a certain knack for it that surprised him. It was simply that he had no desire to go back to prison. Parole, in fact, was the strongest tonic for his problem that had yet been found, a purgative that purified him by eliminating from his mind the poisons of impulsiveness, violence, and a craving for drugs. It did not work by magic but by the very real principle of setting definite limits on his behavior so that he knew in advance what to expect if he exceeded these limits. He knew he would bump into them as surely as if he drove his motorcycle into a concrete wall—getting into trouble meant that he would go back to finish his two year sentence.

At the end of the time period, Mr. Murphy, his parole officer, was pleased to report that Slick had not missed a single appointment and that his monthly urines were clean, being free of any trace of drugs. He was released from parole and suddenly the spell was broken. The structure imposed on his life by the correctional system, the limits that had successfully contained him, evaporated now and he was left to his own devices. It took him only three months to quit his job after an altercation with the shop foreman, whom he felt was picking on him. He began to hang around in bars again, from which he had been excluded during his parole, and was soon arrested for assaulting another youth with a broken beer bottle during a drunken fray over some money he owed. The authorities charged him with assault with a dangerous weapon and being drunk and disorderly, although, had they tested his urine they would have found it strongly positive for barbiturates.

His mother, wondering as usual whether or not her son had been victimized, came down to district court the next morning with the family lawyer for the arraignment. The lawyer was a man not unknown to the court for his close personal relationship with the judge. He called Slick's parole officer, who came over right away. The two of them listened attentively to the distraught woman as she carried on about her son and all of the injustices that he had suffered.

"Vinnie's been so moody since they put him in that awful prison," she complained. "Isn't there something else they can do besides sending him back to jail?" She took out a handkerchief and blotted her eyes, allowed the lawyer to seat her. "He's so old that I can't handle him anymore at home. But ... he really isn't that bad ... I mean, why must everyone pick on him so? The other boys are just as bad or worse, but it always seems like he's the one who's singled out for punishment."

Mr. Murphy nodded gravely. "I understand your position, Mrs. Quinn," he said. "And to a certain extent I'll have to agree with you. It is true that prison doesn't work for a lot of kids. They get in with the real criminals and come out more hardened and antisocial than they were when they went in. I'm afraid, though, that at the rate your son is going, he'll be in again before long." The parole officer glanced at the lawyer. "But perhaps Bruno and I can work something out with the court."

At the trial several months later, the attorney stood up, motioned toward Slick, who was hardly recognizable now with a new suit and a haircut.

"Your honor," he began, "after consulting with several medical authorities, the reports of which are available to the court on request, it is evident that this young man, who comes from a good home, has for the most part what might be termed a psychiatric problem. It is also clear from these medical opinions that ordinary correctional methods have proven to be of little value in his rehabilitation."

The judge was a busy man, and besides, the case had already been settled. It was continued on condition that the defendant see a psychiatrist for as long as necessary. A day later Slick had a seizure and was hospitalized. He admitted to one of the nurses that for several weeks he had been strung out on barbiturates. He was so worried about going back to jail that he popped twelve to fourteen seconals a day until he ran out the very day he appeared in court.

In the hospital, while he was being detoxified from barbiturates, Slick met his psychiatrist for the first time. Dr. Kroll was a sedate, portly man with a round, observant face framed with heavy, black-rimmed glasses. His expression remained emotionless and impassive most of the time, but shifted now and again to a look of startled concern, signalled by the bushy eyebrows arching high above the frames of his glasses. A dark brown, three piece suit matched the sobriety of his demeanor, but a loud silk necktie added a certain, unexpected dash. He wore crepe-soled shoes and moved about noislessly, like a plump, inoffensive shadow. Spilling in behind the desk in his office after seating Slick in a conspicuously threadbare armchair a few feet away, he propped up his watch at a readily visible angle on the desk blotter, and neatly arranged his note pad and pen so they were perfectly parallel with one another. Then he folded his hands, peered through his glasses at Slick, and waited.

After a few moments, Slick began to squirm. "Uh, I guess the court sent me ta see ya. . . ," he mumbled, deciding to say something.

"Yes, I have the report," Dr. Kroll replied. Again there was silence for half a minute as the doctor produced a pipe, stuffed it full of tobacco, packed it with a metal tamper that he unfolded for this purposes. "It seems you're having difficulty staying out of trouble. . . ," he went on, flicking a thin tongue of flame out of a silver lighter and sucking it into the fresh tobacco, raising a great quantity of sweet, pungent smoke that floated upward to hang about him in a cloud.

Slick saw that it was his turn. "I—I guess so," he said.

Dr. Kroll sat watching the youth quietly, as though expecting to hear more. "You must be an angry guy to do many of the things you do," he commented at last, and resumed puffing on his pipe.

Slick tensed at this snide remark, which ordinarily he would not have tolerated from anyone. He recoiled slightly, like a rattlesnake poked in the nose, his mouth twitching into a grin. "I dunno. . . ."

The psychiatrist immediately saw the concealed fury in his client and backpedaled. "Umm, well, why don't you go ahead and tell me a little bit about yourself?" he suggested.

The youth relaxed and shrugged. "Well, I uh—like, what d'ya wanna know?"

"Just . . . tell me what kind of a guy you are. How do you look at yourself?"

Slick snickered silently.

"Why do you laugh?"

"Huh? I dunno—I, ah . . . it's just that I never thought about it, that's all."

"Umm. . ." The therapist puffed thoughtfully while the youth pulled at his chinwhiskers and gazed around the office, distracted by shelves of books reaching up to the ceiling and rows of framed degrees and certificates displayed on the wall behind the doctor.

"I dunno . . . I guess I'm a junkie," he said at last.

Dr. Kroll cocked his head. "A junkie?"

"Yeah, a dopefiend. Everyone hates dopefiends, y'know that?"

The psychiatrist emitted an answering plume of smoke. "I see. And how do you feel about that?"

Slick shrugged. "That's the way it goes, right?"

"But how do you feel about the world hating you because you're on drugs?"

"Huh? I don't give a. . . ." Slick paused and grinned defiantly.

"You don't what?"

"I don't give a fuck, if you'll pardon my French."

The psychiatrist blinked. "You mean, you don't care how people feel about you?"

The youth shrugged again with the same defiant grin. "Naw. Why should I?"

There was a spell of silence. Dr. Kroll sat, waiting to hear more, then gave up, tapped out his pipe, began stuffing it again with fresh tobacco. "Well, why don't you tell me a little about your parents," he urged.

"Huh? Which one?"

"Either one."

Slick grinned.

"Did I say something to amuse you?"

"No. . . ."

"Well, what about your mother?"

"Aw, she's okay."

"How do you get along with her?"

"Great."

"How do you mean, great?"

"She sticks up for me."

"I see, and your father?"

Slick frowned, "He's an asshole, always on my back an' fightin' with my ol' lady. He drinks too, an alcoholic. Never works 'cause he's too busy drinkin'."

"You say your mother sticks up for you. Can you give me an example?" the psychiatrist asked.

Slick pulled at his chinwhiskers again, as if trying to decide on the most appropriate thing to say. "Oh, like that time I got hep three years ago."

"Hep?"

"Hepatitis. You can get it from dirty needles," Slick explained. "I've had it twice already. Anyway, like I was sayin', I was workin' in a park for the city. My ol' lady got me the job through her uncle, who's a city councilman. An' anyhow, I dunno, I told her I got hep from the water where I worked, 'stead of from a needle. I got real sick an' had to go to the hospital. She didn't know I was usin' at the time an' she still don't admit it." He paused for just a moment and smirked with contempt. "So the doctor said that it could have been the water, see? He was real stupid, missed the tracks on my arms an' everything. 'Course I was wearin' a long sleeve shirt at the time. So anyhow my ol' lady gets really uptight an' calls the mayor's office an' says the water from that bubbler is poisoned an' she's goin' to the papers about it. An' so the mayor, who knows my uncle, right, sent a guy out to talk to her an' he straightened it out." Slick grinned with delight and took out a cigarette. "So, then I got over it an' they transferred me to another job. The mayor even wrote my mother a letter of apology, no kiddin'!" His eyes shone with deviltry as he lit the cigarette and puffed grandly. He could still see his mother ranting over the phone while his father drank to hide his embarrassment.

"I see," said Dr. Kroll. "You look quite pleased."

Slick shrugged. "That's my ol' lady. She gets uptight. So does my ol' man. You should see 'em fight. I think they must get some kinda high off it."

The psychiatrist nodded, lit his pipe once more with slow, deliberate puffs, exuding wreaths of smoke. "And how did you say you got along with your father?" he asked.

The youth dropped his eyes and compressed his lips. "Him? Well, he never wants to give me nothin', says I'm a punk, a no good, rotten dopefiend bum. He don't say nothin' to the other kids. But he's the bum, not me. He's a f—, uh, he's an alcoholic."

"Mm-hm. You don't get along with him, then?"

Slick flicked his cigarette vehemently. "Like he used ta beat me when I was a kid. He don't do that now, though. He knows better."

"You would react?" the doctor asked.

The youth let out a breath, looking very tense. "One time I pulled a knife on him," he said. "He leaves me alone now."

Dr. Kroll's eyebrows rose and fell in his look of startled concern, as he reflected calmly, without emotion. "I wonder if . . . maybe you're taking out your anger that you may have toward your parents on others, or on the world in general, perhaps?"

Slick sat motionless and looked at the floor, then shrugged in bewilderment. Meanwhile, the doctor had looked at his watch and was standing up. "Time's up," he announced. "See you next week and we'll go on from there. Goodbye."

No sooner than Slick had begun therapy, Mr. Flynn, his new probation officer, referred him to a state employment agency to find another job. The youth went reluctantly because word was that they never had much to offer. To his surprise, a counselor there interviewed him about his interests and work experience, then gave him a list of jobs to choose from. He decided to apply for a job at an auto parts store because of his hankering for anything on wheels. When he arrived at the store he learned that several applicants had been there ahead of him. He talked with the owner anyway, who eyed him with reservation.

"Ever been in jail or been on drugs. Got a record?" the owner asked.

"No sir," said Slick, realizing that a "yes" would mean immediate rejection, and braced himself for the next question.

"Got any references?"

Slick grinned, almost spelled out the name of his probation officer as a joke, and walked out. He continued to look for work and did find a job at last, jockeying new cars. Now that he had a little money to play around with, he started using downs again, mostly sopors, a non-barbiturate sleeping pill, that he copped off a friend. The next week he scraped up one of the cars while high and was immediately fired. Even though his probation officer had his urines checked periodically to see if they were clean, Slick always brought in a specimen given by a girl he knew who was drug-free. He kept it warm in his pocket and poured it into his cup before giving it to the unsuspecting nurse.

In the psychiatrist's office, where he tried to avoid being stoned, he never ceased to fidget and grin uneasily during his weekly visits. He was told that his therapy would go on for three months this time around, a complete course of what was known as short term psychotherapy. He went along with it and was very cooperative the whole time, agreeing with almost everything the therapist said. He seemed more relaxed during the last few sessions and talked freely about his parents and his girl.

"Me an' my chick get along great when she does what I tell her to," he chatted one day. "But she keeps complainin', tryin' to tell me what ta do all the time an' accusin' me a' doin' dope behind her back an' not sharin' it, an' I don't like that."

"Do you two have any marriage plans?" inquired the psychiatrist.

"Naw, we're too young for that trip," Slick replied with vigorous head-shaking.

"Um-hm. And how would you want your girl to act in order for you to get along with her?"

Silence.

"I dunno. . . ."

"To let you do whatever you want and then stick-up for you whenever you get into trouble, like your mother?" Dr. Kroll spoke firmly at first but his voice softened into well-meaning benevolence as he saw the youth tense and recoil like a rattler that had been stepped on. In the face of such resistance to his interpretations, the doctor resorted to less direct tactics. "Well, tell me, how do you see yourself compared to other people in general," he prodded gently.

Slick's mouth twitched into a grin at this leading question. "How do I see myself with other people?"

"Yes. . . ."

"Uh, like I don't let 'em play me for a sucker, right? Is that what ya mean?"

"Um-mm, um-mm. I wonder if maybe you see others as overwhelming and threatening, out to smother you like your mother, perhaps, or even attack you like your father. And maybe you are always on guard against this, no matter where you are or who you are with." The doctor was speaking carefully with a quiet emphasis. He paused, waited for the youth to reply, then began again. ". . . And because you're on guard, you don't give people a chance. You are suspicious of them, eh?"

"Hey doc, can I borrow your lighter?" Slick said awkwardly and produced a cigarette.

The doctor passed the lighter to the youth and pressed home his interpretation, unable to resist rounding it out. "You don't have to attack people. Wait and give them a chance and if you give them that chance, you may be surprised at what they can give in return. Then you can keep on giving. Do you see how it goes? This is what we call a quid pro quo, or give-and-take kind of relationship."

Slick pondered, then nodded with an empty grin. "Sure, like I give my chick a couple bags an' she lets me ball 'er, right? Yeah, I know what ya mean, doc, everything's give an' take."

"Um-mm." The psychiatrist stared with his mildly startled, concerned look, then lit his pipe, went on speaking doggedly between puffs. "You see . . . others as . . . exploiting you, therefore you must . . . exploit others. You see . . . a relationship as built only . . . on what people can use each other for . . . or barter back and forth to their own advantage."

Slick grinned again, this time with merriment. "Well, ain't that what ya said, doc? Give an take?"

"Yes, but I wonder if you automatically assume that you will be cheated in the process."

"Yeah, someone might beat me, sure, so I gotta beat them first."

The psychiatrist raised his eyebrows once more. "It's better to take advantage of others, then?"

"Sure, why get beat? Why be a sucker?" The youth turned the silver lighter over in his hand then laid it on the desk. "Nice lighter—silver, huh?"

Dr. Kroll nodded and a hint of sadness tugged at his eyebrows as he fumed thoughtfully through his pipe. "I wonder if perhaps you should learn to see people a little differently," he went on mildly. "To see them as human beings who have a capacity for love and sacrifice and who will accept you on your own merits and respect you, rather than trying to 'beat' you, as you call it." He finished with a frank look of disapproval.

This cold look on the older man's face was the one thing that had real meaning to Slick. Here was a man who disliked him and who was talking in riddles at the same time to make him feel stupid. Not even his father talked in riddles. As the doctor's narrowed, slightly concerned and startled eyes peered at him through their black-rimmed lenses, the youth shifted uncomfortably in his seat and grinned innocently. He was thinking how it would be to cut this man with a knife, how he would squeal like a pig and plead for his life. Once he had almost liked this man but now he decided he hated him. For he saw more than just the man, he saw a far more powerful adversary, the indignant eyes of society, of authority and convention, of respect for the law and the rights of others. These eyes were condemning him as he had always been condemned. And if fearful adversaries could not be beaten, they had to be appeased. "Yeah," he agreed, and nodded. "I guess you're right."

In the final interview the youth was very tense. The doctor suggested that he might have come to trust and to have positive feelings toward his therapist and that even though they were terminating the sessions for now, perhaps he could learn to share this trust with others as well.

Slick shrugged sullenly. "Maybe," he replied.

At the end of the session Dr. Kroll stood up and extended his hand. Well, he said warmly, "I think you've made considerable progress. I hope that you don't try to cope with the stresses of life by resorting to drugs again. Now I've decided that we should continue to meet once a month, just so that I can follow you according to the requirements of the probationary period."

"Sure," Slick agreed, trying to hide his mixed feelings. "You've helped me a lot, honest. I don't need to shoot no more dope from now on."

"Fine," said the psychiatrist. "I want you to call my office next month for an appointment. Will you do that?"

"Sure will, doc. An' thanks."

Slick never called. In fact, because he was depressed and out of sorts over losing his therapist, he got off that very day on some good dope, which right away made him feel better. He decided that what the doctor had said about drugs did not matter after all. If it did, then why did he cut him down to one visit a month? What did the doctor expect him to do with four weeks between appointments? Above all, he hoped that Dr. Kroll would write a favorable report to the probation officer. In fact, even though Slick did not go for followup appointments, and despite the evident concern over this fact by the probation officer, the report was evidently favorable enough for Mr. Flynn to recommend that the court take no further action on the case, and it was filed.

47

For an addict to be saved he must renounce that which enslaves him, that thing that owns him. He must recognize this tyrant for what it is and for the harm that it can do, and he must understand his weakness for it. Then with immense will power and great cunning he must plot to overthrow it. The struggle will be fierce and grim, but if he does not succeed, he will live only to see it destroy him. Yet there are some who are so weakened by pain that they almost seek their own self-destruction. They cannot deliver themselves from bondage, can only hope to be rescued by some trick of fate, or by another person who may or may not be well-intentioned in depriving them of that thing which they cannot deprive themselves of. Such was the case with Russ, when he was able at least for a brief period to abstain from cocaine, though certainly not by choice, and not before engaging in the most flagrant abuse of his favorite drug.

He had been on top of the world after returning from New York with a whole ounce of very good snow, worth every nickel of the fifteen hundred dollars he paid for it. Unfortunately at about this time Dolores's business activities began to annoy the landlord, who threatened to file a complaint against them unless they moved out immediately. They were obliged to vacate the premises in the middle of the night in order to avoid paying the rent they owed, and to register in one of the better motels in town where they hoped to find a little business. Their luck improved when, according to plan, Dolores managed to pick up a well-heeled john in the cocktail lounge. A businessman with a lavish expense account, he was far from home and up for some good times. Suggesting dinner and dancing, then back to his place, he offered her a hundred dollars beforehand and if he was satisfied another hundred the next morning.

That evening Dolores was in the best of spirits as she bathed, shampooed, shaved her legs, oiled, powdered and perfumed her voluptuous body, brushed out her long black silky hair, made up her big green eyes, and had Russ zip her into one of her slinkiest evening gowns. She refused to kiss him, afraid of smudging her makeup, and shooed him into the bedroom as soon as the bell rang. At the door she graciously accepted a corsage, and vanished with her date.

Russ did not intend to do any of the cocaine. He tried at first not even to think about it, turning his attention to the television instead. But his mind kept swinging back to his woman, dining out with the trick, the rich, white dude. He pictured a candle flickering between them and his eyes probing hers. Then he could not think any more and suddenly wanted to get high, to blow his mind and render it totally oblivious to everything but the feeling of good coke. Quickly he fixed up, dissolved a pinch of the almost pure, white powder and banged it into his arm. The rush was so powerful that it almost lifted him off his feet. He never wanted to come down again, not as long as the coke held out. After the first high began to fade at the end of about twenty minutes, he did another hit and rode up again, thinking all the while how this drug was the favorite of the jet set, the rich swingers. Here was pure, mellow cheer blended with a sparkling hilarity, the best from speed and heroin rolled into one clean, physically non-addicting high.

He measured out a larger quarter, or twenty-five dollar spoon, still only a fat pinch but when he booted it into his arm he really went flying. Then he did another, and another, and lost track. After a time he stod up, feeling very taught inside, like a steel guitar string about to snap. He was as light as a feather on his feet and his ears were buzzing. His mind was unusually alert and clear, sensitive to even the slightest ripple in his surroundings. He went to the window, looked out suspiciously, sensing an intolerable pressure building up inside his body, a bomb ready to explode at any second. Then he flushed all over, decided to take a shower to try to relax.

He went into the bathroom and closed the door beind him, conscious now of being completely alone, imprisoned within four walls and cut off altogether from the world. The pattering of the shower in the tub reassured him and he stepped in. But as he sat down in the tub and shut the glass shower door, the same stifling feeling seized him again. It was then that he heard a slight noise and looked up to see the shadow of a huge bird hovering with wings outstretched against the glass, trying to get in at him. He yelled in terror, struck out at it blindly, then scrambled out of the tub and started to run as far and as fast as his legs could carry him.

The next thing he knew he was lying in a hospital bed, one arm bandaged up to the shoulder and a unit of blood running into the other arm. Dolores was standing beside him, her pretty face engrained with those deep, ugly, troubled lines that appeared only in times of unusual distress, and which, by their very presence, foretold how she would look as an old woman.

"Won't you ever learn?" she hissed, then took his hand and squeezed it. "Oh, Russ, thank God. . . !" She bit her lip. "Why? Why this when you've been doing coke for years and you know. . . !"

"Huh. . . ?" he mumbled, puzzled, trying to piece together the fragments of his shattered memory.

"You mean, you don't know what happened?" she said incredulously, and bent down close, lowering her voice. "I heard you screaming bloody murder out in the hallway. By the time I talked the trick into letting me up, you'd already run downstairs. There was a trail of blood on the rug and it was even splashed on the walls. I thought, my God, someone cut his throat or something. Then I found you rolling around down in the lobby stark naked, covered with blood and yelling like a wild indian. Three people were holding you down, then you fainted and they called an ambulance." She let out a breath of relief. "It's a wonder we're not in hot water over this."

"I ain't seen no cops," Russ commented.

She levelled a cold stare at him, her green eyes unblinking. "Now, tell me—it was the coke, wasn't it?"

Russ nodded shamefully. "Guess so. Lost track of how much I was shootin'. Man, I coulda died behind that stuff!" He tried to move and winced. "What'd I do to my arm?"

"You slashed your elbow clear to the bone, that's what! Must've hit the shower door. They put in sixteen stitches."

After another embarrassed confession of his complete ignorance of what he had done, he recounted his side of the story, the nightmarish specter of a giant vulture or whatever it was trying to get in at him.

She frowned with skepticism. "No matter what it was you saw, it was still an awful stupid thing to do! I found the rest of the coke and put it away, and took everything out of the motel so we wouldn't have to pay for the damage. It must be a lot—the shower door smashed and all that blood on the carpet. What a mess, and I even lost the extra hundred on that trick! And all because of that lousy coke! You'll land us both in jail again at this rate! You should know better, honestly!"

Apologetically he tried to sit up and take her hand, but the pain held him down. "Hey, baby, I didn't do it on purpose! I just overdid it, that's all. I mean I didn't know where my head was comin' from an' that wasn't cool, y'understan'? Trouble was, I ain't used to such good stuff. I'll cut the rest an' sell it, no lie, soon as I get out baby, I promise!"

Two detectives came in later and questioned him about the incident, investigating the possibility of foul play. Russ gave them a phony name and told them he had been drinking and fell into the shower by accident, cutting his arm, then thought he was bleeding to death.

"You almost did, fella," one replied solemnly. "You owe the motel for damages. What is your address? Do you have any ID's?"

Russ said he had no ID, made up an address, then started in on how grateful he was for their interest. He rattled on about how maybe not everybody appreciated the police, man, but he for one knew that they were there to help people in trouble when there was no other help around and that it was a good thing there were police in this world or it would really go to the dogs in no time. Sufficiently flattered, the two detectives scrawled a few notes and politely withdrew.

He was discharged from the hospital and the next morning and profusely thanked the doctors and nurses for their excellent care, after making sure the clerk had the same phony name and address for billing purposes. Dolores drove him back to a cheap hotel room she had taken. Despite the recent upheaval in their lives, she was bubbly and carefree, not at all her usual fretful self, so that Russ knew right away that she had been sampling some of his coke. He said nothing but the first thing he did when they arrived was to check on how much was left.

"Outa sight!" he exclaimed. "I still got three quarters of an ounce!" In spite of himself he snorted a dime spoon while Dolores was in the other room, feeling ashamed all the while to be wasting it in this way when he should be shooting it by vein. But he reveled in the high and when

Dolores came back he unabashedly invited her to join him. With equal abandonment she accepted and before long they were both buzzing.

"I won't have no hassle gettin' rid a' this stuff," he exuded. "Even after I cut it once or twice it'll still be dynamite."

"Well, don't sell quite all of it," she purred in a sudden reversal of feeling for the drug, captivated by it as she was at that moment. She snuggled up to him impatiently.

He reached out with his good arm, fondled her. "Hey baby, this stuff is so great that I feel like workin' out!"

"Be careful of your arm, honey," Dolores giggled, kissed him on the neck, and tugged at his belt buckle.

They came down within the hour, both a little tired but quite relaxed. Dolores broke out some methadone and shared a few tabs with Russ to lift them out of the vague trough of depression that follows a good coke high. They rested till the methadone warmed their spirits. Then they dressed and went out to eat, for methadone is known to stimulate the appetite, as Dolores's buxom figure suggested. On the way home she dropped him off at a pharmacy to pick up some milk sugar, or lactose. Back in the hotel room, he spread a half ounce of cocaine out on a sheet of aluminum foil. He added an equal amount of milk sugar, hesitated, painfully considered the profits involved, and added another part of sugar to make a two in one cut. He mixed up the new ounce and a half and divided it carefully into fifty dollar or gram bags and wrapped each in foil. At last he was ready to take care of business.

48

Even with the two in one cut it was still good street coke and Russ doubted his customers would be disappointed. He took one more hit of the original coke, snorting it up from the tiny, pearl-handled gold spoon around his neck, then shoved a cut bag into his pocket to use as a sample. In a festive mood he bid Dolores goodbye, hailed a cab and rode down into his old neighborhood. Checking the corners, he spied Louis, a muscular, square-jawed young man who had just gotten out of jail for armed robbery, and ChiChi, slim and sanguine, a renowned pimp who drove a lime green Lincoln Continental with a set of chrome horns glittering on the hood. Not to be outshone by his automobile, ChiChi himself sported a maroon leather suit, sleek lizard shoes and a wide-brimmed, white felt hat cocked at a jaunty angle.

The two young men broke into wide grins at the sight of Russ's familiar face. "Hey, what's happnin', baby? Ain't seen yuh in awhile!"

"Been takin' care o' business. Hey, how ya been?" Russ replied.

"Good, like I'm out on parole, man," said Louis.

"Say, what came down?" ChiChi piped up, eyeing the bandaged arm.

Russ shook his head and chuckled. "Hey, you cats wouldn't b'lieve what I got into! The mos' dynamite coke I ever done! Like, I OD'd on this shit once already, man, it jus' blew my mind! Like I was seein' things, y'understan'? Scared the livin' shit outa me, man, an' I went an' smashed a shower door 'thout even knowin' what I was doin'!"

Their eyes widened at his story. "Hey, ya got any of it left, man?" ChiChi asked.

"Uh-huh, sure do. . . ."

Louis laughed gleefully. "Man, you look like you're still flyin'! I sure would like to try a hit if ya got any on ya."

Russ produced the bag, let them each have a snort. ChiChi used his own pearl-handled, gold coke spoon. He habitually snorted cocaine rather than shooting it and his nostrils were caked with scabs from the constant irritation. "Hey, right on!" the pimp declared, his eyes gleaming with delight. "What's the cut?"

"Two in one," Russ replied. "I met these real heavy dudes in New York, man, an' they had the best."

"How much you wanna get rid of?"

"I got 'bout forty fifty dollar bags."

"Wow, all right!" Louis exclaimed, "I could sell this shit with two more cuts roun' here in dimes an' make out real good."

"Gimme twenty bags," said ChiChi hurriedly. "Them ol' whores a' mine need somethin' to keep 'em goin'."

"I'll take whatever ya got left," echoed Louis. "Where's it at?"

"My place."

"Can you meet us back here in about an hour?"

Russ smiled. "Hey, we talkin' in the neighborhood a' couple grand, man. Tell ya what, I'll put it down in a locker at the bus station, dig, an' when you gimme the money, I'll pass you the key. An' you know me, I don't beat no one."

"Sure, if that's how ya want it," said Louis, his eyes shifting slyly to ChiChi. "You meet us back here in a couple hours with the key, an' everything'll be cool."

They parted company, Russ returning to his apartment where he counted out the foil packets, wrapped them up and stuffed them into two large manila envelopes. He took a cab down to the bus station, deposited the envelopes in a single locker and pocketed the key, returned to the corner at the appointed hour. It was deserted. He went into the barroom, looking for his friends, instead met a taciturn young man who looked familiar but Russ could not place him.

"Louis says to stay put, man," muttered the youth, " 'cause there's some dudes watchin' this place that we think're the pigs. . . ."

Russ looked around in surprise. "Where's ChiChi, then?"

"They both said for me to tell you that they comin' by to pick you up in a little while."

"When?"

"Don' know 'xactly, they jus' tol' me to tell ya. Hey, how 'bout some wine?"

Before Russ could answer the young man brought back two glasses of cheap white port and they sat down. The bar was half empty in the midafternoon lull when the drunks are passed out in the booths or gone home to sleep it off and the working crowd has not yet come bursting in. The patrons seemed to sense the slackness of the hour, the slowness of the drag of time, and yawned, slumped in their seats, blinking in the daylight. An old man reached out with a trembling, gnarled finger and dabbled in the lazy river of infinity, became a child again, rippling the surface of time, watching his reflection melt and disappear. Russ, too, sat immobile, his mind adrift in the neverending present, his thoughts turning aimlessly in this quiet eddy between the past and the future.

Then he felt dizzy. The light shimmered ever more brilliantly on the floor, the checkered tiles quivering, then zig-zagging as he watched in astonishment. "Wow, some wine, man!" he mumbled. "I'm really buzzin'. . . ."

The young man did not reply and his expression froze into a sardonic mask as Russ stared about. Things began to quicken, to come alive. He saw the walls breathe, swelling and contracting like a tired bellows. The beer signs sprouted delicate halos, snowflake fringes, sparkling like exotic comets, silver and gold, green, blue, and fiery scarlet. The patrons along the bar changed subtly, brightened into unreal cartoon figures with curious, muted voices and absurd, almost obscene gestures. He knew well where he was, had been here many times before. It was the psychedelic universe, the wilderness that had once excited him so, but unable to chart it, he had abandoned it. Alarmed, he looked back at the youth once more and saw his ebony face stretched into a sinister, feline sneer.

"Hey . . . wow . . . man. . . ," Russ grunted, feeling as though he were somewhere three feet behind himself. ". . . That was . . . some drink, man . . . tabbed me . . . haw. . . !" He shook his head to clear it but everything kept coming faster as he went up, up, up. "Hey. . . !" he heard himself say. ". . . Don't. . . ." He shut his eyes, saw his voice echoing like silver sheaves flashing through the thousand rooms of his mind. Then the rooms became crypts, locked away, gloomy, terrifying, and he wept, sniveled, tried to gesture, pointed, wagged his head like a floppy scarecrow. "Don' . . . try . . . nothin. . . !" he blubbered.

He rapped his fist on the table, pictured a judge beating his gavel and then the hand of God descending and his majestic, thundering voice puffing out in cloud writing. "S-T-O-P!" The customers along the bar were policemen. One raised his glass and it became a whistle, the shrill orange noise pouring out in a blob to summon a hundred Keystone Cops with empty pink faces charging up to his rescue. "Stop!" Russ mumbled.

"Huh? What you sayin', man? What's wrong?" the young man asked, reaching out like a sneering cat extending a clawed paw.

Cornered, Russ shrank back, imagined himself another cat, arching his back. "Go away! Meow, pfft!" He shut his eyes, saw a thousand cats leap into his mind and crystallize into an intricate, abstract design that was the ultimate in catness.

"C'mon, man," said the young man. "You need some air." He smiled at Russ, his face contorting like India rubber, an inky mask of amused contempt.

A few of the patrons turned around and stared. Russ wanted to shout for help but his voice stuck, a bolus of tangled worms lodged squirming in his throat. His lungs hardly seemed to work at all, as though driven by cheap little electric motors. He found himself mutely struggling for air, then realized through his long experience with acid that it was only a delusion and tried to calm himself. He realized that he had never been this high before and was as helpless as a baby.

"Oh, wow, am I high. . . !" he thought, the amazement of it lofting into space, a creamy geyser of astonishment feathering into shocked whispers, an ivory plume of awe erupting in a vacuum of disbelief, and then others popping up all around. "Wow . . . high. . . ! Wow. . . ! Wow. . . !"

"C'mon, man, let's go outside," someone said and hands grabbed him, supported him and he traveled out of the bar like a toy train on a track, into a make-believe street lined with strawberry frosted cars and chocolate covered houses. He was shoved, lost his balance, fell and rolled onto the soft marshmellow concrete, felt hands jerking at his pockets.

"Hey . . . you . . . motha. . . !" he blurted thickly, and saw the words unfolding in his mind like oriental fans, transformed in another instant into maddening tongue twisters—"'thuluntchy—kaluthunchy—thermaglomadiotch—glomalopaditch"—and the "tch" echoing and re-echoing like dry wood splintering inside his skull. Then he squirmed, covered himself against blows on his face, side, back. ". . . You . . . bla . . . mothfuh. . . !" he uttered.

A foot squashed his face and silenced him and very rationally he decided to lie perfectly still. Alone, he turned his head languidly upward to watch the blue sky. He always liked to get into the sky when tripping because it can do fantastic things on acid. Sure enough it swirled, heaved, contracted—a breathing, living mass. Then he closed his eyes again and saw obscene, color movies flashed in cinemascope before him. The screen was so wide that it seemed to extend away into the distance on both sides, and on it was a sequence of nude figures copulating and performing other acts. He almost recognized them—yes, it was Dolores with her tricks. Fascinated, he watched for a few minutes, then grew bored and wanted to shut it off. For some reason he could not. He opened his eyes again, saw the same sky swirling overhead. Then he began to cry like a bullied, abandoned child, bitterly and angrily, the rivers of salt tears gushing out of his eyes in torrents.

He got up a bit later, reeled back into the bar and splashed cold water on his face, washed off the dried blood. He was still tripping but much less now and his whole body throbbed with pain. He had been robbed, that much he knew, and regretted that he was not the kind of dude who took revenge on people. Certainly, he could not go to the police. He decided it was best to walk home, that perhaps the exercise would help him come down faster. After marching for endless blocks he finally wound up in a diner seated over a cup of coffee. It was late evening and the lights had stopped popping and zinging in front of him. People, objects were looking ordinary again. He could not believe it when the waitress told him where he was. He had gotten lost and wandered clear across town. His legs felt like lead and he had sore spots all over his body. Finding a mirror he saw bruises on his face and noticed that his clothes were torn and dusty. One pocket was slashed open where he had the key. It was missing, and so was his wallet.

49

Dolores was furious at Russ on hearing of his misadventure, and after an initial attemp at self-restraint, she finally spoke her mind.

"Russ, for crying out loud," she burst out angrily. "How come everything you do lately turns to shit? It's that cocaine—I just know it's a jinx!"

He rolled over on his side of the bed in their shabby hotel room, sat up stiffly and yawned. "Aw, c'mon, baby, lemme be!" he begged. "How was I to know I'd get tabbed? That dude musta dropped at least four hits into my glass. I never been so spaced!" He shook his head sadly and examined the bruises on his arms. "Them black motherfuckers ripped me off for all of it! Musta been Louis an' them. 'Course he's a bad motha fucker anyhow an' I ain't gonna mess with him. He'll shoot you as soon as look at you."

"Oh, forget it!" she snapped. "There's nothing you can do."

"You're right, baby," Russ agreed bleakly. "I can't shoot 'em, or call the police, or rip 'em off. Nothin' will get my coke back."

There was a spell of dreary silence. Dolores sat up, moodily lit a cigarette. "If it wasn't for my hustling and my job, we'd be on welfare, that's for sure," she said, sighing out the smoke and staring through the window that framed a bright, busy world outside. "Russ. . . ," she went on, then paused again. ". . . Where is all this getting us anyway. . . ?"

He jerked around, startled at her words. "Huh? What you sayin'?"

She did not answer right away and there was more silence, the unpleasant kind. She was preparing him for something.

"Whaddaya mean. . . ?" he asked again, already planning his counterattack, for he had expected this.

She sighed loudly and faced him, her green eyes cool and accusing. "I mean I'm getting fed up with turning five, six tricks a night, dancing my ass off, and hustling drinks, just so you can coke it up, every penny of it. And that's not all. I'm tired of boostin' and passing your checks and phony tens. No wonder I look like a wreck. It's lucky I'm not in jail again the way I was on account of Cliff."

"Oh yeah?" retorted Russ with indignation. "Jive talk like that ain't gonna get us nowheres, y'understan'?" He studied her grudgingly, stung by the bombshell she had just thrown. He realized he had to retaliate to keep her respect, for as a pimp, handling women was his business. It was a big mistake to let them get out of hand because they always abused their privileges and ended up wearing the pants. Then he was working for them instead of the other way around.

"Now I'm gonna tell you somethin' that I been noticin' but ain't said nothin' about!" he went on sternly. "You been losin' tricks lately, an' you know why? 'Cause you're startin' to look like an ol' street whore!" He reached out, turned her face toward the dresser mirror. "See what I mean? Eyes all sunk an' baggy an' you're pale as a ghost, like death warmed over! An' I think I know why, too—somethin' you been hidin'!"

"What? I don't hide anything from you!" she shrieked and pushed him away.

"You're chippin' heroin again, ain't ya, baby!" he said sharply. "Gettin' fucked up on dope, like maybe somebody's given' ya somethin' extra good an' you jus' forgot to tell your ol' man 'bout it, huh? Here, lemme see your arm!" He rolled over and grabbed her wrist with his free hand as she tried to slide out of bed.

"Get away from me!" she squealed.

He slapped her across the face. "I said, gimme your arm, bitch!" He scrutinized her left arm before she wriggled away. "Well, well, here's a couple tracks! Uh-huh! Goin' down on yer methadone so's you kin do a few bags to get high, huh? Hmm! Pretty soon you'll be ballin' drunks in an alley for five bucks a throw, an' I'll tell you, your ol' man's gonna be long gone!"

Dolores almost uttered something, then caught herself and began to weep, blotting her tears with the bedsheet. "I can't help it!" she moaned. "Only a few bags . . . a trick gives it to me. . . ." She sighed and sniffled loudly. ". . . I—I guess it's my life . . . things are no good anymore . . . and I'm shooting dope over it, even doing pills." She bit her lip. "Russ, can't you see? I want more, so much more out of life!"

"How many bags you doin'?"

"A few a day, that's all—three or four at the most. . . ."

"An' you never told me!" he ranted, confident now that he had her bluffed. "Thought you'd fool your ol' man, huh? Now I been wonderin' if you been stuffin' money on me, too!" In a dramatic gesture he grabbed her by the hair, pulled her down and she flopped sobbing on the pillow, buried her face. "I ought to really whup yo' ass but good! If you was a black whore, I would, too! Now I think I might pull another whore, find one without no man an' bring her in here with you!"

Dolores lifted her face up from the pillow in disbelief, her cheeks pale and streaked with tears. "The last pimp I had turned me onto heroin and got me put in jail," she sobbed. "And now you're gonna blow me just 'cause I'm using!"

"Git out, man!" he scoffed and bounced out of bed in disgust, convinced that she had been put back in her place. And though he tried not to show it, inwardly he felt very sorry for her, realizing that she had a point. He went to the dresser, fumbled around for the plastic bag of cocaine. "I'm almost outa this shit, too," he mumbled as he snorted a dime spoon. His heart began to pound a few moments and his spirits soared. He grinned in spite of himself, went back and sat down on the bed next to Dolores, who had turned away from him, and began rubbing her back. "Hey, I'm sorry baby!" he crooned. "I'm just uptight obout losin' the coke, dig? Things gonna be all right, you wait."

He came down off the cocaine after about fifteen minutes and got up again, paced nervously back and forth across the gray, threadbare carpet. Then he hastily found his works, fixed up and banged a shot into his arm. "Y'know, I don't care if I do run outa coke!" he bubbled almost immediately, untying the rubber tubing from around his bicep. "Here, you try some, baby. It'll make you feel better!"

"No, I want to do some dope, then maybe some coke, okay?" Dolores whimpered unashamedly.

"Anything!" Russ responded grandly, his mood soaring again from the cocaine. "Why, we'll get it together yet, baby, you watch! What you need is a change of pace. Jus' keep workin' at your same job, but no more boostin' or checks or nothin' for awhile. Hang onto your steady tricks, though, the good ones like that carload a' Chinamen that come Sunday night. On an' off like rabbits for twenty-five bucks apiece! Can't beat that! An' keep them high class tricks with bread. As for them young dudes out for a thrill, why I'll pull another whore for them. Know any chick ain't got a man?"

"No, they're all taken care of," Dolores muttered. "Besides, you know how I feel about that."

Sluggishly she rolled out of bed to search for her purse, while Russ watched her nude, voluptuous body with jet-black hair flowing against the pale, almost angelic, white skin. He was moved by her beauty, did not want to destroy her as his kind was wont to destroy women. In fact, he loved her. He might find another girl, but never one this pretty. Yet he thought how it was always the beautiful girls who gave him the most trouble so that their beauty seemed hardly worth it in the long run. Of course, white girls were better for business because the johns were not as wary of them, were less fearful of getting ripped off. Yet some black whores were worth more than their white sisters because they could beat so many tricks, grabbing the roll when they were getting paid, or snaking the big bills out of their customer's wallets after they got in the bed. But Russ himself was not really that kind of pimp, as were some of the younger junkies, who made a practice of roughing up tricks, mugging them in dark hallways, or breaking into their cars for billfolds that had been locked up for safekeeping.

At last Dolores retrieved two bags of heroin from her handbag, borrowed Russ's works and disappeared into the bathroom where she got off on her "wake-up". She did not like needles, but as forlorn and unhappy as she was feeling lately, the rush was worth it, gave her something to relish in life. Then, to hold her for the remainder of the day, and to prolong the high from the heroin, she popped six tabs of methadone. She began to feel relaxed and a sense of peace came over her as her worries faded. A pleasant, sweetness reappeared on her face, almost like the innocence on the face of a child, which prompted Russ to flop down beside her with a loud squeak of the bed springs.

"Hey baby, feelin' better?" he chirped. "Let's work out. Help us relax." He moved against her eagerly but she did not respond.

"I can't. . . ," she said sleepily. "There's something else I didn't tell you. I got them pains again . . . I think I need some more penicillin."

"Oh, gotta see a doc? That ain't nothin'," he reassured her.

She sighed. "Russ, they say you can't have children if you've had VD. Is that true?"

"I don' know. I ain't no doctor."

"Is it true that I could be sterile?" she went on, her face sad and troubled once more. "That's one of the things that I worry about all the time and I'm using heroin because of it. You know, I've had plenty of chances but I've never gotten pregnant. . . ."

Annoyed, Russ reached over, took the set of works. "Who knows, baby? Say, I'm gonna get off on a bag or two myself then, if we ain't gonna do nothin'."

He found the heroin in her purse, sat on the edge of the bed fixing up and probing for a vein. Dolores lay outstretched and motionless, her unnaturally pale skin nearly as white as the linens.

50

Dolores closed her eyes, heavy from the heroin, and dozed while Russ got off. In the trance of a half sleep she remembered how bad luck and bad health had been inseparable in her life and how her real trouble began at the age of fifteen when her mother was ill.

The woman had refused to stop drinking even after her liver failed again, stopping up the poisons in her body that should have been rendered harmless and then eliminated. And as more and more of these raw waste products accumulated in her tissues she was transformed into a pathetic, stooped crone tottering around with an enormous belly, spidery arms, pinched and yellowed skin, and dull, muddied eyes. This had been her mother once, this walking cadaver that could no longer even remember how to get to the bathroom and who stumbled out of the house half naked to be led back by the police. And she was endlessly garrulous in those days, rambling on in vague, fuzzy terms about trivial subjects and yet speaking all the while with great seriousness, as though the nonsense she uttered had deep meaning. Most of all, she stoutly denied that she was forgetful, or even the least bit ill, or that she ever drank a single drop in her entire life, despite the usual array of empty or half-finished glasses sitting forgotten around the house.

"Dee-dee," she croaked one afternoon, her voice almost reptilian in its dry harshness. "Where're my cigarettes? Did you take them?"

"I didn't touch them, mamma," Dolores replied. "I don't smoke, you know that."

"Well ... for God's sake ... I wouldn't lie to you! I haven't ... well if I did ... oh, ah. I had a girlfriend who lied through her teeth ... but, God Almighty, I ... uh, what are these? My cigarettes ... where did you ... uh...." She paused, forgetting completely what she was going to say, and began again. "Where's your sister...?"

"Babysitting—like she said. Now sit down, mamma, before you lose your balance."

"What, oh, thank you. Why, you ... want me to...."

"What?"

"Never mind ... oh, yes...."

"I said sit down, mamma!"

"... Sit down?" quavered her mother, then began rambling on in a monotone. "... Rest your weary ... uh-huh, speak up, tell your mother ... that's what I wanted to ... uh, no-no, don't be a shrinking violet ... a ... hey, what I say, uh, don't let others put, uh, words into your mouth, 'cause ... uh ... I'll be all right, never mind, uh, wait ... got to let out the cat...." She turned mechanically and shuffled into the kitchen.

Dolores heard the clink of a bottle, a brief pause and then a clatter as it was put back on the shelf. She ran into the kitchen, opened the cupboard door, found the half empty bottle of gin and confronted her mother with it.

"Mamma! Where did you get this?" she demanded. "So that really was a cab I saw outside this morning, wasn't it! Don't you understand, the doctor said no more, mamma! No more!"

Her mother stared vacantly back at the girl, eyes twitching, mouth trembling in child-like hurt. "Dee-dee ... I wasn't ... why, now as for things like that ... there are ... people who have ideas, but wh— ... uh, if I say each to his own and all for one ... one for all and all alone ... uh, one and all...."

"Oh, stop it, mamma!" Dolores shouted hysterically. "Now answer me! You had the cab bring it, didn't you! And you must have ordered more than just one bottle! Where's the other one? For Godsake, don't you understand it's killing you?" Disgusted and frightened, she poured the bottle into the sink while her mother stood by, watching dumbly.

Dolores and her sister tried to get their mother into a hospital but she refused to go. Then as her condition worsened the neighbors got involved and called a visiting nurse, who came to the home and tried to get her admitted but at that time there were no beds available. Besides, the sick woman still was unwilling to go. The nurse agreed to follow the family and to return in a few days. Dolores also contacted her welfare worker to ask for a high protein diet for her mother, mainly to get more money, since the one hundred thirty dollars the family received every two weeks was not enough to make ends meet. The social worker said that she would be willing to allot the family the extra money after a physician filled out a certain form that would be arriving in the mail. But after Dolores received the form, her mother was too sick to go to a doctor and they could not find anyone who would make a house call. So the form went unsigned. Instead, Dolores decided it was up to her alone to provide the extra money. With bills piling up and the rent overdue, she dropped out of school and went to work.

She was barely fifteen but pert and physically precocious. Customers at the luncheonette where she worked thought she was all of eighteen or nineteen. She liked her job even though the hours were long and she was always on her feet. Of course, she missed her friends at school but many of them were dropping out also, feeling as she did that their problems were more readily solved out of school than in. And Dolores enjoyed being out in the big wide world. She could meet all kinds of people, and soon had many interested men, all of whom flattered her with their attentions. She responded with an inviting twinkle in her pretty green eyes and an enigmatic smile on her full lips that hinted at some deeper, more exquisite possibility, though at her tender age she was not entirely sure just what this possibility might be. But she avoided open conversation with them, since it was forbidden by her employer and moreover, her basic shyness made it difficult for her to converse with perfect strangers who wanted to get friendly. Over the weeks she did come to know one boy better than the others, a youth of sixteen who worked part time as a stockboy in the same store. His name was Jay, and they found each other such good company that they began taking their lunch breaks together. She accepted his invitation one day to attend a rock concert, and although she enjoyed the evening much more than she had expected, she refused his offer to go out again the following week.

He felt put down until Dolores told him about her situation, that she had to stay home most of the time and look after her mother, who was sick. Relieved that she had not rejected him, Jay asked to visit her at home. She objected at first, embarrassed about the nature of her mother's illness, but at his urging she finally consented. After a few weeks the boy was spending nearly every evening at her home. He was a welcome addition to the fatherless family, acting almost as head of the household, doing repairs and so forth. And her mother and younger sister and brother all enjoyed his company.

But one person who resented his presence was her father, who came by periodically to forage for money and liquor. The first time he saw Jay he rudely ignored him. He was roaring drunk as usual, bullying everyone, yelling at the top of his lungs and demanding money.

"By Christ, if I can't even live in my own house, then goddammit I deserve somethin'!" he bawled. "So gimme a sawbuck an' I'll get the hell out!"

In order to avoid a scene they always gave him the money. Meanwhile he sniffed out any hidden bottle with uncanny accuracy, for he knew all the hiding places, and poured himself a double before leaving. Sometimes he would admonish his wife for having it on the premises, and then confiscate it for his own use.

He saw Jay for the second time some ten days later and gave him an ugly look. "What's this kid doin' hangin 'round here all the time, anyway?" he growled.

"He's a friend of mine," said Dolores.

"Friend, huh!" her father snorted. "That's a laugh! With an ass like yours, you ain't got no friends, lemme tell ya!"

"Fer Chrissake, shut up and—and get out!" squawked her mother. "You and your rotten mouth!"

"Huh? You callin' me rotten?" he muttered scornfully. "You, a cheap, two-bit whore callin' somebody rotten! Cracks me up! Why if it wasn't for you. . . ."

Her mother staggered up, muddy eyes glaring with hatred and her reedy voice trembling with rage. "Get out! Go ta hell, you bastard! Get out before I call the cops!"

Like a goaded bull he lowered his head and glared at her. There was a look of baffled contempt in his eyes, a feeling he had nourished toward her from the day they met nearly twenty years ago. And even though he had somehow married her, he was forever at a loss to explain just why or how he had done this thing that embittered him so. Gradually over the years this bitterness transformed itself into a consuming self-pity that picked away at his very being like a vulture until only a skeleton, a broken wreck of a man remained. And so he scowled at her now, that puzzled, rapt look of fascination at her hideousness never leaving his face.

"Sure, I'll get out," he breathed, and pointed at Dolores. "But she's comin' with me, see? This ain't a healthy place for her. It's a goddam whorehouse, for one thing, an' for another thing, I don't like punks hangin' around here just waitin' fer a chance ta get into her drawers, right punk?" He turned and leered knowingly at the youth.

"Daddy, that's no way to talk!" pleaded Dolores. "He's a nice guy!"

"What the hell do I care! Now you heard me, we're goin' over to your gran'ma's!" He seized her by the arm as she tried to get away.

"Jay, don't let him take her!" screamed her sister.

"Let her go! She's not going with you!" shouted the youth, trying to step between them. He reeled back from an elbow in the face and the three women began shrieking.

"Call the police!" Dolores cried, as her father dragged her struggling out the door, pushed her into a car and drove off.

The police were reluctant to interfere, explaining that this was a family matter and that someone would have to file a complaint before they could act. So the family waited for Dolores all night, and the next day Jay went over to her grandmother's and also searched all of her father's favorite hangouts, but the pair was nowhere to be found. The second night Dolores returned home alone. She looked very tired and her eyes had a strange, hard look that made her appear much older than before. Jay had never seen her like this and it made him uneasy. He greeted her with emotion but she only kissed him tensely and remained silent.

"What's wrong?" he asked, alarmed. "What happened?"

"I'll tell you later," she replied.

"No, tell me now! What did he do? Look, I don't care if he did hit me. The man was bombed out of his mind. He didn't know what he was doing!"

She shook her head and began to cry. "It—it's not that ... I ... I'm. ..."

"What? Tell me? What is it?"

She hung her head. "I—I was raped. ..."

He stared at her and she flashed that hard look at him again and he shrank back.

"Huh?" he replied stupidly. "You mean. ..."

"Yes!" she sobbed. "He beat me and ... then he raped me!"

"I don't believe it!" said the youth, stunned. "Are you sure he really did that?"

"It's true!" she confessed. "I screamed but he slapped me! He said he was going to beat me real bad if I didn't! He was drunk and taking pills! He was crazy...!" She sighed and wept and he took her gently in his arms.

After the incident, which was never reported to the police, she mourned her lost virtue only briefly, then coaxed Jay to sleep with her. She liked him very much and decided that a sexual relationship was the only way to hold him now. He cooperated, though rather reluctantly at first. Still uninitiated, he did not really believe in getting involved without marriage plans. And being so young, he had no plans. He loved Dolores, but it was the kind of puppy love that fades in the face of responsibility. He liked nothing better than making love to her but second thoughts plagued him more and more. She too saw the disadvantages of pregnancy or an abortion and what it might mean in terms of their commitment to one another. They began to quarrel over little things and the relationship cooled. It was heartbreaking for them both when they split up a few months later.

51

Dolores was well into her sixteenth year when she fell into prostitution. Of course she regretted it later but, like many such things, it happened unexpectedly at a time when nothing could have been further from her mind.

Her mother's condition had temporarily improved after several months of abstinence and high doses of vitamins. But she was still very forgetful. She strewed the house with lighted cigarettes and started at least one small fire in her room while smoking in bed, so Dolores and her sister and little brother had to watch her closely. Now that her speech was a bit more coherent she took to sitting around the house, bemoaning her misfortunes in life, her poverty, her bad health. And after a few weeks there was some reason to suspect that she was drinking again by the faint odor of mouthwash on her breath after her "walks". One afternoon in particular she went on at great length about men in general and how every last one of them was no damn good, rotten to the core, and how collectively they had ruined her life.

"Just look at what your father did to me," she rasped. "The no-good, irresponsible bastard. . . ."

Dolores had never mentioned what her father had done to her, and patiently commiserated with her mother. Always a considerate child, she had realized at an early age that her mother had too many of her own problems to be concerned with anyone else's, even her own daughter's. And yet she could not help begrudging her mother for her self-centeredness, and felt more and more an urge to somehow prove to the woman that she was utterly selfish, and to do this even at her own expense if necessary.

An opportunity arose one day when two of the boys from the local barroom paid a social visit to their home. As usual they were affable and extremely thirsty.

"Wh'say, Ella, where ya been hidin'?" one exclaimed with an oily smile. He was dressed gaily in a loud, mod-style sports shirt and corduroy bell-bottoms, a bit outlandish for someone pushing fifty.

The other man was unshaven, in his late forties also. He looked as though he had not changed his work clothes in days and reeked with the strong odor of sweat. "Jeeze," he quipped, scanning the room, "I thought from the sound a' things we'd hafta come over'n bury ya!"

Her mother burst out in a gale of laughter. Suddenly alive again in their company, her complaints of a moment ago were completely forgotten. "That's a riot," she cackled. "Say, can I get you fellas something?"

"Sure, whaddaya got?"

"Just an unopened fifth of bourbon. I've been on the wagon. Just savin' it for a rainy day."

"Oh, hey," said the sharply dressed man, holding up a hand in mild protest. "We kin see how you ain't s'posed ta have nothin', uh, Ellie. Look, we'll just have a cup a' coffee if. . . ."

"Oh no ya don't!" she objected. "I don't want to be no killjoy! Even if I have just a drop it won't make a particle of difference, and you fellas can take the rest along with you if you want."

She disappeared, returned with the freshly unearthed fifth, the full bottle dark and shiny. The two men broke the seal and opened it, their eyes drinking in the tawny fluid even before it touched their lips. It was milk to them. Deprived of it they were but shadows of themselves, tense, sullen, insecure. But a drink or two made them whole again, transformed them into swashbuckling, backslapping buckaroos who would have blessed the pope had he walked in on them.

"Ellie, you're as beautiful as ever," one of them kidded grandly while the other laughed and searched for something to pour into.

"Dolores, honey, get us some glasses and some ice, will you?" her mother asked, trying to ignore this obviously absurd compliment but genuinely tickled at the same time.

"You're not supposed to have any!" the girl retorted. "Remember what the doctor said?" She was standing in the doorway to the kitchen, looking at them with shocked disapproval.

"Yes, I remember, but I'm old enough to take care of myself, don't you think, dear?" her mother replied acidly.

"Well, I won't get it!" Dolores shot back.

The two men eyed the young girl with interest as she turned and disappeared into the kitchen. The one in the loud outfit followed her. "Hold it, I'll get it," he said, entering the kitchen and filling it with the sickening smell of shaving lotion. She stood by uneasily as he jauntily opened the refrigerator and broke loose the ice tray, then glanced sidewise at her. "Remember me?" he whispered with the same oily smile. "Al, down at the grill. You're gettin' prettier every day, y'know it?"

"If you got business, Al, I'll take care of it," croaked her mother from the other room. "Now come on back with that ice an' let's celebrate."

He returned to the front room and her mother stood up, put her arms around him and purred huskily. "Now Al, honey, you know where to come if you want something, don't you? She's a little young for you, I'm afraid."

He shrank back involuntarily at the sight of her approaching face, even more ghoulish without the usual facade of paint, now a pallid wad of wrinkles, like yellowed newsprint. He glanced around at Dolores and his eye gleamed momentarily. "Well, let's pour us a highball an' we'll talk it over," he said, playfully, obviously keen on having as much fun for himself as the occasion would allow.

Her mother obediently clinked ice into the glasses while he filled them generously with the bourbon, clear and amber, so pure that it looked genuinely healthful. He went back into the kitchen for some water and winked at Dolores on his way out. No sooner had they drained their glasses than they poured themselves another round. He sat down next to her mother, his face suffused and glowing now with the same vermillion hue as his clothing, so that he appeared to blushing solidly from head to toe.

"Hey, I got an idea," Al went on lightly, almost joking but not quite. "How 'bout fifty bucks either way. . . ?" He nodded toward the kitchen with a broad, mischievous grin and before her mother could answer he broke into raucous laughter.

"Very funny," her mother rejoined with sarcasm. "Whaddaya think my daughter is, anyway? A whore like I am?"

"You said it, not me," Al replied jovially. There was a pause and he reached back and pulled out his wallet, carelessly counted out five twenties and slapped them on he table. "Got into a good card game last night," he chuckled.

Her mother's jaw quivered involuntarily at the sight of the money, more cash than she had seen in months. She was very low on gin, her favorite drink and knew what would happen if she ran out. She would get the horrors and see things, or maybe go into the DT's—a raving delerium—and wind up back in the hospital, maybe for the last time.

"Rich these days, aren't ya," she observed.

"Uh-huh," he said smugly. "So . . . how 'bout it?"

The other man shifted in his seat, snickered with embarrassment. "Hey, c'mon Al, yer kiddin," he grumbled.

"Who's kiddin'?" said Al, and smirked with the same innocent, playful look.

Dolores moved up to the doorway of the kitchen again to hear what was going on. She thought they were joking until she saw her mother take the money and go into the bedroom with Al as she had done so many times before with so many men through the years. There was a brief silence, then some shouting, and they came out again, Al grinning from ear to ear.

"She can't even undo her buttons!" he said to his friend with a wink. "She's gonzo!"

"Shut up! I can so!" her mother insisted, flustered and obviously very insulted.

"Well. . . ?" Al remarked casually. "I gotta get sumpin' for my dough, don't I?"

There was a tense pause. Eyes shifted to Dolores. The other man tossed off his glass and stood up suddenly. "Aw Al, fer Chrissake, c'mon!" he said impatiently. "She's only a kid! Hey, let's get goin', whaddaya say? I gotta get home. . . ."

"Hey, be right with ya, Ernie," Al said, looking at Dolores hungrily.

"I won't do it, mamma!" Dolores said quietly and stepped back. "You can't make me!"

Her mother gave her a long, sad look. "Dee-dee. . . ," she began imploringly and then paused, not knowing quite how to say it. "We. . . ."

"No, mamma!" Dolores shouted, amazed at what she guessed was on her mother's lips.

Her mother clanked her glass down on the coffee table in front of her and stood up, trembling in a sudden fit of anger. "Goddam you!" she spat. "Here you were playin' around with that stupid kid for six months! Don't think I didn't know it! And look what you have to show for it? Nothing, that's what! And here your poor mother sits flat broke while you're out having your fun every night! Some daughter you are, an' don't try an' come on like no lady! I never was a phony, so by God, don't you be one!"

Recovering from the initial shock at what she had just heard, Dolores felt a fury building up inside her that she had never known before as she stood looking with stupefaction at the shriveled woman. She saw now that her mother was hopelessly selfish and debased, and that her father had been right in many of the things he had said about her. And Dolores perceived everyone in her family being corrupted by this trait of callous self-interest, as though stricken by a kind of grave, hereditary defect, something that they could do nothing about except learn to live with. Just for a moment she wanted to run away, to bolt out of the house. Then a strange, cruel impulse seized her, a vindictive desire to submit to her mother's bidding and to hold her responsible for the rest of her days for whatever suffering it would bring.

"All right, if that's what you want, then I will!" she heard herself say evenly. She stared coldly at her mother for a moment, then spun on her heel and walked quickly past them into the bedroom.

It was much different than with her father. The slap he had given her when she resisted him had numbed the whole side of her face and she collapsed, hardly aware of his heavy hulk that she had known briefly but affectionately as a child, now thrusting and lunging into her with stabbing pain. Even Jay had been rough with her at times, wanting to love her for hours at a time until she got sore. But this man was polite, almost ingratiating in the gentle way that he coaxed her. She cooperated mechanically, partially disrobing and lying back on her mother's bed, hoping oddly that she would not make the same squeaking noises that her mother had made so often in this room with other men for as long as she could remember.

"Relax, sweetheart," Al muttered with excitement, hardly believing his good fortune. "I ain't gonna hurt ya."

The odor of alcohol blended with the powerful scent of shaving lotion almost choked her and reminded her of her father's breath. She grimaced and turned her face away from him, her body rigid. He waited patiently, then probed eagerly until at last he entered her. After a minute or two of rapid thrusting he was spent and she felt him relax, a breathing, sweating mass of flesh oppressing hers.

"Nice, nice, baby!" he panted. "You got it! You really got it!" He rested for a few seconds, then rose obligingly and hoisted his trousers, smiling gratefully. "Boy, was that cherry!" he went on. "I'll see you again sometime, huh?"

She nodded silently, thinking how it had not been as bad or as disgusting as she had anticipated. There was no pain or any real discomfort and he had been very kind. Furthermore, the family's financial worries had been temporarily relieved by the sudden addition of one hundred badly needed dollars, more than she earned in a whole week at the luncheonette. And since Dolores was the breadwinner nowadays, there were others to think of.

There was not only her mother but her sister and brother to take care of and out of necessity she had to put their interests ahead of her own. She concluded that she was being called upon to make the same sacrifice that she now realized her mother had made, despite her seeming selfishness, so that at last the idea became altogether logical and she accepted it.

Al did come back later and brought a friend, who knew someone else, who in turn brought some of his friends. Inside of six months the family had vacated their dreary flat in the rundown neighborhood to take a nice, airy apartment in a much better part of town. That fall Dolores sent her younger sister to a parochial school and hired a woman to look after her mother and little brother. She had quit her job as waitress and spent her time hanging around in downtown hotels and nightclubs with the other girls, most of them quite a bit older than she.

They taught her a lot of shortcuts to satisfying a man without ever having to go to bed with him. She discovered that because she was so young and cute that she needed only to put out her good looks for some of them, or maybe let them take off her bra. Others needed a little more coaxing, and a quick massage or a kiss in the right place finished them off right on the spot, usually in a parked car in a downtown garage. Since she never had to go all the way, the other girls began calling her "the virgin whore". Of course, she was careful, learned to stay away from teenagers, who were too rough, and drunks, who were too slow. She never went for less than twenty-five dollars a trick and the more they wanted, the more she jacked up the price.

After a few more months, however, she began turning regular tricks in order to build up a steady clientele. One convention night she turned eleven tricks and made $500. That week she made $1,800, tax free. One year in the business changed her way of living completely. She drove a new car and had all the clothes she ever wanted. When her thirteen year old brother was arrested while joyriding with his friends in a stolen car, Dolores had the money for a good lawyer. And there was enough for her mother to get proper care and nutrition at home, to the point where she felt well enough to go back to the tavern again. Forever grateful to her daughter for their sudden rise in the world, Ella became a proud, doting mother. Now, for the first time in her life, she could not find enough praise for Dolores's unnatural beauty and cleverness, while she herself was content at last with the happy obscurity of retirement.

Of course, success was not without its hazards. Dolores had a frightening experience one night when a trick who had been drinking accused her of taking money out of his wallet and roughed her up. Next, an undercover cop arrested her for prostitution and she had to stay in jail overnight because of insufficient cash to post bail. It was then that she decided to make a choice between either going out into the suburbs where things were quieter, or staying in town and getting what many of the other girls had, a pimp to take care of her. Because she knew the city and liked to work the big hotels, she put the word out that she was looking for a man.

One night at a party two girl friends introduced her to a powerfully built and extremely charming black man of about twenty-nine or thirty by the name of Cliff. He seemed very interested in her and almost at once she decided she liked him. All the pimps she knew were black and she was not deeply prejudiced.

"Sure baby," said Cliff, flashing a wide grin across his handsome face. "You ain't got a man an' me, I'm lookin' for a woman, 'specially someone young an' cute like you." And he chuckled and once more flashed a very special, inviting grin.

Quickly ousting the woman he was staying with, he moved Dolores into his apartment. As was common practice, he took most of the money but gave her what she needed for clothes and enough for her family. In return he supplied the place where she worked, posting himself in an adjoining bedroom in case of trouble. He also took her around town wherever she wanted to go and was ready to post bail at a moment's notice if she were ever arrested. And he made love to her with feeling, because now he was her man.

52

One evening after she was comfortably settled in Cliff's apartment, another couple dropped by with some good cocaine and began banging it. Dolores had tried snorting it before at parties and developed a taste for it but no more. Because it was psychologically and not physically addicting, she had little fear of sampling it again on this occasion and enjoying the brief, effervescent high. Then someone produced a few bags of heroin.

"Ever speedballed, baby?" Cliff asked her. "It's real groovy. Ya take an' mix smack an' coke together."

"I've never even used smack or done anything by needle," she replied.

"Honey," laughed one of the women, "you don't know what you're missin'! Ain't done smack?" She turned to her gentleman friend. "Marcus, honey, give her a skin pop from that good bag."

"That'll set her on her ass," Marcus replied gleefully. "I better use jus' a tiny hit. It's gold star dope, man, thirty dollars a bag straight from New York."

"Hey, wow, lemme speedball with it, man," said Cliff, reaching for the works.

Dolores had been leery and ready to refuse it. But when she saw Cliff's big hand groping for it and the greedy look on his face, she was both annoyed and impressed. Her first thought was not to let herself be elbowed out by him, for he should be thinking of her or else it was no good between them. And then she reasoned that if he was in such a hurry, then this stuff must be awfully good. She was filled with a natural envy that occurs especially between lovers when one has experienced something that the other has not.

"Wait. . . ," she said. "I want to try some, just a drop, but not in the vein."

Cliff politely yielded, and nodding vigorously, told Marcus to go ahead and give her a skin pop. The slim, effusive young man cooked up half of one bag, drew up only a few drops through the cotton into the syringe and jabbed the needle into the back of her arm. While she sat waiting for the effect, he dumped some cocaine into the cooker, mixed it with the rest of the heroin, drew up the shot and passed it to his girl friend.

"You bang it for me, honey," she insisted, holding out her exposed forearm. "An' I'm jus' gonna sit here an' get high!" As she said this her face relaxed dramatically in an expression of ecstasy.

Marcus tied his girl friend off, milked a vein till it stood out, and popped in the needle. He drew a little blood into the syringe and by working the plunger in and out, mixed it with the fix. Then he slowly injected it back into her bloodstream, carefully because too much at one time could put her right out.

"O-o-o-h, baby, I am high! It's . . . beautiful!" the woman giggled, swooning and lolling on the sofa, again very dramatically, acting the way others expected her to feel.

"I'm next," said Cliff and quickly began fixing up.

Dolores sat expectantly, waiting for something to happen when suddenly she grew conscious of a delicious warmth flooding through her body. She felt wonderfully drowsy, then her flesh started to tingle and she began scratching herself, "I itch all over," she complained dully. "But . . . I sure feel good . . . like I'm floating. . . ."

"That itchin's from the quinine," said Cliff. "It'll go 'way." He looked over at Marcus, a little concerned. "You gave her a pretty good hit."

"She'll be okay," Marcus assured him. "It's just a match head."

Cliff frowned. "Of this stuff? Man, that's like a couple bags a' street dope." He went over to her, let her head flop onto his broad shoulder.

". . . Oh, Cliff, I'm loaded. . . ," she mumbled.

"You ain't as high as I am," the other girl boasted thickly. "I am really flyin' on this coke! You oughta try it this way. . . !" And she lolled luxuriantly on the sofa, aping a sublime smile.

As soon as Cliff got off, Marcus took the set of works and busily began fixing up. "I'm gonna get higher than that!" he declared grandly. "Like, I'm gonna do a whole bag a' dope, man, 'long with a quarter spoon a' coke!"

"You'll OD," said Cliff with an inappropriate grin, his eyes bright with genuine pleasure at the sensation of the cocaine.

"No, man, I done it before. Lotta times," Marcus insisted. "No sweat. I'm gonna blow my mind!" His lean, brown face was composed with the supreme confidence of a man who considered himself a venerable master at the art of getting high.

By now Dolores could hearly hear them. It was as though she were deep in the midst of a dream, swimming in a vast sea of deliciousness, of vanilla ice cream—her favorite flavor—arching through miles upon miles of it like a porpoise. She never knew a feeling like this existed, for she had never as yet experienced the closest thing to it, the fleeting thrill of sexual orgasm. The nearest thing she could compare it to was the relaxed state of well-being after a good nap or a hot bath, both of which she knew and enjoyed. Certainly the feeling was not completely foreign. It seemed to touch upon something deep within her, the memory traces of an early, preconscious experience, a tranquil voyage, bobbing silently, blissfully in the cozy salinity of a primal uterine sea.

She nodded for awhile, then as the sensation waned she longed for it again. And she was aware now of another, completely new feeling, a sudden apprehension that this pleasure could be denied her if she was not careful. In fact, she had inherited an important new craving, a new master of her body and soul.

Impatiently she prodded Cliff. "Gimme one more hit, honey," she said. "I'm comin' down."

He responded with an unnatural grin, pleased that she had just discovered one of the real secrets of life that he had known about all along. Now they could share this marvelous thing together.

"Nothin' like it, huh, baby?" he gloated. "You wouldn't b'lieve jus' that little bit a' white powder could get ya so high, haw! But you ain't seen nothin' yet. You're really gonna dig this. . . ."

He cooked up a small amount of the heroin, tied her off and inserted the needle directly into one of the veins in her forearm, mixing the clear fluid with the blood and squeezing it in very slowly. "Lemme know when ya get the rush—that's from the quinine, baby, an' I'll give ya the rest in a skin pop," he said.

". . . Wow . . . I feel it!" she said dizzily. She almost swooned, then wretched unexpectedly.

"Don't worry 'bout pukin', baby," he assured her. "Jus' means it's good dope."

This time she felt an orgasmic rush that titillated every nerve in her body. She relaxed and then nodded out completely in a beautiful, dreamy sleep that she never wanted to awaken from. And in this repose she found that she no longer despised herself for being a prostitute, an outcast from society. It was all right to be alive again. From then on she was in love, not so much with Cliff as with his heroin. She loved it because it loved her, made her feel better than anyone ever did or ever would.

In succeeding months she chipped from Cliff's supply of dope, at first doing just a few bags now and then. She found it was good for her work, that she could turn more tricks without caring one way or the other. Cliff was naturally aware of this and provided her with whatever she needed. Yet he warned her against getting strung out, fearing she would let her appearance go and lose money. But the more she used, the more she began to notice the unpleasantness of the withdrawal.

"Cliff, do I have the flu?" she asked one morning, shivering under a blanket.

"Ain' no flu, baby," he remarked. "That's the jones. Jus' do a bag an' you'll be straight."

She used more dope to take away the sick and soon had a regular but light habit of five or six bags a day. Then she began to tire of jabbing herself with a needle everytime she needed a fix.

"I hate needles! Just look at my arms!" she complained to Cliff one day, pointing to a line of discolored puncture marks or "tracks" tracing the course of the larger veins.

He smiled with a knowing twinkle in his eyes. "I ain't no dope addict 'cause I can't stand needles either," he admitted. "But I know some cats who get high jus' off'n a point. Needle freaks, we call 'em. Y'see, that's where a junkie's head is at. He digs the needle, makes him feel like a man when he shoots up. But lotta others, like you, maybe don't dig needles an' go for methadone instead. You don't get the same, quick nod behind it like you do heroin. It's a slow buzz, y'see what I mean, but it'll get ya high. Ten or twenty milligrams is about like a bag a' street dope, y'dig? Hey, I'll cop some for you, baby, an' you kin try it. I do it now an' then m'self when I can't find nothin' else, y'understan'?"

She tried the methadone, started off with five of the small, white, ten milligram dolophines, or "dollies", and felt just the kind of gradual high that Cliff described, with the same blissful feeling of warmth and relaxation that she got with heroin. On his advice she popped three more at bedtime and slept all night like a baby. She liked it and found it much more convenient than heroin. It made her placid and content with life, rather than anxious and irritable, and she could stay straight on it all day long, go to work without having to worry about the risk of carrying a set of works in her purse and fixing up again five or six hours later. And best of all, she did not have to put a spike in her arm.

After few weeks Cliff sat her down one evening, his square-jawed, handsome face wearing a slight leer of contempt that she had never seen before. "Baby, you been doin' a lotta dope lately—methadone, plus some heroin an' coke, ain't ya?" he said bluntly. "An' I done been coppin' for ya, dig? Well, now I want you to do for me, y' understan' what I'm sayin'?"

"But I'm turning tricks," she replied. "What more do you want?"

"I know, baby," he went on, nodding at her as though she were a child and smiling ironically. "An' that's cool, but what I really need is fo' a chick kin take care o' business, understan' what I mean? Like boostin' an' passin' a few checks, dig? An' baby, you got a good enough head on your shoulders to get hep to it, see what I mean?"

"Oh no, Cliff, I don't want to get into that," she protested.

Without warning he slapped her sharply across the face. "Who you talkin' to bitch!" he snapped. "Remember, I'm your ol' man an' I'm the one who cops for you!"

She held the side of her face in hurt amazement, her thoughts flying back to the last time she was slapped, by her father. He had been irrational, intoxicated with pills and alcohol and she had to give in to protect herself. Now the same submissiveness came over her. She wanted only to keep the peace and to please Cliff. After all, she liked him and because he was nearly twelve years older, she instinctively submitted to his authority. That he was, in fact almost a substitute father did not enter her mind, nor did she realize that she was simply repeating the same kind of foolish, self-sacrificing behavior as before.

Cliff taught her the art of "boosting," or shoplifting— how to avoid store detectives, cameras and mirrors while quickly rolling something up and thrusting it usually under the skirt and between the legs in one rapid motion. And she was schooled in the intricate techniques of forging and cashing stolen checks. He had a picture ID made up for her to match a set of stolen ID's and she deftly practiced the signature. His efforts paid off. With Dolores working under his direction they made thirty thousand dollars the first year. She was caught shoplifting only once but talked her way out of it. Then she got too hot for the banks and he put her to work passing phony tens, badgering the store clerks for change, acting in a hurry or anything else to distract them from scrutinizing the counterfeit bills.

Now that they were well-to-do, Cliff drove her around in a big El Dorado. He got involved in the traffic of cocaine and heroin and made even more money, but then one night he did not come home and was found the next day slumped over the steering wheel of his car, shot twice in the head. The police were very interested in the circumstances of his death, for it seemed that he was involved with mob figures in a check-cashing and narcotics ring. When they questioned Dolores and linked her to the victim, they went back and found her photos taken by the cameras in various banks when she passed the checks. They put together such a good case of grand larceny against her that she was found guilty and sentenced to two years in the women's house of correction, to be eligible for parole after six months. And, she was required to make restitution for the money she stole.

53

It was just after dark when a solitary man came out of the subway, his gait stiff and cautious from having had one too many. He turned uphill, walking head down, did not see one shadow crouched between two parked cars and another next to a hedge. He was only aware of falling backwards and as he tried to regain his balance something struck him on the back of the head and he knew nothing more.

Ramon jammed the tape-covered pipe into his coat and glanced around while Slick went through the man's pockets, extracting the wallet and removing a ring and wristwatch. Then they ran downhill, across the main street and into the subway.

"That's good for a start," Slick panted as they boarded the train. "Thirty-five bucks and the other stuff oughta be worth ten or twenty. No cards, though." He grinned. "Hey, you really whacked him."

"He'll be okay," said Ramon, secretly proud of the way he put the victim out. He considered himself as good a mugger, if not better than Slick, though both of them were a little small to do the job alone. "Let's switch cars, man, maybe we'll see somethin'."

They got off at the next stop, walked back to a nearly empty car. An elderly couple was sitting at one end and a few other passengers near the opposite end. As the train lurched ahead they sat down across from the elderly couple. The noise of the wheels rose to a loud thundering while the passengers stared tiredly out the windows or poked their noses into newspapers, books. The trainman was sitting in his compartment facing the other way. The elderly couple paid the two youths no attention until they jumped up and put knives to their throats.

"Don't move or say nothin'," said Slick. "Now give us yer money!"

The old man's eyes widened with alarm and he threw up his arms to push the knife away. "Get away! Get out!" he yelled and then moaned, clutched his side where the point of the knife went in. Another slash and his pocket was slit, Ramon grabbing his wallet.

"Please!" quavered the old woman. "Don't kill us! We won't. . . !"

"Shut up!" Slick snapped and jabbed the knife at her eyes to distract her, while Ramon yanked at her purse and snatched out a pocketbook.

The old woman sat shivering in terror while her husband groaned and clutched his side, his face deathly pale. The passengers gawked in terror from the other end of the car, a few huddling together like frightened sheep. The train squealed to a halt at the next station just as the trainman became aware of what had happened. The doors opened and the two youths leapt out and fled.

The old man had reason to resist. He was carrying fifty dollars in his wallet, but the old woman had only four dollars in her purse.

"We gotta do better than this," Slick grumbled with disgust as they rested in a vacant lot.

"Yeah," Ramon admitted. "I came along so's we could really score, right? Well, like I said before, man, let's find a car an' rob a couple stores. That's the only way we're gonna make it."

Slick shrugged. "Anything for dope, right?"

"Right."

They wandered down a side street for a few blocks, careful to avoid being seen. Soon they found what they wanted, a parked Volkswagen bug. Ramon, also an expert car thief, pried open the window, forced the ignition with a pair of sharp-pointed scissors and started the engine. They drove across town to a pharmacy. Unlike many, it had not been hit recently as far as they knew. Parking the car with the engine running, they checked their guns. Slick had his snubnosed, chrome-plated .32 caliber revolver and Ramon a tiny, .25 caliber Beretta automatic. Quickly they peered through the window, sized up the situation. Luckily there were no customers inside and the two men present were standing side-by-side behind the counter.

"You cover the tall guy an' I'll take the guy in white," said Slick. "If anyone comes in, cover 'em an' tell 'em to lay down on the floor."

"Chrissake, I've pulled lotta holdups too," argued Ramon. "I know what to do."

The men behind the counter looked up the moment the two youths entered the store, watching them nervously.

"Hands up an' don't move!" snapped Slick, suddenly whipping out his revolver.

"Aw, come on, fellas!" begged the pharmacist, a smallish, older man in a white coat and thick glasses.

Ramon fired into the ceiling. "We mean it!" he shouted. "All your narcotics an' money, quick!"

The two men started at the shot and edged back, hands up.

"Okay, okay!" said the pharmacist. "We'll do anything you say, just don't shoot!"

He stepped up to the register, opened the cash drawer, reached in and fumbled around. Something clattered and he jerked his arm. At that instant a shot rang out and he flinched, clutched his chest with a look of disbelief, and fell to the floor.

"He had a gun in there, the mother fucker!" yelled slick, and turned his gun on the taller man. "We'll shoot you too, if ya don't give it to us!"

"Hey. . . !" exclaimed the clerk, dazed. "You—you shot him! Why, I've known him for twenty. . . ." He dropped an arm and Ramon shot him in the leg. He looked up, pain and terror written on his face, raised his arms again. "Don't! Don't!" he pleaded and limped over to the narcotics drawer, returning quickly with some bottles of Dilaudid and morphine and put them on the counter.

Slick stuffed the bottles into his pockets while Ramon reached over and seized the money out of the register. They made the man lie down on the floor, then ran out and jumped in the idling car.

"Too bad about that guy," Ramon said as he squealed around the corner.

Slick was leafing through the bills. "Three hundred bucks, just about. . . ." He paused. "Yeah, stupid mother fucker! All that hassle for three hundred measly bucks, but the dope was worth it," he said and patted his coat pocket.

They decided on their next score and drove on in silence for about twenty minutes. Their target was a gas station with a lone attendant sitting patiently inside. He was a very courteous young man and came out immediately to wait on them.

"Yessir?"

Ramon poked the tiny Beretta in his face. "All of it, right now!" he ordered.

Slick got out of the other side and covered the attendant as he lifted his hands, frozen with fear. Ramon pressed the gun against his forehead, leaving a white circle from the imprint of the muzzle.

"Move!"

They shoved him into the station where he pulled a fistfull of small bills out of a drawer. Slick jerked the drawer out, grabbed the rest of the money.

"Hidin' it on us, huh?" he snarled, and held his gun against the terrified attendant's belly. "Where's the shit house?"

"R—round there," gasped the young man.

"C'mon!"

They took him stumbling around to the men's room, pushed him inside.

"We oughta kill 'im," said Slick.

"Please don't kill me!" begged the attendant. "Please don't!"

"Shut up! You can identify us!"

"No I won't, honest, I. . . ."

Slick raised the trembling gun, his knuckles white around the grip.

"Hold it, man!" said Ramon. He drew out his taped pipe and with a lightning stroke, smacked the attendant behind the ear. "That's enough," he went on, stepping over the motionless form of the attendant. "We done too much shootin' already, man. It ain't smart."

"Ah, you got a paper asshole!" sneered Slick, putting his gun away. "You're in this as much as I am! You shot a guy too!"

Ramon was peering out of the men's room and pulled at Slick. "C'mon, let's go—no, wait!" he said and stepped back inside. Another car had pulled up to the pumps, the driver craning his neck, looking for the attendant. The two youths waited a long moment until the impatient motorist drove off, then jumped into the stolen car and sped away.

54

Slick and Ramon's unexpected arrival caused considerable stir in the Quinn household. The moment they entered, his mother upbraided her son for not having called beforehand.

"And where've you been, Vinnie?" she demanded. "We haven't seen or heard from you in over a week. Why I was worried sick. I almost had a nervous breakdown!"

He sneered at her. "Don't get uptight, ma."

She sighed with exasperation, continued shrilly. "I'm not—oh, I hate that word! Now Vinnie, make sense! Can't you see your mother is upset? If you'd only called, why I could have left dinner in the oven! But no, you didn't call so of course you missed it! No wonder you're so thin at the age of twenty-two! No wonder you didn't grow like your two sisters! And it was delicious, that roast, why you would have loved it, and now it's cold—all wrapped up and put away!" She sighed again, then, seeing Ramon's eyes on her, smiled, her voice mellowing. "And who's your friend?"

"This is a buddy a' mine . . . Ramon."

Ramon's single glance had transformed her into another person. Her irritability vanished, replaced now by an oozing coquettishness as she beamed intently at the young man. "Well, come into the kitchen, Ramon," she said invitingly. "Don't be shy. I'll bet you haven't had supper. You look hungry. I'll heat something up."

She sat them down at the table and busied herself laying out the silver. Wearing a partially unbuttoned blouse and an old brassiere, she bent over them, her pendulous breasts dangling in plain sight of Ramon, who stared, while Slick paid no attention.

"I hope Ramon won't mind some of my beef stew," she prattled. "It's the easiest thing to heat up at this hour. And where's that girl of yours, Vinnie?" she asked, her lips turning up saucily in the suggestion of a smile.

"Home, I guess," he mumbled.

She turned away and opened the refrigerator, Ramon's eyes following her movements as she stooped over. "I'm not so sure about her. . . ," she went on, her voice growing shrill again. "But anyway. . . ." She sighed loudly with resignation. "You two go wash up. No telling what you've been up to." She looked back over her shoulder at Ramon with a girlish twinkle in her eye. "And better take your friend with you and get him a towel."

"Sure, ma," said Slick. He stood up, took the revolver out of his pocket, broke it open, snapped it shut and laid it carelessly on the table.

For a moment she gawked at the chrome-plated weapon, then frowned seriously at her son. "Wait till I tell your father you have that gun again!" she warned in a low voice.

"Go ahead an' tell 'im, I don't give a shit," he answered defiantly. "I need it for protection."

She drew herself up in front of him, her bust out and hands on her broad hips. "Vinnie, don't talk to your mother that way! Honestly, sometimes I wish you were someone else's son, the way you treat me!"

"Don't get so uptight, ma!" he interrupted. "What have I done? Just tell me, what have I done?"

She stared at him for a moment, faltering at his argument. "Vinnie. . . ," she went on again. "Please put the gun away before—"

"I am!" Slick growled. "Just wait a minute, will ya?"

His father's voice interrupted them from the hallway. "What's this about a gun?" he asked. The odor of alcohol seeped into the kitchen as he entered, dressed as usual in baggy work clothes and clutching a beer. As though having difficulty focusing his reddened eyes, he glowered around the kitchen, then caught the glint of chrome on the table. "Hey, you can't bring that thing in here!" he bawled. "I won't allow it! What have you been up to, anyway? Out robbin' and stealin'?"

His mother glared at her husband with displeasure. She did not like to see him throwing his weight around in her kitchen. "That's no way to talk to him!" she countered. "He says he needs it for his own protection!"

"He does like hell!" his father yelled, amazed at his own mettle at standing up to her but feeling justified in this case. "According to you this punk never did anything wrong in his life, even though he's been in court a million times an' spent six months in the can! Protection my ass!"

She crossed her arms coldly and spoke with a quiet arrogance that signalled that her patience was at an end. "Why don't you go back to your ball game," she suggested. "Remember, I said you could stay here only if you knew how to behave, and already you're starting all over again. . . !"

Abashed, he took a step backward, then forward again, driven by a reckless self-righteousness that he knew he would have to pay for eventually. "Well, I don't give a shit, to tell you the truth!" he declared. "But I'll say this much—I may be a shit bum and everything else, but that don't matter one bit! What matters is that no kid a' mine's gonna go 'round packin' a rod like some cheap hoodlum, d'you understand, Maureen?" He extended his hand. "Now, gimme the gun, Vinnie. . . !"

"Listen!" she shrieked and moved close beside her son, who gazed insolently at his father. "Why don't you use your head! If someone is after him he has to protect himself, doesn't he? God knows, there are so many nutty people around nowadays! Now why don't you just tend to your own knitting for a change! Think about straightening out your own life!"

"What kinda bullshit is that?" his father wheezed, his bleary eyes popping with anger. He began shaking, both with rage and from his fear of her, and tried to say more but the words stuck in his throat.

Ramon tried to rise from the table but Mrs. Quinn gently crowded him back into his chair. "Don't mind him," she assured the youth. "He's just in one of his moods, that's all." She turned again to her husband, jabbing a finger at him. "You're always poking your nose into Vinnie's business like it was your own!" she chided. "But you! I was talking to father yesterday about you! You know what he said? He said that you're a disgrace to the family, that's what! Now go back in to your ball game and leave the poor child alone! I'll handle this in my own way!"

"Do as she says, pa. . . ," Slick said, grinning slightly, his hand on the gun.

His father's fierce look changed to astonishment as he eyed his son clutching the gun. He drew back, began sputtering. "Huh? Why . . . I'll get you for this, you miserable. . . ! Threaten me with a gun, will you? Why you rotten punk! Why don't you go back out on the streets where you belong! Go ahead—rob, steal, murder, see if I care!"

"Stop it!" screeched his mother.

Ramon stood up abruptly. "I gotta go . . . I'm. . . ."

She blocked his path and he ran up against her soft breasts. "Please stay, Ramon," she pleaded. "Supper will be ready in a jiff. It's no trouble, really. Now come on, sit down!"

Ramon grinned sheepishly, sat down once more.

"Yeah," said Slick. "We ain't goin' nowhere, right? We just got here."

His mother pushed his apalled father out of the kitchen and into the front room where they had another violent tiff. She reappeared, took a quart bottle of ale out of the refrigerator, snapped off the cap and brought it back to him. After quieting her husband down she returned to the kitchen and got supper. The boys ate quickly, Ramon chatting politely with Mrs. Quinn and trying to avoid her cleavage with his eyes. She enjoyed his bashfulness immensely and treated him like an honored guest. But the occasion was marred by the sight of Slick's gun still sitting in plain sight on the table through the entire meal, and though her eyes darted to it frequently she said nothing more.

After supper they went into Slick's room to count the money and divvy it up. All told they had nearly seven hundred dollars. Then they took turns in the bathroom getting off on some dilaudids. Slick placidly said goodbye to his mother, promising to return later but he did not know just when. He rolled his Harley CH out of the garage, kicked the starter down with all his might and the engine crackled to life with a loud, throaty roar. They strapped on their helmets, Ramon climbing on the back, and shot down the street, headed for a "dope house", a deserted structure next to a park where local addicts gathered to shoot up, especially in bad weather. Here they met some other people, sold the morphine and some of the dilaudid, and got high, lolling on the grass beside the building in the warm, night air. Ramon had given a free hit to a girl he knew whom he felt sorry for because she was nursing her newborn baby at the time and could not go out and hustle. She was wearing rags, thin and sickly looking, and the infant was filthy and apathetic, staring with wide, unseeing eyes at its littered surroundings. Yet as long as she was high, the young mother seemed not to care and lay nodding on an old, urine-soaked matress ignoring her wailing baby.

The two youths stayed loaded all night and returned to Slick's house late the next morning to eat. They got off again in the bathroom, slept until evening, then went back to their "get off" spot in the park to repeat the same performance. After two days of shooting prodigious amounts of dilaudid, cooking up to nine of the four milligram tablets in a single shot, they exhausted their supply. The evening of the third day they began to yawn frequently, an early sign of impending dopesickness. They rode down to The Prophet where they found Martin Shine slouching lazily in the corner of a booth. He wore dark glasses as usual even though the place was quite gloomy, so that he could close his eyes and nod without anyone noticing. Slick poked him and imperceptibly he came to life.

"Yeah, man?" he muttered.

"Seen Dom around?"

"Dom? He's in New York."

"What for, connection?"

Martin shrugged and looked away, plainly annoyed by their intrusion. "I guess so," he replied. "Who knows?"

"When's he comin' back?" Slick went on.

"Tonight. Look, I got somethin', if that's what you're lookin' for."

"Yeah?" Slick laughed drily. "I'll bet it wouldn't make a pimple on the ass of the stuff Dom's bringin' back."

"Maybe not," sighed Martin impatiently, thinking how these kids were ruining his high and how he hated his life as a dealer, even though it was the easiest way to support his voracious habit. "Look if ya want what I got, fine, otherwise forget it, huh?"

"You high, Marty?" Ramon observed.

"Um-hm."

They both looked at him with envy, remembering that only yesterday they too had been this high.

"Give us a half load," Slick said at last.

"Fifteen bags? That'll be sixty-five bucks—special deal."

"If it's like it was before, it oughta go fer nothin'."

"Usual price," Martin said sleepily.

Slick clenched his teeth and gave the fat man a terrible look. "We junkies bust our balls, go out an' steal, get into trouble an' hurt people so's you bastards can beat us an' shoot all the good dope yourselves, an' that really sucks!"

Martin took off his dark glasses and smiled, wide awake now. He knew they were both armed and sick, and he also knew there was nothing more dangerous in this business than armed, dopesick junkies. "Look," he said blandly. "I know ya both got pieces and so I certainly ain't gonna argue with ya. Now, let's cool it, huh fellas, whaddaya say? I'm sorry Dom ain't back, okay? Now, wait here an' I'll be back in a few minutes. Have a beer or somethin'. It'll settle your nerves."

The two youths split up the fifteen bags of dope they copped from Martin and headed for the park again. Slick dumped five bags into his cooker and booted the fix, unafraid because he had a big habit and knew this dope was probably only around one percent heroin. Ramon followed suit, cooked up another five bags but shot it more slowly.

"You gettin' off?"

"Nope. . . ."

"Me neither."

"Sonofabitch, it's garbage!" Slick muttered. "We got burned!"

"When are we gonna learn?" said Ramon sorrowfully.

"We should go back an' shoot the cocksucker!"

"Aw, it wouldn't be worth the bullet, man," Ramon sighed. " 'Sides, some junkie would rat on us to the cops for a couple bags."

They fixed up again and shot the rest of the junk, then lay back on the cool grass and enjoyed the high, such as it was. At least the dopesickness was gone, plus all the pain and agony of life, and existence was once more a pretty picture, a dreamland.

After a long silence Slick spoke up, his voice mellow. "We ain't even got a bag left between us . . . so we gotta find Dom before he unloads that dope, don't ya think?"

"I'll bet it's uncut," said Ramon wistfully. "Or maybe stepped on only one or two times . . . maybe he'll even sell us a whole quarter piece. . . ."

"We'll wait for him at his pad," Slick concluded. "All night if we have to."

They stayed about two hours until the nod wore off, then got up, unchained the bike and roared off through the summer night to Dom's rooming house.

55

The plane skimmed high over the blue shelf of the Atlantic and circled back overland to the south, tilting the horizon. The city came into view again, far below him now, a volcanic scar gouged into the land, leaden fingers of sky scrapers jutting up through sooty mist, and miles of suburbs flowing away in every direction like oozing streams of lava, swallowing up the green hills. Even as he hurtled southward at fifteen thousand feet, Dom felt hemmed in by the city, smothered in its noisome atmosphere. Psychologically his world had remained unchanged, for he was only flying from one city to another bigger one. He sat back, tired but unable to relax, unexplainably broke into a cold sweat and mopped his face with his sleeve.

A middle-aged woman sitting beside him turned and he felt her eyes on him. "Is it too hot for you?" she asked. "Turn on the air, why don't you?"

"Thanks, I will," he said and obligingly twirled the knob above his head, opening the valve and hearing the hiss of air, feeling it soothe his face. He smiled at her briefly.

Avoiding further conversation, he turned to look out the window, saw the aircraft knifing through a ragged, gray curtain of cloud to pursue the fading light of a sinking sun. In a way he wanted to fly on forever and never reach his destination. He had arrived enough times in enough places only to wish he had never come. And his thoughts raced back again to another flight through the clouds, this time in a Cobra gunship during the torrential monsoons in Vietnam.

They had not expected such heavy rain. It spilled like a cataract out of the hot, metallic tropical sky, nearly six inches in two hours at division headquarters. Then as the rain let up they climbed aboard the chopper, streaked low over the sodden jungle and flooded paddys back to Loc Nan. Forty minutes later they swooped over the last circle of hills ringing the village. The gunship took some hits, the rounds whacking into the fusilage, and the pilot banked away. Luckily no one was injured.

"Looks like bad news," he observed. "That VC battalion may be in the area."

He radioed division and was about to sign off when the copilot prodded the pilot and pointed. Explosions were erupting in the center of the village, one then another and another, bright flashes and geysers of mud and smoke.

"They're hitting us!" Dom yelled, craning his neck for a better look as the pilot veered away to avoid ground fire. The copilot radioed division for an air strike, then Dom had him contact the village command post. The voice of Lieutenant Trager crackled in reply, high pitched with excitement.

"This is Alpha One! Charley broke in . . . he's holed up in that big shed about fifty feet due west of the tower! Request fire support, over!"

"This Lancer One. Roger, wilco. Out." replied the pilot.

The gunship turned to make the pass. Dom pointed the target out to the gunner, watching as the fifty caliber machinegun began pounding above the whine of the turbine engine. Mud flew up around the building below them as the hail of slugs found it, tearing off chunks of sheet metal and kicking them into the air. On the second pass the roof collapsed and the building caught fire. Two men with weapons darted out of the smoke and the gunner caught them with a long burst and sent them sprawling. The ship banked away from the village and proceeded to make passes along the treeline, strafing suspected enemy positions and firing rockets that slammed into the forest in twin spouts of flame and smoke.

Dom felt something wet on his face and touched it, saw blood on his fingers. He thought he had been hit until he looked around and saw the crew chief lying on the floor in a pool of blood. The gunner stopped firing, knelt beside him as the pilot veered over the ridge top.

"It's getting rough!" he yelled. "We better get back to division!"

He radioed Trager but got no response.

"Something's wrong down there!" Dom cried. "Put me down in the village!"

The pilot shook his head negatively, was about to say something, then pointed. Two Phantom jets streaked out of the clouds, shot past them. The pilot radioed, swooped in to drop smoke grenades and the jets returned, winging in low to release cannisters of napalm. Part of the strike hit the hillside in a sheet of flame but the remainder went wide into the paddy.

"Sonofabitchin' weather!" said the pilot. "They can't even see what they're doin'!"

On the next pass the jets fired rockets that flashed into the forest like Roman candles, then vanished in the clouds.

"Can't take you in there!" the pilot continued.

Dom felt a flush of anger. "Well put me down out here then!"

The pilot swung the ship around, headed for the middle of a paddy and hovered down just long enough for Dom to sprint out from under the beating rotors toward the village. Rounds came in at him out of nowhere and he ducked, crawled, ran once more until he reached the perimeter. Here he found himself entangled in the concertina of barbed wire and was in danger of setting off a land mine. As more rounds buzzed around him he thought his luck had run out until three ARVN soldiers jumped out of a bunker and pulled him in.

"Let's go!" Dom shouted and motioned for them to follow as he dodged from house to house and at last reached the command post. He saw smoke drifting through the entrance of the demolished bunker. The body of a Vietcong sapper lay nearby, apparently caught in his own explosion. Peering inside he saw more bodies half-buried in the debris. A satchel charge had destroyed everything, including the radio.

The firing continued from the other end of the village, long, staccato bursts of M-60 machinegun fire and single sharp reports of M-16's. Then the firing ceased and after a few minutes a militiaman appeared, followed by Captain Trung.

"Nous gagnons!" he exclaimed with a triumphant, toothless smile. *"On fait bien le guerre, non?"*

A few minutes later three more American gunships arrived, hovered over the village until Dom waved them in. They landed one by one, disgorged several inquisitive officers and a fresh platoon of ARVN troops. The medevac choppers followed, began ferrying out the casualties. The medics recovered the bodies of Lieutenant Trager, Specialist James, and Major Huong in the shambles of the command bunker.

Women, children and old men came out of their bunkers, gathered in the rain to stare at the smoking huts and to sort through the debris. An old woman ran up to Dom, wailing and gesturing. He was talking to a Major Lambert, filling him in on what he had seen, but the woman kept begging him to follow her. He excused himself and with a sense of foreboding went with her to one of the smoking ruins. It was the large building they had directed the fire at from the gunship, now a smoldering mass of scorched sheet metal and embers steaming in the rain. Soldiers were poking around, dragging out the burned corpses of women and children. Weeping relatives were identifying them and when Dom stepped up he saw one small body unclaimed. Gently he turned the head, looked at the seared, puffed face, then picked it up and held it in his arms.

They lined up the six slain Vietcong soldiers side-by-side for official ARVN photos. The rain was increasing now and washed their faces clean of blood and dirt. They were young faces, innocent and serene in death. The remainder of the squad of enemy sappers had escaped in the heavy rain. Dom learned that, despite a request from Lieutenant Trager, Major Huong had elected not to send out a patrol, insisting that the enemy would never attack in such bad weather.

Sick with grief and tortured by the throbbing pain in his arm that he had been forced to use while crawling, Dom realized with apprehension that all the morphine had been kept in the ruined command bunker. Then he remembered where James had stashed his heroin and went to get it now. He dissolved a match head of the white powder in a teaspoon just as he had seen James do. But he did not mainline it, only injected it under the skin, like the morphine. The drug was strong. He felt less pain and despair, could go on now despite the smell of smoke and burned flesh, the sight of the fresh corpses and the row of caskets, one of them containing the body of Little Dom. He lay a wreath on the casket, said a silent prayer, watched the mourners weep. They were mostly women. He was a soldier and did not weep.

56

As soon as the plane landed at the air terminal in New York, Dom contacted the middleman by phone. After a long wait the man appeared at the appointed spot, a heavyset Puerto Rican who observed him from a distance, then approached cautiously.

"You Tony's boy?" he asked.

Dom nodded. After another long moment of scrutiny the middleman led him to a waiting cab. They rode into the city, through the deepening shadows of skyscrapers towering up everywhere like canyon walls of stone and glass, cut by asphalt rivers and clogged with machines—a growling, roaring torrent of metal and grease and rubber sending up an acrid mist.

"You live here?" Dom asked.

"Spanish Harlem, where we're goin'," came the reply.

The buildings fell away into cluttered brownstones, decrepit brick tenements, the streets narrower and darker. Idle youths loitered on corners, older folks slumped on the stoops, and flocks of children scurried and played between parked cars. The middleman told the cab driver to stop and he indicated a sooty dwelling advertising "rooms."

"Check in here," the middleman said. "I bring it back in an hour."

"They told me I have to go there and pick it up," Dom explained quickly.

The man frowned, left the cab to make a phone call. He returned, directed the cab another few blocks and told the driver to wait. They got out and Dom followed the middleman up a dingy tenement stairway. After a knock and a few staccato words of Spanish they were admitted and escorted down a dark hallway into a brightly lit room. A man stood just inside with a shotgun, guarding what looked like a scene from an operating room.

Three women wearing surgical masks were seated at a long table working with the brown, South American heroin. One was cutting it with a mixture of probably about five parts milk sugar for weight, two parts quinine for the "rush," and one part mannite to fluff it up for bulk. The second woman was weighing out "short ounces" on a set of scales. The third was bagging the now brownish-white speckled dope with the aid of a playing card, dabbing it into the small glassine envelopes with deft, practiced strokes. They wore the masks because a good whiff of the nearly pure heroin could put them under.

A man with a thin mustache sat unsmiling behind a desk and studied the young man keenly. "This guy Tony sent you, huh? Yeah, you fit the description he gave us. He wants half a pound, huh? Let's see the money."

Dom unlocked the attache case, dug out the manila envelopes and opened them, dumping the bundles of bills onto the desk. The man counted it quickly, holding a few of the bills up to the light.

"Ten grand. Okay. He's getting good stuff for his money. You tell him. It can take four cuts easy. You gonna taste it?"

"No," said Dom.

The man barked an order in Spanish and one of the women spooned some of the cut heroin into a plastic bag.

Dom counted the spoons, tablespoon sized, nine ... ten, then the man distracted him with a remark, purposely perhaps and he lost count. She checked the bag quickly on the scale, handed it to him. He took it, avoided hefting it even though he was suspicious that the ounces were short, realizing that the declared weight was normally reduced at each change of hands.

He wrapped a towel around the heroin, stuffed it deep into the attache case and turned to leave. The middleman blocked his path.

"My commission," he said quickly.

Dom handed him a hundred dollar bill but he only frowned. "For a ten grand connection I get three, four hundred," he complained angrily.

"Sorry, but that's all I have," Dom replied. "You'll have to talk to my boss."

Abruptly he went downstairs to the waiting cab. When the sullen Puerto Rican followed, he knew he had problems. He got in and closed the door, saw the middleman get into a parked car.

"The airport, quick," said Dom, looking back and seeing the car following them as they pulled into the traffic. "Faster!" he urged. "I'm in a hurry!"

"Look, I can only go so fast, okay?" the cab driver grumbled.

They stopped at a traffic light next to a big department store, the other car right behind them. Taking a gamble, Dom jumped out of the cab with the attache case and bolted into the store. He tried to lose himself in the throng of shoppers while searching for an exit when he saw the middleman shoving through the crowd toward him. Finding a door at the far end of the store, Dom catapulted out onto the street, his long legs driving hard, and sprinted flat out for four blocks, turning at each corner, then lost his wind and ducked into a hotel. He looked out through the window, saw nothing. After waiting nearly an hour, he checked the street again carefully, called a cab and rode to the airport, this time Kennedy International, where he would be harder to find.

After an hour's flight the jet skimmed over the runway lined with blue lights, landed with a great rushing of engines and coasted into the brightly lit terminal. Dom, attache case in hand, nodded to the stewardess and descended. He walked quickly through the glaring corridors swollen with an endless procession of travellers crowding one another like tireless runners in a never-ending marathon of departure and arrival, caught in that millrace of time that swallows them until they surface again at their individual destinations. Looking at a clock, he saw that it was almost midnight. He glanced around quickly to see that he was not being followed, then hailed a cab. He got in and at last allowed himself to relax.

Arriving at his rooming house, he rode twice around the block, waited a minute or two before getting out and paying the driver. He stood alone on the darkened street, suddenly aware of extreme fatigue and a growing dope-sickness. He wanted to get off on just a match head or two of the good dope, then he would call Motto. As he walked into the inky shadow of the dooryard, a familiar voice called his name and stopped him short.

"Wh'say, Dom?"

Slick stepped out of the shadows, grinning, Ramon just behind him.

"Nothing much," said Dom, his stomach tightening. He had no gun. "What's up?"

"We heard you made a connection down in New York," Slick remarked.

"We wanna cop a quarter piece," said Ramon.

They stared at him in the pale streetlight, their eyes glittering with that queer, distracted look of dilated pupils. Dom knew they were sick and that he was in a very tight spot. He began to edge past them.

"That's right," he answered casually. "I just dropped it off a few minutes ago. My man should have some ready by tomorrow afternoon. I'll meet you, say, at five in the club, okay?"

"You just come from the airport, huh?" Slick asked.

"Yeah, I told you. . . ," Dom faltered as Slick drew out his revolver.

"What's in the case?"

"But. . . ."

"The case, drop it an' don't move!"

"Listen, don't be stupid," Dom persisted. "My man picked it up already. Now c'mon, let's. . . ."

"Drop that case, you motherfucker or I'll blow your brains out!" Slick warned.

Dom let the case clatter to the ground and Ramon snatched it up, began disemboweling it, then hesitated, pulled out the plastic bag of white powder.

"Jesus. . . !"

"Tried to bullshit us, huh?" Slick snarled, his voice taught with rage. "You could've let us have somethin', but no, you don't give a fuck! You're just lucky I ain't gonna pull this trigger, man! Just because you're a dealer you think you can fuck over everyone, right? Well, the shoe is on the other foot now, man!"

Ramon kept a gun on Dom, who prudently remained silent while Slick pulled his bike out of the shadows and kicked it over. They jumped on and tore down the street leaving Dom standing dazed beside the empty, hinged shell of the attache case.

57

Slick and Ramon rode out to one of the dingier, more historic suburbs, well-known for its local drug scene, where they intended to get high on the dope and later cut some of it to sell to the local addicts. They checked into a cheap motel and Ramon opened the plastic bag, snorted a pinch. In a minute he was straight and they knew it had been stepped on only once or twice and therefore was not only very good but dangerous.

"Let's do a couple match heads an' see what happens," said Slick, his hands trembling with anticipation. He fixed up, shot up very slowly, even skin-popping the last few drops because he was already starting to feel the rush. His face lit up with elation. "Wow, we really scored!" he yelped. "This is dynamite! Shows ya how bad the street dope really is around here. . . ."

Ramon, who had OD'd many times, was not as cautious. He shot a good bag, vomited and went right into a nod. Two hours went by. Slick came down a little, stood up, stretched, urinated, felt hungry and decided to go out and get something to eat. He tried to rouse his sleeping partner with some slaps but Ramon scarcely stirred. Slick laughed silently, thinking how back in the city there were junkies he knew who would strip him of everything he had, even his clothes, and dump him down a laundry chute somewhere. Slick went to work again with brutal slapping and kicking, then when Ramon still could not be aroused he found a syringe, filled it with a solution of table salt, injected it into his vein and Ramon opened his eyes. After more slapping, Slick pulled him up, glassy eyed but awake.

"You almost went out, you stupid asshole!" he said. "I'll go out an' get you some coffee."

He jumped on his bike, rode over to an all night hamburger place, wolfed down the special and a chocolate frappe, then called up his girl friend, Sherry.

"What are you doing calling at this time of night?" she answered, her voice sleepy and irritable.

"I split from Comeback," he replied.

There was a pause. Her voice grew cold and distant. "Well, I've kicked here at home and I don't want anything to do with dope anymore, or with any friends who do dope."

"Don't get uptight," he returned tensely, trying to hide his anger. "I gotta see ya about somethin'. It's real important. I'll come by tomorrow 'round noontime, okay?"

"Tell me now. . . ."

"I can't over the phone."

Reluctantly she consented on condition that he stay no longer than a few minutes. This made him all the more furious and all the more resolved to get even with her for her sudden independence. He arrived the next day, just in time for lunch. Luckily for him she was home alone, her parents having gone to the hospital very early for rounds. Slick sensed that Sherry was still recovering from the throes of kicking, judging from her nervousness, her distracted look of fatigue and sleeplessness.

"My father doesn't want any of my junkie friends coming over or he'll kick me out," she warned with noticeable vexation almost before he entered.

"Aw, c'mon, be a good kid an' fix me a bite ta eat," he said amiably. "I'm hungry as hell, ain't had no breakfast."

She watched him with distrust. "All right, but promise you'll leave right after."

He agreed and sat down in the kitchen while she made him a sandwich. She brought it over and suddenly froze in her tracks, eyes wide.

"I wonder if I should get off first. . . ," Slick was saying, opening a bag of dope, his works on the table. He looked up and grinned at her and she bit her lip.

"You bastard!" she gasped.

He caught her arm as she tried to move away. "Wait!" he said. "This ain't no ordinary dope! This stuff'll knock you on your ass! It's almost pure, straight from New York."

"W—where'd you get it?" she asked in spite of herself.

"Can't say, but I got about a half pound . . . me an' Ramon. Uh, 'scuse me. . . ." He dumped the powder into the cooker, got up and added a few drops of water and heated it briefly with a match. "Don't need to cook it much at all, it's so pure. . . ." Drawing the clear, tawny fluid up through the wad of cotton, he tied off, tapped a vein, shot up and got off in front of her. "Wow, I'm loaded. . . !" he murmured, his eyes half-shut with contentment.

She watched as if spellbound, an expression of hungry fascination on her face. Then she frowned angrily. "You're a real son-of-a-bitch!" she cried.

"Hey, don't get pissed," he responded blandly, grinning with a mischievous, almost elfin look of merriment. "I know you're kickin'. But here, I'll leave ya a couple bags just in case ya want somethin' ta help ya sleep at night.

Not enough to do no harm. But watch out ya don't OD on this shit. . . ."

He took four foil packets out of his pocket and tossed them onto the table. She tensed at the sight of them, shook her head as if struggling inwardly and finally stepped back.

"No—I—can't! I promised!" she exclaimed.

He shrugged. "Have it your way. You can take 'em anyhow. I got plenty, a whole half pound, like I said."

There was a long pause. He watched as she approached, her hand reaching out almost involuntarily, then jerking back but reaching out again to grasp the packets. "I—I'll flush them down the toilet just so you can't use it. . . ," she muttered and left the room.

Slick picked up the sandwich and devoured it, then smiled languidly at the sound of Sherry wretching in the bathroom upstairs. After a few moments she returned, pale and a little sleepy.

"Ya got off, didn't ya," he said.

She nodded faintly, looked at him with sadness. He stood up, grinning.

"You're still a fuckin' dopefiend just like I am, ain't ya!" he sneered, his face oozing with contempt.

He kept leering at her in this way until she told him to get out, and he left without another word. As he rode away he thought with satisfaction that no more than a couple of days would pass before she would be calling him. After all, he had so much dope now and he hated to do it all alone. Sherry was his partner in this. They had always enjoyed getting off together, sort of like having sex, only this was something much better. It was everything almost, had to be because they had given up everything for it. It was food and drink, fun and laughter, fame and fortune. It was a sense of manhood or womanhood. And it was love—boundless, oceanic love.

58

The second evening after Slick's visit, Sherry lay curled up on the sofa, her thin body covered with a woolen blanket, unusually warm for midsummer. Her father came in, his face drawn with fatigue after a long day at the hospital.

"Your mother won't be home until late, I'm afraid," he began. "She has. . . ." He paused, noticed her shivering slightly. "What's the matter? You're not ill, are you? I saw thirty-five patients today, and now you? My God, it seems like everyone's sick. I don't even feel well myself. . . ." He rubbed his eyes, glanced at his watch. "Do you want any supper? I can order something."

"I don't feel like eating," she murmured.

Concerned, he came over and touched her forehead, then stopped suddenly, studied her eyes. ". . . Your skin is moist and your pupils are dilated," he declared. He felt her pulse and observed her rate of breathing while glancing at his watch. "Your vital signs are increased. . . ." He eyed her keenly. "Sherry, have—have you been using heroin again? Answer me!"

He squeezed her arm and she drew away. "Leave me alone!" she whimpered.

"Let me see your arm!" he exclaimed and looked at the white skin of her thin forearm while she struggled vainly. "There! That's a needle mark! You must be injecting into that same place. . . !" He released her arm and stood over her, a look of anguish twisting his face. "Oh, my God, Sherry, have you been out on the streets again? Please, please you mustn't do it! Think of us, your parents! Your poor mother is at her wit's end! Do you know what she said? She prayed and said, 'God forgive us and God forgive her . . . we've got to keep our daughter at home from now on!' "

He looked at her again desperately and she nodded, her eyes staring, glittering. "Yes, father, you told me that once before. But I'm not doing anything! Look, I'm grown up now, almost twenty-one. I can take care of myself! So please, don't worry! Just leave me alone and I'll be all right!"

He shook his head in disbelief, a glimmer of under-standing coming into his eyes. "I—I see now how sick you really are," he said slowly. "At last I realize . . . you need extensive psychiatric help! I'm taking you to a hospital where they can treat you!"

She laughed softly. "Don't be silly, father! Now, I have to get some things together. I'm going to visit a friend for a. . . ."

"Oh no you're not! he shouted. "This is the last straw! You go to your room and stay there, young lady! Tomorrow we're flying out to the west coast, as far away from all your drug addict friends as we can go! I'll get you into a hospital out there!"

She twisted out of his reach as he approached. "Please! You don't understand!" she cried.

He nodded vigorously. "Oh yes, but I do understand! I understand only to well! You're not my daughter anymore, not that sweet, quiet little child that was granny's favorite. You've changed since she left. I can see it now that I think back—those temper tantrums, staying alone in your room, not going to school, and then hanging out with young hoods and acting like a tramp! And nothing has helped, nothing! I can see what they mean now—I thought it was just a crackpot expression, but it's true what they say—you are a dopefiend!"

She shrieked in protest as he seized her and wrestled her up to her room. He pushed her onto the bed where she lay sobbing under his sorrowful gaze, then he turned and walked out, shutting the door. Almost as if to apologize for his show of temper, he brought up some supper an hour later but she was too dopesick to touch it. Her refusal to eat upset him and once again he left the room in an ill humor.

She waited till he closed the door to his study to eat alone and read journals. Carrying her shoes, she stole out of her room, entered her parents' bedroom and took some checks and sixty dollars in cash. Then she crept down the back stairs and went out through the servants' entrance. She ran down the street, thumbed a ride into town and made a phone call. Hailing a cab, she climbed in and sat shivering in the back seat. The old driver seemed in another world as he wheeled his lumbering vehicle through the sluggish, midevening traffic.

"Please hurry," she said. "It's important."

With a droll glance reflected through the rearview mirror he picked up a little speed. "Sure," he replied. "Funny how everyone's in a rush nowadays. For what? That's what I keep wonderin'. We all get there sooner or later, y'know. ⁻. ."

She did not respond but the driver, roused into conversation, continued his monologue while she sat, shivering and sniffling. "Hurry, hurry, hurry! Humph! Tell me, where does it all end? Superhighways, supersonic jets, you name it, just so we can go all the faster. I tell ya, it's a helluva world we live in, huh?"

She mumbled an almost inaudible reply, her mind elsewhere, and gazed out the window of the cab. The sun had sunk over the horizon, draining the daylight from the city. Man-made suns blazed in its place, pushing back the web of darkness just enough to produce a cheap imitation of day, with harsh contrasts between infinite blackness and brilliant, carbon-arc illumination. She shut her swollen eyes and tried to sleep. It seemed only a moment later that the cab stopped. She opened her eyes and rubbed them, saw the diminutive figure in a leather bike jacket walking out of the motel. He opened the door, let her out.

"Ya didn't waste much time," he said thickly, trying to conceal his delight. "C'mon inside an' join the party—jus' me an' Ramon."

The motel room was small and shabby, like a dozen other rooms she had seen where people were getting off. There was the same clutter of empty bottles, food wrappers, cigarette butts, the same stink of stale air and smoke, human sweat and urine. But she did not mind as long as the dope was good, for that was all that mattered.

Slick gave her two match heads, even fixed up for her and she got off, a dreamy look on her face as she felt the rush. "Wow ... it's pisser...! Where'd you get it, anyway?" she asked.

He grinned. "Promise not to tell? We ripped off someone, how else?"

"Who?"

"Someone real stupid."

"I don't want to know," she said and lay back, closed her eyes. "Was it Marty...? she went on dully after a pause.

He grinned again, the way he does when annoyed. "You kiddin'?" he said. "His dope ain't worth stealin'."

"Then I'll bet it was Dom...."

"Hey, forget it, man!" Ramon interjected. He was against her coming in the first place because in his opinion women were nothing but trouble and always brought bad luck.

"Was it really him?" she went on, her eyes opening again.

Slick nodded and half-smiled. There was an uncomfortable silence, Sherry lolling on the bed, the two youths sprawled in chairs.

"You shouldn't have...," she finally managed to say, though without much concern. She was preoccupied with her high, the nod, and nothing else had much meaning.

Slick sneered at her words. "Aw, he'd fuck me if he had the chance, right? So, why shouldn't I fuck him?"

"Hmm ... isn't this the second time you ripped him off?" she queried, a bit accusingly, then tensed at the contemptuous look he gave her and tried to change the subject. "It is terrific dope," she purred.

"Look, I rip a lotta people off," he scoffed. "But him, he shoulda been more careful, right? He's stupid for bein' a dealer. It's a wonder he ain't dead by now."

"If they legalized heroin, we junkies wouldn't hafta rip nobody off to get a fix," argued Ramon. "We could jus' get high, man, mind our own business with no hassle...."

"Wow, that would be super," Sherry agreed.

"Not me," said Slick. "I like to do hustles. I don't know nothin' else. It's my life, right? The straight world sucks an' I don't want no straight dudes tellin' me how much dope I'm gonna shoot and when, right?"

"Don't sweat it, man," said Ramon with a smile. "There's plenty a' dope around an' there always will be. Them farmers in Turkey are stashin' opium an' now they're growin' poppies in Asia, man. The dope is comin' through Hong Kong by the shitload. Even from South America, man, it's comin' from all over."

"I don't care as much as you kids do," Sherry asserted. "Honest, I hate to say it but I'm gettin' kinda sick of this whole dope scene. My father was going to fly me out to California tomorrow and get me into a hospital where I could kick and stay clean for good."

"Ha, that's a laugh!" Slick jeered. "There's dope out in California too—plenty of it, brown dope from Mexico. They sell it by the balloon for twenty-five dollars. It's about the same as three or four real good bags."

She shot him a quick look of resentment. "Maybe I'd have a chance without you around to turn me on all the time!" she said cuttingly and fell into a pout.

He grinned uneasily and said nothing. Tired of talking, the three of them turned on the television, smoked, nibbled chocolate, then got off and nodded once more. They were content, knowing that their perpetual life of ecstasy would continue for at least as long as the dope held out. And they had a huge supply, enough to last for weeks. Meanwhile Slick and Ramon intended to cut a few ounces three or four times, sell it to the local kids for ten dollars a bag, and end up fifteen or twenty thousand dollars richer.

59

It was well past midnight when Ramon sat up with a start, jammed a finger into his mouth. A burning cigarette had scorched his hand while he was nodding. Hungry, he got up, made a peanut butter and jelly sandwich and ate it, watching Slick and Sherry slumbering on the bed. They were scarcely breathing, almost dead to the world. He wondered if they might have OD'd.

"Hey, you guys okay?" he said loudly.

They hardly moved, even when he nudged them. He made another sandwich and kept an eye on them as he nibbled, watching and thinking. Even though he was high he could still reason. And it occurred to him that since Slick was the kind of junkie who ripped everyone off, why should he stop now? The more Ramon thought about it, the more certain he was that Slick planned to somehow deprive him of his rightful share of the heroin. Therefore it made sense to Ramon to act first. At last, he decided, it was Slick's turn to be ripped off. With all the money he could get from selling it, Ramon would go back and see his grandparents in Puerto Rico who were very poor. He would give them enough to live out their lives comfortably, then maybe find a nice girl and get married.

He found his jacket and gathered up the dope. He even went through Slick's and Sherry's belongings and took all the money he could without awakening them, then very quietly departed. As he trotted through the darkened streets he realized that too many people would be looking for this dope. He had to leave now, before dawn. He finally found a cab and rode back into town to a garage in his old neighborhood of crumbling rows of red brick apartment buildings that made up the Puerto Rican section of the inner city. Picking up a few tools, he continued by cab to a much nicer section of town, an affluent area of modern, high rise, concrete and glass apartment complexes. After prowling around on foot for a few minutes he found what he wanted, something big and fast, a Lincoln Mark IV with no sign of an alarm system.

Quickly and expertly he thrust his long, bent screwdriver into the vent, pried it open enough to get at the latch, and jimmied it with a quick snap of the wrist. He got into the car, screwed the threaded tip of his dent-puller into the ignition lock, slammed the ten pound weight backward to the end of the shaft several times until the ignition cylinder broke out. Then he gingerly guided a small, specially filed screwdriver into the empty socket, turned it, and the engine started.

He drove fast, the big car eating up the road effortlessly. At two o'clock in the morning he crossed the state line, reached the next city at three. No longer as high now, he felt tired and stopped at a diner to stretch and have a quick cup of coffee. Afterwards he went into the men's room and got off again on a match head. Climbing back into the idling car, he nodded for what seemed like no more than a minute, until aroused by someone rapping on the window. He opened his eyes, saw three or four people staring at him. One man was trying to open the door. Ramon glanced up and saw that he was blocking a parked car. Disconcerted, he threw the shift into drive instead of reverse and lurched forward, striking the car. Now he shifted into reverse and flew backward, the people scattering. He grazed another parked car before squealing off down the road.

Back on the highway, his blurred vision picked out the fluorescent speedometer needle climbing to seventy, then ninety as he passed everything in sight. One hundred—too fast, the thought, but the big car skimmed smoothly down the road like a clipper ship under full sail on the high seas and he could not seem to slow it down. A whirling blue light closing less than a mile behind him jolted his mind back to reality. In a detached state of semiawareness he realized that he was in serious trouble and would escape only by a miracle. His best chance was to try to outrun them, one reason why he had picked the big car to begin with. He floored it, watched the speedometer needle dip down to the limit, one hundred thirty miles per hour. The road rushed under him like a smooth chute of black water as the car planed ahead, passing other cars as if they were standing still. He saw that the blue light had fallen back. He had a chance. He kept the pedal glued to the floorboard, thinking only about speed and more speed. Then a car ahead suddenly pulled out in front of him to get around another car and he scarcely had time to step on the brakes. He was too late, cut the wheel, struck the car and left the road.

He woke up in a hospital, an oxygen mask on his face. His body was numb. Once more he blacked out and when he opened his eyes again it was day. The mask was gone. After an hour or so two detectives and a highway patrolman came to his bedside, accompanied by a doctor and a nurse.

"Ramon Perez?" asked one of the detectives. "You are under arrest." He went on crisply to advise him of his rights, then his voice softened. "Look, kid, you're going to be all right, the doc tells me. You were real lucky. But a little girl was fatally injured in that car you hit. . . ." He paused, looked at the youth with unwavering gray eyes, anglo eyes. "And there's another reason why we're holding you. You're wanted for at least two armed robberies. A police officer was shot in one of them."

The group of people studied the youth and he closed his eyes. "I don't know nothin'. . . ," he groaned.

"Oh, you don't eh?" said the other detective, his voice harsh. "Well, you'd better start remembering. Unless you tell us all you know you'll spend the rest of your life in prison, I can guarantee it! And keep this in mind—possession of narcotics and transportation of a stolen vehicle across a state line are both federal offenses. Plus we have manslaughter and possibly murder. You're in the worst kind of trouble, son."

"Why don't ya cooperate with us, whaddaya say, Ramon?" crooned the first detective. "You tell us where that heroin came from and who you're working for, and we'll try to arrange it so you can plead to a lesser charge."

"It's your only chance," said the other detective.

Ramon said nothing.

"He's still in a state of shock," protested the doctor, "Why don't you postpone your questioning until we discharge him."

The detectives politely obliged, left the trooper to guard the prisoner. The next afternoon Ramon was released from the hospital and transferred to the county jail. They waited patiently as the sickness came over him more strongly—the chills, leg cramps, violent nausea and explosive diarrhea. That night they took him out of his cell, led him trembling to an interrogation room.

One of the detectives smiled at the bruised and deathly ill young man, held up a single glassine bag of heroin before his eyes. "It's all yours, this and as much as you want, boy," he said soothingly. "Just tell us who the big dealer is. Who are you working for? Tell us everything."

Ramon hesitated for only a moment, then the dry heaves began again and he doubled over, rolled off his chair onto the floor. They hoisted him up, sat him down again, their faces like masks of granite as they watched him without pity.

"L—let me get off first. . . !" he gasped.

"Tell us now!" one of them snapped and shook him until he fell off his seat again, crashing to the floor.

Again he was picked up, dropped back onto the seat of the chair. He had been beaten up by cops before and could take it when he was not sick. But he was sick, unbearably so, and was going to get much sicker unless he had something. In short, breathless phrases he began to talk, while one of the detectives switched on a tape recorder and adjusted the mike.

60

Dolores was only nineteen when she went to prison for passing bad checks. From the very beginning, the experience hardly seemed real to her. Even as she stood in the courtroom hearing her sentence, the judge's stern words had little meaning. She lapsed into sort of a daze and was led away, taken far from the city and deep into the green countryside to the women's house of correction. This cluster of red brick dormitories enclosed by a six foot cyclone fence topped with barbed wire was to be her new home, yet it seemed impossible somehow. Only after weeks of waking up morning after morning in the close, bare-walled room of her cottage and seeing the light stream in through the window checkered with heavy wire mesh did she come to realize that she was actually a prisoner, a convicted criminal. Something that had started out innocently enough, prompted by someone she loved and wanted to please, had been her undoing. Cliff forgot to tell her about this part of it, about what happened to those who were caught.

Her mother could not believe it either. But then she did not really try, managing to erase any deep awareness of her daughter's imprisonment by going on another alcoholic binge that started even before the trial, and which once again transformed her into a piteous, gibbering creature hardly able to get out of her own way. The sick woman visited her daughter only once, during the first week. She came hobbling into the visitor's room, led by Dolores's sister and brother. She seemed bewildered at having to sit well apart from Dolores, unable to comprehend that any kind of physical contact was forbidden.

"But . . . but . . . ," she sputtered. "What do . . . they think I am. . . ?" She paused, peered around the hall while Dolores studied her with concern.

"Are you still drinking, mamma?" she asked with a note of impatient distress. "I'm not at home to stop you now, am I!"

Her mother seemed not to hear, perhaps because she did not want to. She kept staring this way and that as though she had never had the faintest idea of what the inside of a prison looked like. "Jesus. . . ," she mumbled. ". . . Look at all them coloreds . . . you all right in here?" She turned back to Dolores and gave her a doubtful look.

"I'm not happy to be here at all, mamma, but I'll be okay," the girl confessed, her eyes slowly filling with tears.

"How's the food?" her little brother piped up.

"Shutup!" scolded her younger sister, who had remained in a state of cowed silence.

"It's not that bad," said Dolores, then began sobbing. ". . . Mamma . . . I . . . I hope you don't think I'm no good."

Her mother's expression changed slightly to mild surprise at her daughter's outburst. "No good...? she muttered and shook her head negatively. "... Uh-uh ... him ... your father ... he was no good ... and I knew it, too, but ... god damn men all ... plain no good ... I ought to know, Dee-dee ... I ought to know. ..." She stopped and heaved a sigh, seemed to forget what she was saying and turned to her daughter after a long pause. "When, uh ... when does the bus leave. ..?"

"It took us two hours to get out here on the bus," her brother spoke up again.

"No it didn't!" scolded her sister. "Only an hour and a half."

Her mother dropped her head to gaze at the floor in silence, now and then glancing sidewise with suspicion at the other inmates and their families. She stayed this way for several minutes while Dolores chatted with her sister and brother, catching up on the latest neighborhood gossip. The news about people she knew cheered her, restored a sense of belonging to the world outside. She dried her eyes and looked back at her mother.

"Are you all right?" she asked and gave her sister a worried look. "I think you'd better go to the hospital, promise?"

The woman only nodded sleepily, seemed a thousand miles away. Even the officers stared at her with concern when she was escorted off by her children, shuffling like a blind woman out of the visitor's hall. Dolores did not know it then, but it was the last time she would see her mother alive.

Her worries about her mother's condition preoccupied her for the first few weeks in prison. She felt miserable because of her helplessness in caring for the woman at a time when she was obviously failing. The downcast, gloomy look on her pretty young face soon attracted the attention of some of the female officers who became worried about her. One of them in particular was Miss Cunningham, a buxom woman of about forty, who always seemed to be one step ahead of the others in doing little favors for Dolores to cheer her up.

"Here, see what I brought?" she would cluck. "Some chocolates. They had none in the canteen so I got some in town." She bent low, patted Dolores on the cheek. "Smile now! It's part of my job to keep you happy. After all, my dear, we have a long time to get to know each other, so why not make the best of it?"

With such encouragement, Dolores stopped moping, began to adjust to the prison routine. She was assigned to the flag shop where she spent eight hours a day at a machine stitching gold fringe on American flags. In the shop she got to know another inmate, Janet, a husky black girl who had been in for several months on two counts of larceny. Although the black and white inmates usually kept to themselves, Dolores felt that she had little in common with the tough, white girls against whom Janet sometimes stuck up for her in an argument. The two ate together every day and gradually Janet oriented Dolores to the system.

"You gotta watch out for them officers," she warned one night at supper in a low voice. "Every cute little chick that comes in here gets picked off sooner or later."

Dolores looked at Janet in bewilderment, unsure at what she was trying to say. But by the cynical look in her eye the meaning was clear.

"But Miss Cunningham just wants to help me," Dolores argued. "She's nice—she gets me anything I want. . . ."

Janet's face grew taut and she smiled. "I heard about her. Like I said, play it cool."

"I'm not worried," Dolores insisted, but again she was made uneasy by the cynical, almost pitying look that her friend gave her.

After a time she found that she had more in common with the other inmates than she realized. For example, most of them were from working class homes, as she was. They all liked the same TV shows that she liked, and all knew about the facts of life as thoroughly as she did. Dolores came to know Sally, a white girl and one of the prettiest in the cottage. As with many beautiful women who enjoy one another's company, each seemed to find their own attractiveness mirrored in the face of the other, which served to strengthen their mutual admiration. Sally had also been into drugs, had become a prostitute and was convicted on several counts of larceny, like Dolores. The two of them used to get together and point out to one another where they had gone wrong. They both agreed that it was because they did not think for themselves enough and allowed other people to sway them. Then one day Sally mysteriously did not show up at the supper table.

"She isn't sick, is she?" Dolores asked Janet.

"No," whispered Janet, again with that cynical, almost tragic smile. "She's probably in max for not cooperating."

"Not cooperating?" Dolores replied, still unwilling to accept it.

"It's just 'cause you're new here, so you don't under-stan'," Janet explained. "But it's part of the system, dig? Most everyone does cooperate, 'cause we don't want no hassles." She bent over her tray of institutional food, forked the perpetual mashed potatoes and artifically colored gravy into her mouth and refused to talk about it any further.

After worrying about Sally for several days, Dolores decided to put the whole thing out of her mind. After all, even with all of the bad breaks that she had in her young life she basically trusted everyone. And certainly she would not go along with anything she did not approve of, which as she and Sally had agreed, had been their cardinal error from the very beginning. Dolores wanted only to make the best of it here and to be paroled as soon as possible.

It was only a few days later that Miss Cunningham came to her room with the usual supply of chocolates. When she left she slipped a note under the door. Dolores caught her breath when she read it.

"My dearest Dolores. Since I've gotten to know you, I like you more and more. I feel very close to you. Isn't it strange yet wonderful that I love you so dearly? Not as a little girl but as a woman. It is because you are so beautiful and such a sweet, wonderful person. I hope that I'm as special to you as you are to me. With deepest love, Loretta C."

She got two more notes the following week and decided to ignore them, hoping, like the proverbial ostrich, that by sticking her head in the sand the problem would go away. All the while Miss Cunningham also said nothing and flitted around Dolores, lavishing her with little presents and fond gazes. When the girl still showed no sign of responding, the older woman grew irritable. One afternoon she sat down and looked at Dolores longingly.

"Did you get my notes?" she asked.

Dolores was so confused by this remark that she started to say something, then stopped and averted her eyes.

"Then you know how I feel—and I don't want you to be afraid of me. There's no reason. . . ," Miss Cunningham went on earnestly.

Dolores blushed. "I—I'm not afraid of you," she replied, looking up at the woman quickly, yet feeling a sense of dread deep inside, the kind of disturbing uneasiness that comes from discovering the abnormal.

"I'm so glad to hear you say that," returned the matron and placed an eager hand on the girl's rigid shoulder. "Because I've gone out of my way to be nice to you, you know that. And you can help me, too. Yes, you really could if you wanted to. Because one hand washes the other in here, my pet. And I promise that if you care for me the way I do for you, nothing will ever happen to you as long as we're together."

Moving closer, Miss Cunningham threw her arms around the startled girl and hugged her so tightly that she could hardly breathe. Then she stepped back, gazed at Dolores full in the face for several seconds, her round, almost sad brown eyes fairly melting with adoration.

Even though she was somewhat repulsed by the woman, at the same time Dolores was flattered that someone really cared about her so intensely. She sat motionless for a moment, the combination of opposing feelings leaving her perplexed. She did not know whether to push the officer away, whom she pitied, or to accept her. Then she remembered how Sally had mysteriously disappeared and Janet's cynical explanation. If it were true then Dolores knew that her own situation would be just as difficult unless she cooperated.

"What happened to Sally?" Dolores asked Miss Cunningham pointedly, deciding to settle the issue.

The officer's eyes narrowed and lost their gleam of affection for a second, as though the question was out of place. "I wouldn't know," she replied curtly. "She's in maximum security, I think. Why do you ask? That is none of your business, my pet."

Dolores gave a slight frown as she looked back at the older woman, thinking how it must all be true. "Sally's my friend," she said. "Can't you help her get out? It would mean an awful lot to me." And she kept her eyes on the older woman for a long moment, not only to impress upon her the urgency of the request but also in subtle recognition of Miss Cunningham's indisputable control.

The response was immediate in the officer's faint smile. "I'll look into it," she replied. "Sometimes the girls are put in for some small thing and kept there longer than necessary." She paused and her voice softened. "I'll come back later tonight and let you know. And remember, I am your friend!" Her smile broadened, as if intending that Dolores should smile also. And by this very expression of uninhibited warmth she seemed to be saying, "Then it is settled!" with no room for disagreement. Because to disagree was to affect ill humor, which she knew Dolores did not want.

Later that evening after bed check, the lock clicked on Dolores's door. It opened and someone entered. By the large, ponderous figure and the familiar tinkling of keys, she knew immediately who it was.

"Are you in bed?" whispered the officer.

"Yes."

The door closed and the lock clicked, shutting out the light. The girl lay in the dark as if in a trance, hearing the woman unzipping herself and struggling out of her uniform.

"Please," the officer whispered, approaching the bedside. "Let me lie next to you, my darling."

The much heavier, older woman rolled into bed with a noisy squeaking of springs as the girl moved to one side, then let herself be taken in an embrace. She noticed the muscles first. Miss Cunningham had more of them than most men she had known. It was like being in bed with a strong man.

"Love me, oh sweetheart. . . !" the woman was moaning, kissing the girl and guiding her hand between her huge thighs. "Touch me more, more, oh, don't stop. . . !" The woman bent low and Dolores felt her hot mouth and prying tongue, so much more than any man had ever done. Herself a professional at making people happy, Dolores almost reflexively massaged the woman and thrust up her own hips expertly in a passionate response. At last the officer grunted, squeezed the girl's hand between her thighs and lay still, breathing hard.

"Oh, my love. . . ," she panted, and kissed Dolores gently on the lips. She relaxed for a moment, perspiring heavily. Regaining her breath, she kissed the girl several more times on the lips and breasts. Then she got up and dressed hurriedly. "I must go now, my darling," she whispered. "I'll be back tomorrow night. Oh, and your friend Sally will be released from maximum security in the morning. Goodbye."

She rattled the keys, unlocked the door and departed. Dolores lay alone, curiously frustrated and haunted by a vague sense of shame and revulsion that she had never experienced before with her usual, male clientele.

Miss Cunningham treated her royally after that first night. In fact, the whole staff became more lenient toward her. The few male guards in the prison never interfered with what went on, since they had it in with the matrons, too. But if there was ever anything the women could not handle, the men were called. Dolores saw them in action only once. A matron had beaten a girl in her room and a day later three girls jumped her and injured her badly. A riot broke out in the cottage, the girls overturning beds, throwing mattresses out in the hallway and shouting out how bad the food was. Then someone set fire to one of the mattresses and a dozen girls burst out into the courtyard.

There they found themselves milling around, choking in a cloud of teargas. A phalanx of male guards wearing gas masks charged in, towels wrapped around their fists, and pummeled the girls, some of whom were every bit as tough as the guards themselves. There were few visible bruises on them the next day, even though the girls could hardly get out of bed.

Dolores stayed out of the fray. After all, she was a pet, not a rebel, and hoped to be paroled soon on good behavior. Meanwhile Miss Cunningham loved her more and more, saw her practically every night and waited on her hand and foot. At last she proposed marriage, which caught Dolores completely by surprise. Exasperated, she put the women off in a heavy-handed manner. The officer was visibly wounded by the rejection but far from discouraged. She kept badgering Dolores about how heppy they would be together, and so on. This worried the girl all the more. She realized now that the whole thing had gotten way out of hand and had been a mistake from the very start. Sally had been right, had followed the advice they gave to one another not to be swayed. But for some peculiar reason that she could not understand, Dolores had once more failed to be prudent, even though she acted in order to save her friend.

Quite unexpectedly her problems with Miss Cunningham were solved one day when her younger sister came alone for a visit. She wore a downcast, pale look of tragedy that can only been seen in the sensitive face of a child, an unconcealed look of pain and sadness. Even before she spoke, Dolores's blood was frozen by it.

"What's wrong?" she demanded, knowing what the reply would be.

"Mamma died," her sister announced simply.

"Oh, Debra, when!" Dolores gasped and the two sisters looked at one another in anguish, then the younger one began to weep. "Was it in the hospital?" Dolores went on, trying to comfort her.

Her sister nodded. "This morning . . . and the wake is on Saturday. Are you . . . can you come?"

Could she come? To Dolores the question seemed so simple that it hardly needed answering. Yes, she could come, of course she could, and she became aware of a stoic sense of duty, yet without sentiment. "Mamma's dead," she kept on thinking. "Then why don't I feel it?" And the more she tried to feel the less emotion she had. Only an awful, wooden numbness took hold of her and she found herself responding mechanically, like a talking doll. "Yes...," she heard herself say in a toneless voice. "I'll see if I can." Then unexplainably she smiled, felt embarrassed and hastily went on to ask about the details of her mother's death.

Her sister kept brushing away her tears, barely able to speak. "She took sleeping pills. An overdose...," she explained. "I found the empty bottle next to her bed this morning. She was ... hardly breathing and so cold ... I called the police and they took her to the hospital and when me and David got there they—they said she was...." The girl broke off and began sobbing again, gave Dolores a look of despair.

Dolores nodded and paused, then in a very matter-of-fact tone went on to ask who was going to take care of her sister and brother. She learned that they were staying with a neighbor but would be placed in a foster home tomorrow or the next day. Then the bell rang. The visiting hours were over and people rose, said goodbye. Dolores wanted to kiss her sister but could not, promised to call her that evening.

One of the officers who had been standing nearby accompanied Dolores out of the visiting area. "Did I hear you say that your mother just passed away?" she asked and looked at her with pity. When Dolores only nodded the woman went on. "My goodness, what a shame! I'm sorry to hear it. It's hard, I know, bein' here an' all, but they do let you go to the wake, y'know."

Dolores remained silent until they reached the cottage, then stopped and glared at the sympathetic officer. "She took an overdose—on purpose, that's what!" she blurted out and her lip quivered. The matron gave her an incredulous, frightened look and quietly withdrew.

The story spread through the cottage, the girls commiserating, trying to console Dolores. Accompanied by two matrons, Dolores went to the funeral several days later where she showed little emotion. Everyone was very impressed by how well she took it. After three weeks of moodiness and quiet she was herself again. Only one thing changed. She grew cold toward Miss Cunningham and stopped seeing her.

As soon as the disappointed officer was sure that their affair had ended, she retaliated quickly. Dolores spent nearly two weeks in maximum security, locked up directly after each working day, but still the girl did not change her mind. And as news of the split got around, some of the other officers also grew hostile, harrassing her whenever they could and making her stand inspection every morning before work. Despite this unpleasantness she was paroled on good behavior after serving six and a half months of her sentence.

61

Because she had nowhere to go, Dolores was sent to a post-release, halfway house under the supervision of her parole officer. There she obtained employment as a waitress through the job placement program, working full time and meeting with her parole officer every month. After eight months, half of her parole was completed and things looked good for her rehabilitation as a useful, productive member of society. This might have come to pass had it not been for one thing—her remarkable physical charm that caused her to be so irresistible to strangers.

Despite her initial efforts at ignoring men, at last she could not resist flirting back at them. It thrilled her to know that she could entice them so effortlessly—it made her feel important and desirable rather than downtrodden and disreputable. Now that her vanity was starting to blossom, she began dating a few of them but not the type she was looking for. Still young, she had her ambitions in life and meant to rise in the world and to meet the right people. But to do this she needed money, an apartment, and some new clothes. So when a date half-jestingly offered her a hundred dollars to spend part of the night with him she accepted. Of course, she only intended to do it this once, but the money ran through her fingers like water and she accepted another proposition, and then another. She was fired from her job when the management got wind of what was going on. But Dolores had only brief misgivings over the loss of her waitressing job, which was never her line anyway. She had already obtained permission to leave the crowded, noisy, halfway house to take a decent apartment which she filled with attractive rented furniture. She bought a new wardrobe and began to frequent the big hotels again. This, she decided, was what she wanted—not the obscure servitude of a working girl who could never expect to get to the top no matter how hard she tried. With such beauty Dolores felt she was entitled to more of everything, more social status, luxury, gaiety, freedom, and eventually more in the way of security. But even though she attended parties and met a lot of classy men, she had trouble making friends. For one thing, she tended to look at most men as potential clients. And they in turn saw something in her that prevented them from taking her seriously. Whether it was her lack of education or a certain quality of hardness that worked against her striking charm and basically accommodating nature she did not know. What she did know was that despite her numerous admirers, all of whom were clearly impressed with her beauty, she was lonely. She needed one man, someone she could depend on, yet who would be willing to give her a certain amount of freedom to go on working and meeting new faces.

And so she met Russ. He seemed to understand her position, which was his position also, and overnight they became fast friends, then lovers. It was not the heavy-handed, pimp-whore relationship that she had endured with Cliff. For the first time since Jay she had that rare and satisfying experience of knowing that someone knew and cared about the real person inside her. And she in turn fell deeply in love with Russ.

One of the common bonds that cemented their relationship was a mutual appreciation for the drug experience. Unlike Cliff, Russ was the more gregarious type of druggie who wanted to share his high with others. For him, doing dope was a part of socializing, a way to compare feelings, thoughts, impressions. He liked to prepare his guests by carrying on beforehand about how good the stuff was and how high everyone was going to get on it. Then he would set the pace for the evening by bragging about his own high, giving them a running account of whether he was going up or coming down, or if everything was cool, groovy, or out of sight.

Dolores had not touched drugs during the entire eighteen months of her parole. But the memory traces of the old craving remained strongly ingrained in her mind. So when he wanted to include her in the fun and kept offering her some of whatever he had, she finally gave in. Then life took a sudden twist for her, became stimulating, almost fascinating. She let Russ lead her by the hand, the two of them wandering like children out of their everyday world into a vast, exotic wilderness, a place unknown to most, filled with unimaginable and undreamed of experiences. It was another reality altogether, completely distorted from the one they knew. Between bangs of speed, cocaine, heroin, or acid and mescaline, Russ would philosophize about this experience to Dolores and their friends, who were usually too high to understand him and could care less.

"Man, dig this," he exclaimed one night at a party. "When ya do drugs, 'specially acid, you feel real spaced, right? But that gets ya uptight, too, 'cause you can see how fine the line of sanity is, understand? You realize that the mind is just like a TV with the knob stuck on one channel. But jus' unstick that knob an' change channels an' you got a whole new picture, a new reality. But like, things themselves ain't really changed, it's just our way a' seein 'em is changed, can ya dig it? So who can really say what is real an' what is unreal, see what I mean? You don't know whether to b'lieve the world when you're high or when you're straight. An' who knows what sanity is, or insanity? We jus' call somethin' real 'cause most of us agree on it, y'understand what I'm sayin'?"

If she were awake Dolores would start a friendly debate, intentionally expressing her own naive feminine view just to provoke him. "I don't even think about what's real," she responded. "All I know is what I see. That's all I care about."

"Well now, that sure is a simple way a' lookin' at it, ain't it?" Russ scoffed. "Like, take race prejudice. Now white folks see me as just another nigger 'cause I'm black an' that's all they see and so that's all they care about. But they don't even know me—I may be just like them, a human bein', flesh an' blood. Now, I see myself as beautiful, man, can y'dig it? 'Cause black is beautiful an' that's where my head is at, understan'?"

"Beauty is in the eye of the beholder," Dolores recited and the rest of the group mumbled in agreement.

Even when Russ was nodding on heroin he liked to ramble on about the nod and would try to keep the others awake long enough to pose some questions as they sat, heavy-lidded, neglected cigarettes glowing into long ashes between their fingers.

"How come life can't be like this all the time, man?" he proposed. "Like, it would be a whole different trip altogether. We wouldn't be hassled. We'd be so cool we wouldn't need no dope."

"But who could live like this?" Dolores argued, lolling sleepily on the sofa. "We couldn't survive 'cause we'd be too high all the time."

"Huh? What you sayin'? This really is livin'," he insisted. "It's beautiful—no pain, no grief, everything is cool when you're high." He paused, reflected, then remembered his cigarette nearly scorching his fingers, took a puff and poked it toward the cat sleeping under a chair. "I'll bet that cat don't get uptight an' down on everything like humans do. So it don't hafta get off on no dope to get feelin' good neither, right?"

"Cats get high on catnip," someone observed.

He snorted. "Yeah? But cats, as a rule, don't get uptight, right? That's what I'm sayin', when we talk about 'this cat, man,' we mean someone who knows where his head is at an' ain' no one gonna give 'im no jive 'cause he's too cool, understan'?"

"But Russ, honey, the cats you're talkin' about all do dope!" Dolores pointed out with amusement.

He closed his eyes. "Well, that's what I'm sayin'—how come everybody don't do dope?"

"That's not what you said. You're going around in circles," she teased.

"Heck, let's roll another joint," he suggested, not caring.

As the months passed Russ and Dolores grew jaded with the novelty of drugs and settled down to the humdrum of an everyday habit. They tapered off on the mind-expanding drugs like LSD and mescaline and did more heroin and cocaine, drugs of subjective indulgence. Questions about the immediate reality of their lives and where they were going began haunting them more and more. Being young, they wanted to feel life and experience it to its fullest, but at the same time they had to think of the future. Dolores especially did not intend to remain a prostitute forever. After all, it was a young woman's profession and offered no security in the long run, as she saw with her mother. And Russ, too, had similar misgivings about his station in life. Yet neither had any definite plans for altering their increasing monotonous and purposeless lives from which they knew drugs were only a temporary escape. And the more the thought about it, the more they needed respite from thinking, from the distress of self-examination. She found it in the pleasing, languid warmth of methadone and he in the heady exhilaration of cocaine.

62

The slap was so hard that Dom scarcely felt it, then he was punched once in the belly and again in the face and he doubled over. Another blow on the temple knocked him down and he lay in a gray daze, unable to move or breathe. They dragged him up and pushed him into the back seat of the car. He opened his eyes at the sensation of a gun in his ribs. Were they going to kill him? He saw Motto's face, blurred at first and then focusing into a menacing, reptilian scowl, the hard eyes narrowed into slits under the puffy lids.

"You better tell us where it is, kid!" he snapped, his voice sharp and high-pitched with rage. "You got ten seconds!"

"I—I told you. . . ," Dom mumbled, fighting for his breath and getting ready to die. "I—got ripped off. Honest I did. . . !"

"Balls!" Motto roared. "You got a lotta balls to tell me sumpin' like that! Why that stuff was good for fifty grand, easy! What am I gonna tell the guys that put up the money? Yeah, big men, respectable, who put their trust in me! Am I supposed to say, 'Sorry fellas, but I wuz ripped off'!" He lit a cigar, disgustedly blew smoke in Dom's face, then poked it at him, nearly burning his eyes and causing him to flinch. "You fucked up but good, kid! I'm tellin' yous right now, this is it! I ain't gonna front ya no more! From now on, you fuck up on your own!"

Dom wiped the blood from his swollen mouth and looked at Motto's angry face. Here was someone who could kill him, he thought. Both by a bullet or by refusing to give him any heroin, for he was desperately sick and would risk his life at this point to get something.

"Look," he said weakly, swallowing salty blood. "Dope is tight. Whatever you give me I can sell for at least six times what it's worth, I swear it! Give me just one ounce and I'll show you. . . !"

"I said, forget it!"

"But—but I'm sick as hell! Please. . . !"

"Yous're gonna be dead if you don't get outa this car an' start walkin'!" Spanky warned and prodded him in the ribs with his gun.

"Mr. Motto!" Dom went on imploringly. "Look at all the money I made for you—how hard I worked! Can't you give me a couple bags just to hold me . . . can't you do that?"

Motto studied him closely, the slits of his eyes narrowing even further, then turned to his strong-arm man, Spanky. Even Joey, the driver, looked back in surprise.

"Hey, this kid can't take no for an answer, can he?" growled Motto.

"Yeah," Spanky agreed. "He could be dangerous, go to the cops, rat for a bag. . . ."

"You know I'm no rat!" Dom insisted.

"You kiddin'? You're no different from the next junkie!" Motto spat and then paused, gave an emphatic nod of his head that signalled an irreversible decision. "Okay, kid. . . ." He turned to Spanky. "Give him a couple bags. Like he says—the good stuff."

They dropped Dom off near his rooming house. Relieved by their sudden change of heart, he waited for the runners to return. He was shaking all over from the dopesickness and had the dry heaves. At last he saw the rented car return and circle the block, stopping to drop something onto the pavement, then roar away. He ran over and picked up the two small foil packets and quickly walked down the street into an alley.

Crouching behind some trash cans he took out his works and opened one of the packets. He dumped the whole bag into the bottle cap and added a few drops of water from a rain puddle at his feet. It was a stormy, windy day and he had trouble burning a match long enough to cook it up. In his effort to shield the flame and because of his trembling hands, he spilled some of the half-dissolved powder on his fingers. Cursing, he licked it off, then sat bolt upright, his mouth afire. He fell face first into the puddle, spitting and gagging and rinsing his mouth out again and again.

"Battery acid. . . !" he sputtered, his tongue raw and swollen. "They tried to kill me. . . !"

Faint from fear he poked at the white powder, realizing he had been a fool to trust them. He had never seen any hot dope before but heard that it was either battery acid or rat poison. Sure enough, this stuff looked and cooked up just like real heroin. Only after shooting it would he feel the burning stab like a hot poker, see the red streak racing up his arm, and know that he had only a few seconds left to live. As soon as it reached the lungs he would die of asphyxiation, choking, eyes bulging, his face purple and bloated. The rat poison, or strychnine, took longer. He would have gone into convulsions first. He knew of someone unlucky enough to have been saved from it, alive but completely paralyzed.

He picked up the other bag and put it in his pocket, gathered up his works with shaking hands, the tremor of fear gradually giving way again to the tremor of dope-sickness. No longer solely concerned with supporting his habit, he saw himself drawn once more into a life and death situation, the kind he had been in overseas in Vietnam. Instead of faceless brown men, Motto and his men were the enemy now, and as in war, Dom realized that he would have to defend himself. To do this he needed allies, and the only one he could think of that was as strong as Motto was the law. And yet he did not want to engage in that low form of revenge known as ratting. His strategy would require more ingenuity and probably more risk.

In the meantime he had to find some dope, and since he had no money he was obliged to go out and steal. The quickest and safest way was to find a partner and break into a drugstore, basically a nonviolent crime. Ideally he wanted someone with experience but without any "tick-ets" or warrants against him that might tempt him, if arrested, to rat in order to reduce the charges. He decided to give Rolf a call. This kid was careful, rarely got caught and had never been in jail. Yet he was an expert thief. The only problem was that, like many people from the "other side," he got wrecked on pills now and then to relieve his chronic depression that comes from being different from most of society.

As Dom had hoped, Rolf was interested. He did not want the hard stuff as much as he did the pills, the ups and downs, worth around fifty cents apiece on the street and in great demand among his friends. Most junkies did them too, as well as the neighborhood teeny boppers still working their way up the drug ladder. Rolf agreed to meet Dom at The Prophet in about an hour and a half. This meant another hour and a half of dopesickness that was becoming almost unendurable.

Dom needed something now. He did not have time to wait till dark to do a "crash job"—kicking in a window, rifling the "narco" drawer and running for it while the alarm went off. Instead he remembered a hustle that with luck would work. He found a neighborhood pharmacy, entered and waited until the pharmacist's back was turned. Then he moved behind the prescription counter and huddled in a corner next to the shelves of medications. Spotting the Darvon, although he would have taken cough syrup, he shoved it into his pocket and moved back to the counter. The pharmacist had already seen him and came running over.

"Hey, what're you doing in here!" he yelled.

Dom swayed, peered around as if searching for something, then staggered a few steps. "Where's the bathroom?" he asked thickly, his speech slurred. "I gotta go bad. . . !"

"Bathroom?" the pharmacist replied indignantly. "I'm sorry fella but we don't have one! Now you'd better get outa here! Go down to the gas station!"

Dom reeled out under the angry gaze of the pharmacist. But he followed his advice by loping a few blocks to a gas station and going into the men's room. Opening twelve of the red and gray capsules, he discarded the white powder and took out the BB-sized "sour balls", one in each capsule. He dissolved these in a small amount of water, letting the white particles settle out. Then he shot the clear solution into his arm. It did not make him high, only straight enough now to hold on until he could find something better.

Entering The Prophet, the first person he recognized was Sam, his short, broad figure seated at the bar. Before he could avoid him, Sam caught his eye and waved him over.

"Jeeze, what happened to you!" he exclaimed, noticing the bruises on Dom's face and the stiffness of his movements.

"Got roughed up by—" Dom stopped, then went on carelessly. "By some people I worked for."

An appropriate expression of concern crept over Sam's face and he shook his head. "How 'bout a drink?" he asked briskly. "Shot n' a beer?"

Dom shrugged, nodded, and Sam ordered the drink, then turned back with a quizzical look.

"Anything I can do to help?" he offered. "If there is, lemme know."

Dom was not interested in getting sympathy from anyone. He smiled ironically and tossed down his shot of whisky then quenched the burning in his abdomen with a long draught of beer. "All's I need is ten grand. . . ," he joked in a toneless voice.

There was a pause. "Ten grand?" Sam echoed. "You know, maybe I can help. It so happens that I got a call from this dude that I used to do business with before I got into trouble. He's looking around for some good heroin, real weight if it's quality. If you can use the bread or if it'll make your life any easier, I'll cut you in on it, that is if you can get it, if you see what I mean."

Dom was glancing around the room for Rolf and the words registered slowly. Yet somehow he had expected Sam to come out with this sooner or later, knew that it was inevitable. It was as certain as the greening of that oak tree every spring, a thing that was beyond his will and meant something more than his own feeble struggle to live. He paused, struck by what he had heard, and felt suddenly that he was a part of this larger thing, caught up in it to move unerringly along some given path as surely as everything in the universe moves along its course.

He glanced back, startled, almost as though he had been propositioned and had discovered an unexpected weakness within him that he was ashamed of. Sam was smiling now, as if aware of it also. Dom was alarmed, perplexed. He drained the glass of beer, thanked him, and walked away.

63

Rolf arrived at The Prophet some minutes later, Dom catching sight of the towering, Herculean figure standing near the entrance. They greeted one another with the special, thumbgrip handshake reserved for "in" people.

"Wow, what'd ya do, get in a beef?" Rolf asked, seeing the marks.

"Motto's muscleman," Dom replied bitterly. "It's lucky I'm even alive. I made a connection for 'em and got ripped off by that asshole Slick and Ramon. So y'see? You can't win."

Rolf shook his head sadly. "If you're smart you'll quit this dope game while you're still ahead," he advised. "Those people are animals. I should know. . . ."

"Say," Dom interrupted, ignoring the warning, "before we get started I have to cop. I did a few Darvons but I need something else to hold me."

"You should've told me before," replied Rolf. "I have some blues at home. Jackie does them once in awhile but she doesn't have a habit, just chips maybe a couple times a month." He looked around. "Wait a second, that kid over there oughta have something."

They approached a slim, boyish youth sitting alone and asked him for anything—junk, dollies, valiums, sopors, reds. The youth nodded.

"Gimme ten bucks an' I'll be right back with a wafer of methadone," he said.

Rolf handed him the money and the youth went toward the rear of the club and disappeared. "Wait a minute!" Rolf exclaimed and ran after him.

Dom followed, got held up in the crowd and finally reached the alley. There was Rolf, holding the much smaller youth up in the air by the collar with one hand.

"Don't hit me!" the youth screamed. "I wasn't gonna take off, honest!"

"The hell you weren't!" Rolf snapped. "You did the same thing to a friend of mine, ya little prick!"

They found valiums in his pockets but no methadone. Rolf took these, plus the ten dollar bill, and told him to get lost. The youth called him a name but when Rolf tried to grab him again he fled.

Dom popped six of the pale blue-colored, ten milligram valiums and his sick waned somewhat. He even got a slight buzz off of them, although they were not opiates. He knew people who had developed big valium habits on top of dope because valium made the high last longer and had the same pleasant, relaxing effect. But Dom wanted something more and was lucky enough to locate some methadone inside the club. He took two forty milligram wafers and, boosted with the valiums, he got high. He was not loaded but felt good, as though instilled with a new confidence in himself. Now he was ready to do the store.

Rolf, jittery from the excitement, copped some reds and popped three at a single gulp. Dom watched with apprehension, noting that his partner probably had a sizeable barb habit, and he hoped that it would not make trouble for them.

After it got dark they set out on foot, roamed about the streets in search of a car. Rolf pried open the vent of a VW with a screwdriver, then lifted the hood, crossed the wires to start the engine and taped them together. They picked up Rolf's tools and drove way out, almost into the country to the drugstore they had planned to hit. It was located in an old building on a deserted corner with very little traffic around. They parked the car a half block away and Rolf unhooked the ignition wires. After checking to see that all was clear, they went to the front door.

"Looks like there's just one lock," Rolf observed. "We could jimmy this easy with a couple of long screwdrivers and the bar, or bust it with a shoulder, but I'll bet it's wired." He indicated an alarm box just above them.

"Why not go up on the roof and come in through the skylight?" Dom suggested.

"Nope, that's probably wired too. C'mon, follow me." Rolf moved around into the alley in back and found a boarded up cellar window in an adjacent store, but still in the same building. "This is where we'll go in," he said. "Beauty parlors don't have alarms the way drugstores do."

They fetched the tools from the car. It was about one o'clock when they pried the sheet of plywood from the low window, climbed down into the cellar of the beauty parlor and replaced the panel behind them. As they flashed a light around they saw something common to the cellars of such buildings. The walls were not solid up near the floor joists. Here a two foot space was filled with loose brick and planking. A few deft strokes with the crowbar dislodged these and they made a hole large enough to climb over into the cellar of the pharmacy.

Once inside, they did not try to force the door at the top of the stairs, knowing that it, too, was hooked into the alarm system. Dom flashed the light around, looking for an electrical outlet. It always fascinated him how neat and clean these little stores were upstairs and how filthy and cluttered they were downstairs. Certainly if the customers ever had occasion to go down into these cellars they would quickly take their business elsewhere.

Plugging in the extension cord, Dom hooked up the power drill and stood by while Rolf got up on an old chair and gently tapped the flooring overhead with a hammer. He knew the layout of the store already and after shifting the chair several times he finally picked a spot to go through. The powerful youth took off his coat, wrapped it around the drill to muffle the noise and began boring through the two-by-six subflooring along the joists. After a few minutes he was covered with sawdust. He tiredly handed down the overheated drill and asked Dom for the keyhole saw. He whipped the narrow blade furiously with his big arm, cutting between the holes until the boards fell free and clattered nosily onto the concrete cellar floor.

"Shhh. . . !" said Rolf.

They waited for a long moment, heard nothing outside. Then Rolf resumed working. The heavy carpet on the floor of the pharmacy was the hardest part of the job. He had to resort to the power drill again and finally slashed at it with a knife to raise a flap.

"Okay, ol' pal! Make it quick!" he said softly.

With his partner boosting him up, Dom snaked his lean frame into the black interior of the pharmacy and flashed a penlight around. Rolf had been right on target. He was standing near the middle of the store, in front of the prescription counter. A few feet behind it were the shelves of prescription drugs—cough syrups, laxatives, antibiotics, birth control pills, and so on. He stepped carefully around the counter, hoping that there was no pressure alarm system under the rug. Now he stood in the area where the prescriptions were made up. The narrow beam of his penlight stopped on a small, locked metal cabinet against the wall. Taking the crowbar out of the burlap sack, he popped the door and marveled at the contents inside.

First he scooped up the biggest prize—bottles of 100 dilaudids in the tiny white two and four milligram tablets, and in the sixteen milligram "footballs", plus powder for injection. Next he grabbed the boxes of aqua-blue, ten milligram numorphans, twelve in each box, and some ampules for injection. He also found bottles of his old friend, morphine sulfate. Though just as potent, it was not quite as valued because shooting it by vein caused a "pins-and-needles" sensation. Finally, there were a few quaint, old fashioned apothecary bottles with cut glass stoppers, two of tincture of opium and one of pure cocaine crystals, or "snow". Not a cocaine user himself, he recalled with amusement that like heroin, cocaine was once a recommended treatment for morphine addiction in the latter half of the nineteenth century. He took the bottles, knowing he could sell them to someone.

The pills that Rolf wanted were in separate locked drawers under the prescription counter. The first drawer that gave way to the crowbar contained the "downs". These included large bottles of barbiturates—one hundred milligram seconals in red capsules, or "reds", yellow nembutals, or "yellows", blue and pink tuinals, and sky blue amytals. Then there were the non-barbiturates, of which methaqualone, or "sopors", and doridens were the most popular. He also located the valiums, a favorite of many addicts, especially methadone users and junkies. The "ups" were locked up in two more drawers, also easily jimmied with the bar. Mostly diet pills, there were the shiny black biphetamine capsules, or "beauties", the green dexedrine capsules, or "Christmas trees", blue and yellow desbutal tablets, or "bombers"—a potent amphetamine-barbiturate combination—some lavender benzedrine capsules, or "bennies", also in pink, heart-shaped tablets, and other varicolored amphetamine preparations. There were hundreds upon hundreds of them in large plastic bottles. He noted with irony that there had to be an awful lot of addicts around to consume so many pills, whether legally or illegally, and that certainly all of this prescribing and taking of ups and downs, or whatever else, could only benefit the drug companies in the long run.

He pried open a few more drawers looking for per-codans and found them at last. A synthetic opiate, they were much less potent than the first line of hard drugs, but addicts used them to keep down their sick. He also took a bottle of codeine, an even weaker opiate that was very little used since it worked only in great quantities. And he discovered one small bottle of one hundred, ten milligram dolophines, or methadone, and was surprised to see this big league synthetic opiate kept down with the minors.

Having emptied the drawers, he flashed the penlight across the store and spotted an old fashioned soda fountain through the maze of display counters, the spigots looming up like the skeletal spines of some extinct species of dinosaur. Dom was too young to remember that serene era when another generation of youth congregated here to sip frothy, ice cream sodas for the biggest high of their evening. Now, twenty-odd years later, his own generation had grown much more specialized in the fine art of self-indulgence. Yet the carryover of a craving for sweets remained within him. Impulsively he went over to the gleaming rows of spigots and inspected them. He had never seen a deserted soda fountain before and had an urge to dive in and go hog wild. A soda, or several of them, would taste good after such hard work. He put down the bulging bag of drugs, went behind the counter and found an ice cream scoop. Digging blindly into the barrels of ice cream, he filled a couple of glasses, added squirts of syrup and some fizz. Returning to the hole in the floor he gingerly handed a soda down to his partner.

"Hey Rolf, have one on me!" he whispered.

"Huh, what's this?" he replied, fumbling at it, and took a sip. "Mmm! Tastes like Hawaiian punch and Coca-Cola. Kinda weird but it hits the spot. Gotta straw and a spoon?"

Dom went back, got straws and spoons, passed everything through, then dropped down into the cellar. They stood, drinking the sodas hurriedly. Rolf was already digging at the last scoop of ice cream.

"Wow," he went on, his mouth bulging, "I dunno whether this is moca or peppermint, but who cares, it sure is good. Hey, what is it with you junkies anyway? You always dig sweets. You're gonna get caught one day, not with dope but with a hot soda."

They wiped the glasses clean of prints, took up their tools and the sack of drugs and climbed back over the cellar wall and out of the building. After checking around they went to the car and drove out of the neighborhood to a main road. They followed it for ten miles or so and finally stopped in a wooded area to take a closer look at the contents of their haul.

"Pisser!" Rolf exclaimed joyously, like a child at Christmas time as he shuffled through all the boxes and bottles. "Looka that stuff! What a score! Think I'll do a few a' these nembutals right now."

"And I'll get off on a couple footballs," said Dom.

Finding the bottle of white, fifteen milligram dilaudids, Dom got out of the car, scooped some water out of a ditch and cooked two of them up in his bottle cap, drew the solution through the cotton and shot it straight away. Rolf, who was more of a pill freak then a dopefiend, borrowed the set of works, cooked up a couple of nembutals, or "yellow jackets", and banged them. Meanwhile Dom began to shiver, his teeth chattering like dice in a crap game.

"Foreign body reaction!" he groaned. "Boy, do I have the chills. . . !"

"Cotton fever, huh?" Rolf asked. "Gotta headache?"

"Wow, better believe it. . . !"

"Hey, now I feel shitty, too!" Rolf complained. "That ditch water must've been awful dirty, probably ran through a cow pasture or somethin'."

Dom was miserably sick, but higher than a kite on the dilaudids. "We'll feel better in a couple hours," he said. "Let's get going."

"I'm gonna do a desbutal first," said Rolf, his speech growing more slurred. "Maybe that'll help me." Groping around in the bag, he found them and ate not one but two, and even snorted a pinch of the cocaine crystals. "I can't believe it," he laughed, his eyes staring wildly. "Wow, this is really outa sight. I'm really ripped. . . !"

"You sure you can drive?" Dom asked uneasily. "Better let me. . . ."

"Huh? You kiddin'?" Rolf cut in loudly. "No sweat, man, ol' Rolfie really has his shit together. . . !"

After a lot of fumbling around he crossed the wires and started the bug. Pulling out onto the highway he floored it and began chuckling and bantering rapidly about how well they had scored. But by now his speech was so sloppy that Dom could hardly understand him. He would have made Rolf pull over and stop had he not been so sick and tired and high at the same time. He was stiff from the beating he had received from Motto's goon, and had a bad headache and hot and cold sweats. The nod from the dilaudid lulled him into drowsiness and his eyes closed despite the wild ride and the jabbering of his partner. He was sound asleep when there was a lot of bumping and then a sharp jolt, something striking him in the face. Stunned, he opened his eyes. The car was sitting tilted in the middle of the woods and his nose was bloody.

He saw Rolf wriggle out through the window like a huge sloth, cursing and then laughing. "Hah-hah, shit! How d'ya like that! Whadda gas! Musta hit a tree! Y'okay, ol' pal? Hit the windshield, huh! Look—cracked the hell out of it! Hah-hah, sonofabitch!"

He grasped the car with both hands on Dom's side and righted it with one terrific heave, then yanked open the door and helped Dom out. The two of them staggered thirty feet through the woods, fell into a swamp at the edge of the road and crawled out onto the highway. Dripping wet and covered with mud, they tried to thumb a ride but there was very little traffic at this time of night and they were too stoned and filthy for anyone to pick them up, except maybe the police, who would be very interested in the contents of the sack they were carrying. So they went back to the car, got off again, got sick again from the swamp water, and slept until dawn to the delight of every mosquito that flew by.

64

Dom searched the seedy crowd in The Prophet until he found the short, stout figure of Sam Thornton seated as usual at the bar talking to another youth. Again he noticed that no matter how hard Sam tried to fit in, there was something inperceptibly different about him, an aura of robust wholesomeness that set him apart from the others. As Dom approached, he turned as though already aware of his presence, and broke into his habitual polite smile.

"Hi? Have a beer? How 'bout a shot?" he asked agreeably.

"Sure," Dom replied, "only this time let me buy." Avoiding Sam's eyes he ordered a round from the bartender.

"Thanks," said the youth. "Hey, what's up? Haven't seen you since the other day."

"Nothing much," Dom replied evasively.

"You haven't told me yet what you thought about my offer," Sam went on and paused, then began again, a bit nervously. "Are you interested? Do you know of anyone who might have something?"

Dom wanted to laugh at the awkwardness he felt, a kind of professional embarrassment that one experiences around an amateur. "Uh...," he hedged, feeling himself boxed into one of those searching dialogues where to say even one word was to betray himself completely. He looked away, felt Sam's eyes on him, then became aware of the same irresistible urge to give in, despite all of his instincts to the contrary, that had come over him and frightened him the last time they had spoken. He sighed and turned, looked Sam squarely in the face for just a moment.

"I ... might," he heard himself say, and felt an unexpected relief, as though some great tension that had racked his mind for years had suddenly been released.

"Can you introduce me to him?" Sam asked abruptly.

Dom smiled faintly. "You mean, introduce you to ... to my man?"

"Yes, if he wants to do business. I want to meet him face to face."

"Let's go outside and talk," said Dom, lifting his glass.

They drank up, pushed through the throng of young but old faces, their words inaudible under the pulsing refrain of hard rock, and emerged into another crowd of busy, intent people encased in machines, gliding through the streets to an equally frenetic beat, the clamorous tempo of the city.

"If you could arrange it I'd really appreciate it," Sam went on insistently above the hiss and roar of the traffic. He had lapsed back into his polite manner with the stiff smile. "Y'see, I need some cash myself, and like I said, this guy's lookin' for weight. He's a big dealer out in the suburbs, sells to the rich kids out there. He'll pay top dollar as long as the quality is good. I think he said twenty-five percent." He paused. "... Of course, I don't know how you feel about your man, since he gave you such a hard time and all. But if you can hang in there, why, we'll both make some bread."

Dom squinted in the sunlight as they strode along the sidewalk, annoyed at Sam's impatience. "I'll think it over," he replied simply. "It could be a big hassle. Like you say, me an' my man are not exactly on the best of terms."

"Can you give me his name and address," Sam prodded. "Maybe I can approach him myself. . . ."

Involuntarily Dom glanced at Sam with concern, then gazed around at the passing cars and pedestrians. He felt caught between this sea of anonymous, uncaring faces and his inquisitive, agreeable companion intent on cordially dragging both of them to certain destruction. But then he saw that the one was as impersonal as the other, the faceless crowd as unfeeling and as gray as death itself. He was resigned to it and no longer thought of restraints, of treading a fine line for safety's sake. Now they could get on with it.

"Tell you what," he said. "I'll see you here tonight around nine, okay?"

"Sure, sure," Sam responded with a hint of apology, clearly not meaning to rush things or to put anyone out.

Though they had hardly spoken to one another until today, the two young men parted company with scarcely a word or gesture, like old partners who understood each other's thoughts almost as if they were their own.

Dom went back to his room, got off on ten four milligram dilaudids. Because he had not slept the night before he was exhausted and wanted to crash, to sleep for days. But there was still work to do and he had to stay awake. He found some of the diet pills that he had not yet sold, the black beauties, and popped three of them. He began to feel dizzy and he remembered that he had not eaten in over twelve hours. But he was just too tired to go out again. Then after a few minutes the biphetamines picked him up, lightening his leaden body so that at last he felt bouyant, even sprightly. All sorts of clever thoughts began racing through his mind and he decided to put them to good use by writing his family. He went to the sink and splashed his face with cold water, glanced at himself indifferently in the mirror. He was not surprised at how wasted, how thin and pallid he looked since he first started using dope, how his teeth had turned chalky and were rotting in the gums. He had the look of an old man.

He sat down and began scribbling furiously on a note pad, going on about anything that came into his mind. Then he stopped, tore off the sheet, crumpled it up and tossed it away. He did this once more and again sat staring at a blank sheet of paper. He wanted something magical to flow from the pen, words that his parents would understand and accept, an explanation why he had failed them even while standing at the very door of success. The pen weighed heavily in his hand like a splinter of stone. He had nothing to say. He had lived his life as he had lived it and whether it was successful or not meant little to him now. He saw how life as he knew it only concealed a deeper, more awful truth, an emptiness not meant to be seen by anyone for fear they would shrink back from it in terror. For life must feed and thrive upon itself, and to sense that great, bleak void of nonbeing beyond it is to know of its own extinction. Dom had discovered this in the agony of his addiction, understood that not to believe in himself or in life and to see instead that terrible nothingness and to know it and feel it close upon him was to suffer the unendurable pain of dying.

He put down the pen, stood up and stretched. He would have supper and then come back and sit on the front steps before going to bed. The lilting voices of children playing in the warm summer evening would float through streets hushed with shadow. And as the night rolled in deeply round about and everything grew still, the crickets would sing in the hedges for as long as he wanted to listen.

65

One of the best places to take care of business is in the bus depot. Crowded and noisy, much can be accomplished without exciting undue suspicion, and the comings and goings of passengers arriving and leaving through various entrances make police surveillance all the more difficult. Dom had been here often enough before, picking up deliveries or dropping off cash. He had done it mostly for Motto over two long years with never a single arrest for dealing. Maybe that was the reason why his boss had agreed to accept him back once more. Either this ordinarily ruthless, hard-nosed businessman was remorseful over what he had done, or tried to do, or else he was simply attracted by the prospect of ten thousand dollars clear profit, with no more than the usual tolerable risk. Whichever the reason, and Dom suspected it was much more the second than the first, Motto had agreed to send Joey, his driver, down to the bus station with a sample for the prospective buyer.

The thin, shadowy man appeared at one of the entrances, slipping through the crowd toward Dom with a hurried, anxious step, as though not at all secure about meeting them here and wanting to get it over with as quickly as possible. Naturally a very cautious, skittish man, he felt much safer behind the wheel of an automobile than out in the rough and tumble world afoot. And it was even harder for him when it involved something he did not approve of. He had objected to this connection, to selling weight to total strangers at a time when there was a lot of heat around, and in his own quiet way he had tried to communicate these feelings to the boss. But quiet men, no matter how wise they may be, are not always heard. And this had been the curse of his life, because he always ended up dissenting from but at the same time acquiescing to the mad schemes of others.

"Here's the key," he grumbled, his voice conveying unmistakable disapproval. "Tony wants ya to give him a call tomorrow night. He can deliver ten pieces for fifteen hundred hundred each, got it?"

After a narrow look of distrust, the runner slipped away and Dom walked across the depot. He and Sam opened the locker, removed a manila envelope and returned to Dom's room where they shook out the two sample bags. Warily Dom tasted a speck of it, was reassured by the bitter-sweetness of the mixture of heroin, quinine, and milk sugar. Too eager to take any more precautions, he went into the bathroom, cooked up a bag and got off. He felt a good, solid rush, waited till it had subsided before reentering the room. Sam's inquiring eyes followed him as he sat down and all the while Dom was thinking how strange it was that, under the influence of the drug, this collision course with trouble that they were following seemed no more than a lark, a light-hearted prank. In spite of himself he grinned at Sam, vaguely aware that he looked a little stupid.

"It's good stuff, all right," he declared thickly. "Take a two-cut anyway. Here—for your man. . . ."

Dom tossed the other bag to Sam, whose faint frown of annoyance at seeing his ordinarily level-headed friend so intoxicated never left his face. He looked down at the small packet of white powder in his open hand, a little chagrined at handling a substance that had just trans-formed someone into a semiidiot before his very eyes.

"Look," Sam began crisply, his lips compressed in doubt. "You still haven't told me who I'm doing business with."

Hearing this bald question posed for the second time, Dom responded with a droll, lazy look and hesitated for a long moment. "All right," he assented. "His name is Motto—Tony Motto. At least, that's the name he goes by. He doesn't use himself and deals strictly in weight. Gets it mostly from New York as far as I know. His stuff is usually quality. I used to buy two pieces a week from him, cut it once and it was still the best stuff around."

"I've heard his name before," Sam confessed. "And I know all the kids really dig your stuff. They say it's the best. But tell me, is this guy an independent operator or part of an organization?"

"I don't know," Dom replied. "Except that some big men in town back him financially, legitimate businessmen, but he never mentions any names."

"Yeah, that's the way it is," Sam affirmed with a nod. "No one would ever suspect that they're investing in dope. I guess sometimes they don't even know it themselves 'cause they don't ask any questions about how you can get twenty-five or fifty percent interest on your money."

"Huh. . . ?" said Dom who had just closed his eyes and then opened them.

Sam hesitated and smiled nervously at Dom's inattention, shrugging his shoulders as he went on. "I mean . . . that's the way a lot of these cats operate, right? Take my man—he's anonymous, too. Like I said, even I don't know his name and I've never met him." Sam lit a cigarette, offered one to Dom, puffed rapidly and continued. "You know, dope is big business, one of the biggest and richest, and I guess it has been for a long time. I was reading that in the last century English and American traders addicted millions of Chinese to opium and made a real killing off it. Then around 1840 the Chinese government stepped in and destroyed thousands of chests of opium and that started the Opium War. The British won and forced the Chinese to pay for the opium. Then they went back to selling it again, even more than before. Heavy, huh?"

Dom smiled. "Looks like now the shoe is on the other foot. The Asians are the ones who are getting rich off our habits." He shook his head thoughtfully, went on with a note or irony. "But after all, it's human nature to want to feel good, right? And life is no bed of roses. That's why your addict just wants to stay high, no matter what nationality he is, because he doesn't think life is worth living otherwise."

"Yeah, you can't change human nature, I suppose," Sam agreed. "But you can control it up to a point, don't you think? Seems to me people should be protected against themselves if they're that weak. Take gambling—some guys can't help it, they're just compulsive gamblers. So we need laws to protect them from professional gamblers, right?"

"Sure. Take me for example," Dom admitted. "If someone would throw away my works and take me a thousand miles away from dope, or else got rid of all the dudes who were selling it to me, then I could get a fresh start. What the hell, I don't want to be a dopefiend for the rest of my life, but the stuff is around so I use it."

Sam shrugged. "That's up to you. A lot of kids chip but they don't get strung out, and if they do they kick and give it up for good. But all I want right now is to make this connection. I need the bread—wanna buy a new bike."

"What kind ya gonna get?" Dom asked, letting the rest of his remark slide by. Obviously this kid had never been hooked on anything.

"I'm not sure, maybe a BMW," Sam replied.

"I don't ride, but I know that's a good one. Say, I'm gonna crash now," Dom went on, hardly able to keep his eyes open. "See you tonight at the club. Lemme know the time an' place."

After Sam left, Dom lay down, let the heavy lids close over his eyes. He heard the steady roar of a distant jet passing over the city, growing fainter as it circled in toward the airport a few miles away. And then it all came back to him again as it often did when he was alone and heard a big plane rumbling through the sky. He was on that long, transcontinental flight again that took him home to Brenda, to that first night he saw her. And like a frenetic machine his mind began to unravel the sequence of events, running faster and faster until the series of memories of her whirled like a bewildering delerium that he hardly would have believed, had it not really happened. He, with his lucky star, had never expected it.

66

The military air transport jet had taken off from Saigon in the dead of a hot tropical night. Midway over the Pacific it collided prematurely with the dawn. He saw it through the window—the ocean, a dark floor under the wing, first tinted with silver and then running pink along the horizon as a luminous sun heaved into view, lying like an angry cinder on the water. Burning white hot it began to climb, shedding the airy light of day and rolling the shadows away westward.

He blinked, rubbed his swollen eyes. Like a blind, subterranean creature suddenly unearthed in the full glare of daylight, he wanted only to burrow back again into the dark comfort of an eternal night. Rising stiffly from his seat, he stretched and went down the aisle past rows of still slumbering soldiers to the lavatory. He urinated, washed up, shaved, brushed his teeth, and then got off. By the time he reached his seat, a stewardess was passing out breakfast trays.

Too high to eat much, he sat looking out at the new day, the clean white wisps of cloud, the deep bold blue of the Pacific Ocean. It was peaceful down there, the stillness of the ocean imparting the same unearthly calm that he knew in heroin. After the morphine was used up he had switched to it, doing only a match head at first, then more. Even though his arm had healed months ago, other scars had not. And the heroin was so good and so easy to get that, as with Spec-4 James, his life had begun to revolve around it, for somehow it helped to redeem the tropical, battle-cursed hell he lived in. Now, far away from it all, here above the quiet sea, he wanted to hover like a serene bird, to float silently and to stay as high and as peaceful forever as he was at this very moment.

Thousands of miles and many hours later they touched down at Travis Air Force Base in California. He out-processed, made a long distance call, then took the bus to

San Francisco Airport and went on military standby. All
the while he had been extremely uneasy because of the
half kilo of potent Vietnamese heroin he carried taped
around his waist and stuffed deep inside his pockets. He
got off again in the men's room at the airport to relieve his
tension, reasoning that the more relaxed he was, the less
suspicious he would look. But he overdid it, nodded for an
hour and missed his flight. He had to make another phone
call to his family to tell them he would be late. Two hours
later he boarded a jet east. After takeoff he sat smoking a
cigarette, glancing down at the cotton roof of clouds
sheltering the land—his land that he believed in, a place
that had never been invaded, had never known the rain of
bombs, of fire and death since its birth. And it puzzled
him how one faraway nation had to lie bleeding and
broken in the jaws of war in order for his own to remain
safe and prosperous. But he was a soldier. His job was to
fight rather than to ponder.

His attention turned to a couple sitting beside him.
They had been watching him, had noticed the medals he
was wearing.

"Back from Vietnam?" the man asked politely.

"Yes, sir."

"Y'know, it's a great thing, what you guys're doing over
there," he drawled and clamped his heavy jowls shut in
solemn respect.

Dom nodded a reply.

The woman, a bleached blond in her early forties,
looked past her thickset husband with wide, admiring eyes.
"My, look at all those medals," she declared. "I'm proud
of you. I don't care what they say, it must be very hard,
what you boys have to go through over there. We've seen a
lot on television."

"Thank you," he said and smiled politely, picking up a
magazine to discourage further conversation. He felt a
little guilty about being flattered and did not want to
offend them. They were well-meaning people, but he,
having lately come back from hell itself, did not know just
how to respond to praise.

On his arrival home he cut quite a figure stepping off the plane, lean and tanned in his bemedaled, dark green Class A's. Nothing really betrayed his addiction. The sunken eyes and listlessness could have been from fatigue or the tropical climate, and the mild tremulousness from the excitement of being home. He walked rapidly across the runway, saw his father, mother, and sister just inside the terminal, met them in a flurry of hugs, kisses.

"Dominick!" his mother cried. "You're so thin! What have they been feeding you!"

His father beamed with admiration. "You've lost weight but you look fine! Thank God you're all right! We certainly missed you son, all of us!"

"You look good, too," Dom said and smiled at them. "I'm sure glad to be home, let me tell you. Say, where's Brenda?"

There was a pause, then his sister spoke up. "Her mother said to call. She isn't in. . . ."

"I'll bet you're exhausted," his mother broke in. "Why don't you come home, rest, and I'll fix you something to eat."

Impatiently he called Brenda's house from the airport. Her mother answered, welcomed him brightly, said that she would have Brenda call him just as soon as she got in. Then his family drove him through town, scarcely changed in the short time he had been away. Somehow he had remembered it as a cleaner, more prosperous place than it actually was, and the houses larger than they appeared now. A big sign in the front window of his home brought a grin to his face. It said, "Welcome Home, Dom."

He talked with his family awhile, then called Brenda's house once more but still she was not in. Exhausted, he lay down, tried to sleep but could not, kept thinking of her, of holding and kissing her and hearing her voice in his ear. To ease his mind he got off once more and took a hot bath. Relaxed and feeling much better now, he dressed in his old athletic shirt, dungarees and running shoes and went downstairs. He was greeted by the familiar aroma of Italian cooking, an aroma that had haunted him during his whole hitch overseas.

"I'm making something you like," his mother clucked. "It will be a surprise." She paused, noticed the pitted scars. "Was your arm hurt very bad, dear?"

"It doesn't bother me that much, mom," he said and patted her shoulder.

His father called him into the front room to meet a few neighbors who had dropped by to welcome him.

"We're proud of you," said one of his father's close friends. "So many question the war but, somebody has to go. After all, we went in 'forty-one. Y'know, they oughta send them peace freaks over there, shove a rifle in their hands an' make 'em fight, fer Chrissake!"

"Yeah? Well I sure hope they end it soon," said another, older man. "I don't see any sense in it, to tell you the truth. No reflection on you, Dom, I know you've done your darndest over there, but what's the point? We're not getting anywhere, so why waste lives?"

Dom nodded politely, shook their hands, tried to avoid being dragged into heavy discussions about the war, pro or con. Besides, he had the funny feeling that even though he had been there and they had not, whatever he said would have been wrong. Sensing his reticence, the neighbors politely excused themselves. Then his uncle arrived and the family sat down to a gala supper.

"To our hero, our Dominick!" said the uncle, raising his glass and they all toasted him.

It was the best food he had eaten in twelve months, and in spite of his poor appetite he had seconds and thirds, washing it down with glassfuls of Chianti. It was a wonderful sight to see them all sitting at the table again, faces he had missed so much. He was surprised to see them so well, so hale and hearty, again a contrast to what he was used to seeing overseas.

After what seemed like endless after dinner talk, mainly neighborhood gossip, he managed to get away. The family understood, were in fact waiting for him to excuse himself. He took his car and drove the familiar route to Brenda's house. Her mother answered the door.

"Dom! You look fine!" she chirped. "Brenda's not in yet but why don't you come out back and wait with us. It's so wonderful to see you again!"

Her mother had always liked him. In fact, he got along better with her than he did with Brenda, and fancied that she secretly desired him. She escorted him through the house that he knew so well and out into the patio. Her father, a little heavier now, was stretched out comfortably, watching the ball game.

" 'Lo, Dom!" he boomed. An amiable man, he admired Dom for his athletic prowess. "Welcome back. Say, how's the arm?"

"Okay, I hope."

"Good. And how was it over there? Rough?"

"Rough enough," he replied, supressing an urge to really open up to this man, whom he considered a second father almost. "But I'd go back again if there wasn't a war going on. They're friendly people, basically, but they just want to be left alone."

"I can certainly understand that," her father agreed heartily, and turned back to the television. "Sox're ahead four-nothing. They may take the pennant this year...."

Dom tried to focus his attention on the game, but the painful thought of whether or not he could still pitch preoccupied him. And he was still attuned to small sounds—the crickets in the flower beds caught his ear. They sounded almost like the tree frogs in the jungle, and instinctively he waited for them to cease, a sign of the enemy nearby. Something rustled in the shrubbery and he jerked around in alarm.

"It's just the cat," her mother assured him. "Would you like a beer?"

At that moment the unmistakable crackling of tires on the gravelled drive out front sent him to his feet. "That must be Brenda!" he exclaimed.

"Why don't you wait here and you can surprise her," her mother said quickly.

He paid no attention, but leaped across the yard to the gate at the side of the house and vaulted it. In front the headlights blinded him for a moment, then he heard the car door open and she stepped lightly out, turned to say something to the driver. The car backed away and she stood, her figure silhouetted, waving a hand in the swinging beams. Breathlessly he realized that she had come to life again, was no longer the tantalizing dream that haunted him day and night overseas. And yet suddenly she seemed very far away, further than the dream, and he saw now that the two, the real person and the dream, were altogether different. With an uneasy reserve, he stepped forward.

"Brenda!"

She stopped short, turned and smiled.

"Dom!" she blurted. "So that is your car!"

"You mean already you've forgotten what my car looks like?" he kidded. Instantly he regretted saying it, stepped closer to embrace her and they kissed. It was then that he knew. He let her go, smiled, "I called but you weren't in," he went on mechanically. "Flew in about three hours ago."

"I'm sorry, Dom," she said earnestly. "How was your trip?"

"Not bad, uh. . . ." He paused, his voice tightening, motioned toward the street. "Who was that, anyway?" Even as he questioned her he found himself worshipping her. She was still just as beautiful, still the girl of his dreams.

Avoiding his eyes, she moved her lips slightly, the words caught inside. ". . . It's something I—couldn't explain in my letters because I didn't want to upset you, Dom. He's—just a guy I met a month or two ago and we've—just been dating off and on, that's all. . . ."

"That's all? That's enough!" he exclaimed. "It—it isn't serious. . . !"

"I don't know," she said. "I'm kind of confused right now. . . ."

Stunned at her words, he drew a deep breath. ". . . Well, what about you and me. . . ?"

She gave an answering sigh and looked directly at him, as though annoyed at his question. "You've been gone for a whole year," she argued. "Things change. . . ."

"Huh? Then why did you say you loved me in all your letters?" he demanded.

Her expression turned to sadness and she tried to say something but he interrupted.

"It hasn't changed with me, sweetheart!" he went on, his voice trembling with emotion. He caught her, kissed her once more, hard, with the hunger of a love-starved soldier. And again he knew, by her answering kiss, that she no longer wanted him. He stepped back, struggling with panic, with overwhelming desperation. "I have to go. . . ," he mumbled. "I—we'll talk again, okay?"

She responded with a wave of her hand. "I did miss you, Dom. Call me. . . ."

He drove around the streets, his mind deadened by the thought of so much love lost with nothing that could be done to save it. Like the death of the little boy, whom he had also loved, he could not accept Brenda's words. It seemed strange, fictional, something that would pass in time. Almost without thinking he took out his set of works and got off on a good bag, so pure he did not even have to cook it. He got high on the dynamite Vietnamese dope and the pain slackened. Nodding like a child in a sweet dream, he found a paradise where no one else could follow.

67

Before his thirty day leave was up, Brenda agreed to see him again and they dated briefly. Then he had to report to his new unit stationed out in the midwest. He endured the monotonous grind of stateside duty, of endless work details, paperwork, inspections, and changing of the guard, inspired only by his desire to be with her again and by the undying hope that she still might want him. A big moment came when she called him on his birthday. But she forgot to say how much she loved him and this conspicuous ommission gnawed at him for weeks.

Up till then he had cut his habit down to only a few bags a day and had plans to kick. Now her apparent coldness caused him to start using more. After all, it was easy to get. He had it in with a few of the blacks as well as with some troops who had arrived directly from Nam, and between all of them there seemed to be a never-ending supply of dope. Then one quiet morning at 0500 hours the brigade commander called an alert. The battalion stood inspection in the billets while the CID came through and searched everyone. Within two hours a wide assortment of drugs, from marihuana to heroin, had been uncovered in the sleeping areas of nearly fifty men in Dom's company alone, stashed in lockers, mattresses, field jackets, helmets, gas masks. Twelve men, eight of them Vietnam veterans, were arrested by the MP's for possession of narcotics, in this case heroin, and marched to the stockade. Dom was among them.

The following morning a young medical officer, a psychiatrist, interviewed each man individually. "Have you ever received psychiatric treatment?" he asked them. "Ever heard voices or had thoughts of people trying to harm you? Were you previously a drug user or did you become addicted while in the service? Did something in the line of duty compel you to use drugs or did you use it on your own volition? Did another soldier turn you on or was it a Vietnamese national? Would you have been able to function overseas without drugs?"

The doctor needed this information for his report, and for the line of duty determination. Line of duty "yes" implied a service-connected psychiatric illness and the veteran would be entitled to a medical discharge and disability. But uncomplicated drug abuse was considered not in the line of duty.

Dom was dopesick and nervous in the interview, and in the face of so many questions he had trouble communicating with the young doctor, who evidently had never been to Vietnam. He could not explain what it was really like over there, that it was not a war in the conventional sense, with enemy and allied lines clearly demarcated on a wall map. It was not a war where special uniforms and insignias identified the friendlies from the aggressors. Instead it was confusion and frustration, the dread of never quite knowing who or where the enemy was, yet being maimed and killed by him without warning. It was the suspicion that he could be a ten year old child with a hidden grenade, or a sixty year old woman acting as a spy. It was knowing that the enemy could be the farmer, the fruit vendor, the bus driver, or the monk. And it was hating this faceless enemy and lashing back at it with an equally cruel and impersonal holocaust of massed fire-power. It was counting the dead, losing friends to bullets, mines, booby traps. It was being sent into an ambush by young, boot lieutenants to save indecisive allies. And it was valiantly fighting under a foreign flag for the honor of one's own country, only to create discord at home and abroad.

"I can't explain it, sir," he said after a long pause. "I just got hit, that's all, started taking morphine for pain in the arm and shoulder, and then because heroin was so cheap and easy to get I got turned on to it by another GI and developed a habit. I'd like to kick if I could. . . ."

After the interview the psychiatrist dictated a report that was almost identical to his reports on the eleven others.

"There is no evidence of organic brain syndrome or psychosis.

Diagnosis: Drug dependency, secondary to passive-aggressive personality. Cleared for administrative separation."

A judge advocate officer, a young second lieutenant, visited the stockade a few days later to provide legal counsel. He spoke with self-assurance as he addressed the pitifully dopesick soldiers, telling everyone just about the same thing.

"Take my advice," he said to Dom, who was trembling and sniffling and suffering from dry heaves and explosive diarrhea. "If you're court martialled you may end up in Leavenworth for possession of narcotics. It would be a lot smarter to take an undesirable discharge, in which case the court martial would be waived."

Dom did not want to go to prison. All he wanted at this point was to get out. And an undesirable discharge was not the same as a dishonorable. It only meant the loss of certain veteran's benefits. So he agreed and was released from the stockade. One month later a board of five colonels assembled in brigade headquarters. Dom stood before them and in less than twenty minutes he was out of the army.

His family was more than a little surprised when he showed up one day unannounced in civilian clothes and said he was out. He insisted that it was due to his wounds, the shrapnel in the arm and shoulder. As if to prove his point, he tried pitching through the old tire out in the back yard but his arm hurt and the throws went wild. Subsequent days of practice only worsened the pain and he gave up. But despite the bitter loss of his pitching skill he still hoped to bring it back again, perhaps after another year of rest. And there was still his girl—he would get her back now. He was clean, had kicked in the stockade after ten hellish days of leg aches, nausea, diarrhea, hot and cold sweats, and worst of all, no sleep. But now the service was behind him, like a bad dream. He had the future to live for.

Work was tight for young veterans just back from the war, most of whom had not gone to college and had no trade. But Dom was fortunate. His father got him a job in a men's clothing store, where he planned to work until he decided what he wanted to do. Tall and lean, he cut a good figure in a suit and the customers wanted that lithe, athletic appearance for themselves. And his pleasing, informal manner endeared him to middle-aged customers, who often resented youthful salesmen. Business began to pick up at the shop and he was given a small raise.

Even more encouraging, Brenda saw him regularly now, though she still wanted to date other boys. Her affections filled the void left by heroin, so he did not crave it. But she seemed distant and kept putting him off when he tried to make love to her. After a few months his patience grew thin and he began badgering her about it. She made vague excuses, then one night under pressure she broke down and wept, announced that she was two months pregnant by the same boy he had seen her with his first night home from overseas.

"I've decided not to get an abortion," she sobbed. "... It would hurt my parents too much if they ever found out—so—I'm getting married next month. Oh, Dom, Dom! I'm sorry it had to work out this way—I'm so sorry. ..!"

She clung to him, he dumbfounded, not believing it. And as he held the weeping girl he had the strange awareness that she was crying more for herself than for him.

He stayed in his room for most of two weeks after that. His mother thought he had a virus, wanted him to see a doctor, and made him little cups of broth. He needed more than broth. He had not thrown away his works, kept looking at them in his top drawer. Every time he saw them he had an intense desire to get off. One night he went in town and nosed around. He had been drinking some but the alcohol gave him little comfort. In fact, it only made him want to hurt her—he had to stifle thoughts of laying for the two of them as he had been taught to do with the enemy in the jungle. Heroin was what he needed and impulsively he made a connection and copped some bags.

Because the street dope was not much good, his new habit was small at first but grew steadily along with his tolerance, from six bags up to ten or twelve. Spending sixty to seventy dollars a day, he rapidly exhausted his savings. He was forced to filch money at work just to stay straight, pocketing the cash from a sale instead of ringing it up. Of course, he intended to pay it all back. It was several months before the accountant picked up the error on the books. The company quietly ran a security check on every employee and discovered Dom's undesirable discharge from the service. They put a few facts together and confronted him.

"I hate to say it, but we think you're the one," the boss said. "You're a Vietnam veteran and a lotta those boys got hooked on drugs over there. Now tell us, have you been taking the money? Don't worry, I won't press charges."

Dom admitted it and the boss looked at him sorrowfully. "I can't believe it," he said. "I've known your family for thirty years and you were one of the best kids around. I just don't know what to say. . . ."

They agreed that Dom would pay the money back and in return the boss would not say anything about it. Of course, he was let go.

Unknown to him, word somehow got around the neighborhood that he was a dope addict. The first he knew of it was when some of his old friends no longer trusted him in their homes. He would drop over to visit, only to find that they would not answer the door, or would put him off and find a reason not to let him in. Then he heard that he had been blamed for a theft in a neighbor's home, even though he himself knew who had done it. He came to realize that he was an outcast, that he had lost his old popularity.

Since he valued his friends more than drugs and also feared that he might end up in jail if he continued using, he decided to apply immediately to the nearest VA hospital for treatment. At the outpatient clinic a fortyish, male social worker in a loud coat and tie interviewed him.

"Sorry, but we can't accept you until you're drug free," he announced brusquely. "Besides, all we really have here is a day care program, and it's full right now, though we can put you on a waiting list. Our detoxification unit upstairs is also full at the moment, but they will call you when they get a bed if you want to wait a few days."

"How long would I have to wait?" Dom asked.

The social worker shrugged. "Who knows? A week or ten days, maybe longer. Just depends."

This offhandedness did not inspire confidence in the youth. At last he saw clearly that being a veteran of an unpopular war somehow made him a second class citizen, even here at the VA, the sole agency created to help him but which seemed to be catering more to Second World War vets, who soldiered in a "good" war. He left his name and a telephone number anyway but after ten days of waiting he changed his mind. He decided instead that kicking in the stockade had been pure hell and he did not want to go through it again just now, even though he had a much smaller habit. He did not think he was ready to stay clean anyway, mainly because he was not on his feet emotionally.

A few nights later his family got worried when he stayed in the bathroom for over two hours without making a sound. After shouting vainly, his father kicked in the door and found him lying on the floor, scarcely breathing, a hypodermic syringe stuck in his arm. He was rushed to the hospital by ambulance, where the doctors hooked him up to a respirator and injected Narcan, an opium antagonist, to restore his breathing. The next day he was discharged. His parents were silent until they arrived home, then his mother spoke up, her voice strained.

"Dom, the doctor says you're a drug addict! Is it true? Was he right? I told him he must be wrong! I said it can't be because I know my son and I know he could never...!" She faltered, then went on softly, her eyes wet with tears. "But the doctor said—it probably happened overseas, like so many of the boys—but—is it really true...?"

Her shining eyes gazed at him imploringly, asking for just one sign of reassurance, one word to put her mind at ease. But he said nothing, only looked at her stricken face with pity.

"Please, mamma, stop it!" his father exclaimed, seizing her by both arms. He looked at her earnestly, shaking her as he spoke. "Everything will be all right, don't worry! Dom will stay here with us and I'll get the best doctors in the country to cure him! He'll be okay, you'll see! God will help us!"

But his parents did not understand. He was no longer the same person, not the promising young athlete, the soldier-hero, or the young lover. Life had changed him beyond their comprehension. He left for the city a few days later, where dope was easier to get and where he could freely roam the darkened streets.

68

The Prophet catered to those patrons burdened with time, with endless long evenings that needed to be filled. Here the pain of monotony was dispelled by illusion, by unending music, dancing, colored lights, and a variety of intoxicants. Time was broken, stirred into a pleasant effervescence, the hours fizzing away like bubbles in a glass. The youthful guests took in this heady atmosphere almost like an anesthesia, numbing themselves against their own emptiness, against a world outside that seemed to exclude them. Only when something from that nether world touched them or their friends personally did they bother to respond, and then they did so with apathy, or with a shallow display of emotion.

Dom, Russ, and Danny were sitting together, busily staring into their drinks and otherwise reacting with customary cynicism to the news of Rolf's and Jackie's separation after someone had slashed Rolf with a knife. Rolf evidently did not press charges and Jackie left immediately for New York in the company of an ex-boyfriend.

"They were doing an awful lotta pills," Russ commented. "An' them things're a thousand times worse'n junk, man."

"Right," Danny agreed, peering unblinkingly through his thick, wire-rimmed spectacles. "Rolf didn't like that kid to start with. He was making all kinds of passes at Jackie."

"So you think he was copping and Rolf beat him with baking soda just to get even, huh?" Dom asked.

"Wow," Russ breathed with a quick, knowing smile. "Ain't no better way to get someone down on ya. Only thing is, Rolf can take care of himself. He prob'ly jus' wanted to start somethin' so's he could do a number on that kid." He shook his head with great solemnity. "Lotta marriages fuckin' up these days. An over little things, too, like a bag a' dope, can y'imagine?"

"I saw Slick today," Danny remarked. "He says dope's tight as hell, wanted to know where he could find something. Even Martin was out. And, get this, he said Ramon ripped him off for a whole half pound."

Dom shifted in his seat, his face taught. "That's a laugh," he cut in ironically. "After they both ripped me off for it."

"Serves ol' Slick right, if y'ask me," Russ declared energetically. "He rips everyone off."

"He'll have a helluva time finding anything right now," Dom observed. "The last thing I got from my man was a couple of hot bags. So I had to go out and do a store with Rolf."

"Wow, what a bummer!" Danny exclaimed in his loud monotone. "I still can't believe it, after you'd been working for them so long."

"Yeah, it kind of shook me up, all right," Dom admitted. "After I made over fifty grand for 'em, too. . . ." He paused and compressed his lips in a straight line of troubled reflection. "Y'know, I've been having these really weird dreams since that happened, like the one last night. . . ."

He took a sip of beer while they leaned forward to listen, and noticing their attention, he went on. "It was far out, I tell ya. I was somewhere over in Nam I think, walking across a big field. Then I saw the most beautiful sight I'd ever seen in my life—purple and white poppies everywhere, just like the ones they grow over there. They were tall, way above my knees, some with only those bulbs that they draw the milk out of. And I thought, wow, like these are real opium poppies, man, an' I could get off by just standing here and breathing the air. Then I got scared because I heard you could OD in a poppy field, and so I started walking fast to get the hell out of there. But there was no place to go. The poppies were everywhere as far as I could see. It bummed me out 'cause I figured I was going to die. Ever had that feeling?" He smiled at the pair of spellbound faces.

"That's heavy," said Danny. "A nightmare. God, I know how it is. I have nightmares when I'm dopesick."

"That's what it was," agreed Dom. "I must have been sick in my sleep."

"Them poppies are beautiful but deadly," Russ observed ruefully. "Same as a woman. Prettier she is, the more she'll fuck your head over. Mushrooms same way, the more beautiful the more poison they got in 'em."

"If I was in that poppy field, I'd get down on my knees and pray," said Danny. "I'd pray to be saved by a miracle or something."

"Hmph!" Russ scoffed. "I'd rather jus' sit back an' enjoy the high. Go out in style, dig? Ain't no time for religion, 'less it's your thing, understan'?"

Danny grew excited, his eyes widening and voice getting louder. "No really, I'm serious. You can get off on religion, too," he argued. "Just like you can on junk. You can even get high just by helping people and watching their faces light up with gratitude. Now, when I kick, I'm thinking of going into missionary work, so that I'll be getting high off the right things instead of the wrong things."

"You? A preacher?" Russ laughed. "Danny, the Jesus freak!"

"I'm not like you think I am," Danny blared in protest. "Sure, I did a lot of acid and speed a few years back to expand my mind, my self-awareness or whatever you call it, then I did heroin just to come down again. You know, I did eighty or ninety acid trips until I saw shadows crawling around and bright lights on things same as I saw on acid and I had to go see a shrink and he put me on Thorazine. But now. . . ." He paused and raised both hands toward the ceiling. ". . . I know that God has a plan for me because he revealed it to me when I was tripping one day. He said he had a plan for me just like he had for everyone and even every addict, no matter how down and out they were."

"I heard it all before," Russ said with a sigh.

"And like I'm really into Buddha, too," Danny went on, ignoring Russ's sarcasm. "Jesus and Buddha are both dynamite people who came from the same God. They can get it together because they understand human suffering. And if we don't let them help us, we'll be lost forever, that's for sure—man will perish from the earth."

"Hey, you been gettin' into this thing too heavy, man," Russ chuckled. "Jus' like all the heads I know, makin' like they was some kind of guru. Acid does that to your head, don't it? I was even into that bag when I was doin' it. But now to me, drugs jus' show you another side of reality. Fact is, ain't nobody knows where we're at or where we're comin' from, so we jus' have to take care a' business the best we can, man."

"But I've gone further," Danny insisted. "I'm into faith now."

"It is the truth that we're destroying ourselves," Dom spoke up, after listening to their argument with interest. "I mean all of mankind. I think you're right, Danny. The human race is going to overpopulate and pollute itself right off the face of the earth, unless maybe we can find other planets to settle, but where? And even as individuals we're sort of destroying ourselves, just pissing our lives down the drain. The whole thing doesn't make any sense. . . ."

"Right, it doesn't," Danny admitted. "As for me, I'm tired of screwing around. I don't want to be a heroin addict all my life. I want to do something worthwhile, to help people and make something of myself. But it seems like no one will give me a break. As soon as they find out I've done drugs they drop me. Like I can't even get a decent job because of it, so now I just help my old man. He's in the tile business and I make deliveries for him. Me, with three years of college. And I wanted to go to law school. . . ."

He stopped and stared at the crowd and was about to begin again when they were interrupted by a newcomer. It was Sam, his face strained, without a trace of his usual smile.

"Hey Sam, what's happnin'?" Russ spoke up.

"Sit down," said Dom. "What's the matter?"

"Wait'll you hear what came down," Sam said quickly. "It's Martin. I—I went over to his pad to look him up and he didn't answer, so the door was unlocked and I went in. Something just told me to go on in. And there he was lying on the sofa. I knew he wasn't asleep—I could tell that right away. When I went up and poked him he didn't move. He was stiff as a board. Been dead for hours, I guess. . . ."

"Must've OD'd, huh?" said Russ, after a shocked silence. They sat immobile in their chairs, not touching their drinks, in a gesture of respect for their departed friend.

"I dunno," Danny reminded them. "He's burned a lotta people."

"I'll bet I know," Dom said softly, his voice barely audible above the steady thud of the music. "Yesterday he came over to cop some drugstore dope from me 'cause he was completely out of junk. I had a few blues left and he also asked for some barbs. He wanted them to hold down his sick. Anyway he said he was really depressed because there was no dope around since the panic started at the beginning of the summer, and he was tired of being sick all the time. He went on about the good old days twenty years ago, about how much good heroin there was then, so much that it sat around in the back rooms of drugstores in big boxes like sawdust. And then he made some kind of freaky remark about wanting to see what was on the other side, but he dropped the subject."

"Uh-huh," said Russ. "An' you can't do much dope and barbs together 'cause you'll go right out."

"I'll bet that's what happened," Dom concluded. "But you'd think he'd know better. He's done dope for over twenty years, for cryin' out loud."

"You think maybe he did it on purpose?" Danny suggested.

They considered this remark for a moment with cynical grimness.

"Who knows?" Russ said at last. "Cops come?"

The trace of a polite smile crept onto Sam's face again, twitching the corners of his mouth. "Yes, I had to call them," he confessed. "But I played dumb, like I hardly knew him."

"They'll be comin' 'round askin' questions now," Russ went on, looking genuinely worried. "Them detectives, Collins an' what's his face, Feeney, they're real bastards. Caught me in an alley one time, threw me up against a wall, put a bag a' dope in my pocket an' a gun to my head. 'You're under arrest!' they said, wanted me to fink on some buddies a' mine but I wouldn't, 'cause I knew they were goin' to bust me anyhow."

"If the cops want you, they'll get you, that's for sure," said Danny, his monotone sounding all the more serious. "Like when a friend of mine was doing drugstores and they couldn't catch him but they knew it was him. So one day they busted him just walking down the street for being disorderly." He shook his head slowly and sighed. "Anyhow," he went on, "I liked Marty. He was a nice man."

Everyone nodded in sober agreement and there was silence. They had run out of the few words they had to say about his passing. Quiet reflection seemed more proper. There was no deep regret. They accepted it because it was inevitable. Marty dying a natural death would have surprised them more. Dom looked at Sam, who averted his eyes while Russ tapped his finger slowly to the heavy beat of the music. Danny blinked around at the crowd through his thick, wire-rimmed spectacles, as though searching for some great truth that would explain it.

69

Dom paced unhurriedly along a row of suburban shops, crossed the street and lingered on a corner. He lit a cigarette and watched the smoke drift off in a light summer breeze. It was blowing off the bay a few miles away and he welcomed its freshness. He found himself breathing deeply, noticing how much cleaner and more bracing the salt air was than the tainted air he was accustomed to.

He looked around once more at the parked car that had been watching him a block away and now forgot about the simple pleasures of life, his stomach knotting involuntarily. The car waited for another few moments before pulling up. He caught sight of Spanky and Joey up front and Motto alone in the back seat, his face more puffed than usual and broken into a disgruntled frown.

"Climb in, kid," Motto directed and looked away. "What's the news?"

"No problem," Dom explained quickly. "He wants ten pieces of the same stuff as the sample and he'll meet your price of fifteen hundred each. It has to take at least two cuts. He wants me to taste it when you drop it off. If it's good, he can use more in a few weeks."

Motto bit off the end of a cigar, jammed it into his mouth and hunched over to light it. He seemed relieved but did not want to show it, disguised it instead behind a mask of perpetual displeasure. "Yeah, well tell me, who is this guy?" he asked.

"I don't know," Dom replied simply. "His own runner doesn't even know who he is."

"Who's the runner, some kid?"

"Yeah, he's just a kid," Joey offered from the front seat, and he and Spanky both turned around but avoided looking at Dom, he seeing the sullen sneer on both their faces.

Motto thought for a moment, chewing ruminant-like on his cigar. "There's an awful lotta heat around right now," he went on. "I don't know these guys an' I don't like to take too many chances. If I was stupid I wouldn't have lasted this long in the business, see?"

"Look," Dom insisted. "This kid has the same thing in mind. He wants to be real careful. That's why he's gotta do business face to face, so he can get what his man wants. He trusts you. I told him he's got nothing to worry about."

Motto stabbed his cigar at Dom. "You're the one who's stupid, y'know that, kid? The more I hear about this thing, the more it stinks!" He looked away, went on muttering to himself. "Sonofabitch, what a rotten business. . . ! Never a moment's peace! No one's ever happy either—the junkies ain't happy 'cause they want a better cut on the junk, the investors ain't happy 'cause they want a better percentage on their dough. On top of that ya gotta pay off the right people, pols, cops, judges, you name it, just to stay in business." He waved his cigar contemptuously, his high pitched voice growing harsher. "Then—they all turn around an' point at you, say you're wors'n a murderer for corruptin' our young! That's a lotta baloney! If parents spent time with their kids nowadays like they did when I was growin' up, there wouldn't be no dope business, fer Chrissake! But instead, they blame me for it! Whadda buncha jerks!" He paused, began mumbling again. ". . . Christ-o-mighty, all this rumpus—sneakin' around like a common thief for a few measly hundred grand a year an' then worryin' about the time if they pick ya up! I wish ta hell I'd stayed in the bookie business. All we had to worry about there was a raid now an' then just ta keep the public happy!"

He stopped, glanced around defiantly, as though daring someone to disagree. No one did. "Well, whaddaya think, boys?" he snapped to the two men in front.

The driver flinched at the question. "I think it's takin' a big chance," Joey said quietly after a pause.

"Okay—Spanky?"

The big man raised his ham hands in protest. "I'll go along with you, Tony, but to tell ya th' truth, I don't like it. We oughta just drop it somewheres an' take a chance on gettin' beat fer it."

"Well," Motto mused out loud, and looked sharply at the youth. "My guys don't like it. So whaddaya think a' that, kid?"

Dom sat motionless on the seat of the automobile, mesmerized by the ugly look of scorn on Motto's face, by the evil, reptilian eyes of a fiend in human flesh who had tried to kill him, who thought nothing of snuffing out a man's life if it suited his interests.

"But there's one thing my boys gotta remember," Motto went on deliberately, half turning toward them. "That's what they're paid to do, ta take a few chances now an' then, right fellas?"

He darted a keen glance at the two of them and they looked uneasily away, saw the passing countryside sweeping by on both sides of the moving car, for they were out on the freeway now, speeding between suburbs. They said nothing to disagree.

"Tell ya what," Motto continued, turning back to Dom and poking the stub of his cigar at his face. "I'll admit I need the dough, 'cause one a' my daughters is gettin' married. Gonna have everything for the girl, y'know how it is. So you come up with the fifteen grand an' we'll come up with the ten pieces. Only if anything happens, you ain't gonna see the light a' day, understand?"

"As long as I get what I want for dealing," Dom replied simply. "I'll do anything."

"Yeah, well dead men don't use no dope, remember that!" Motto pointed out.

"Yeah, ain't it the truth," Spanky chuckled. "Ha-ha-ha-ha!"

"Shaddup, will ya!" snapped the boss. "Joey, turn this thing around and let the kid out."

Minutes later Dom was standing alone on a residential street bordered with smooth lawns and neat beds of gaudy flowers. The suburbs were certainly nice in the summertime, he thought, and the people out here must be happy and content with life, not living everyday in fear the way he did in the city. Yet he knew there was a lot of dope out here in the suburbs. Wherever there were kids, there was dope.

He walked down a few streets to the square and hailed a cab, rode as far as the subway stop. There he took a train back into the city. All the while he kept thinking how Motto was too smart for him and that, just as he had feared, he was risking his own skin more than he had intended. He could not help but feel contempt for himself at thinking he could ever get even with a man like Motto for having him beaten and then nearly killed. But he had made up his mind to go through with it anyway. Even if he failed he would be better off taking whatever grim consequences might be in store for him, rather than to continue suffering this sting of self-humiliation that had tormented him ever since the day he got hooked on heroin, and which had become unendurable with Motto.

He went straight to The Prophet. His haul of drugstore dope exhausted, he had to try and cop. Fortunately he was far from broke, had made a lot of money from selling what he did not use. A few pills and a drink or two would kill the sick until he could locate some junk or methadone. He found Dolores, Russ, and Danny perched together at a table like a flock of convivial crows. Ordering a 'ball and a beer at the bar, he pushed in among them. Immediately he noticed that Dolores looked very tired and pale.

"What's wrong with you?" he asked. "Got the bug?"

"We think she's got hep again," said Russ. "I'm takin' her to the hospital in a little while."

"Cigarettes taste lousy? That's one of the signs," Dom added.

Dolores nodded mournfully. "They taste awful. I'm sure I have it. My urine was real dark this morning."

"I might have it too, man," said Russ, " 'cause me an' her been usin' the same set of works."

"Maybe you just have a slight case," Danny remarked, peering quizzically through his thick spectacles. "Do you feel tired?"

Russ shrugged. "A little, but that's from doin' coke all night long."

There was silence. Everyone sipped their drinks, stared aimlessly around the room, tuned in on the music whining and rumbling about their ears.

"Did you read about the election poll?" Danny piped up at last. "It was in this morning's paper. Mayor Rowen has a big lead. He'll probably be reelected."

"Hey, all right!" Russ exclaimed. "Let's hope the dope stays in too. 'Course, it's tight now, but once all the elections're over, just watch it come in again! Why, it'll be beautiful!"

"They're setting up more of these methadone clinics," Danny went on. "I might apply. I'm tired of copping, tired of the whole scene. I'd like to get off of drugs, but then again I'm afraid of getting strung out on methadone."

"I might go," said Dolores, "if they'll give me my methadone everyday. But I couldn't give it up, ever. It's like a good friend. I'm just not happy without it. . . ."

"You're really hooked on that shit, ain't ya," Russ chided. "Why, the way you talk, you'll still be on it when you're old an' gray."

Her green eyes snapped feebly in their muddy whites and she would have given him a piece of her mind, even though she was ill. She would have berated him for suggesting that she was a hopeless addict, as nearly all methadone users do. After all, methadone was considered a "cure" for heroin addiction. It was prescribed by doctors and nurses and other highly trained professionals, just as they once prescribed cocaine and later heroin for morphine addiction near the turn of the century, until the G-men raided them. So by definition, how could she be called an addict when she was taking the cure?

But what she could not really admit to herself was that she would always be an addict, even after years of drug abstinence. Because opiates were bigger than she was, and left her weak and helpless. And she did not understand also how others preyed on this weakness—not only the syndicate and the local pushers, but also the drug companies, psychiatrists, nurses, social workers, counselors, and everyone else who depended on her continued addiction for their livelihood. She was the patsy of every hoodlum and a pawn in the fly-by-night, drug treatment game.

There was a phone call at the bar for Dom and he went to answer it. He returned a moment later, sat down again with a peculiar slouch that drew everyone's attention. "That was Slick," he remarked slowly.

"Him calling you? After what he did?" Dolores said with surprise.

"He's got awful big balls," said Danny. "What did he want, dope, like everyone else?"

"That's right."

"What did you tell him?"

"That I'm out. But he doesn't believe me."

"Now that he knows you're not home I'll bet he's gonna rip off your pad, man, right while you're sittin' here," Russ speculated. "Too bad—he won't find nothin'."

"He might," Dom muttered.

"Huh? I thought you didn't have nothin'?"

"I don't—just that hot bag I told you about. . . ."

Dom tossed down his beer casually while the others looked up in alarm. Dolores was the first to speak.

"Someone better tell him!" she declared quickly.

Russ, seeing what was in store for him, tried to dissuade her. "Aw, he'll know it when he sees it, baby," he said. "No sweat!"

"Maybe not," Danny argued. "It depends on how sick he is at the time." He leaned forward and stared at them owlishly. "Look, I know he's a bad dude who's been ripping off everybody and all that but still, somebody oughta tell him before he or maybe somebody else puts it into their arm, don't you think?" He focused his stare at Dom.

"Who knows," Dom replied with a shrug. "He may not even find it. It's under the mattress. But even if he does, tough shit, it'll be his own fault." He lit a cigarette, blew the smoke out casually. "Think I'll have another beer. Anyone else want one?"

Distressed at his callousness, they ignored him as he got up and went back to the bar. It was unlike Dom not to care about people, and they were puzzled by it. After some urgent persuasion, Dolores pulled Russ up out of his chair and they hurried out together.

"Where'd they go, over to my place?" Dom asked when he returned, irked that they had gone before he could find out if they had anything to sell him.

"Uh-huh," Danny replied. "They've got a car. They'll call us if they see Slick, otherwise they'll leave a note for him under your door. That's about all they can do. Hope you don't mind."

"Hell no. . . ."

Dom sat down again, poured out his beer, watched it foam up and spill over the top of his glass. He tossed down the other half of the shot and chased the burning in the pit of his stomach with the beer, quenching it. A little light-headed from the alcohol, he still felt dopesick and began to look around for other people to cop from. The fact that someone could die because of his indifference had little impact—and it dawned on him at that moment that he was just as bad as Motto, whom he reviled for the same, callous selfishness. At last he had sunk as low as the most fiendish of men, and the awareness of it brought only a fleeting, cynical sense of bemusement.

"Any dope around?" he asked.

A few minutes later Russ and Dolores arrived at Dom's room but found nothing out of the ordinary. He door was locked and the room, quiet. They called out Slick's name but got no answer. They checked in back of the house but saw no jimmied or broken windows. Then, with Russ still protesting about the foolishness of it all, Dolores slipped a note with Slick's name on it under the door, and they left.

It was nearly dark when they reached the old hotel. The shadows in the hallway were deep, barely pushed back by a single, naked bulb. After Russ and Dolores left the elevator they heard footsteps behind them and when they stopped, the footsteps stopped. When they started again the footsteps started.

"Someone's behind us," whispered Russ, catching her arm.

Reflexively he pulled whatever drugs he had out of his pockets and flung them into the dark corners of the hallway, while Dolores did the same. Just as they reached the door to their room they looked back, into the guns of a detective and two state troopers.

"Put your hands up and don't move, both of you! Russell Reed and Dolores Marden?"

"Yes, sir," Russ said discretely.

The detective approached. "You are both under arrest! You have the right to remain silent. Anything you say can and will be used against you in a court of law. You have the right to consult an attorney of your choice. If you cannot afford an attorney one will be provided by the court."

"What are you arresting us for?" Dolores asked indignantly.

"C'mon, up against the wall!" the detective snapped, ignoring her.

"Go ahead an' fish us if ya want" said Russ. "We ain't done nothin'."

The troopers frisked the two of them and were exasperated to find absolutely nothing. They flashed a light around and to their chagrin they discovered a bag of cocaine, a set of works, and some methadone tablets lying in the shadows of the hallway.

"These yours?" demanded one of the troopers.

"No sir," answered Russ.

"All right, let's go inside," the detective ordered.

He produced a John Doe warrant, and they were handcuffed and pushed into the apartment. The troopers started rummaging through the rooms, turning everything upside down, while the detective asked them some questions.

"Ever know a guy by the name of Ramon Perez?"

"Nope," Russ uttered, his heart leaping up in his throat. What he feared all along had come to pass. At the age of twenty-four, he had witnessed the end of his youth and the beginning of his old age in the twinkling of an eye.

The detective's expression hardened. "Well, he knows you, Reed. He told us everything. They picked him up down in Rhode Island." He turned to Dolores. "You're an accessory as far as we're concerned," he added.

"Hey, she ain't done nothin!" Russ objected. "I can—"

"Russ, be quiet!" warned Dolores and he obeyed after giving her a quick look of anguish.

The search produced another set of works and some more methadone. Satisfied, the lawmen took the couple downstairs past the surprised clerk, and drove them over to the city jail. There they were skin-searched separately, booked, and locked up pending bail.

Sometime later, near midnight, Dolores was led out of her cell by a matron and into an interrogation room where the detective who arrested her and another man, who identified himself as a detective from the city police department, were waiting.

"Dolores, your boyfriend told us all about you," the first began gently. "How you use methadone and heroin and support your habit by prostitution. So why don't you come clean with us and tell us everything you know about him? Who's he working for, what are his connections? We already know he's a cocaine addict and small time dealer. Remember, if you cooperate, things'll go much easier for you. And we also want whatever you know about this kid Vincent Quinn, who we know was in on that supermarket holdup where that officer was shot."

They both watched her expectantly as she gaped at them in disbelief. "Russ wouldn't rat on me like that!" she shrieked. "You're lying!"

The second detective raised a hand to quiet her. "Hey, sweetheart, don't take our word for it," he rasped with sarcasm. "Go ask him yourself. We're just tryin' to help you. You'd better think of yourself for a change, instead of trying to cover up for Reed. We just might be able to get you off with probation and then get you into a treatment facility somewhere. But him, he's goin' away for a long, long time. We already have all we need even without your testimony."

She grew pale and slumped back in her chair. "Look . . . I have to go to the hospital," she groaned. "I think I've got hepatitis. . . ."

"Oh, ya do huh?" the first detective said cuttingly. "Well, we'll worry about that later. Now look sister, get smart! We'll slap you with so many charges you'll never get out of jail—possession and accessory to two counts of felony, including attempted murder of a police officer. Good for fifteen to twenty at least, even with concurrent sentences. Why, they'll lock you up and throw away the key!"

"After all, you already have a prison record," added the other detective.

Dolores caught her breath and sighed. She had a violent headache and felt weak, with cramps in her stomach, then waves of nausea. "I'm going to be sick," she gasped.

The matron whisked her into a restroom where she vomited. Then she was led back into the interrogation room. The two detectives had their jackets off and were relaxing, smoking cigarettes, as if ready for a long night. The smell of the smoke made her want to throw up again. The lights burned her eyes and she wanted to lie down and sleep forever. In a feeble, halting voice, she gave them what little information she knew and then begged to be taken to a hospital.

70

Slick kicked down the stand of his CH and chained it to the back porch of his house. He was tired and disgusted. It had been easy enough to get into Dom's room, but he found only one bag of dope, hidden in the most obvious of places, under the mattress. And with him and Sherry both sick, it was simply not enough.

At the slam of the screen door, his mother called out from the kitchen, her voice shrill and peevish. "Vinnie, I was wondering when you were coming home! I don't know how in the world you expect me to cook for you when you don't show up at mealtimes! I just put everything away!"

"Aw skip it, ma!" he grumbled. "I ain't hungry."

In order to evade her he continued on into the living room where his father was watching television, a half-quart can of beer balanced on one knee.

"Well, well, are you ever in the dog house!" his father rasped. "Sit down, why don't ya, and have a beer."

"Where's Sherry?"

"She don't feel good, went in your room to lie down. Got the flu or somethin'," his father replied and drained his can of beer.

He was half way out of his chair to fetch another when Slick's mother appeared in the doorway, wearing slacks and a sweater fitted so tightly that at first glance she looked almost naked. She stood, frowning angrily at her son. "Don't you run away from me when I'm talking to you, Vincent!" she scolded.

"Aw, leave the kid alone, Maureen," begged his father.

She moved in front of her husband, blocking his way as he tried to get into the kitchen. "Pete, will you mind your own business?" she grated. "If I want any advice from you I'll ask for it! God knows, you have enough troubles of your own! Look at you—stiff as usual!"

His father raised an arm in protest. "Look, was I botherin' you? Fer Chrissake, all I ask is to be left in peace! That's all! Just to die in peace!"

"Stop feeling so sorry for yourself!" she taunted. "As if you're the only one here! Think of us, why don't you? Think of your son!"

He gazed at her as he always did when she was scolding him, his puffed eyes blinking in astonishment, like a sleeping man waking out of a bad dream. Then he turned and regarded his son, squatting gnome-like on the divan, grinning. He shook his head and let out a weary wheeze.

"Look, Maureen," he began, trying to sound reasonable, but the anger creeping into his voice made it shake. "You're so busy gettin' on my back you don't even know what this kid is up to. Why don't you ask him if he's been out robbin' an' stealin', or muggin' people? But no, you're blind to it all."

"Aw, screw you, pop!" Slick shot back.

His father's head jerked around and his eyes bulged with fury. "Shut yer mouth, you dopefiend bum, you, why. . . !" He stepped toward him but his mother shoved him back.

"Leave him alone, I said!" she shrilled. "I've had enough of your yelling! You're leaving this house tomorrow and that's final! I'm finding you a room and you're getting out for good this time! I'll see my lawyer tomorrow and get a restraining order!"

Cowed by her ultimatum, his father swallowed his words, shuffled into the kitchen and opened the refrigerator.

"I'm goin' in to see Sherry," Slick said, getting up. "Pop said she. . . ."

"She's all right," insisted his mother. "Just tired, that's all. She didn't eat much, but then I don't think she likes my cooking. After all, it isn't kosher cooking, you know, but then I don't know what to feed her." She sidled up to him, put her hand on the back of his neck and stroked it. "Come on now, sit down here with me for awhile and watch TV. There's a good movie on. I'll make you a sandwich."

"Later, ma," he muttered and pulled away, went into the bedroom where he found Sherry huddled under a heavy blanket. She sat up abruptly when he entered.

"I thought you'd never come in," Sherry whined softly. "Like, I'm really sick! Did you find anything?"

"Just one bag," he replied.

"One bag? Is that all?"

He shrugged. "Who knows, it may be good dope." He took it out of his pocket and held it up. "See? I ripped it offa Dom's pad."

Smiling, she got up from the bed and came to him, huddled against his shoulder, her body trembling. "I like you for an old man," she whispered and kissed him on the ear.

He pushed her away. "Sure, 'cause ya like my dope, that's why!"

"No, that's not it! I love you!"

She came back, tried to throw her arms around him but again he brushed her aside, then searched for the set of works.

"Lemme alone, will ya?" he snapped irritably.

"Please, can't I get off first?" she pleaded. "Just this once! I'm so sick. . . !"

"I said get outa here!"

She gave him a hurt look, went back and lay down on the bed sobbing and trembling, while he opened the packet, transferred most of the contents to the bottle cap, added water, and struck a match under it. He drew the solution through some cotton into the eye dropper and fitted on the needle.

"If you don't shut up," he went on, "all you'll get is the cotton shot, an' that wouldn't even make a mouse high."

400

He was tying off when his mother came to the door and called insistently. "Vinnie! I made you a sandwich! Now come and eat it before I give it to your father!"

"Go ahead, I don't give a shit!" he yelled.

Just as the door knob turned he hid his works and his mother came bursting into the room.

"Don't you talk to me like that!" she exclaimed, looking around and narrowing her eyes at Sherry on the bed. "What are you two doing in here anyway? It must be very important if you don't even have time to eat!"

Slick glared at her. "Fer cryin' out loud! Whaddaya have ta come buttin' in for, huh? Okay, where's the goddam sandwich?"

"Out in the kitchen."

He did not want to get off only to be disturbed by his mother. And of course she did not know that he was too dopesick to eat. "Don't touch nothin'!" he said to Sherry and left the room behind his mother.

In the kitchen his father had already taken a bite out of the sandwich and another argument broke out.

"Pete! Did I say that was for you?"

"You didn't say nothin'!"

"Go ahead, pop! I said I didn't want it!"

"Honestly, Pete, I'll be glad when—"

A scream from the bedroom interrupted them. Slick dashed in to find Sherry rolling on the floor, choking, the needle in her arm. He plucked it out and held her up just as his parents came in. Horrified, they watched as her face turned a dusky purple, her eyes bulged out and her tongue swelled, protruded toad-like. She kicked, struggled in Slick's arms while his mother began screaming hysterically.

"Vinnie! Vinnie! Oh, my God! Pete! Call an ambulance!"

"No, no she's ... better call the cops!" his father bawled, kneeling and staring at the stricken girl.

Sherry gasped and lay still, barely twitching, a whitish foam bubbling from her mouth. Slick put her down gently, then examined her arm and saw the tell-tale red streak of battery acid following the vein. With a terrible look he picked up the dropper and flung it against the wall, where it shattered.

"Sonofabitch, a hot shot! That dirty motherfucker!" he cursed.

"Huh? So that's it!" yelled his father. "I thought so! You must've killed her with that shit, ya little murderer!"

"Pete, what are you saying!" shrieked his mother.

"I'm callin' the cops!" his father shouted again.

He rushed down the hall to the telephone in the kitchen, had just picked it up when Slick appeared, holding a gun.

"Hang up that phone, pop, or I'll shoot!" he ordered.

"Wait, Vinnie!" his mother was shouting, running up behind him. "Oh, what are we going to do? I think she's dead, Vinnie—she's really—!"

Slick reeled back suddenly as his father lunged for the gun and wrestled him to the floor. There was a muffled blast as they struggled, then his father tore the gun out of his son's grasp. Slick rolled over and got up slowly, holding his side, his shirt stained with blood. He leered like a cornered animal at the gun in his father's hand.

His mother screamed at the sight of the blood. "Pete! You shot him! Vinnie! Are you all right? Pete! You're the murderer, not him! Oh, Vinnie!"

She pulled at her husband and threw him off balance. With his free hand he turned and pushed her against Slick, then pointed the gun at the two of them, while they huddled together.

"Both a' you cut it out!" his father yelled. "Now, I'm gettin' the cops!"

As soon as he bent down to pick up the telephone, Slick dodged out the back door. His father went after him, his mother following them, shrieking and pulling at her husband, and he shoving her back again. He caught up with his son just as Slick was throwing the chain off his motorcycle. He stood up stiffly and turned, looked at his father fearfully, then seeing the gun he leered with hatred.

"Go ahead, pop!" he taunted. "Finish the job!"

His father held the gun trembling in his hand as he glared at this grinning imp of a son whom, along with his own wife, he knew despised him. It had always seemed that everything weak and loathesome in himself had been passed on to this boy, and now he saw this cursed self, this spineless, shiftless bum grinning back at him in the face of his own son. And as it mocked him, he standing with eyes bulging in dismay, he saw that he was the one who hated himself more than anything in the world. His jaw quivered as he tried to speak, and he lowered the gun. His wife was beside him wailing and seizing his arm, he shouting at her. Then they both stopped at the sound of a sharp command, saw the flash of blue uniforms and the glint of the officers' drawn revolvers.

71

Motto was plainly upset as they waited in the rented sedan parked off the road. He spoke to no one, not to Dom seated beside him, nor to the driver, but muttered under his breath between short puffs on his cigar. Every few moments his head jerked up almost involuntarily, his narrowed eyes scanning the dark woods around them.

The driver tensed, rolled down the window at the sight of a huge shadow approaching.

"There's a motorcycle out front, that's all," Spanky grumbled.

Motto glanced at Dom. "That kid rides a bike, don't he?"

"Right, a Triumph," Dom answered.

"Then that must be his. No cars?"

"I didn't see none," said Spanky.

Motto stubbed out his cigar, jabbing at the orange sparks. "Okay, now I'm gonna have a look."

Driving a quarter mile further along the deserted, tree-lined road, they stopped near the beach at a point where the cottage was visible about two hundred yards distant. Dom saw that it was not the same quaint Cape Cod cottage that a few months ago had been the scene of one of the wildest bashes that anyone could remember.

Now it jutted like a stark silhouette out of the dunes above an invisible sea. A single lighted window beckoned them, casting a weak glow onto the sandy path winding to the front door.

Motto lifted a pair of binoculars, scanned back and forth, hesitated on a neighboring cottage.

"It looks quiet, don't it?" he observed. "An' I don't like it when it's this quiet." He turned to his strong-arm man. "Tell you what. Spanky, you an' the kid go up an' check the place out. Knock on the door an' ask who's there. See if they got the money. Nothin's gonna jump up 'cause you ain't got nothin'. If it looks okay, c'mon back an' make the connection. But if anything looks fishy, lemme know."

The driver turned the car around, pulled it over to the side of the road with the engine running and the lights out. Dom got out with Spanky and they started walking, their footsteps muffled in the sand at the shoulder of the road. He had been sick with nausea and hot and cold sweats up to now but the fresh salt breeze found his nostrils and revived him. The sea lay everywhere in front of him, the murmuring surf barely audible in the darkness. It was the night sea, enchanting in its emptiness, another world of serenity eclipsed in blackness. It beckoned him gently to come and surrender himself, to be taken and embraced in it. But a conscious purpose directed him onward toward the dimly lit cottage, shuffling through the sand together with the big man beside him.

The door yawned open and Sam stuck his head out, his jack-in-the-box face painted with a stiff smile as he searched the yard behind them.

"This is Spanky," Dom announced. ". . . Sam."

The strong-arm man glanced past Sam into the cottage, then eyed the youth gravely. "Lemme see the money," he said abruptly.

"Where's your boss?" Sam returned with a slight, cordial nod of his head. "I want to do business with him face to face. My man insists on it."

Spanky continued to regard the youth for a long moment with a forbidding stare, as though conveying an unspoken warning. "What's it to yous where he is?" he grumbled at last. "Now let's get on with it. We ain't got all night."

"I thought—" Sam caught himself, his eyes darting down to the hand in the big man's pocket. He let out an involuntary sigh. "All right—just a second," he said.

He disappeared into another room, returned with an attache case, placed it on a table near the doorway and opened it. Spanky stepped inside the cottage, shuffled through the bundles of bills and nodded.

"Looks like we're in business," he said. "Be right back. Kid, you stay here."

The two young men were left alone in the room together, facing one another. Suddenly Sam snapped the attache case shut and removed it to the other room. When he returned, Dom was smiling ironically.

"I wouldn't rip you off," he remarked.

"No one said you would," Sam replied.

There was an uncomfortable silence, then Dom spoke again. "You really want to meet him, Motto, I mean."

Sam's eyes conveyed a keen look of disappointment. "Sure. I thought you were going to have him here."

"Well, he's waiting outside in a car, but he won't come in."

"Can't you persuade him?" Sam almost demanded.

Dom shook his head. "It's like Motto himself said. If he wasn't careful, he wouldn't be in this business, right?" He waited for Sam to agree but drew only the same disappointed frown. "It's men like him, and some are a lot bigger and more reputable, you know, who run the dope game," he went on to explain, as though apologizing for his failure. "But then again, I guess they don't really run it because it runs them. The money I mean—they'll do anything for it, no matter how rotten, as long as they can get their hands on it. You might say they have a money habit, because it gives them a real high to make it big and spend it big. They're as sick as any other addict, even a dopefiend. But we don't understand that. We respect them because they're rich and never have to go to jail. But their habit feeds on all the other habits—dope, gambling, broads, booze, you name it. That's why one of these guys is worse'n a thousand junkies."

Sam nodded and his face brightened, betraying a feeling that Dom had never seen there before. They shared something very personal at a glance. It was more than a love for the truth or a belief in human dignity. In fact, it was the will to stand by these ideals and to defend them at any cost, and the awareness of this conviction drew them closer together now than ever before.

Before Sam could reply, the strong-arm man stamped back into the cottage with an attache case, opened it and placed ten plastic bags of brown and white speckled powder on the table.

"This is Mexican stuff," he explained. "Only thing around since the panic. It's good though, take two, three cuts easy. Go ahead, let the kid taste it if ya want."

"Yeah, lemme taste it for you," Dom said impulsively.

"I haven't got time," Sam objected.

"You better let him taste it," Spanky insisted. "Just so's we'll know. Go ahead, kid."

Dom took a pinch out of one of the plastic bags, fixed up and recklessly shot up. He felt what he expected and hoped for, a gratifying rush, and his sickness vanished.

"It's dynamite," he boasted. "Like Spanky said, it'll take at least two cuts, maybe three or four."

The strong-arm man had been counting the money and shut the attache case with a loud snap. "We all set?"

"I still want to meet your boss," Sam requested. "Is he outside?"

"He ain't here," Spanky said nervously. "C'mon kid, let's go."

"Stop! You're under arrest!" came a sharp voice and two strangers stepped into the room with drawn guns.

Spanky ducked behind Dom, fired from his pocket and one man staggered backward while the other fired. There was a flurry of shots, Sam fumbling at his boot and then collapsing to the floor. Dom dove and rolled sideways as several more men appeared, one of them putting a gun to his head. The others ran out the door and there was more shooting, then someone shouted, "Hold your fire!"

While Dom was being frisked, he saw Sam sprawled motionless on the floor. He was not breathing and the

406

plastic bags of brown and white speckled powder were strewn around him. Dom had a strange feeling of numbness, brought on partly by all the shooting, by the powerful drug, and by the shock of witnessing the certainty of death, as he had seen it so many times in Vietnam. He would never get used to it.

Parked out on the road nearly a half mile distant, they could not make out the cottage through the trees, only a faint glimmer from the single lighted window. At the sound of the shots, Motto cursed, threw away his cigar and jerked the binoculars up to his eyes. Again he saw only the same lighted window, larger now, glowing through the dark leafy branches of the trees.

"Let's get outa here!" he yelled.

The tires squealed as the driver gunned the car down the road. Glancing back through the rearview mirror, he saw the dreaded headlights of a pursuing car, and stabbed the pedal down to the floorboard.

"Slow down and turn right at this next intersection," Motto ordered, also looking back.

The car skidded around the corner. Joey turned again at the next junction and then made a third turn.

"I think we lost 'em," he said, slowing to eighty.

"C'mon, keep movin'!" Motto yelled gruffly. "We're not outa this yet! Musta been a setup! Musta got Spanky! He was a good man, too! That lousy punk, I knew he was up to somethin'."

"He'll put the finger on us," said Joey, keeping his eyes on the road.

Motto coughed nervously. "Better head for the state line. Our people are gonna be very upset about this, y'know it? I'll call 'em tonight and get a contract out on the kid. Donohue can bail him out tomorrow so they can make the hit."